PRAISE FOR THE TERRIFYING NOVELS OF F. PAUL WILSON

REBORN

"THIS ACCOMPLISHED THRILLER, THE FIRST IN A PROJECTED TRILOGY, IS A PAGE-TURNER!"
—*Publishers Weekly*

"FOUR STARS . . . CHILLING!"   —*Rave Reviews*

THE KEEP

"A BATTLE BETWEEN GOOD AND EVIL THAT STAGGERS THE IMAGINATION, WITH AN ENDING AS DRAMATIC AND EXCITING AS ANY HORROR FAN COULD WISH!"
—*Providence Journal*

"*THE KEEP* WILL BE READ AS LONG AS ANY HORROR NOVEL WRITTEN IN THE LAST QUARTER OF THIS CENTURY!"
—J. M. WILLIAMSON, *The Best of Masques*

"A TENSE AND TERRIFYING PAGE-TURNER."
—*Cleveland Press*

"A SUPER HORROR NOVEL . . . THE BEST!"
—*Nashville Tennessean*

"MUCH, MUCH MORE THAN JUST ANOTHER HORROR STORY. . . . *THE KEEP* IS AN EXCEPTIONAL BOOK AND WELL WORTH THE READING!"
—*THRUST: Science Fiction in Review*

Continued . . .

THE TOMB

"THIS NOVEL WORKS ON ALL LEVELS . . . A SPLENDID HORROR YARN!"
—*West Coast Review of Books*

"WILSON DISPLAYS THE SAME CLEAN WRITING STYLE AND REALISTIC CHARACTERIZATION THAT MADE *THE KEEP* SUCH AN ENGROSSING READ. . . . *THE TOMB* IS A FAST-MOVING THRILLER THAT STANDS HEAD AND SHOULDERS ABOVE MOST OF THE HORROR FICTION CURRENTLY AVAILABLE."
—CHARLES DE LINT

"A ROLLICKING GOOD TIME . . . SUPERB."
—*UPI*

"A GOOD STORY, AN ENTERTAINING TALE . . . IT READS ALONG AT A FINE CLIP."
—EDWARD BRYANT, *Mile High Futures*

"A CHARACTER AS REAL AND AS FASCINATING AS ANY OF KING'S OR LUDLUM'S BEST. . . .YOU WILL NOT BE DISAPPOINTED. MY HIGHEST RECOMMENDATION!"
—*Fantasy Review*

"VERY WELL DONE!"   —*Science Fiction Chronicle*

"FAST ACTION!"   —*Locus*

THE TOUCH

*And now
the nightmares continue
with . . .*

REPRISAL

REPRISAL

F. Paul Wilson

JOVE BOOKS, NEW YORK

REPRISAL

A Jove Book / published by arrangement with
the author

PRINTING HISTORY
Jove edition / March 1992

ISBN: 0-515-10589-9

Jove Books are published by The Berkley Publishing Group,
200 Madison Avenue, New York, New York 10016.
The name "JOVE" and the "J" logo
are trademarks belonging to Jove Publications, Inc.

PRINTED IN THE UNITED STATES OF AMERICA

10 9 8 7 6 5 4 3 2 1

ACKNOWLEDGMENTS

The Marquis de Sade for his warped philosophy; George Hayduke, whose *Make My Day* inspired certain dirty tricks in this novel; and as usual to Steven Spruill and Albert Zuckerman for their invaluable input.

CONTENTS

PART I

NOW

SEPTEMBER

ONE

Queens, New York

Rain coming.

Mr. Veilleur could feel the approaching summer storm in his bones as he sat in a shady corner of St. Ann's Cemetery in Bayside. He had the place to himself. In fact, he seemed to have most of the five boroughs to himself. Labor Day weekend. And a hot one. Anyone who could afford to had fled upstate or to the Long Island beaches. The rest were inside, slumped before their air conditioners. Even the homeless were off the streets, crouched in the relative cool of the subways. The sun poured liquid fire through the hazy midday sky. Not a cloud in sight. But here in the shade of this leaning oak, Mr. Veilleur knew the weather was going to change soon, could read it from the worsening ache in his knees, hips, and back.

Other things were going to change as well. Everything, perhaps. And all for the worse.

He had been making sporadic trips to this corner of the cemetery since he had first sensed the *wrongness* here. That had been on a snowy winter night five years ago. It had taken him a while, but he had finally located the spot. A grave, which was perfectly natural, this being a cemetery. This grave was not like the others, however. This one had no marker. But something else made this grave special: Nothing would grow over it.

Through the past five years, Mr. Veilleur had seen the cemetery's gardeners try to seed it, sod it, even plant it with various ground covers like periwinkle, pachysandra, and ivy. They took root well all around, but nothing survived in the four-foot oblong patch over the grave.

Of course, they didn't know it was a grave. Only Mr. Veilleur and the one who had dug the hole knew that. And surely one other.

Mr. Veilleur did not come here often. Travel was not easy for him, even to another part of the city he had called home since the end of World War II. Gone were the days when he walked where he wished, fearing no one. Now his eyes were bad; his back was stiff and canted forward; he leaned on a cane when he walked, and he walked slowly. He had the body of a man in his eighties and he had to take appropriate precautions.

Age had not dampened his curiosity, however. He didn't know who had dug the grave or who was in it. But whoever lay down there below the dirt and rocks and weeds had been touched by the Enemy.

The Enemy had been growing steadily stronger for more than two decades now. But growing carefully, staying hidden. Why? There was no one to oppose him. What was he waiting for? A sign? A particular event? Perhaps the one buried below was part of the answer. Perhaps the occupant had nothing to do with the Enemy's quiescence.

No matter—as long as the Enemy remained inactive. For the longer the Enemy delayed, the closer Mr. Veilleur would be to reaching the end of his days. And then he would be spared witnessing the chaotic horrors to come.

A shadow fell across him and a sudden gust of wind chilled the perspiration that coated his skin. He looked up. Clouds were moving in, obscuring the sun. Time to go.

He stood and stared one last time at the bare dirt over the unmarked grave. He knew he would be back again. And again. Too many questions about this grave and its occupant. He sensed unfinished business here.

Because the grave's occupant did not rest easy. Did not, in fact, rest at all.

Mr. Veilleur turned and made his unsteady way out of St. Ann's Cemetery. It would be good to get back to the cool apartment and get his feet up and have a glass of iced tea. He tried to believe that his wife had missed him during his absence, but with her mind the way it was, Magda probably hadn't even realized he was gone.

TWO

Pendleton, North Carolina

Conway Street was nearly at a standstill. Like a parking lot. Between fitful crawls, Will Ryerson idled his ancient Impala convertible in the stagnant traffic and watched the heat gauge. It was staying well in the safe range.

He patted the dash. *Good girl.*

He glanced at his watch. He'd already had a late start for work this morning, and this was going to make him later. He took a deep breath. So what? The grass on the north campus at Darnell University could wait a few extra minutes for its weekly trim. Only problem was, he was in charge of the work crews this morning, so if he didn't get there, J.B. would have to get things rolling. And J.B. had enough to do. That was why he had recently promoted Will.

Will Ryerson is moving up in the world.

He smiled at the thought. He'd always wanted an academic life, to spend his work days on the campus of a great university. Well, for the last three years or so, his wish had come true. Except he didn't travel there every day to immerse himself in the accumulated knowledge and wisdom of the ages; he came to tend the grounds.

Of course, with his degrees, he could have been at Darnell as an academic, but proving his qualifications would require him to reveal his past, and he couldn't do that.

He glanced in the rearview mirror at his long, salt-and-pepper hair, still wet from his morning shower, pulled tight to the back, his scarred forehead, bent nose, and full, graying beard. Only the bright blue eyes of his former self remained. If his mother were still alive, even she'd have trouble recognizing him now.

He peered ahead. Had to be an accident somewhere up there. Either that or the road department had picked the town's so-called A.M. rush hour to do some street repairs. Will had grown up in a real city, the city with the king—no, the *emperor* of rush hours, and this little bottleneck couldn't hold a candle to that.

He killed time by reading bumper stickers. Most of them were religious, including a fair number of worn "PTL CLUB" stickers, and others like, BORN AGAIN, LISTEN FOR THE SHOUT—HE'S COMING AGAIN, YOUR GOD DEAD? TRY MINE: JESUS LIVES, A CLOSE ENCOUNTER OF THE BEST KIND: JESUS, and Will's favorite, JESUS IS COMING AGAIN AND BOY IS HE PISSED.

I can dig that, Will thought.

He considered turning on the radio but wasn't in the mood for the ubiquitous country music or the "new music" that dominated the university's student station, so he listened to the engine as it idled in the press. A quarter-century-old, gas-guzzling V-8 but it purred like a week-old kitten. It had taken him a while, but he'd finally got the timing right.

Will noticed that the right lane seemed to be inching forward faster than the left, the one he was in. When a space opened up next to him, he eased over toward the curb and made slightly better time for half a block. Then he came to a dead stop along with everybody else.

Big deal. He'd picked up fifty feet over his old spot in the left lane. Hardly worth the trouble. He peered ahead to see if the next side street was one he could use to detour around the congestion. He couldn't make out the name on the sign. He glanced to his right and froze.

There was a telephone booth on the sidewalk not six feet from the passenger door of his car.

Usually he could spot one blocks away, but this one had been hidden by the unusually large knot of people clustered at the bus stop next to it. He'd missed it completely.

Panic gripped the center of Will's chest and twisted. How close was he? Too close. How long had he been stopped? Too long. He couldn't stay here. He didn't need much, just half a car length forward or back, but he had to *move,* had to get away from that phone.

There was no room in front; he had pulled right up to the rear bumper of the car ahead of him. He lurched around in his seat, peering over the trunk. No room there either. The car behind was right on his tail. Trapped.

Get out of the car—that was the only thing to do. Get out and walk off a short distance until the snarl loosened up, then run back and screech away.

He reached for the door handle. He had to move now if he was going to get away before—

No. Wait. Be cool.

Maybe it wouldn't happen. Maybe the horror had finally let go. Maybe it was over. He hadn't allowed himself near a phone for so long, how did he know it would happen again? Nothing had happened yet. Maybe nothing would. If he just stayed calm and stayed put, maybe—

The phone in the booth began to ring.

Will closed his eyes, set his jaw, and gripped the steering wheel with all his strength.

Damn!

The phone rang only once. Not the usual two-second burst, but a long, continuous ring that went on and on.

Will opened his eyes to see who would answer it. Someone always did. Who'd be the unlucky one?

He watched the commuters at the bus stop ignore it for a while. They looked at each other, then at the phone, then back down the street where their bus was stuck in traffic somewhere out of sight. Will knew that wouldn't last. No one could ignore a phone that rang like that.

Finally, a woman started for the booth.

Don't, lady!

She continued forward, oblivious to his silent warning. When she reached the booth she hesitated. It was that ring, Will knew, that endless continuous ring that so jangled the nerves with its alienness. You couldn't help but sense that something was very wrong here.

She looked around at her fellow commuters, who were all staring at her, urging her on with their eyes.

Answer it, they seemed to say. If nothing else you'll stop that damned incessant ring!

She lifted the receiver and put it to her ear. Will watched her face, watched her expression change from one of mild curiosity to concern, and then to horror. She pulled the receiver away from her head and stared at it as if the earpiece had turned to slime. She dropped it and backed away. Another of the commuters—a man this time—began to approach the booth. Then Will noticed the car in front of him begin to move ahead. He gunned the Chevy and stayed on the other car's bumper as it pulled away.

Will kept his sweaty hands tight on the wheel and fought the sick chills and nausea that swept through him.

And he didn't look back.

Lisl Whitman sat in her office in the math department at Darnell University and stared at her computer screen while trying to ignore the insistent beeping of her watch.

Lunchtime.

She was only a little hungry now, and she was really rolling on these calculations. A very productive morning. She didn't want to see it end just yet. This was good work. She had a feeling that it was going to make people sit up and take notice.

But that one o'clock advanced calculus class wouldn't wait, and a couple of those eager Darnell undergrads wouldn't let her get away for at least another fifteen minutes after class, which meant she wouldn't get free until well after two. She'd be famished by then and maybe even a little shaky. And when she got that hungry, she always ran the risk of going into a feeding frenzy.

And so what if I do?

One more binge wasn't going to matter. She was already at least twenty pounds overweight. Who'd notice a few more? Will Ryerson might, but her weight didn't seem to matter to him. He accepted her for who she was, not how she looked.

Lisl had never had a weight problem until her late twenties. Until after the divorce. She was thirty-two now and knew she'd let herself go in a big way. She'd been lonely and depressed, so she immersed herself in her doctoral thesis. And food. Food had been her only pleasure. And somewhere along the line she became a compulsive eater. She'd binge, hate herself for it, and then binge again.

Why not? She'd been considered a math nerd all her life, and nerds were supposed to look rumpled and slovenly. It came with the territory, didn't it? She'd never allow herself to look slovenly, but the loose clothes she tended to wear did lend her a rumpled look. She rarely wore makeup—her high coloring didn't require it—but she took scrupulous care of her naturally blond hair.

Eat now, she told herself. *Now!*

Maybe her weight didn't matter, but she had to draw the line somewhere.

She hit the SAVE button and watched the monitor return to the READY screen. Satisfied that her work was now safely stored away in the memory banks of the university's Cray II, she shut off the monitor and looked out the window. Another bright, warm, glorious September day in North Carolina.

Now. Where to eat? Four choices. Here in the math department—either alone in her own office or joining Everett in his—or in the caf or al fresco. Actually, there were only three choices. Alone could be more company than Ev. Still, he was the only member of the department still on the floor and she guessed she owed him the courtesy of asking him to join her. It was a gesture that risked nothing, and she sensed that Ev genuinely appreciated it whenever she asked.

She stepped across the hall to his open door. EVERETT SANDERS, PH. D. ran in black across the opaque glass. He was hunched over his computer keyboard, his narrow back to her. His shiny pink scalp gleamed through his thinning light brown hair. He was dressed in the Ev Sanders uniform: short-sleeved white shirt and brown polyester slacks. Lisl didn't need to see his front to know that a nondescript brown tie was tightly knotted around his neck.

Lisl tapped on the door glass.

"Come," he said without looking around.

"It's me, Ev."

He turned and rose from his seat to face her. Always the gentleman. Only in his mid-forties but he looked older. And yes, another of his muddy brown ties was cinched up high under his Adam's apple.

"Hello, Lisl," he said, his watery brown eyes peering at her through his wire-rimmed glasses. He smiled, showing slightly yellowed teeth. "Isn't it wonderful?"

"What?"

"The article."

"Oh, yes! The article. I think it's super, don't you?"

U.S. News & World Report's annual college issue had given Darnell University a top rating, even going so far as to call it "the new Harvard of the South."

"I'll bet John Manning's sorry now that he left for Duke. All we need to complete the picture is a Division I basketball team."

"And you can coach it," Lisl said.

Ev gave one of his rare, *heh-heh-heh* laughs, then rubbed his palms together.

"Well, what can I do for you?"

"I'm going to lunch now. You want to come?"

"No, I don't think so." He glanced at his watch. "I'll be stopping work in two minutes. After that, I'll be eating lunch here and catching up on some reading. You're welcome to join me."

"That's okay. I didn't bring anything today. See you later."

"Very well." He smiled, nodded, and reseated himself at his computer console.

Relieved, Lisl turned away. Asking Ev to lunch was a private game she played. He always brown-bagged it, always ate in his office. It was a safe courtesy to ask him to join her. He never accepted. Ev Sanders was nothing if not predictable. She wondered what she'd do with him if he ever did accept.

She grabbed the vinyl-covered cushion from behind her office door and headed for the caf.

The caf's lasagna was good as a rule, but the weather was a little too warm for a hot lunch. She picked out a fruit cocktail and a turkey on white.

There. That looked sensible.

Then she came to the dessert counter and snatched a piece of coconut cream pie before she could stop herself.

Who'll notice?

She scanned the tables in the faculty room and saw no one she cared to sit with, so she headed outdoors to the grassy knoll behind the caf. She hoped Will would be there.

He was. She spotted Will Ryerson's familiar figure leaning against the wide trunk of the knoll's only tree, a battered old elm. He was sipping a can of pop and reading, as usual.

Her mood buoyed at the sight of him. Will was a tonic for her. Ever since she had started dabbling with this idea of submitting a math paper, Lisl had found that her insides tended to twist into tight little knots of tension when she was working on it. Her underarms would dampen from the intense concentration, like someone doing hard physical labor. All that tension uncoiled within her now as Will looked up and saw her. A welcoming smile lit through his graying beard. He closed the little book in his hand and slipped it into his lunch box.

"Beautiful day!" he said as she joined him under their tree. *Their* tree. At least that was the way she thought of it. She didn't know how Will thought of it.

"That it is." She dropped the cushion on the mossy ground and sat on it. "What were you reading there?"

"Where?"

"When I came up."

Will suddenly seemed very interested in his sandwich.

"A book."

"I gathered that. What book?"

"Uh . . . *The Stranger*."

"Camus?"

"Yeah."

"I'm surprised you haven't read that one by now."

"I have. I thought I'd try it again. But it doesn't help."

"Help with what?"

"Understanding."

"Understanding what?"

He grinned at her. "Anything." Then he took a savage bite out of his sandwich.

Lisl smiled and shook her head. So typical of the man. She'd once heard something described as an enigma wrapped in a mystery. That was Will. The philosopher groundskeeper of Darnell University.

Lisl first met him two years ago under this very tree. It had been a day like today and she had decided to sit outside to correct some test papers. Will had come up and informed her that she'd taken his spot. Lisl had looked up at a tall bearded stranger in his late forties. His accent was definitely from somewhere to the north, he smelled of motor oil, his hands were heavily callused and looked to be permanently stained with engine grime, his green overalls were dusty and sweat-stained, his work boots were clumped with grass clippings. He had clear blue eyes and long, dark brown hair heavily streaked with gray, pulled back and fastened into a short ponytail with a red rubber band, a nose that had been badly broken, and a wide scar on the right side of his forehead. An aging hippie-type handyman who'd managed to land himself a steady job, she'd thought as she smiled and moved exactly three feet to her right. He'd seated himself and produced a sandwich and a Pepsi. Again, typical. But when he pulled out a copy of Kierkegaard's *Sickness Unto Death* and began reading, Lisl had to revise her assessment. And she *had* to talk to him.

They'd been talking ever since. They became friends. Sort of. She doubted Will had a true, deep friendship with anyone. He was so secretive about himself. The most she knew about his origins was that he was from "New England." He would tell her his deepest thoughts on life, love, philosophy, religion, politics— and listening to him it was quite apparent to her that he had done a lot of thinking in those areas. He would expound on any subject but Will Ryerson. Which made him all the more intriguing.

Lisl sensed that he was a lonely man and that she was one of the few people in his life with whom he could communicate on his own level. The other groundskeepers weren't in Will's league, or he wasn't in theirs. He had often complained that as far as his coworkers were concerned, if it wasn't in the sports section or didn't have big breasts, it didn't really matter. So he used his lunchtimes with Lisl to ventilate the thoughts that had accumulated during the time they were apart.

That was why she couldn't understand why he was being so evasive about the book in his lunch box. She was sure it wasn't *The Stranger.* But then what was it? Porn? She doubted it. Porn wasn't his style. And even if it were, he'd probably want to discuss it with her.

Lisl shrugged it off. If he didn't want to tell her, that was his business. He didn't owe her an explanation.

She watched him tear into his lunch. It was one of those belly-buster subs he favored, where anything within reach was sliced up and piled between two halves of a loaf of Italian bread and splattered with oil and vinegar.

"I wish I were like you."

"No you don't," he said.

"Metabolism-wise, I do. Lunch-wise, at least. Good Lord, look at the size of that sandwich—and I can imagine what you eat for dinner. Yet you don't put on a pound."

"I don't sit at a desk all day either."

"True, but your body does a far better job than mine of burning calories."

"Not as good a job as it used to. I'm nibbling around the edges of fifty now and I can feel the machine slowing down."

"Maybe, but men age better than women."

Will was aging pretty well in Lisl's estimation. Maybe it was because he carried his weight so well: very lean and muscular, a good six feet in height, maybe a little more, with broad shoulders and no gut. Maybe it was his long hair and beard, both of which had grown grayer over the past two years, although his clear blue eyes remained mild and gentle—and impenetrable. Will had equipped the windows of his soul with steel storm shutters.

"Men just don't worry about it as much," he said. "Look at all the guys on the maintenance crew with beer bellies."

Lisl smiled. "I know what you mean. Some of them look eight months pregnant. And if I put on any more weight, so will I. If only I could shed the pounds like you."

Will shrugged. "I guess it's just like everything else about us—opposites. What you can't do, I can. What I can't do, *you* can."

"You know, Will, you're right. Together you and I make one well-rounded, well-educated person."

He laughed. "What I said: I know next to nothing about the sciences, and you might well be classified as culturally deprived as far as the humanities go."

Lisl nodded, agreeing fully. These pastoral lunch hours with Will had made her realize how painfully lopsided her education had been. She had her Ph.D., yes, but it was as if she had gone through high school, college, and graduate school with blinders on. Science and math, math and science—they'd been her whole life, all she'd cared about. Will had shown her how much she'd missed. If she had it all to do over again, she'd do it differently. There was a whole other world out there, rich, colorful, filled with stories, music, art, dance, schools of thought on ethics, morals, politics, and so much more that she'd missed. Missed completely. She still had plenty of time to catch up. And with Will as a guide, she knew it would be fun. Still, the thought of all that wasted time irritated her.

"Well, thanks to you, I'm certainly less deprived than before we met. Can we keep this up?"

She sensed his face soften behind the beard. "As long as you want."

Just then, Lisl spotted someone waving from the base of the knoll. She recognized Adele Connors's stout, compact figure.

"Yoo-hoo! Lisl! Look, y'all! I found them!" she said in her squeaky voice.

She trundled up the slope jingling a set of keys in the air.

"Your keys?" Lisl said. "Oh, good!"

Adele was one of the stalwarts of the secretarial pool. Lisl had found her wringing her hands and lamenting the loss of her key chain yesterday. Adele had searched most of the afternoon with no luck. Finally, since she couldn't start her own car without her keys, she'd asked Lisl to drive her home.

Which had vaguely annoyed Lisl. Not that she minded doing Adele a favor, it was just that the secretaries tended to treat her like "one of the girls." And Lisl wasn't "one of the girls." Although she wasn't tenured yet, she was an associate professor in the university's mathematics department and wished sometimes they'd treat her as such. But she had herself to blame. Being the only female in the department, perhaps she'd become too chummy with the secretaries when she first arrived. Unaccustomed to being in a position of authority, she'd been oversensitive about coming on as a tight-assed bitch with the secretaries. Plus, a little girl talk had come in handy—she'd got the lowdown on everyone in the department without even asking.

But still . . . as useful as the camaraderie had been, there'd been a price to pay. She couldn't help noticing how the secretaries addressed all the other Ph.D.s in the department as "Doctor," while she was always "Lisl." A minor point, but an irritating one.

"Where'd you find them?" she asked as Adele reached the top of the knoll.

"Right behind my seat cushion. Isn't that something!"

"I thought you said you searched the entire area."

"I did! I did! But I left out one thing. I forgot to ask for the Lord's help."

Out of the corner of her eye she saw Will pause in mid bite. She groaned inwardly. Adele was a Born Again. She could go on interminably on the subject of Jesus.

"That's great, Adele," Lisl said quickly. "By the way, this is Will Ryerson."

Will and Adele exchanged nods and hellos, but Adele was not to be turned from her favorite subject.

"But let me tell you how the Lord intervened for me," she said. "After you dropped me off home last night, I got big Dwayne and little Dwayne together and we knelt in the middle of our living room and prayed for the Lord to help me find my keys. We did that twice last night, and once again this morning, just before the school bus came for little Dwayne. And you know what?"

Lisl waited. Apparently it wasn't a rhetorical question, so she took a wild stab.

"You found your keys."

"Praise the Lord, yes! When big Dwayne dropped me off this morning, I went to my desk, sat in my chair, and felt a lump under my cushion. I looked and—Praise the Lord—there they were! It's a little miracle, that's what it is! Because I know they weren't there yesterday. God found them and put them where I was sure to happen across them. I just know he did. Isn't the Lord wondrous in his ways?" She turned and started back down the slope, bubbling and babbling all the way. "I'm spending the whole day just witnessing and praising Him, witnessing and praising my wonderful Lord. Bye, y'all!"

"Bye, Adele," Lisl said.

She turned to Will and saw that he was leaning back against the tree and staring after Adele's retreating figure, the sandwich lying forgotten in his lap.

"Incredible!" he said.

"What's the matter?" she asked.

"People like that make me lose my appetite."

"*Nothing* makes you lose your appetite."

"The Adeles of the world do. I mean, how empty-headed can you get?"

"She's harmless."

"Is she? I mean, where's her perspective? God isn't a good luck charm. He's not there to help you find your keys or make it a nice day for the church's Labor Day picnic."

Lisl sensed the growing heat behind Will's words. He usually avoided the subject of religion—anything else was fair game, but he didn't seem to like to talk about God. This would be good. She let him roll.

"God helped her find her car keys. Great. Just great. Praise the Lord and pass the mashed potatoes. Where's her head, anyway? We've got thousands—no, *hundreds* of thousands of people starving in places like Ethiopia. Desperate fathers and mothers kneeling over the bloated bellies of their starving children, crying out to heaven for a little rain so their crops will grow and they can feed their families. But God's not answering them. The whole damn region remains a dust bowl with children and adults alike dropping like flies. Adele, however, sends up a couple of quick Our Fathers and God hops right to it. He locates those lost keys and shoves them under her seat cushion where she's sure to find them first thing in the morning. There's still no rain in Ethiopia, but Adele What's-her-name's got her goddam car keys." He paused for breath, then looked at her. "Is there something wrong with that scenario, or is it just me?"

Lisl stared at Will in frank shock. In the two years she'd known him she had never heard him raise his voice or become angry about anything. But Adele obviously had touched a raw nerve. He was seething; the scar on his forehead was turning red.

She patted his arm.

"Calm down, Will. It doesn't matter."

"It does matter. Where does she get off thinking that God's ignoring prayers for rain in the Sudan to go put her car keys where she can find them? It's not fair for her to go around telling everybody that God's answering *her* ditsy prayers while prayers for things that really matter go unanswered!"

And suddenly it was clear to Lisl. Suddenly she knew why Will was so angry. Or at least thought she did.

"What did you pray for, Will? What did you ask for that didn't happen?"

He looked at her, and for a moment the shutters were open. In that moment she had a glimpse into his soul—

—and recoiled at the pain, the grief, the agony, the disillusionment that welled up in his eyes. But mostly it was the overriding fear that shook her so.

Oh, my God! Oh, my poor Will! What happened to you? Where have you been. What have you seen?

And then the shutters slammed closed and once again she faced a pair of bland blue eyes. *Opaque* blue eyes.

"It's nothing like that," he said calmly. "It's just that the childishness and superficiality of that kind of religion gets to me after a while. It's so prevalent around here. You hear of bumper-sticker politics, but it seems to me they've got bumper-sticker religion in these parts."

Lisl knew from what she had glimpsed in his eyes that it was much more than that, but sensed it would do no good to probe. Will was shut down tight.

Lisl added another mystery to the mental list she'd been keeping about the enigmatic Will Ryerson.

"Not just around these parts," she said.

"Yeah," he sighed. "Ain't that the truth. It's all over the country. Televangelism. God as game show host. A heavenly *Wheel of Fortune.*"

"Except the money comes *from* the contestants instead of *to* them."

He looked at her. "You've never said much about it, Leese, but I gather you're not very religious."

"I was raised a Methodist. Sort of. But you can't get too far into higher math and stay very religious."

"Oh, really?" he said with a smile. "I've looked into some of those journals you bring up here. I'd say it takes quite a leap of faith to get involved in that stuff."

She laughed. "You're not the first person to feel that way."

"Speaking of higher math," Will said, "what about that idea you had for a paper? How's it coming?"

Just thinking about the paper started a buzz of excitement within her.

"It's going great."

"Good enough for Palo Alto?"

She nodded. "I think so. Maybe."

"No maybes. If you think so, you ought to enter it."

"But if it gets rejected—"

"Then you're right back where you started. Nothing lost except the time you spent working on it. And even the time isn't completely lost because you'll no doubt learn something. But if you don't do the paper, and don't submit it, you're betraying your potential. It's bad enough to let other people stifle you. But when you stifle yourself—"

"I know, I know."

They'd been over this ground before. Lisl had grown so close to Will over the past couple of years. She'd opened up to him as she had to no man before, more even than to Brian during their marriage. She never would have believed she could be so intimate with a man without sex edging into the picture. But that's the way it was.

Platonic. She'd heard of platonic affairs but had always thought them fantasies. Now she was living one. Once she had broken through Will's shell, she'd found him warm and accepting. A great talker and a better listener. But she'd remained wary of him. The deep discussions during lunch hours here on the knoll during the week, the long, aimless, languorous drives on weekends . . . through them all Lisl had stayed on guard, dreading the inevitable moment when Will would put the moves on her.

And dread really said it. The nightmare of divorcing Brian had been still too fresh in her mind, the wounds had barely stopped bleeding and were a long way from healing. She hadn't wanted another man in her life, no way, no how, especially not someone about twenty years older. And she knew—just *knew*—that Will was going to want to expand their relationship beyond the purely intellectual to the physical. Lisl didn't want that. It would back her into the position of rebuffing him. And what would that do to their relationship? Wound it, surely. Perhaps even kill it. She couldn't bear that. She'd wanted things to stay just as they were.

So Lisl had faced each of those weekend drives-to-nowhere with growing anxiety, waiting for the inevitable invitation back to Will's place for "a couple of drinks" or where they could "be more comfortable." She waited. And waited.

But the other shoe never dropped. Will never made that "inevitable" pass.

Lisl smiled now at the memory of her own reaction when it had finally dawned that Will wasn't going to put the moves on her. She'd been hurt. *Hurt!* After spending months afraid he'd make a pass, she was wounded when he didn't. There was no winning this game.

Of course, she'd immediately blamed herself. She was too dumb, too frumpy, too dull, too nerdy to attract him. But then logic reared up and asked, If he truly saw her that way, why would he spend so much time with her?

Then she blamed Will. Was he gay? But that didn't seem to be the case. As far as she could figure, he had no men friends. No friends at all other than Lisl.

Asexual? Maybe.

A lot of maybes. One thing had been certain, though. Will Ryerson was the kindest, gentlest, deepest, *weirdest* man she had ever known. And despite all his quirks—and there were quite a few of them—she'd wanted to know him better.

Over the two years, Will gradually had assumed the role of tutor and Dutch uncle, conducting mini seminars on the knoll as he casually guided her through the terra incognita of philosophy and literature. He was a good uncle. He demanded nothing of her. He was always there for her, to give advice when asked for it or merely serve as a sounding board for her problems and ideas. And always encouraging. His opinion of her capabilities was always far more sanguine than hers. Where Lisl saw limits, Will saw endless possibilities.

Lisl liked to think that their relationship wasn't just a one-way street, that she gave something back. She wasn't sure why or how, but she sensed that Will had benefited almost as much as she from their interaction. He seemed far more at ease with the world and with himself since they'd first met. He'd been a bleak, melancholy, almost tortured man then. Now he could make jokes and even laugh. She hoped that had been at least partly her doing.

"Go for it," Will said.

"I don't know, Will. What will Everett think?"

"He'll think you're making a bid to get tenure in the department, just like he's doing. Nothing wrong with that. And why on earth should you defer to him? You both joined the department the same year. Even if you are younger, you're his equal in seniority, and you're his match—if not his better—in ability. And besides, you're a hell of a lot better-looking."

Lisl felt herself flushing. "Stop that. That's irrelevant."

"Of course it is. But no more so than any of those cop-outs you allow to hold you back. Go for it, Leese."

That was Uncle Will: supremely confident that she could attain any goal she set her sights on. Lisl wished she could buy into his unabashed enthusiasm for her abilities. But he didn't know the truth—that she was a fake. Sure, she'd earned her Ph.D. and managed to be the first woman accepted into Darnell's traditionally all-male department of mathematics, but Lisl was sure that some sort of fluke had let her slip past the review board, some sort of affirmative action thing that had opened the doors for her. She wasn't that good. Really.

And now Will was pushing her to try to move up in the department. The International Congress of Mathematicians was meeting in Palo Alto next spring. Ev Sanders was submitting a paper for presentation there. If it was accepted, he'd be the fair-haired boy in the department, a shoo-in for tenure. And tenure was getting harder to come by. Darnell had been tightening up on the number of tenured positions the past few years, and now that it was being called "the new Harvard of the South," the situation was sure to become even tighter. But John Manning had left his tenured professorship in the department last month to take that position at Duke, which meant math had an open spot. If Lisl's paper was also accepted, Everett would no longer have the post position. And if Lisl's paper was accepted *instead* of Ev's . . .

"You really think I should?"

"No. I just like the sound of my own voice. *Do it, dammit!*"

"All right! I will!"

"Good. See? Wasn't that easy?"

"Yeah. Sure. Easy for you. You don't have to deliver a paper."

"You'll do it."

"Uh-huh. Can I call you when I get stuck?"

"You can try."

"Oh, right. The man without a telephone. How could I forget."

Even after all this time, Lisl still could not get used to the idea that Will managed to live in the modern world without the benefit of a telephone. She realized no one would ever get rich as a groundskeeper, but the men had a union that had bargained them up to decent wages and good benefits. So Will's lack of a phone could not be due to a lack of money.

"You've *got* to get a phone, Will."

He finished off the last of his sub. "Not this again."

"I'm serious. A telephone is an essential tool of modern living."

"Maybe."

"And I know they've got phone lines out there on Postal Road."

After realizing she had nothing to fear from him, Lisl had visited his home a number of times. He lived in an isolated cottage but it wasn't in the boonies. "What if I call the phone company for you. I'll even pay—"

"Forget it, Lisl."

She sensed from his tone that he wanted her to drop it but she couldn't. No phone . . . it was crazy. Unless . . .

"You're not one of those Luddite types, are you? You know, antitechnology?"

"Now, Leese, you know better than that. You've seen the place. I've got a TV, a radio, a microwave, even a computer." He looked at her. "I just don't want a phone."

"But why on earth not? Can't you give me a hint?"

"I simply do not want one. Can we leave it at that?"

His voice carried only mild annoyance, but his eyes surprised her. Just before he looked away, she could have sworn she caught a trace of the fear she had seen before.

"Sure," she said quickly, hiding her concern and the curiosity that burned inside her. "Consider it dropped. When I hear that my paper's been accepted, I'll let you know immediately—by carrier pigeon."

Will laughed. "You'd better drive right out and knock on my door. Promise?"

"Promise."

"What's up in the faculty world?" he said in an obvious attempt to steer the conversation away from the subject of telephones.

"Not much. Dr. Rogers is having his annual Welcome Back party Friday night and he invited me."

"He's in the psychology department, isn't he?"

"The chairman. The party's just for his department, but since I helped him out with some tricky math glitches he was having over the summer, he says I'm an honorary member. So I'm invited."

"And knowing you, you turned him down, right?"

"Wrong," she said, lifting her chin, glad to be able to surprise him. "I've decided to show up with bells on."

"Good for you. You need to get out more with the rest of the faculty instead of spending your free time with a broken-down groundskeeper."

"Right. You're positively decrepit, and intellectually backward as well."

Will glanced up at the faculty office building.

"Will Professor Sanders be going?"

"No. Why would—?" she began, then broke off as she caught his meaning. "Oh. Is he watching us again?"

"Yep. Having his after-lunch cigarettes."

Lisl glanced up at the second-floor window of Ev's office. No face was visible in the dark square, but at regular intervals a puff of white smoke would drift out through the screen.

Everett Sanders stared down at Lisl Whitman and the groundskeeper as they sat together beneath the tree. They seemed to be staring back at him. But that could be no more than coincidence. He knew he was invisible to them when he stood this far back in his office.

He drew deeply on his cigarette, his sixth for the day, his first after a lunch of eight ounces of tuna salad, a cold potato sliced and smeared with mustard, and a medium-sized peach. The same lunch he brought every day and ate right here at his desk. He kept rigorous track of his nutrition, and balanced it carefully. His fourth cup of coffee cooled on the desk. He allowed himself a dozen cups a day. Excessive, he knew, but he'd found he couldn't function well on less. He smoked too much too. Twenty cigarettes a day—opened a fresh pack of Kool Lights every morning and finished the last just before bed. Coffee and cigarettes—he wanted to give them up, but not yet. He couldn't give up *every*thing. But maybe in a few years, when he was more confident about his level of control, he'd try to get off tobacco.

He watched Lisl and wondered again at the type of man with whom she chose to spend her precious time. Here was one of the most brilliant women he had ever met wasting her lunch hours dallying with a common laborer—one with a ponytail, no less. A mismatch if he ever saw one. What could they possibly have in common? What could a man like that possibly have to say to interest a mind like hers?

It plagued him. What could they talk about, day after day, week after week? *What?*

The most frustrating aspect of the question was knowing that he would never have the answer. To obtain that he would either have to eavesdrop on them or join them, or ask Lisl directly what they talked about. None of which he could do. It simply wasn't in him.

Another question: Why on earth was he wasting his own time pondering such an inconsequential imponderable? What did it matter what Lisl and her big gardener friend discussed at lunch? He had better things to do.

And yet . . . they looked so relaxed together. Ev wished he could be so relaxed with people. Not even *people*—he'd settle for just one other person in the world with whom he could sit down and feel perfectly at ease discussing the secrets of the universe and the inconsequentials of daily existence.

Someone like Lisl. So soft, so beautiful. Maybe she wasn't beautiful in the accepted modern sense, but her golden blond hair was thick and silky smooth—he wished she'd wear it down and loose instead of twisted into that French braid she favored— and her smile so bright and warm. She was small-breasted and carrying too many pounds for her frame, but Ev wasn't impressed by exteriors. Appearances meant nothing. It was the inner woman that counted. And Ev knew that beneath Lisl's dowdy, pudgy shell was a wonderful, brilliant woman, sweet, sincere, compassionate.

What did that handyman see when he looked at her? Everett sincerely doubted the other man was attracted to Lisl for her mind. He didn't know him, of course, but it seemed that the groundskeeper possessed neither the values nor the depth of character that would set him in pursuit of a woman's mind.

So what was his angle?

Were they sexually intimate? Was that what it was all about? Pleasures of the flesh? Well, there was nothing wrong with that, as long as it didn't interfere with Lisl's future. Tragic if she were drawn away from her career. A brilliant mind such as hers did not belong at home all day changing diapers.

And of what concern was any of this to Everett Sanders?

Because I want to be where they are.

Wouldn't that be wonderful. To have her as a friend, a confidante, a sharer. To have almost *anyone* to share even a few hours. Because, Everett knew and freely admitted to himself, he was lonely. And although loneliness was far better than other problems he had known in the past, it could be a terrible burden at times, a constant gnawing ache in his soul.

Lunches with Lisl, silly chitchat with Lisl. It was more than he could hope for.

More than he *would* hope for.

The whole idea was ridiculous. Even if it were feasible, even if it were possible, he couldn't allow it. He couldn't permit himself to become involved in an emotional relationship. Emotions were too unpredictable, too difficult to control. And he couldn't let any area in his life slip from his control. Because if one area broke free, others might break loose and follow. And then his whole life might slip free from the iron grip in which he clutched it.

So let Lisl Whitman dawdle with her groundskeeper friend and/or lover. It was none of his business. It was her life and he had no right to think he should control it. It took all his resolve to control his own.

Besides, he should have been reading instead of wasting time at the window like this. Especially on a Wednesday. He had the weekly meeting tonight so he had to do his daily page quota on this week's novel earlier in the day. It was *Daddy* by Loup Durand. A few years old, but someone had recommended it to him as a thriller with a twist. And indeed it did have a twist. More than one. He was enjoying it immensely.

Everett had come to find fiction a welcome relief from the constraints of working with numbers all day, so years ago he had resolved to read one novel a week. And he did. He started a new novel every Sunday. Faithfully. *Daddy* was 377 pages long. So, to finish the novel in a week he had to read 53.85 pages a day. This was Wednesday, which meant that he had to reach page 216 before he slept tonight. Actually, he was a little ahead of the game today because he had gone past his daily page increment last night and continued to the end of the chapter. That wasn't a bad idea in itself, but he didn't like breaking his own rules.

He stubbed out his cigarette and lit another immediately. He allowed himself two in a row after lunch. He opened the book to the top of page 181. Thirty-five to go. He settled himself at his desk and began reading.

THREE

Will glanced at his watch. Almost quitting time, but he wanted to get this tractor-mower running before he knocked off for the weekend. That way it would be ready to roll first thing Monday morning.

He looked across the gently rolling field of the lower campus where the soccer and football teams were practicing on the freshly mown grass. Keeping the campus pruned and trimmed was an endless task, but Will loved it. Never thought he'd end up a groundskeeper—not with his background and education—but he had to admit it had its rewards. He found a very real satisfaction in doing simple labor with his hands. Weeding, edging, pruning, doing motor maintenance, it didn't matter. While his hands were busy, his mind was left free to roam. And roam it did. It occurred to him that he had done more heavy-duty thinking in the last few years than he had done in his entire life, and that was pushing half a century.

But still he hadn't found any answers. Only more questions.

Back to the tractor. The old John Deere was one of the crew's workhorses and it had been kicking up all week, coughing, sputtering, stalling. He thought he'd heard something that sounded like a bad wire. He'd replaced it. Now came the test.

The engine started on the first turn of the key. Will listened carefully. He could tell a lot about an engine just from the way it sounded. It was a knack he'd discovered back when he began fooling around with cars as a teenager.

"Hey, Willie! Sounds great!"

Will looked up and saw Joe Bob Hawkins, the foreman of the grounds crew, standing over him. He was younger than Will—about forty or so—but his receding red hair and big, burly barrel-chested physique made him seem older.

"Bad wire," Will told him.

"You got that magic touch, I tell ya. Ain't never seen a body could fix an engine the way you do. Y'all got a degree in motor medicine or something?"

"You got it, Joe Bob. I'm an M.D.—a motor doctor."

"That you are, guy," he said with a laugh, "that you are. Tell you what. You stow that thing in the garage and then join me in my office. I'll buy you a TGIF snort of sour mash."

Will thought about that. A drink would be good about now, although he'd have preferred a cold beer to a shooter. And some simple conversation with an affable good ol' boy like Joe Bob would be good, too. But he couldn't risk it.

"Aw, I'd love to, J.B., but I've got to hit the road as soon as I'm off. My ma's been kinda sick and so I'm heading north for the weekend."

"That's too bad. She's not bad sick, is she?"

"Yes and no. It's her heart. Sometimes it acts up and sometimes it don't. Lately it is."

Will hated the easy way the lies tripped off his tongue, but this story was so well practiced he almost believed it himself.

"Well, okay," Joe Bob said. "I reckon y'all better get hustlin'. I hope she's all right. If there's anything I can do, you know, if you need some extra time off to stay with her or anything like that, you just let me know."

"I hope it won't come to that, but thanks for offering."

Will was touched by Joe Bob's genuine concern, which made him feel worse than usual for lying. But there was no way he could go kill a half hour or more sitting and sipping in the foreman's office.

There was a telephone there.

Will drove the tractor over to the garage and stowed it away for the weekend, then headed for the parking lot.

On the ride home, Will cruised Conway Street and thought about the day. He hadn't connected with Lisl today, so at least he hadn't had to lie to her again about rereading *The Stranger*. Couldn't let her know what he really was reading. She'd ask too many questions. Questions he couldn't answer.

Pretty foolish stunt, bringing it to work with him. Almost as if he wanted her to see it, wanted her to ask those questions. Was that it? Was his subconscious deliberately nudging him into exposing his past, pushing him to get off the dime and into motion instead of marking time here year after year?

Maybe. But no matter what his subconscious wanted, Will knew he wasn't ready to surface again. He still had a ways to go before he could even consider going back.

Maybe he'd never go back. He liked it here in N.C.; he was fitting in, and Lisl was a big part of that comfortable feeling. She made him feel good. Yet she had her share of hang-ups, the most glaring being her lack of self-esteem. She was bright, warm, real, so free of pretense, a refreshing trait these days on the campus of "the new Harvard of the South." She'd had no trouble convincing Will of her brilliance, her sweetness. Why couldn't she see it?

Somebody had done a real number on Lisl. The most obvious culprit was her ex-husband, but Will sensed that it went deeper than that. What were her parents like? How had they raised her? Stuck her in front of a TV? Like so many people he met these days, Lisl seemed to have been raised with no values. She was brilliant, but she lacked focus. She was incomplete, vulnerable, and lacking a vital piece: someone to love. The right someone could make it all come together for her. The wrong someone— again—could unravel her. Will knew he was one of the wrong someones.

He wished he could help her, but didn't know exactly what to do with her—pulling her closer, pushing her away, wanting to open up to her the way she had opened up to him, yet knowing he couldn't really open up to anyone ever again.

Lisl parked her car in her assigned space and got out. The sun was well on its way down the sky, but the early September air was still warm and slightly hazy with the humidity. Hazy enough to mute and blend the various shades of green on the trees and the wild splotches of color from the bunches of mums blossoming all over the grounds. Only the aging garden apartments kept the scene from being an Impressionist's dream.

Brookside Gardens was a set of two-story brick apartments, occupied for the most part by young marrieds, many with kids. It could get noisy here on Saturday afternoons. But Brookside adequately suited Lisl's needs. Her one-bedroom unit offered security and comfort, was the perfect size, and didn't strain her bank account. What more could she ask?

Right now? Maybe a little company. She wished Will lived nearby instead of out in the country. She had this urge to drop in on someone and plop into a chair and talk about nothing over a glass of wine. But there was no one here she knew well enough for that.

That was one problem with Brookside. She had no real friends here. She didn't fit in with the young marrieds surrounding her. Sure, they welcomed her to their parties and cookouts on holiday weekends, and she'd drink and talk and laugh with them, but she never felt at ease with them, never really felt she *belonged.*

Well, it wasn't really relevant tonight. She had to get herself spruced up for Dr. Rogers's Welcome Back party.

In the old days, it might have been called a faculty tea. Nowadays it was a cocktail party. Lisl really didn't want to go. She wouldn't know anyone there. After all it was the psych department, not math. She and Ev had only helped them with a few snags over the summer. No big thing. No reason to invite them to the party. Of course it would have been a little easier to take if Ev were going. At least she'd have someone to talk to. But Ev never went to parties.

Lisl wasn't a party person either. She saw herself as the dullest of people. A rotten conversationalist who could think of nothing to say once she'd covered the weather and general comments about the incoming student body. Then there'd be these long uncomfortable silences and she and whoever she was with would slowly drift to different rooms.

Funny, she never seemed to run out of things to say to Will.

But Will wasn't going to be there, so forget that. If tonight followed the usual pattern, she'd wind up alone, standing by the bookshelves, nursing a plastic tumbler of too-tart chablis as she sneaked looks at her watch and pretended to be interested in what titles and authors were stacked on the shelf. Usually the selection was as uninteresting as she felt.

But this past summer had proved an unusually solitary one. She'd shuttled between her apartment and her office six days a week with little or no deviation in pattern. Over a long, lonely Labor Day weekend she had decided it was time to force herself into some sort of social . . . what? Whirl? Her social life would never *whirl.* And she wasn't sure she wanted it to. A social *crawl* was more her speed. She'd settle for that. Gladly.

And so the old Lisl was determined to become a different

Lisl, a new, improved, socializing Lisl. She would turn down no invitation to a social gathering, no matter how dreadful she thought it might be.

Which was why she was determined to show up at Cal Rogers's party tonight.

But the most immediate problem was what to wear. These things were casual but Lisl didn't want to be too casual. Most of her comfortable clothes fell into the too-casual category; and her good stuff really didn't fit her anymore. She'd gained more poundage over the summer and was now weighing in at one-sixty-five.

You're a cow, she thought, looking in the mirror.

She rarely looked in the mirror. What for? To check how she looked? She wasn't all that interested. Since the divorce she hadn't been able to dredge up much interest in anything besides her work. Certainly not much interest in men. Not after what Brian had put her through. Six years later it still hurt.

Brian . . . they'd met as freshman in calculus class at U.N.C., both of them aiming toward a B.S., Brian a premed in biology, Lisl a math major. A tentative courtship, a growing affection blossoming into love, at least on Lisl's part, and then sexual intimacy, the first time for Lisl. They were married immediately after graduation and moved to Pendleton where Lisl went to work teaching high school math while Brian started his stint at Darnell University medical school. Lisl supported him through most of those four years, taking occasional night courses toward her masters in math. During Brian's fourth year in medical school she discovered that he was having an affair with one of the nurses at the hospital. That would have been bad enough, but she learned from one of the other nurses that since he had begun his in-hospital clinical training, Brian had been bedding any female employee who would have him.

Lisl felt her throat constrict at the memory. God, it still hurt. After all this time, it still hurt.

Lisl filed for divorce. This seemed to infuriate Brian. Apparently he had wanted to be the one to do the dumping. Lisl's lawyer told her that he was probably terrified, too, because of a recent legal precedent in which a wife who had supported her husband through medical school could demand a share of the future proceeds he reaped from that diploma.

Lisl wanted no part of that. She only wanted out. And she had gotten out.

But Brian made sure he had the last word.

When all was said and done, when all the papers had been signed and notarized, Brian had caught up to her as she'd fled the attorney's office.

"I never loved you," he said, then walked away.

No amount of physical abuse, no tirade of vituperation, no stream of curses, no matter how long, how loud, how vile could have hurt Lisl nearly as much as those four whispered words. Although she had said nothing and had walked coolly and calmly to her car, inside she'd been shattered, completely, utterly.

I never loved you.

The words had been echoing down the empty hallways of her life ever since.

Even now she felt her knees wobble with the hurt. And the worst part was that he was still around. He lived on the other side of town and was now on staff as an orthopedist at the county medical center.

Shaking off the memory, Lisl searched deep in her closet for something to wear, but stopped when she came across a familiar-looking shoe box. She lifted the lid and found her old shell collection from childhood. She smiled at the memory of how she'd once wanted to be a marine biologist.

Shells. All through her life she'd assigned shells to the people in her life. She picked up a beautiful brown-striped chambered nautilus. This was Will—big, mysterious, hiding who-knew-what in all those inner chambers; and secretive, withdrawing and snapping his lid shut whenever anyone got too close. The razor clam was Ev, thin, sharp edged, smooth-surfaced, unadorned, what you saw was what you got. And here was Brian, a starfish, gentle and appealing on the surface, but it survived by trapping a mollusk with its arms, boring through its shell, and sucking out the soft parts inside, leaving an empty husk.

Like me, Lisl thought, picking up a chowder clam shell—common, uncollectible, its pale, dull surface windowed by a starfish burr hole. *Me.*

She lidded the box and continued her search for something to wear. She wound up squeezed into a pair of cream-colored slacks topped with an oversize lightweight sweater. She felt like a sausage from the waist down but it would have to do. A little makeup, five minutes with the curling iron, and she was set. All she had to do was get through the evening without splitting a seam.

Someday soon she was going to do something about these extra pounds.

* * *

Lisl noticed him as soon as she walked through the front door.
She'd never seen him before. Young, not tall—no more than
five feet ten, she guessed—and very slim. Hardly prepossessing
physically, yet he was the first man she noticed. His movements
were smooth, relaxed, and graceful. With his neat mustache, Latin
coloring accentuated by the perfectly pressed white slacks and
shirt that fit as if they'd been made just for him—and perhaps
they had—he stood out in the crowd of paunchy, shaggy, patch-
sleeved academics like a prince among peasants. This young man
had style.

He was handing drinks to a pair of faculty wives who were
blatantly gushing over him. As he turned from them, his eyes
brushed past her, then returned. He smiled and gave her a tiny
bow. Unaccountably, Lisl blushed, pleased that he had picked her
out for a personal welcome.

Probably does that to every woman who comes through the
door, she thought as he turned away to speak to someone.

Lisl sidled through the press of guests in the living room,
nodding, smiling, saying hello to the faces she recognized. Her
immediate goal was the bar—a card table laden with beer, jug
wine, soda, mixers, and a few bottles of hard liquor. Lisl didn't
drink much, but a half-filled glass in her hand made her look and
even feel like someone who belonged.

As she moved, she noticed from the corner of her eye that the
stylish young unknown seemed to be watching her. Who was he?
Somebody's son?

At the bar she found Calvin Rogers, the host, a portly, jovial
sort, an aging Puck who sported a goatee to offset the hair he was
losing on top. He held up a glass and smiled.

"Hi! Want a drink?"

Lisl could see by his expression that he knew her face but
couldn't quite connect it with a name.

"Sure."

"Wine, beer, or booze?"

"A white wine, please."

"Great!" As he poured from a two-liter bottle of Almaden
he said, "House rule: I make you the first; after that you're on
your own."

"Fine," Lisl said. "No limit?"

He raised his eyebrows and grinned.

"Oh, it's going to be one of *those* nights, is it?"

"Not really," Lisl said with a laugh. She hesitated a moment, debating whether she should ask him, then decided to plunge ahead: "Say, I see some new faces here. Some young ones."

"Yeah. I invited a couple of the new graduate students."

"I see," she said, glancing at the dark young man.

"That's Losmara," Rogers said, following her gaze. "Rafael. Bit of a dude, isn't he? But a brilliant mind. Brilliant. Comes out of Arizona State, which isn't exactly a heavy hitter in psychology, but he sent this proposal for a paper outlining a cybernetic model for schizophrenia that just blew me away. I knew right then this was a guy who was going somewhere. And wherever he was going, I wanted him to come from here. I couldn't offer him money—I understand his family's half as rich as Croesus—so I played coy and conned him into choosing Darnell for his doctorate. Figured he might teach the rest of *us* something before he's through. I invited him and the other grads tonight, figuring they won't drink much and it'll make them feel more at home with the department."

"That's nice of you."

He smiled and handed her the glass of wine. "I'm a nice guy. Or so they tell me."

Lisl wandered the cramped living room–dining room area, looking for someone she knew. She avoided the bookshelves, figuring she'd have plenty of time to inspect them later. One full circuit and she found herself standing alone by the sliding glass door that opened onto the backyard.

This wasn't working. She felt more out of place than usual here because there wasn't a single other person from her own department. She looked around and envied all these people with the knack for conversation. Nobody else seemed to be having problems. They all made it look so easy. Why couldn't she just stop by a group, listen in for a while, and then join the conversation?

Because I can't.

She stepped out onto the small flagstone patio. After examining what few of Cal's roses hadn't been eaten by beetles, she turned to go back inside.

And found the dark young man next to her.

"Hello," he said. His voice was velvet, deep but soft, melodious. His teeth were so white under the dark mustache, his eyes almost luminous in the dark. "I hear you're from math."

So simple. So perfect.

Small talk. Rafe—that was how he introduced himself—seemed to be a natural at it. Relaxed, exuding self-confidence, he gave her the feeling that no subject could be inconsequential if he was discussing it. They stood side by side for a while, then moved to the redwood bench by the picnic table. Rafe had a lot of questions about campus life at Darnell, especially as it related to graduate students. Lisl had a good store of knowledge on the subject because she'd earned her own doctorate here.

He listened. Really *listened*. Whatever Lisl had to say, her insights, her opinions, all seemed important to him. A part of her was on edge, ready for the brush-off, waiting for him to smile, excuse himself, and move on after he'd learned what he wanted to know. But Rafe stayed by her side, asking more questions, drawing her out, freshening her wine when he replenished his own bourbon and water. He left her from time to time, but only briefly.

Although he was much too young for her—he was twenty-three, tops—Lisl found him stimulating. He exuded a maleness, almost like a scent, a pheromone. Whatever it was, she knew she was responding to it. This would never go anywhere, but it was exciting to be with him. He was making the party for her.

Throughout the evening she noticed inquisitive glances from other women as they passed in and out through the patio door. She could almost read their minds: What was the most interesting-looking man at the party doing with that frump who's got to be a good ten years his senior?

Good question.

Idly, she sorted through the pretzels in the bowl between them on the picnic table, and picked out one to eat.

"Do you always do that?" Rafe said. His gaze was flicking back and forth between the pretzel in her hand and her eyes.

"Do what?"

"Take the broken ones."

Lisl looked at the pretzel in her hand. Half a pretzel. A loop and a half. She vaguely remembered picking out broken ones all evening. She always picked out the broken ones.

"I guess I do. Is that significant?"

He smiled. A warm smile, showing off those white, even teeth.

"Could be. What matters is why."

"I guess I don't want to see them go to waste. Everybody grabs the whole ones and leaves the broken ones. They're like old maids. When the night's over they'll probably get thrown away. So those are the ones I take."

"In other words, you're existing on other people's leftovers."

"I wouldn't call it existing—"

"Neither would I." Rafe pulled an unbroken three-ring from the bowl and offered it to her. His voice was suddenly serious. "*Never* be satisfied with leftovers."

Intrigued and fascinated by his intensity, Lisl took the pretzel and laughed. A bit too shrilly, she thought.

"It's just a pretzel."

"No. It's a decision, a statement. A paradigm of life, and how one chooses to live it."

"I think you're reading too much into this." He was, after all, a psych grad. "Life is a little more complex than a bowl of pretzels."

"Of course it is. It's a bowl of choices. A series of choices you make from moment to moment from the time you are volitional until you die. Each choice you make mirrors what you are inside. They say where you've been, they tell where you're going."

His intensity was just a tiny bit intimidating, yet exciting, stirring something within her.

"Okay," she said, not wanting to argue yet unwilling to let him get off without a qualifier. "But *pretzels?*"

Rafe picked another whole three-ring from the bowl and took a savage bite out of it.

"Pretzels."

Laughing, Lisl took a big bite of her own.

Yes. One very intense young man.

Too soon the crowd began to thin. People were leaving so early. This had to be the shortest party Lisl had ever been to. She glanced at her watch and was shocked to see 1:06 on its face.

Impossible. She'd just got here. But a check with the mantel clock inside confirmed it.

"I guess I'd better be going," she told Rafe.

"I'm sorry for monopolizing all your time," he said.

Monopolizing her time—that was a laugh.

"Don't worry. You didn't."

"You have a ride?" he said, his eyes holding hers.

"Yes." For an instant she wished she didn't. But as much as she wanted to continue their party-long conversation, driving off with him would look like she'd been picked up, and that would be all over the math department before she arrived Monday morning.

"Good," he said, "because I feel obligated to give Dr. Rogers a hand cleaning up."

"Of course."

Lisl had difficulty picturing Rafe Losmara, dressed all in white as he was, emptying ashtrays and rinsing glasses. But the fact that he was cheerfully willing to pitch in said something about him.

He walked her to the front door where he took her hand as if to shake it, but did not let go.

"This would have been a pretty dreary affair without you," he said.

Lisl smiled. *Took the words right out of my mouth.*

"You really think so?" she said.

"I know so. Can I call you sometime?"

"Sure." *Sure you will.*

"Great. Talk to you soon."

Right.

Lisl did not expect to hear from him again. Not that it would really matter, anyway. A nice evening. No, more than nice—the most interesting, stimulating evening she'd had in longer than she cared to compute. A shame it had to end, but that was that. Rafe, that fascinating grad student, had seemed genuinely interested in her. *Her.* And she'd held up her end of the conversation effortlessly. Such a good feeling. But it was over. Take it for what it was worth and go on from here. She was glad she'd decided to come. If nothing else, this evening had bolstered her resolution to become more socially active.

Party-hearty Lisl—that'll be me.

Back in her apartment, Lisl groaned with relief as she released herself from her slacks and readied for bed. She reached for the amber, safety-topped bottle of Restoril, then stopped. She didn't want a sleeping pill tonight. She preferred the idea of lying awake for a while and savoring memories of the evening.

The phone rang as she slipped under the covers.

"Hi. It's me," said a soft voice.

Lisl recognized it immediately. She wondered at the rush of warmth that surged through her.

"Hello, Rafe."

"I escaped Dr. Rogers's place and got home, but I'm still kind of wired. Feel like talking?"

Yeah, she did. She felt like talking all night. Which they damn near did.

Before hanging up, he asked her if they could have lunch together tomorrow. Lisl hesitated—she was faculty, after all, and he was a grad student—but only for a second. She was feeling more alive tonight than she had in years, and now an opportunity to extend it was being offered to her. Why turn it down?

"Sure," she said. "As long as they don't have bowls of pretzels sitting around."

His laugh was music. "You're on!"

The man in the white shirt and pants hung up the phone and leaned back on the white sofa in the white living room of his condominium townhouse. He smiled and traced letters in the air. His fingertip left trails of depthless black as it moved: L . . . I . . . S . . . L.

"Contact," he said in a voice that was barely a whisper.

He rose and walked to his back door, glided down the pair of steps to his backyard, and stood barefoot in the moist grass. He smiled again as he gazed up at the wheeling constellations in the moonless sky. Then he spread his arms straight out, level with the ground, palms down.

Slowly, he began to rise.

Everett Sanders jerked upright in his bed and stared at the window.

He'd never been a good sleeper and tonight had been just like all the rest: a series of catnaps interspersed with periods of wakefulness. He'd been lying here with just a sheet covering him, tilting on the cusp of a doze, when he thought he saw a face appear at his window.

He rubbed his eyes and looked again. Nothing. The window was empty. Nothing there but the screen, nothing moving but the drapes swaying gracefully in the breeze.

Nothing there at all. But then, how *could* a face have been there? His apartment was on the third floor.

He lay back and wondered if it had been a dream or an hallucination. He'd hallucinated years ago. He didn't want to go through that again.

Everett Sanders rolled onto his side and searched for sleep. But he remained facing the window, opening his eyes every so often to check if the face was back. Of course it wouldn't be. He knew that. But it had seemed so real. So real . . .

Will Ryerson awoke sweating. At first he thought it might be another of his nightmares, but he couldn't remember dreaming. As he lay there in the dark he had a strange, uneasy sensation, as if he were being watched. He got up and went to the window, but there was no one outside. No movement. No sound except the crickets.

Yet the sensation persisted.

Slipping into an old pair of loafers, Will grabbed a flashlight, turned on the yard lights, and went out to the front yard. He stood there in his undershirt and Jockeys and trained the flashlight beam into the dark recesses of the tree-lined lot. Somebody was out there. He was sure of it.

Why? Why would someone be watching him? He was sure no one knew about him. If someone did, they'd surely turn him in. So who was out there?

He sighed. Maybe no one after all. Maybe just his paranoia getting the best of him. But why tonight? Why now, after all these years?

The phone call. That had to be it. In the three days since it had happened, his subconscious must have gone into overdrive. He was beginning to feel the effects tonight.

As he turned to go back inside, he glanced up and froze.

Far above him, a white cross floated against the stars.

It was moving, drifting toward the south. As Will squinted upward, it appeared less like a cross and more like a man—a man all in white, floating in midair with his arms spread.

Will felt his saliva dry up as his palms began to sweat. This wasn't happening. This couldn't be happening. A nightmare—*this* was the nightmare. But after his real-life nightmare experience in New York five years ago, he knew that the rules of reason and sanity were not constant. Sometimes they broke down. And then anything could happen.

Far above, the man cross-drifted over the trees and was gone from sight.

Trembling with dread, Will hurried back inside the house.

THE BOY
at six months

May 19, 1969

Oh, Jimmy—what's wrong with you?

Carol Stevens stared down at her sleeping son and wanted to cry. Lying prone in his crib, pudgy arms and legs spread wide, round-faced with soft pink cheeks, wisps of dark hair clinging to his scalp, he was the picture of innocence. She studied the delicate venules in his closed eyelids and thought how beautiful he was.

As long as those eyelids stayed closed.

When they were open he was different. The innocence disappeared—the *child* disappeared. The eyes were old. They didn't move like the eyes of other infants, roving, trying to take in everything at once because everything was so new. Jimmy's eyes stared, they studied, they . . . *penetrated*. It was unnerving to have him watch you.

And Jimmy never smiled or laughed, never cooed or gurgled or blew bubbles. He did vocalize, though. Not random baby noises, but patterned sounds, as if he were trying to get his untrained vocal cords to function. Since his birth, his grandfather Jonah would sit here in the nursery with the door closed and talk to him in a low voice. Carol had listened at the door a number of times but could never quite make out what he was saying. But she was sure from the length of the sentences and the cadence of his speech that it wasn't baby talk.

Carol turned away from the crib and wandered to the window where she looked out on the Ouachita Mountains. Jonah had brought them here to rural Arkansas to hide until the baby was born. She'd followed his lead, too frightened by the madness she'd left behind to do anything else.

If only Jim were alive. He'd know how to handle this. He'd be able to step back and decide what to do about his son. But Jim had been dead a little over a year now, and Carol could not be cold and logical and rational about little Jimmy. He was their son, their flesh and blood, all she had left of Jim. She loved him as much as she feared him.

When she turned she saw that Jimmy was awake, sitting in the crib, staring at her with those cold eyes that started out blue but had darkened to brown within the past few months. He spoke to her. It was a baby's voice, high and soft. The words were garbled but clear enough to be understood. She had no doubt about what he said: "I'm hungry, woman. Bring me something to eat."

Carol screamed and fled the nursery.

FOUR

Manhattan

"Letter for you, Sarge," said Potts, waving the envelope in the air from the far side of the squad room.

Detective Sergeant Renaldo Augustino glanced up from his cluttered desk. He was reed-thin with a ruddy complexion and a generous nose. His dark hair was combed straight back from his receding hairline. He took a final drag on his cigarette and jammed it into the crowded ashtray to his right.

"The mail came a couple of hours ago," he told Potts. "Where you been hiding it?"

"It's not regular mail. Came over from the One-twelve."

Great. Probably another late notice for dues to a PBA local he no longer belonged to. He'd been transferred to Midtown North over two years ago and they still hadn't got the message yet.

"Chuck it out," he said.

"Could be a bill of some sort," Potts said.

"That's what I figured. I don't even want to see the damn thing. Just—"

"A phone bill."

That brought Renny up short. "Local?"

"No. Southern Bell."

His heart suddenly thudding in his chest, Renny was out of his chair and across the squad room so fast, he frightened Potts.

"Give me that."

He snatched the envelope from Potts's fingers and strode back to his desk.

"What gives?" said Sam Lang, leaning over Renny's desk, slurping coffee from a foam cup.

They'd been partners for a couple of years now. Like Renny, Sam was in his mid-forties, but balding and overweight. Everything Sam wore was rumpled, tie included.

As Renny sped through the text, he felt the old anger rekindling.

"It's him!" he said. "And he's up to his old tricks!"

Puzzled creases formed in Sam's doughy brow.

"Who?"

"A killer. Name of Ryan. Nobody you'd know." He scanned the letter again. "Any idea where Pendleton, North Carolina, is, Sam?"

"Somewhere between Virginia and South Carolina, I imagine."

"Gee, thanks."

Renny seemed to remember something about a big university there. No matter. He could find out easily enough.

Almost five years now . . . the kid, Danny Gordon . . . left for dead by some sicko bastard. Renny had been assigned to the case. He'd seen a lot of gut-wrenching things in his years on the force. When you spent your nights turning over rocks in a city the size of New York, you got used to the slimy things that crawled out. But something about that boy and what had been done to him had grabbed Renny by the throat and wouldn't let go. Still hadn't let go.

His mind leapt back across the years, images flashed before his eyes. The white, pain-racked little face, the hoarse screams that wouldn't stop, and other horrors. And the priest. So horrified, so shattered, so lost, so convincing in the lies he told. Renny had fallen for those lies, had allowed himself to believe, to get sucked into that bastard's trap. He'd come to like the priest, to trust him, to think of him as an ally in the search for Danny's mutilator.

You worked me beautifully, you son of a bitch. Played me like a maestro.

Renny knew he was being hard on himself. The fact that he had once been an orphan like Danny Gordon, growing up in the same orphanage as Danny, raised a Catholic with endless respect for priests, all of that had made him an easy mark for that slimy Jesuit's lies.

Until it had become clear that Danny Gordon was not going to die. Then the priest had acted in desperation to save his worthless guilty hide.

And then, in one night, the whole case had gone to hell. As a direct result of that, Renny had lost his rank. An indirect result of the whole mess had been the loss of his marriage.

Joanne had been gone three years now. When the Danny Gordon case fell apart and Renny's career took a dive, he took it out on everybody around him. Joanne had been around the most so she bore the brunt of his rage and frustration and growing obsession with bringing the killer to justice. She took as much as she could—two years worth. Then she folded. She packed up and left. Renny didn't blame her. He knew he'd been impossible to live with. Still was, he was sure. He blamed himself. And he blamed Danny Gordon's killer. He added the Augustino marriage to the list of the killer's victims.

One more thing I owe you for, you bastard.

But what was really going on here? Now. Today. Had the killer priest he'd been chasing the past five years finally surfaced, or was this just a coincidence? He couldn't tell for sure. And he wanted it so bad, he didn't trust his own judgment.

He decided on a second opinion.

He placed a call to Columbia University and arranged to meet Dr. Nicholas Quinn in half an hour. At Leon's, Midtown North's watering hole.

Dr. Nick arrived just as Renny was downing the last of his second Scotch. Not bad time, considering the guy had to come all the way from Morningside Heights. They shook hands—they didn't see each other often enough to forgo that formality—and moved to a table. Renny carried his third Scotch along, Nick brought an eight-ounce draft.

Renny savored the dark and the quiet, not minding the mixed odors of stale smoke and spilled beer. Not often you could have a quiet drink or three in Leon's; only when it was mid-shift, like now. But in forty-five minutes, when the first shift ended, look out. Most all of Midtown North would be here, three deep at the bar.

"So, Nick," Renny said. "What're you up to?"

"Particle physics," the younger man said. "You really want to hear?"

"Not really. How's the love life?"

Nick sipped his beer. "I love my work."

"Don't worry," Renny said. "It's just a phase you're going through. You'll get over it."

Renny smiled and looked at his companion. Dr. Nick, as he called him—or Nicholas Quinn, Ph.D., as the people at Columbia called him—was an odd-looking duck. But weren't physicists supposed to be weird? Look at Einstein. There'd been a strange-looking guy if there ever was one. So maybe Nick had a right to look weird. From what Renny had been able to gather, Nick Quinn had an Einstein-league brain. And under all that unkempt hair, an Elephant Man–shaped skull. He also had bad skin, pale with lots of little scars, as if he'd had a severe case of acne as a teenager. And his eyes. He was wearing contacts these days, but Renny had a feeling from their wide stare and the flattened look of his eye sockets that he'd probably worn Coke bottle lenses most of his life. Thirtyish, thin, a little stooped, and developing a paunch. Not surprisingly, he was single. A true nerdo from the git-go. But who knew? Maybe someday he'd find himself the perfect nerdella, and together they'd raise a family of nerdettes.

"How's by you?" Nick said.

"Couldn't be better, kid. Took me five years, but I'm a detective sergeant again."

"Congratulations," Nick said, hoisting his beer.

Renny nodded but didn't drink. It was old news. And besides, he never should have been busted down in the first place.

"And Joanne found herself an insurance salesman out on the Island and got remarried."

Nick didn't seem to know how to take that.

"Don't worry, kid. That's good news too. No more alimony payments."

Renny did take a sip for that one, but there was no celebration inside. Joanne. Remarried. The finality of the news had taken a while to sink in: She'd nailed down the coffin lid on any hopes of a reconciliation.

"Speaking of news," Nick said, "why'd you want to see me?"

Renny smiled. "Anxious?"

"No. Curious. I've been calling you regularly since it happened, and for years now it's always the same answer: nothing new. Now you call *me*. I know you like to keep people dangling, Mr. Detective, and I've been dangling long enough. What've you got?"

Renny shrugged. "Maybe something, maybe nothing." He pulled the letter from Southern Bell from his pocket and slid it across the table. "This came today."

He watched Nick study it. They'd met five years ago, during the Danny Gordon case. But they'd stayed in touch since. That had been Nick's idea. After Renny had blown the Gordon case, Nick had shown up in the squad room—Renny had been working out of the 112th in Queens then—and offered to help in any way he could. Renny had told him thanks but no thanks. The last thing he needed was a nerdy citizen getting in the way. But Nick had persisted, pulling on the common thread that linked the three of them.

Orphans. Renny, Danny Gordon, and Nick Quinn—they'd all been orphans. And they'd all spent a good part of their childhood in the St. Francis Home for Boys in Queens. Renny had lived there in the forties until he was adopted by the Augustinos. Nick had spent most of the sixties there before being adopted by the Quinn family, and had known the killer-priest well. That alone made Nick an asset. But on top of that, Nick was brilliant. A mind like a computer. He'd sifted through all the evidence and run it all through his brain, and had come up with a theory that was hard to refute, one that made the suspect, Father Ryan, look clean . . . up to a point.

What Nick's scenario couldn't explain was the eyewitness accounts of Father Ryan carrying Danny Gordon from the hospital and driving off with him, never to be seen again.

In anybody's book, that was called kidnapping.

Renny felt his jaw muscles bunching even now as he thought about it. He'd liked that priest, had even thought they were friends. What a jerk he'd been. Allowed himself to be set up so the priest could pull an end run around him and leave him looking like a Grade-A asshole. An empty-handed asshole who'd let some sicko bastard snatch a child victim from right under his nose. The memory still sent icy fury howling through him like a hungry wind.

"North Carolina," Nick said, looking up from the letter. "Think it might be him?"

"I don't know what to think. It sort of came out of the blue."

"How—?"

"A long-term gain on a short-term investment, you might say."

Five years ago, when Father Ryan had taken off with the boy, and seemed to have got away clean, Renny had put out a man-and-a-boy description of the fugitive pair, but had added a new wrinkle. Through the FBI he'd asked the East Coast phone companies to be on the lookout for complaints about a certain kind of prank phone call that Renny had come to associate with the missing priest. There'd been a fair amount of returns on that at first, and for a while Renny had thought they were zeroing in on Ryan, but just when he'd been sure they were going to run him to ground, he disappeared. Suddenly, Father Ryan was gone, vanished from the face of the earth as if he'd never existed.

Nick dropped the letter onto the table and reached for his beer.

"I don't know. It's so vague. Isn't there some way you can talk to anyone down there?"

"Already have. Couldn't get anything firsthand, though. It happened on the street near a bus stop. The people who'd actually listened to the phone had boarded their bus and gone home by the time the police and emergency squads had arrived. But there seemed to be a definite consensus that the call was from a child in trouble."

Just like the other calls, Renny thought, his mind leaping back five years to the waiting area outside the children's ward at Downstate. He still had nightmares about that endless week in hell, the door to Danny's hospital room looming before him, drawing him forward, opening to reveal the horrors that lay behind it. And he remembered that phone call.

He'd been sitting there with Father Ryan, a man he had come to trust, even to admire. They were both on tenter hooks, alternately sitting and pacing, waiting for the docs to give them the latest news on Danny Gordon, when the phone rang.

A NYNEX pay phone, bolted to the wall, like a million others around the city. But Renny had never heard a phone ring like that before. It just *rang,* steadily, on and on. Something about it made his hackles rise. Against the priest's warnings, he'd answered it. What he'd heard over that wire still echoed in his brain on those too-frequent nights when sleep wouldn't come. He'd been horrified, mystified, sickened. But when the priest— his new friend, Danny's supposed guardian—had hiked off with the kid, he realized it had all been a scam, a sleazy attempt to direct suspicion elsewhere.

And it might have worked, too.

You were good, you bastard, Renny thought. The Marlon Fucking Brando of the priesthood.

"Low specificity," Nick said.

"Say what?" Renny said, yanking himself back to the present.

Nick smiled. "Scientist talk. It means that the incident under review resembles the sought-after phenomenon in only the most general sense. What about that bizarre ring of the bell you've told me about?"

"Like I said: I couldn't talk to the folks who picked it up, so I don't know. Wish I could. If they confirmed that long drawn-out ring, I'd be on a plane heading south right now."

Nick glanced at him, then looked away.

"You still think he killed the boy?"

As Renny replied, he watched Nick closely. He'd had a feeling all along that Nick knew more about the whereabouts of the priest than he let on. That was why Renny kept an eye on him. One day Nick might slip, and then Renny would have the break he'd been waiting for.

"I'm sure of it," Renny said. "It's the only way he could get away clean. If there's one good thing about working in Manhattan, it's that it's an island. There's only so many ways you can get off. We screened every bridge and tunnel for a man and a boy. Pulled over every man-and-boy combo we found. Danny and the priest weren't among them. Yet we know he slipped past us, through Staten Island is my guess. And as far as I'm concerned, that means he offed the kid and dumped his body—maybe in a construction site, maybe in the East River. Wherever it was, it was a good spot. We haven't found him yet. But Danny Gordon is dead. That's the only way that bastard could have gotten away."

"How about a boat?" Nick said.

Renny shook his head. He'd already shuffled through this deck. Many times.

"Uh-uh. Not in that weather. And anyway, there were no boats reported missing or stolen. No, Nick. Ryan eliminated the only witness who could finger him."

"And then disappeared himself," Nick said. "The point of eliminating a witness is to obviate flight. You're saying he did both. That doesn't make sense."

"Nothing about this whole case has made sense from the start," Renny said, finishing his Scotch. "And whose side are you on, anyway?"

"It's not a matter of sides. I'm pulling for Danny Gordon, that's for sure. But as for the rest . . ."

"You mean you're keeping a soft spot for that pervo priest?"

Nick's eyes blazed. "Don't say that. Nobody's ever even hinted—"

"I'm sure that was behind it. When we finally turn over all the rocks, that's what we'll find. And it won't be the first time, believe me."

"He was good to me," Nick said, his throat working as he looked away. "Damn good."

"Yeah," Renny said, sensing the turmoil in the younger man, and feeling for him. "I know what you mean. He fooled us all."

"So what are your plans?" Nick said after a while.

"Not sure. That's why I called you. What do you think?"

Renny trusted his own instincts, but he'd learned over the years that you could get too close to a case—you could get so fixed on the leaves that you lost sight of the tree. That was where a "third eye" came in handy. And since no one at Midtown North really gave a damn about the Danny Gordon case—after all, it was almost five years old and really belonged to the 112th in Queens—Renny used Nick as a sounding board. Besides being brilliant, he was interested.

"I'd wait," Nick said. He tapped the letter. "There's not enough to go on here. Odds are extremely low that it was him. And even if it was, he might have been just passing through. Wait and see."

Renny nodded, pleased because Nick's assessment jibed with his own.

"I think you're right. But if I get another notice like this from North Carolina, I'm out of here. I'm southbound."

Nick nodded slowly and sipped his beer, a faraway look in his eyes. Yeah, this rocket scientist knew more than he let on. Definitely.

Nick Quinn's mind raced ahead of him as he left Leon's and hurried back to Morningside Heights. He didn't know if he should be worried or not. If that telephone incident in North Carolina was connected to Father Ryan, it could mean real trouble for the priest. If only he had some idea where Father Bill was. But he didn't even know if he was still in the country. He could be in Mexico or Staten Island, or anywhere in between.

It made no difference, really. Nick knew how to get in touch with him. And he also knew that Father Bill was no killer, no matter what Detective Augustino or the NYPD or the FBI thought. The man had practically raised him. He couldn't be a killer.

As soon as he got back to his office, he locked the door and sat at his desk. He turned on his Macintosh and dialed into the DataNet network. When he'd accessed the bulletin board, he left a brief message for the priest.

TO IGNATIUS:
YOUR AUGUST OPPONENT GOT WORD OF AN ABERRANT RING-
A-DING IN DUKE COUNTRY. THAT YOU, IGGY? HE'S STAYING

PUT FOR NOW, BUT YOU BE EXTRA CAREFUL. HOPE YOU'RE
WELL. PLEASE STAY SO.

EL COMEDO

Nick leaned back and sighed. Even after five years he still felt
the loss of a dear friend.

Please be careful, Father Bill—wherever you are.

THE BOY
at one year

November 29, 1969

He'd stopped sleeping.

It had frightened Carol at first, but she was getting used to it now. Somewhere in his tenth month he'd begun to stay up all night reading. He'd been reading books and newspapers ever since he could manipulate the pages. He would give her lists of books to buy or take from the library in Dardanelle. An omnivore of information, the child read voraciously, almost continuously. And when he didn't have his nose in a book, he'd settle himself in front of the TV.

Carol stood in the doorway now and watched Jimmy, clad in his Bullwinkle pajamas, as he sat before the TV. Legs folded beneath him, he rested on his heels, his feet pigeon-toed inward, crossing under his buttocks. His dark eyes were alive with interest, a small smile played along his lips. But he wasn't watching *Romper Room* or cartoons. He was watching a story about Viet Nam on the ten o'clock network news.

"All that fear and destruction and death over there," he said with shocking clarity in his toddler's voice. "And all the rage and strife here at home. All over a worthless, tiny clump of dirt on the other side of the world." He turned his head and smiled at Carol. "Isn't it wonderful!"

"No," Carol said, stepping forward. "It's awful. And I don't want you watching it."

She turned the set off and lifted him under the arms.

"How dare you!" he cried. "Put that TV on! Put me down!"

She held his tiny body away from her, out of reach of his flailing arms and kicking legs.

"Sorry, Jimmy! You may not be like any other baby in the world, but I'm still your mother. And *I* say it's past your bedtime."

She placed him in his crib, closed the door to the nursery, and tried to block out his screams of rage as she walked back to her bedroom. He was still too small, his arms too weak to pull himself over the crib railing. Thank God for small favors.

She sat on the bed and tried for the thousandth time to sort out her feelings for her son. Despite everything there was love—at least on her part. He was Jim's child, and carrying him within her for nine months had forged a bond that would not break, no matter how bizarre his mental abilities and his behavior. And yet there was fear too. Not fear for herself, but fear of the unknown. Who *was* Jimmy? Carol wanted desperately to be a parent to him, but that had proven impossible. He seemed like a fully developed adult in a toddler's body. He'd been born with an encyclopedic knowledge of the world and its history and he was ravenous for more.

Suddenly the screams from the nursery stopped. Carol stepped out into the hallway in time to see the tall, lean figure of Jonah Stevens leading Jimmy toward the den.

"Jonah!" she said. "I want him in bed. He needs his rest."

Here was another skirmish in what had become a constant battle between mother and grandfather: Whatever Carol denied Jimmy, Jonah would give him. He almost worshiped the child.

Jonah smiled condescendingly. "No, Carol. He needs to learn all he can about the world. After all, it's going to be his someday."

Jimmy barely glanced up as he toddled past her to the den. Carol leaned against the wall and fought the tears as she heard the news begin to blare anew from the TV screen.

OCTOBER

FIVE

North Carolina

"What a wonderful piece of filmmaking!" Rafe said as they left the auditorium.

Lisl smiled at him. "I can't believe you've never seen *Metropolis* before."

"Never. Those sets! How much have I missed by ignoring silent films? I've always avoided them—all those histrionics. But that's going to change. Next stop: *The Cabinet of Dr. Caligari*!"

Lisl laughed. She'd been seeing a lot of Rafe since Cal Rogers's party. She felt comfortable with him. More than that, she felt *confident* with him. Never a dull moment, never a lag in the conversation. Always something to talk about—some new idea, some new theory about anything that struck his fancy. His mind was a voracious, restlessly foraging omnivore, always on the prowl for new game, new fields in which to graze. She'd come to see their pretzel conversation that night at Cal's as a paradigm of so many of their conversations over the past few weeks. Rafe found significance in every little action of an individual. "The increments of personality," he called them. He said he planned to devote his career as a psychologist to tallying, quantifying, grouping, and analyzing those increments. His doctoral thesis would be his first step along that path.

As the weeks passed, they'd progressed from lunches to dinners to long walks in the parks to tonight's special screening. Rafe hadn't put a move on her yet and she wasn't exactly pleased about that. Not that she wanted a physical relationship with him, and she was sure the thought had never crossed his mind. She was too old and frumpy to appeal to someone like him. But it would do wonders for her ego to politely turn him down.

But would she turn him down? *Could* she?

Lisl caught herself. Sexual feelings for Rafe? Preposterous. Dreaming of a sexual relationship with him? Impossible.

First off, he was too young. Ten years was simply too much of a gap in time and experience and maturity . . .

But he *was* mature. Rafael Losmara was not the typical graduate student, not someone who had passed through the college experience yet was still in a state of becoming. Rafe seemed to be *complete*. God, there were times when he seemed so much older than she, when she felt like a child learning at his feet. He seemed to see everything so clearly. He had this ability to cut through all the layers of pretense and get to the core of whatever matter was at hand.

But even if she could forget the years between them and acknowledge that he was mature enough for a serious relationship, Lisl still had to ask herself a very basic question: Why?

Why should someone as wealthy, bright, talented, and good-looking as Rafe Losmara, who could cut a sexual swath through the female graduate students and the hordes of nubile undergraduates as well, want to get involved with an older woman? A dumpy divorcee, no less.

Good question. One not easily answered, because Rafe wasn't chasing other students, graduate or undergraduate. As far as Lisl knew, she was the only woman in his life at the moment. The thought had crossed her mind that he might be gay. But he didn't seem interested in men, either.

Recently she had noticed little touches, sidelong glances that seemed to hint at something bubbling beneath his cool exterior. Or was she reading too much into them, looking for something she hoped might be there?

He was a lot like Will. Maybe they were both asexual. Why not? And what did it matter? They had a nice platonic relationship, one that brightened many a day for her. Very much like the one she shared with Will. She decided to be satisfied with that, because it was unrealistic to the point of delusion to think it could be anything more.

Rafe took her hand and squeezed it. A tingle ran up her arm.

"Thank you, Lisl. Thanks for suggesting this."

"Don't thank me. Thank Will."

"Will?" Rafe's brow furrowed. "Oh, yes. That intellectual groundskeeper you told me about. Thank him for me."

"If he's here, you can thank him yourself."

"I'd love to meet him. He sounds interesting."

Lisl searched the small crowd of attendees and immediately spotted Everett Sanders's reed-thin figure passing nearby. She waved him over and introduced him to Rafe.

"An impressive film, don't you think?" Rafe said.

"Extraordinary."

Lisl said, "We're going over to the Hidey-hole for a drink. Want to come along?"

Ev shook his head. "No. I have some work to do. And speaking of work, I understand you intend to submit a paper for the Palo Alto conference."

"I thought I'd give it a shot," she said, suddenly uncomfortable. Even though she had every right in the world to submit a paper, she felt as if she were crashing his party.

"I'm sure it will be brilliant," he said. "Good luck."

"Sure you won't have that drink with us?" Rafe said.

"Positive. I must be off. Good night."

"A bit stiff, don't you think?" Rafe said as they watched Ev stride away.

"Maybe that's why I like him," Lisl said. "When he's around I feel like a swinger."

She resumed her search for Will but he wasn't anywhere to be seen.

Strange. He'd seemed so enthusiastic about the university film society's acquisition of a fully restored print of the Fritz Lang classic, telling her all about the recently discovered dream-sequence footage. Yet this afternoon he'd said he was going to *try* to make it. There had been a hint of melancholy in his voice, as if he knew there was no chance of his being there. Too bad. He'd have loved it. Lisl had once seen a shorter version on TV and hadn't been too impressed. But tonight, in a theater, in the dark with a full-size screen, the scope of the images had been mesmerizing.

To Rafe it had been some sort of epiphany.

"You know," he said, raising his voice as they walked out into the night, "I wonder if adding sound to films really improved them."

"It forced the acting to improve, that's for sure."

"True. All that mugging and those exaggerated gestures were no longer necessary. But not having sound forces the filmmaker to use the visual medium to the max. It's all he has. He can't tell you things, so he's got to *show* you. My new theory of film criticism:

If you can close your eyes and still follow the story line, maybe they should have saved the celluloid for some other feature and performed the script on the radio. If you can plug your ears and follow the story with your eyes only, there's a damn good chance you've got a good movie on your hands."

The couple walking ahead of them obviously had been listening, for the man turned around and challenged Rafe's theory with the titles of a number of Academy Award winners. Lisl recognized him from the sociology department. A few more of the filmgoers chimed in and within minutes Lisl found herself in the heart of a friendly but vigorous debate moving across the east campus. The whole group gravitated to the Hidey-hole where they commandeered one of the big tables and went through round after round of drinks discussing Rafe's theory and *Metropolis* itself.

"Visually stunning, yes," said Victor Pelham from the sociology department. "But the class-war politics are positively archaic."

"And a rip-off of H. G. Wells," said a doctoral candidate from English. "The idle rich frolicking above and the oppressed workers toiling below—it's the Eloi and the Morlocks from *The Time Machine.*"

Pelham said, "I don't care *who* he ripped off—a socialist like Wells or Marx himself—that class-war bullshit has been passé for ages. A shame, too. It hobbles the film."

"Maybe it's not as passé as you think," Rafe said.

"Right!" Pelham laughed. "Will the real Overman please stand up."

"I'm not talking about anything so crass as Overmen and Undermen," Rafe said softly. "I'm talking about Primes and non-primes—or, for the sake of simplicity and clarity, Creators and Consumers."

The table fell silent.

"That's where the real division lies," Rafe continued. "There are those who innovate, invent, modify, and elaborate. And there are others who contribute nothing, yet enjoy all the benefits of those innovations, inventions, modifications, and elaborations."

"Sounds like another variation on the Eloi and Morlocks," someone said. "Creators on top, consumers below."

"Not so," said Rafe. "That implies that the Consumer masses are slaves to the Creator overlords, but it doesn't work that way. The Creators are in fact the slaves of the masses, providing them with all the benefits of art and modern science. The Wellsian cliché of the Eloi elite owing their comfortable life-style to the labor of the Morlock masses is backward. The Consumer masses owe their health, their full bellies, and the comforts of civilization to the efforts of the small percentage of Creators among them."

"I'm confused," someone said.

Rafe smiled. "It's not a simple concept. Nor is it a clear-cut division. The dividing line is nothing so obvious as economic status. Creators have often reaped fame and profits from their work, but throughout history there have been countless Creators who've lived out their entire lives in obscurity and abject poverty. Look at Poe, at Van Gogh; think of the mathematicians and physicists whose work Einstein studied in laying the groundwork that led to his theory of relativity. What are their names?"

No one answered. Lisl glanced around the table. All eyes were fixed on Rafe, everyone mesmerized by his voice.

"And far too many of the wealthiest among us are nothing more than overfed Consumers. Those who have merely inherited their wealth are the most obvious examples. But there are others who've supposedly 'earned' it who are just as useless. Take the Wall Street types—the stockbrokers and arbitrageurs: They spend their lives buying and selling interests in currencies or in concerns that actually produce things, they pocket their commissions, they cash in on the spread, but they produce nothing themselves. Nothing at all."

"Nothing but money!" Pelham said, evoking a few muted laughs.

"Exactly!" Rafe said. "Nothing but money. A whole life of six, seven, eight decades, and what besides a big bank account have they left behind? After their assets are gobbled up by their greedy little Consumer heirs, what mark have they left in their wake? What evidence is there to indicate that they ever passed this way?"

"Not much, I fear," said a middle-aged woman with red hair. Lisl recognized her as being from the philosophy department but couldn't remember her name. "If I may quote Camus: 'I sometimes think of what future historians will say of us. A single sentence will suffice for modern man: He fornicated and read the papers.' "

"And if I may paraphrase Priscilla Mullin," said Rafe. "Speak for yourself, Albert."

Amid the laughter, Pelham said, "Are you serious, or are you just trying to rattle the cage as you did with your sound-as-a-detriment-to-filmmaking theory?"

"I'm quite serious about both."

Pelham stared at him, as if waiting for Rafe to smile and laugh it all off as a joke. Lisl had a feeling he might have a long wait.

"Okay," Pelham said finally. "If all this is true, why haven't these Creators taken over the world?"

"Because they don't know who they are. And because too many of them have learned over the years not to reveal themselves."

"Why on earth not?" Lisl said.

Rafe's eyes poured into hers.

"Because they've already been crippled or damaged by the masses of Consumers who try to destroy any trace of greatness in others, who do anything they can to douse the faintest spark of originality, no matter where they find it. Even in their own children."

Lisl felt as if a bell were chiming in a remote corner of her past, toning in resonance to Rafe's words. It made her uncomfortable.

"I've *consumed* too many drinks to *create* a cogent rebuttal," said someone at the far end of the table. He turned to his date. "Want to dance?"

They headed for the postage-stamp dance floor and began to sway to a slow tune on the jukebox. A few others followed; those who didn't said good night and departed.

And left Lisl and Rafe alone at the table.

Lisl glanced around the dimly lit tavern, at its college memorabilia –strewn walls, at the dancers on the floor. When she turned back to Rafe she found him staring at her over the rim of his glass. His eyes glistened in the neon light. The scrutiny made her uncomfortable.

"Care to dance?"

Lisl hesitated an instant. She never had been much of a dancer—always had thought of herself as clumsy—and had never had many opportunities to learn. But the two and a half glasses of wine in her system had lulled her inhibitions and she was too surprised to say no.

"I, uh . . . sure."

He led her from the table, took her in his arms, pressed himself against her, and led her expertly around the tiny floor. They moved as one. Light presses and pulls from his left hand on her right or from his right hand against the small of her back told her precisely which way to move. For the first time in her life she felt graceful.

"Where did you learn to dance like this?" she asked. "I thought it was a lost art."

He shrugged. "My folks made me take ballroom dancing when I was a kid. I found it came easily. I was the best in the class."

"How did you do in your modesty lessons?"

He laughed. "Flunked every time."

As she became used to the sensation of gliding around the floor, she became aware of another: Rafe's body against hers.

Deep within her, old emotions stirred. At first she wasn't sure what she was feeling. So long since she'd felt much of anything. After the number Brian had done on her in the final days of their marriage, and the nastiness of the divorce, she had simply turned off. She'd wanted nothing to do with another man, and women didn't interest her that way in the least, so she'd gone into a sort of sexual coma.

What was happening now? Was that what she was feeling? Was she waking up? She couldn't deny how good it felt simply to have someone hold her. She was surprised at the emotions awakening in her, churning to life after years of dormancy. Human contact. She had forgotten what it was like. She had thought she no longer needed it. Maybe she was wrong.

She pushed the thought away but stayed close to Rafe. The contact was too enjoyable. He was holding her tight against him. She became aware of the sensation of her breasts rubbing against his chest; their two bodies seemed joined at the pelvis.

Warm. Very warm where they met. And the warmth was spreading. She found her body pressing itself more firmly against his, as if it had a mind of its own. Well, not a mind, perhaps, but most definitely an agenda of its own.

It wanted him.

Rafe leaned back from Lisl and looked at her.

"Let's go to my place," he whispered.

Her mouth was dry. "Why your place?"

"It's closer."

The logic of that simple statement struck her as utterly flawless. Lisl nodded.

It wasn't far from the tavern to Parkview, the upscale development where Rafe owned a condo. They walked quickly, in silence. Lisl was afraid to speak, afraid it would shatter the mood and taint the delicious excitement coursing through her. The last thing she wanted or needed now was to stop and think about this. No common sense, no cold hard facts, no prudence, no worries, no doubts or second guesses. None of that. The excitement was too wonderful. So long since she had felt anything like this. Like a teenager. She didn't want to let it go. And she wouldn't. She'd flow with it, let it take her where it was going, do something impulsive for once in her life.

But she had to hurry before she changed her mind.

The brisk walking pace graduated into a jog, which evolved into a gallop. When they reached the door to Rafe's condo, they were both breathing hard, perhaps not wholly from the exertion. Lisl leaned against the railing while he fumbled with his keys. Then the door was open. They ducked inside, slammed it shut, and then they were in each other's arms. Rafe's lips found hers. Lisl's arms went around him as his fingers slipped lightly up the sides of her face and ran through her hair, down to her shoulders, coming to rest at the top button of her blouse. He unbuttoned it and moved to the second.

Lisl experienced an instant of panic. *Too fast! This is happening too fast!* Then his tongue probed hers and her apprehensions melted away.

When he had her blouse open, he slipped it off her shoulders, then reached around and unfastened her bra. As that fell away, he pulled his lips from hers and ran them down her neck to her breasts, his silky mustache tickling her along the way. She groaned and leaned back against the door as his tongue found a nipple.

"Oh, God, that feels good."

Rafe said nothing. His hands never stopped moving. While his lips and tongue pleasured her breasts, his fingers caressed her back, her abdomen, and then they were working on her belt, the buttons to her slacks, pulling them open, pushing them and her panties down until they sank to her ankles.

And then Rafe, too, began to sink. He drew his tongue between her breasts, down her abdomen to her navel, circled it, then continued downward. His lips slid into her hair down there, his tongue probed toward the swelling heart of all her sensation but didn't reach it. Lisl spread her legs. She felt wanton, she felt wonderful. She entwined her fingers in the silky black waves atop his head and pushed his face more tightly against her. So close now . . . he had to reach it. Rafe gripped her right leg behind the thigh and lifted it so that it rested on his left shoulder. It felt fat and heavy there. She was glad the lights were out, she wished she were slimmer, she wished—

"Ahhh!"

He'd found it! Bolts of white-hot pleasure shot down her legs and up through the rest of her body. She shuddered with delight, not wanting it to stop, not wanting it ever to stop.

Too fast! she thought again as her breath hissed in and out through her teeth at a steadily increasing rate. *It's going way too fast!*

But the night was only beginning.

THE BOY
at five years

February 12, 1974

"You've been neglecting my money," Jimmy said at breakfast one day.

"*Your* money?" Carol said. "I didn't know you had any."

She and Jimmy had reached a sort of equilibrium. She had grown used to his almost unearthly precocity and adapted to it. Adapted as well as one could to a forty-inch child whose brain seemed to hold the accumulated wisdom of the ages. Five years of daily life with him had closed off areas of feeling; and questions she'd asked had gone unanswered so long her mind had stopped asking them. He was imperious, intolerant, inconsiderate, insufferable at times, but he could be charming when he wished. There were times when she almost liked him.

"The inheritance. The eight million dollars' worth of assets my father inherited from Dr. Hanley."

"So Jim's 'my father' now, is he? I thought he was 'merely the vessel.' "

"Whatever. The fact remains that my birthright has been lying around, moldering, static, when it could have been growing all these five years. I want you to rectify that immediately."

"Oh, you do, do you?"

He was in his insufferable mode but Carol found him amusing nonetheless. Despite everything, he was still her son. And Jim's.

"I want you to go back to New York and start converting everything—the mansion, *everything*—to cash. I will then advise you on how it shall be invested."

Carol smiled. "How good of you. The Bernard Baruch of *Sesame Street.*"

His dark eyes blazed. "Don't make fun of me. I know what I'm doing."

Carol realized her remark had been gratuitous. But understandable in light of their ongoing battle of wills.

"I'm sure you do."

"One thing, though," he said, his voice soft, almost hesitant. "When you get to New York—"

"I didn't say I was going."

"But you will. It's your money too."

"I know. But we can't spend the interest we get on the bonds and C.D.s we already have. Why fool with it?"

He favored her with one of his rare smiles. "Because it will amuse me to see how fast I can multiply it." Then the smile faded. "But when you get to New York . . . be careful."

"Of course I'll—"

"No. I mean, be wary. Beware of anyone who asks about your child. Tell them you miscarried. No one must know I exist, especially . . ."

There was something in Jimmy's eyes. Something Carol had never seen before.

"Especially who?"

Jimmy's tone was grave. "Be alert for a man in his mid-thirties with red hair."

"I'm sure there'll be a fair number of those in Manhattan."

"Not like this one. His skin will have an olive cast and his eyes will be blue. There is only one like him. He will be looking for me. If such a man approaches you, or tries to speak to you, or even if you merely see someone like him, call me immediately."

Carol realized that Jimmy was afraid.

"Call you? Why? What will you do?"

He turned and stared out the window.

"Hide."

NOVEMBER

SIX

Lisl glanced at her desk clock as she finished grading the last calculus test. Noon. Perfect timing. She was starved. She pulled on her jacket, picked up her cushion, and stepped out into the hall.

Al Torres, a tenured associate, was passing by, shrugging into a light sports coat as he headed for the stairs.

"Going to the caf, Leese?"

"Brown-bagging it today, Al."

"Again?"

"The diet. Can't make it work if I go to the grease pit."

He laughed. "You're really sticking to this one. And it's working. Good girl!"

Lisl was tempted to call him on that "good girl" business—she was thirty-two, for God's sake—but knew his heart was in the right place. He had two young daughters and probably used the phrase a lot.

She pulled her lunch bag from the department's ancient refrigerator and looked inside: four ounces of cottage cheese mixed with pineapple chunks, two carrots, two celery stalks, and a diet Dr Pepper. She stuck out her tongue.

Yummy-yummy. I can hardly wait.

But it was working. With a three-mile jog every morning and a strict diet the rest of the day, she'd dropped fifteen pounds in just six weeks. She was feeling more fit now than at any time in her life.

She headed for the elm tree. Will was there ahead of her, sitting on the newly fallen leaves, unwrapping a huge sandwich. Her mouth watered at the sight of the inch-high stack of corned beef between the thick slices of rye.

"You buy those things just to torture me, don't you?"

"No. I buy them to torture *myself.* You southerners don't have the faintest idea of the proper curing of corned beef. This thing may look good, but taste-wise it's a pallid reflection of the kind of sandwich people eat every day in New York. What I wouldn't give for a hot pastrami from the Carnegie Deli."

"So go back and get one."

Will looked away for a moment. "Some day I just might."

"You sound like a born-and-bred New Yorker. I thought you grew up in Vermont."

"I lived all over the Northeast before moving south." He suddenly leaned forward and stared between her breasts. "A new necklace?"

Don't think I don't know when you're changing the subject away from your past, she thought as she smiled and lifted the shell hanging from the fine gold chain.

"Yes and no. The chain's been in my jewelry box for years and I've had the shell forever. I just decided one day to put them together."

"What's the shell? It's a beauty."

"It's called a cowrie. The South Seas natives actually use them for money."

This was her Rafe shell. A few weeks ago she'd dug into her shoe box and pulled it out. A glossy cowrie with an intricate speckled pattern on its back. Beautiful—just like Rafe. She'd had a jeweler drill a hole and voilà, she had a necklace. Only Lisl knew who it represented.

A moment later Will was staring again, this time at the impoverished contents of her lunch bag as she laid them out on a paper napkin.

"Still hanging in with that diet, I see."

"Hanging is right—by my fingernails. Six weeks of gerbil food. I just love it. I jump out of bed every morning looking forward to the myriad gustatory delights that await me."

"You're getting results. I mean I can really see the difference. Maybe you've lost enough to merit a treat once in a while."

"Not till I've reached my target weight."

"And what's that?"

"One-thirty. Fifteen pounds to go."

Whoops. She just gave her weight away. Not that it would matter with Will. She had a feeling that he was something of a sphinx when he wasn't with her. But it was not a number she wanted to slip out too often.

"I think you're fine the way you are now."

"So do the actuarial tables. According to them, a five-five, medium-frame female like me should weigh one-forty stripped. Maybe that's optimal for maximum life span, but it's not right for the clothes I want to wear."

"You still look fine to me."

"Thanks." But she knew her looks didn't really matter to Will. "I'll tell you one thing, though. Besides freeing me of some excess baggage, all this dieting has given me some real empathy for those people with lifelong weight problems. I can't imagine fighting the pounds year in and year out. It's so *depressing!*"

Will shrugged and took another bite of his sandwich.

"Just self-discipline," he said around the mouthful. He swallowed. "You set yourself a goal and you go after it. Along the way you make choices. The choices you make are determined by what you value more. In the dieter's case it comes down to choosing between a full belly or a trim figure."

Strange. He almost sounded like Rafe.

"It's not that easy," she told him. "Especially not when there's people around—like you, for instance—who seem to be able to manage both a full belly *and* a trim figure. When have you ever had to make a sacrifice hour by hour, day by day, week after week, month after month?"

Will stared at her, and for a moment something flashed in his eyes, then he looked away. His gaze found the horizon and rested there. Again, the question flashed through her mind: *What have you seen, what have you done?*

"Don't . . ." Lisl's voice faltered. "Don't brush it off until you've had to do it."

"I wouldn't think of it," he said.

They ate in silence for a while. Lisl finished her cottage cheese and veggies and was still hungry—as usual. She nursed her diet Dr Pepper.

"Didn't you tell me this was your first diet?" Will said.

"Yes. Rafe says it will be my last. I hope he's right."

"Is this Rafe fellow pushing you to lose weight?"

"Not in the least. As a matter of fact, he wishes I'd ease off because we don't go out to eat anywhere near as often as we used to. He says he liked me just the way I was when he met me."

She felt a little smile flicker across her lips as she remembered Rafe telling her how his taste in the female figure tended to run on a line with Reubens's. But that hadn't stopped her from starting her get-in-shape program.

Will grunted.

"What's that for?" Lisl said.

"It means that he doesn't strike me as the type who leaves well enough alone."

"How can you say that? You don't know him."

"Just an impression. Maybe because he's too good-looking and appears to have had too much money for too long. Those kind tend to think the rest of the world exists for their exclusive use."

"Well, you know the old saying about books and covers. Look at yourself. Who'd believe you've done the kind of reading you have?"

"Touché."

"Rafe is very deep for his age. You'd like him if you got to know him."

"I'm hardly in his league. He drives a brand-new Maserati; I drive a Chevy that's almost as old as he is. He doesn't seem the sort who likes to hang out with groundskeepers."

Lisl hid her growing annoyance with Will's attitude.

"If you had something interesting or intelligent to say, as you usually do, he wouldn't care what you did for a living."

Will shrugged again. "If you say so."

Lisl wondered at Will's hostility toward Rafe, a man he'd never met, and then she realized: *He feels threatened!*

That had to be it. Lisl was probably the only person in Will's small world with whom he could communicate on his own level. And now he saw Rafe as a rival for her attention, someone who might take her from him altogether.

Poor Will. She searched for a way to reassure him that she'd always be his friend and be here for him, a way that wouldn't let on that she knew what was eating him.

"I'm planning a Christmas party," she said.

"It's not even Thanksgiving yet."

"Thanksgiving's only days away. And besides, everybody starts planning Christmas around Thanksgiving time."

"If you say so."

"I say so. And I also say that you're invited."

She sensed rather than saw Will stiffen.

"Sorry."

"Come on, Will. I'm inviting people I consider my friends, and you're at the top of the list. You'll finally get to know Rafe. I really think you two will hit it off. He's a lot like you. You're both deeper than you seem."

"Lisl . . ."

She played her ace: "I'll be very hurt if you don't deign to make an appearance."

"Come on, Lisl—"

"I'm serious. I've never thrown a party before and I want you to be there."

There followed a long pause, with Will staring into the distance.

"Okay," he said with obvious reluctance. "I'll try to make it."

" 'Try' isn't good enough. You were going to 'try' to make it to *Metropolis* last month. I don't need that kind of try. I need a promise."

Lisl caught a trace of hurt in his eyes that contrasted sharply with his smile.

"I can't promise. Please don't ask me for something I can't deliver on."

"Okay," Lisl said softly, hiding her own hurt. "I won't."

As they finished what was left of their lunches in uncharacteristic silence, Will thought about Losmara. A strange character. A loner. Didn't seem to have any friends but Lisl.

Like me.

He'd seen him from a distance and hadn't been impressed. His recurring nightmare was that the close-up Rafe would be a limp-wristed, foppish Latin-lover type with a pencil-line mustache, reed thin, draped with half a dozen gold chains, wearing a blousey, open-necked, lacy-cuffed white shirt.

Lisl deserved a Clint Eastwood; Will was afraid she'd wound up with Prince.

And if she had, so what? As long as he made her happy, as long as he wasn't taking advantage of her vulnerability.

And she was so very vulnerable. He'd sensed that the first day he'd met her. Like a gentle forest creature who'd been cruelly treated, she'd drawn her defenses tight around her and tried to seal herself off from further hurt. But her defenses were thin. Behind her buzz of constant activity, Will saw a lonely woman, aching to love and to be loved. An oblique approach, clothed in gentle words telling her what she wanted to hear, and Will knew she would respond. Treated with a modicum of warmth and tenderness, she would open like a flower to the morning sun.

Love was what she needed most. Romantic, sexual love. And

that was the one thing Will could not offer her. He could work at opening her mind, but not her heart. He could offer her anything but that kind of love.

Not that the idea hadn't occurred to him more than once. Many times, in fact. Though he was almost two decades older, there had been a phase during his relationship with Lisl when he had sensed that the time was ripe for a joining of more than minds. But that was not the way for him to go. He was gearing for other things, slowly retooling himself to return to the life he had left behind. There was no place for a woman in that life.

So Will was glad that someone had found the key to Lisl's heart. He fervently hoped it was the *right* someone. Lisl was very special. She deserved the best. He did not believe in meddling in other people's lives, but if it became evident that this Rafe Losmara was taking advantage of her vulnerability, of her trusting nature, he would have to step in.

He could not allow anyone to hurt Lisl.

Will was startled by the thought.

Me. Protector of the defenseless. I can hardly take care of myself!

Yet why shouldn't he have strong protective feelings toward Lisl? She had grown to be an enormously important part of his life over the past couple of years, his only friend in the world— at least the only one he could talk to. In his own way he loved Lisl. What she possessed was rare and precious, and demanded protection. Will would do his best to provide that protection.

Will smiled again. Lisl had told him so many times how much she thought she owed him for opening the worlds of philosophy and literature to her. If she only knew. She had done more for him than he could ever do for her. Her unstudied combination of sweetness, innocence, intelligence, and vulnerability had gone a long way toward restoring his faith in humanity, in life itself. When all had seemed blackest, she had provided a ray of sunlight. And as a result, Will's whole world was brighter now.

Lisl left the campus early that afternoon. The days were getting shorter and she reveled in the autumn coolness. When she reached Brookside Gardens, she realized she didn't want to be in her apartment. She sat in her car in the lot and wondered what to do with the extra time she'd found this afternoon. She told herself she should invest it in her paper for Palo Alto, but that didn't appeal to her. Too restless to sit in front of a computer terminal.

Restless. Why?

Then she knew.

Lisl didn't feel like being alone today.

This wasn't like her. She'd always been a loner, always with so much on her mind that she could keep busy enough not to miss human company. But not now. Today she felt the need to be with someone else.

And not just anyone.

A memory of what she had come to think of as "*Metropolis* night" wafted through Lisl's mind and she shuddered. She and Rafe had spent many other nights together since then, all of them wonderful, but that particular night remained special because it was the first, and because it had awakened an almost-overwhelming appetite in her, one that could be temporarily sated, but never for long. She was a sexual being now, a whole person, and she reveled in it. And Rafe . . . Rafe was like a satyr—always ready.

Probably ready even now.

Instead of restarting her car, Lisl got out and began walking toward the park. She cut across its grassy southwest corner to Poplar Street. From there it was four short blocks to Rafe's condo in Parkview, the town's haven for yuppies who either didn't want or couldn't yet afford their own home.

But as she entered the development and walked among its contemporary two-story row house condos finished in blue-green stained cedar clapboard, a tiny knot of apprehension began to form in her stomach. He might not be there, of course, but that wasn't it. This was going to be a surprise visit. What if she were the one who wound up surprised? What if she found him there with another woman? What would she do then?

Part of her said she'd die right there on the spot. And another part of her whispered that she wouldn't die at all. Why should she? She'd been betrayed before—in spades. And being betrayed by someone like Rafe would be no more than she should have expected, no less than she deserved.

Stop it! she told herself. Negative thinking. Rafe had warned her time and again about tearing herself down like that. And Lisl tried. But it was a habit. And lifelong habits were difficult to break.

Once a nerd, always a nerd.

And what was a nerdy broad like her doing trysting with a younger man like Rafe Losmara? Handsome, brilliant—what could a man like that see in her?

Yet he did see something in her. Had to. They'd been a "thing" on campus for almost a month now. They did their best to keep it a discreet, off-campus affair, but it was impossible to hide a relationship as intimate as theirs in such a close-knit community.

Lisl was sure some of her fellow faculty members and their wives tsked and shook their heads when they saw them together downtown, but no one had told her to cool it and drop him. She was sure it would have been a different story if Rafe were doing graduate work in her department. Their relationship then would be perceived as a blatant conflict of interest and she had no doubt that Harold Masterson, as chairman of math, would have come down on her like a ball of fire. But since Rafe's work was overseen by the psychology department, their relationship was tolerated, viewed not with disdain, but rather with wonder and astonishment.

Go ahead and stare, she'd think with a smile. *I've got mine, you get yours.*

But did she really have hers? Or was she only fooling herself?

She loved him. She didn't want to. She hadn't wanted to place herself in that vulnerable position again, but there was no helping it. And she couldn't help but wonder how he felt about her. Was he stringing her along, playing with her?

Lisl paused as she stood before Rafe's door, unannounced. He was so young—she could not let herself lose sight of that fact. Would he tire of her? Could he ever be truly satisfied with her? Was somebody else inside with him now?

Only one way to find out.

Taking a deep breath, Lisl knocked. And waited. No one came to the door. She tried again with no result. Maybe he wasn't home. Or maybe he wasn't answering the door because . . .

Better not to know.

But as Lisl was turning away, the door opened. Rafe stood there with dripping hair and a bath towel around his waist. He seemed genuinely surprised.

"Lisl! I thought I heard the door but I never dreamed—"

"If—if this is a bad time—"

"No! Not at all! Come in! Is anything wrong?"

The *whiteness* of his condo never failed to strike her—the walls, the furniture, the rugs, the picture frames and most of the canvases within them—white.

"No," she said, stepping in. "Why should there be?"

"Well, it's just that this is so unlike you."

She felt her confidence draining off. "I'm sorry. I should have called."

"Don't be ridiculous. This is great!"

"Are you really glad to see me?"

"Can't you tell?"

She glanced down at his towel and saw how it was tented up in front of him. She smiled, her spirits lifting. That was for her. All for her. Hesitantly, she reached out and loosened the knotted portion of the towel at his hip. It fell away.

Yes. For her. Just for her.

She stroked him ever so gently with her fingernails, then knelt before him.

"I don't deserve this," Lisl murmured.

"Don't deserve what?" Rafe whispered in her ear.

She sighed. She was so happy and at peace now she could almost cry. The exhausted afterglow of their lovemaking was almost as delicious as the lovemaking itself.

"Feeling this good."

"Don't say that," he told her. "Don't ever say that you don't deserve to feel good."

They lay side by side, skin to skin, on his white king-size bed. The waning sun was beaming through the window, suffusing the pallor of the room with red-gold light.

"Want me to pull the shade?" Rafe said.

Lisl laughed. "A little late for that now, don't you think? Who-ever's out there looking has already gotten quite an eyeful."

"No worry about that."

Right. Rafe's bedroom was on the second floor. There were no other windows in sight from the bed.

Making love in the day or with a light on had bothered Lisl at first, back when she had been a pudgette. She'd preferred then to cloak the excess fatty baggage on her body in darkness. But now that she had slimmed down some, she didn't mind. In fact, it was kind of exciting to exhibit her new, trimmer proportions for him.

"You've lost more weight," he said, running a hand along her flank.

"You like?"

"I like you any way you want to look. What's more important is how you like the thinner you."

"I love it!"

"Then that's all that matters. I'm for anything that gets you thinking better of yourself."

"And I'm for anything that makes you enjoy looking at me as much as I enjoy looking at you."

Lisl loved looking at Rafe. He'd told her that his mother had been French, his father Spanish. His features favored the Spanish side—his almost-black hair, the thick lashes around his eyes, and the irises of a brown so very dark they, too, seemed almost black. His smooth café au lait skin was utterly flawless. She could have resented that skin. Its perfection was almost feminine. She could have wanted it for herself.

But there was nothing feminine about the way he approached sex. Lisl had only made love to one other man in her life: Brian, who she considered, in her limited experience, to be good a lover. After her first night with Rafe, she had learned just how limited her experience had been. She thought that maybe there was some truth after all to that old cliché about Latin lovers.

He put his face between her breasts.

"You're a Prime. You deserve to feel good about yourself. You've allowed the host of lesser creatures around you to determine what you think of yourself."

Primes—Rafe had called them Creators when he'd broached the subject after *Metropolis* in the Hidey-hole Tavern, but that had been for simplicity's sake. In private he divided the world into Primes and everyone else. Primes, he'd told her, were unique people, like prime numbers, divisible only by one or by themselves. It was his favorite topic. He never tired of it. Always pointing out examples. After weeks of listening to him, Lisl was beginning to be convinced that it might have some validity.

"I'm not a Prime," she said. "What have I created?"

Rafe was a Prime, no doubt about that—*Homo superior* in every way. But Lisl? Not a chance.

"Nothing yet, but you will. I sense it in you. But let's get back to what you think you don't deserve. *What* don't you deserve? And why not?"

"Don't you think . . ." she began, then paused as Rafe nuzzled one of her nipples and sent new chills up and down that side of her body, "a person should have to do something special to merit feeling so happy and content? It's only fair."

Rafe lifted his head and looked into her eyes.

"You deserve the best of everything," Rafe said. "As I said, you're a Prime. And after the kind of life you've had until now, after what you've put up with, you're long overdue for some good feelings."

"My life hasn't been so bad."

Rafe flopped onto his back and stared at the ceiling.

"Right. Sure. A lifetime of being knocked down and kicked

around by the people who should have been supporting you and encouraging you to keep going. That's a long way from 'not so bad.' "

"Since when do you know so much about my life?"

"I know what you've told me. I can guess the rest."

Lisl rose up on one elbow and looked down at him.

"Okay, wiseguy. Tell me all about me."

"All right. How's this? Nothing you ever did really pleased your parents."

"Wrong. They—"

Rafe overrode her. "They were always on your case, weren't they? Even though all through grammar school and high school you got straight A's. Right?"

"Right, but—"

"And I'll bet your project took first place at the science fair, didn't it? Even though you did it all on your own. With no help from your folks—who always seemed to have better things to do— you beat out all those other kids whose fathers and brothers and uncles—who also had better things to do, by the way, but who gave a damn—did most of the work for them. And how did your folks respond when you came home and showed them your blue ribbon? I'll bet it was 'That's nice, dear, but do you have a date for the prom yet?' Am I far off?"

She laughed. "Oh, God! How do you know?"

"And I'll bet your mother never let up on you. 'Put down that book, get up, get out, meet boys!' "

"Yes, she did! She did!" This was uncanny.

"What single phrase during your developing years most typified her attitude toward you?"

"Oh . . . I don't know."

"How about, 'What's the matter with you?' "

The words pierced her. That was it. God, how many times had she heard that through the years?

She nodded. "How—?"

"Your mother never paid you a single compliment, I'll bet. An insecure bitch who couldn't bring herself to say that you looked nice, couldn't stoop to bolster your confidence. You got the message: 'Sure you're a brainy kid, but so what? Why don't you date more? Why don't you dress more in style? Why don't you have popular friends?' "

Lisl was getting uncomfortable now. This was striking a little too close to home.

"All right, Rafe. That's enough."

But Rafe wasn't finished yet.

"And when it wasn't something they said or did that cut you off at the knees, it was what they *didn't* say, *didn't* do. Never went to parents' night to hear your teachers gush about you. I'll bet they never even went to the science fairs to see how your project stacked up against the others."

"That's *enough*, Rafe."

"But somewhere along the line, late in the game, I'll bet, your father became a believer. Throughout most of your adolescence he was afraid you'd become a spinster schoolmarm and hang around the house forever. Then somebody told him that your SAT scores made you prime scholarship material, that you could qualify for a free ride at one of the state universities. Epiphany! Suddenly he got religion and became Lisl's big booster!"

This was becoming too painful. "Stop it, Rafe. I mean it."

"Suddenly, for the first time in his life, he was bragging about his daughter, how she was going to tap into the state for big bucks and get him back some of the taxes he'd been paying all those years."

"Shut up!"

It was true—too true. She'd seen it then, she'd known it all along, but she'd never faced it. It had hurt so much she'd buried it in some deep, dark recess. But now Rafe was digging it up, rubbing her nose in it. Why?

Rafe smiled. "Suddenly Daddy was standing foursquare behind his precious little academic meal ticket!"

"Damn you!"

She swung a fist at him. He didn't turn, didn't try to block it or fend her off. She felt her knuckles land square on his chest with a meaty impact, saw him wince.

"He was a creep!" he said.

She hit him again. Harder. Again, he took the blow.

"He drained off your self-esteem like a drunk guzzles beer. So what did you do? You hooked up with a creep in college who was the same. Good old Brian! He proposed and you accepted. He let you support him through med school and then he dropped you the first time a pretty nurse smiled at him!"

Lisl was almost blind with fury now. Why was he doing this? She rose to her knees and began slapping at him, scratching him, pounding on him. She couldn't help herself. She hated him.

"God damn you!"

But Rafe wouldn't stop.

"They all dumped on you! And you know why? Because you're

a Prime. And all those petty nothings who raised and educated you hate Primes. But worse than that, you're a woman! A woman who dares to be intelligent! Who dares to think! You can't do that! You can't be better than them! Not unless you're a guy! And even then, don't be *too* much better!"

Lisl kept slapping, scratching, pounding. Rafe flinched with each blow, but took it all.

"Go ahead," he said in a lower tone. "Get it out. I'm you're mother. I'm your father. I'm your ex-husband. Beat the shit out of me. Get it *out!*"

Like smoke in a gale, Lisl's anger suddenly dissipated. She continued striking Rafe, but the blows were fewer and lacked their previous force. She began to sob.

"How could you say those things?"

"Because they're true."

Lisl gasped when she saw the scratches, welts, and bruises on his chest.

I did that?

"Oh, Rafe, I'm so sorry! Did I hurt you?"

He glanced farther down and smiled. "Not so's you'd notice."

Lisl followed his gaze and gasped. He was erect again. Hugely so. She let him pull her atop him. He kissed away her tears as she straddled him, then he slipped smoothly inside her. She sighed as her turbulent emotions faded and became lost in the misty pleasure of having him so deep within her. She couldn't be sure, but he seemed bigger and harder than ever before.

"I can see we've got a lot of work to do," Rafe said as Lisl got dressed.

Lisl's hands shook as she rolled her panty hose up her legs. Never had she experienced anything like their second bout of lovemaking today. Numerous smaller eruptions had led to a final explosion that had been, well, almost cataclysmic. She was still weak.

"I don't know about you, but I think we've got that down pretty near perfect."

Rafe burst out laughing. "Not sex! Anger!"

"Who's angry?"

"You are!"

Lisl looked at him. "Rafe, I've never been happier or more content in my entire life."

"Perhaps." He sat down beside her on the mattress and put his arm around her. "But way down deep inside, where you don't let anybody go but you, you feel you really don't deserve it and you're convinced it's not going to last. Am I right?"

Lisl swallowed. He was right. He was so right. But she didn't want to admit it to him.

"Lisl, you've said as much, haven't you?"

She nodded.

"And you don't want to feel that way, do you." It was not a question.

She felt a tear form in each eye. "No."

"It makes you angry, doesn't it."

"I hate it."

"Okay," Rafe said. "Now we're getting somewhere. You 'hate' it. That's the key, Lisl: anger. You're riddled with it. You seethe with it."

"That's not true."

"It is. You've bottled it up so well behind this placid exterior of yours that even you don't know it's there. But I do."

"Oh, really?" His know-it-all psych grad student attitude was beginning to annoy her now. "How do you know?"

"Recent experience," he said. "Like maybe half an hour ago."

She glanced at his chest. The wounds she had inflicted—the scratches, the welts and bruises—were almost completely gone. She ran her fingers over the near-normal skin.

"How—?"

"I'm a fast healer," he said quickly, pulling on a T-shirt.

"But I hurt you!" She stifled a sob. "Oh, Jesus! I'm so sorry!"

"It's all right. It's nothing serious. Forget about it."

How could she forget about it? She frightened herself.

Maybe Rafe was right. Now that she thought about it, she did resent her parents for the way they had managed to denigrate all her interests and cheapen her accomplishments. And Brian—God knew she had reason enough to hate her ex-husband.

"It'll never happen again, I swear it."

"I didn't mind, believe me. As a matter of fact, I *want* you to take some of your anger out on me. It's good for both of us. It binds us more closely to each other."

"But why . . . why would you want to put up with that?"

"Because I love you."

Lisl felt her heart swell within her. It was the first time he had said it. She threw her arms around him and hugged him to her.

"Do you mean that?"

"Of course. Can't you tell?"

"I don't know what I can tell. I'm so mixed up now."

"We're going to have to fix that. We're going to have to find a way to cleanse you of all that anger."

"How?"

"I don't know just yet. But I'll think of something. You can count on that."

THE BOY
at ten years

December 8, 1978

Two patrol cars and an ambulance in her driveway. Carol dashed toward the kaleidoscope of red and blue flashing against the front of the house.

More than a house. A three-story mansion. The former pride and joy of an oil company executive, with a pool, lighted tennis courts, even an elevator from the wine cellar to the third floor. They'd bought the place last summer. In the five years since he'd begun managing the inheritance, Jimmy had increased their net worth to twenty-five million dollars. He no longer felt the need to remain in the Arkansas boondocks, so they'd moved here to the outskirts of Houston.

"What happened?" Carol cried, grabbing the arm of the first policeman she saw.

"You the mother?" he said.

"Oh, my God! Jimmy! What's happened to Jimmy!"

Shock ran through the fear coiling within her. Jimmy was so self-contained, so self-sufficient, she couldn't imagine anything happening to him. He seemed almost indestructible.

"That's some boy you've got there," the cop said. "He's fine. But his grandfather . . ." He shook his head sadly.

"Jonah? What happened?"

"We're not sure. He was in the elevator shaft. Why, we don't know. But whatever the reason, he was trapped in there when the car came down."

"Oh, God!"

She pushed past the policeman and ran toward the open front door. She stopped when the ambulance attendants appeared, pulling-pushing their wheeled stretcher. A black body bag was strapped atop it. Blood oozed from one of the zippered sides.

Carol pressed a hand over her mouth to keep from screaming. She'd had her differences with Jonah, and many times had wished he'd pack up and move out on his own. But this!

She slipped past the stretcher and into the house. Something had been going on between Jonah and Jimmy lately. Jonah's previous deference and almost slavish devotion had undergone a strange transformation during the past year or so. His attitude had become challenging, verging on threatening.

"Jimmy!"

She spotted his short, slight figure, dwarfed by the pair of policemen flanking him. Her impulse was to run to him and gather him in her arms but she knew he'd only push her away. Affection was repugnant to him.

"Hello, Mother," he said softly.

"Some boy you've got here," one of the cops said, tousling the boy's dark hair. Only Carol saw the glare Jimmy leveled at him. "Kept his cool and called us as soon as he saw what happened. Too bad we couldn't get here in time."

"Yes," Jimmy said with a slow shake of his head. "He must have been in such terrible agony for so long. If only I'd found him sooner."

His eyes reflected none of the sadness in his voice.

"What happened, Jimmy?" Carol said when the police and the ambulance were gone.

"Jonah had an accident," Jimmy said blandly.

"*Why* did he have an accident?

"He made a mistake."

"It wasn't like Jonah to make mistakes."

"He made a serious one. He was supposed to be here to guard me. But he started believing he could *be* me."

As a numbing frost gathered in Carol's marrow, Jimmy turned and walked away.

DECEMBER

SEVEN

Lisl had just finished addressing the last invitation to her Christmas party when the phone rang.

"How's my favorite Prime?" Rafe said.

Warmth flowed through her at the sound of his voice.

"Pretty good. Glad to be just about done with these invitations."

"Feel like doing some Christmas shopping?"

Lisl thought about that. December had barely begun. She had a small list of people to buy for and usually she waited until the last minute. Purposely. She'd found that the trials and tribulations of last-minute shopping—the crowded malls, the clogged parking lots, anxiety over the very real possibility that all the good gifts would be gone—added a certain zest to the Christmas holidays.

But this wouldn't be just shopping. This would be a day with Rafe. They were together almost every night. But daytime together was rare. He had his studies to keep him busy, and she had her classes and her Palo Alto paper.

"Sure. When?"

"I'll pick you up in half an hour."

"I'll be ready."

As she stamped the invitations, Lisl double-checked to make sure she'd addressed one to everybody on her list—she had—and then she thought of Will. He wasn't on the list because he'd be a waste of an invitation, but dammit, she wanted him at her party. So why let him get off easy by not inviting him? Quickly she addressed one last envelope, added a personal note to Will, and shoved the stack into her purse. Then she hurried to get dressed.

She thought of the Thanksgiving she and Rafe had spent together.

For the first time in her life, Lisl hadn't shared the traditional turkey dinner with her folks. She had Rafe to thank for that. One result of her combative encounters with Rafe was a deeper insight into her childhood. She was beginning to understand her parents better, to see them in a new light. And she didn't like what she saw. As a result, it had been only mildly traumatic to call her folks and make up an excuse why she wouldn't be there this year. They'd been very understanding. She'd almost wished they'd been less so.

Rafe confessed that he'd had little experience with Thanksgiving Day. His Spanish father and French mother had never celebrated the holiday. But since he considered himself a full-blooded American, he now wanted to join in the tradition. So Lisl had baked a breast of turkey with all the usual trimmings. They'd drunk two bottles of Riesling during the course of the evening and wound up in another bout of traumatic lovemaking.

Their time together had become a bit strange. Rafe would start out gentle and loving, then begin to probe her past. He knew all the weak points in her armor, all the most sensitive areas of her psyche. He'd probe and poke until he provoked her to violence. And then they'd make love. She'd be left feeling exhausted and ashamed for physically lashing out at him. But he encouraged the violence, seemed to want it, and she had to admit that afterward she felt somehow *cleansed.*

A strange relationship, but one she did not want to quit. Rafe said he loved her and Lisl believed him. Even amid all her nagging insecurities, despite the tiny insistent voice that kept whispering, *Watch out, he's going to hurt you,* she sensed his deep interest in her. She needed that. Slowly, steadily, Rafe was filling an emptiness within her, a void she only vaguely had been aware of before now. His mind challenged her, his heart warmed her, and his body pleasured her. And now that she was beginning to feel complete, she couldn't bear the thought of facing that emptiness again.

"Where are we going?" Lisl said as she slipped into the passenger seat of Rafe's Maserati.

"Downtown," he said, leaning over and kissing her on the lips. He was wearing gray wool slacks and a pale blue shirt under a cranberry cashmere sweater; black leather driving gloves, as tight as a second skin, completed the picture. "I thought we'd try the new Nordstrom's."

"Sounds good to me."

Downtown was festooned with Christmas decorations—animated Santa mannequins in the windows, giant plastic candy canes on the corners, tinselly arches over the streets of the shopping district, all under a bright sunny sky and temperatures in the balmy mid-sixties.

"Pretty garish," Rafe said.

"And it gets more garish every year. But that's the shopkeepers' doing. That's not what Christmas is about."

"Oh? And just what *is* Christmas all about?"

Lisl laughed. "I can buy the fact that your family didn't celebrate Thanksgiving, but Christmas?"

"Of course we celebrated Christmas. But I want to hear what *you* think it's all about."

"It's about all the good things in life—giving, receiving, sharing, friends gathering, good fellowship, brotherhood—"

"Peace on earth, goodwill toward men," Rafe said. "And so on and so forth."

Something in his voice made Lisl pause. "You're not some sort of Scrooge, are you?"

As they pulled to a stop at a light on Conway Street, Rafe turned toward her.

"You don't really believe all that brotherhood of man stuff, do you?"

"Of course. We're all on this planet together. Brotherhood is the only way we'll all come out of it in one piece."

Rafe shook his head and stared ahead.

"Man, oh, man, did they ever do a brainwashing number on you."

"What are you talking about?"

"Brotherhood. It's a myth. A lie. 'No man is an island'—the *Big* Lie."

Lisl had a sinking feeling.

"You don't really mean that," she said, but deep within she sensed that he did.

"Look around you, Lisl. Do you see any real brotherhood? I see only islands."

The Maserati was moving again. Lisl watched the people on the crowded sidewalks as they flowed by. She liked what she saw.

"I see people walking and talking together, smiling, laughing, hunting for gifts for their friends and loved ones. Christmastime draws people together. That's what it's all about."

"What about the children starving in Africa?"

"Oh, come on now!" Lisl said with a laugh. For a moment he reminded her of Will. "You're not going to drag out that hoary old cliché, are you? My mother used to pull that on me to make me finish my brussels sprouts."

Rafe didn't return her smile.

"I'm not your mother, Lisl, and I'm not giving you a line to make you finish your greens. I'm talking about a real country. I'm talking about real people, really dying."

Lisl felt her own smile fade. "Come on, Rafe . . ."

He pulled into a municipal lot just as someone was backing out of a space.

"He must have known I was coming," Rafe said. He pulled into the slot and turned to Lisl again. "What about the continuing geno-cide in Laos? What about the daily brutalization of the female half of the populace in any fundamentalist Moslem country?"

"Rafe, you're talking about the other side of the world".

"I didn't think brotherhood was limited by distance."

"It's not. But you simply don't dwell on those things day in and day out. They're so far away. And the numbers are so staggering they don't seem real. Like it's not happening to real people."

"Exactly. You've never seen them, never visited their lands, and what happens to them does not affect your life." He gently poked her shoulder with his index finger. "That puts you on an island, Lisl. A big island, maybe, but still an island."

"I don't accept that. I feel for them."

"Only when someone reminds you—and even then only brief-ly." He gripped her hand. "I'm not putting you down, Lisl. I'm the same way. And we're no different from anyone else. We all need a certain amount of insulation from what our fellow humans do to each other."

Lisl stared out the window. He was right, dammit.

"Let's go shopping," she said.

They locked up the car and headed for the new Nordstrom's. Rafe put his arm around her shoulder.

"Okay now," he said. "Let's move closer to home. Look around you at these houses, these apartment buildings. They look peace-ful, but we know from statistics that there's a certain amount of violence and brutality going on behind those walls. Wives being beaten, children being sodomized."

"But I can't feel anything for statistics."

"What about that three-month-old in the paper this morning?

Scalded to death by his mother yesterday. I believe his name was Freddy Clayton. He's more than a statistic. Think how that child felt as the person he depended on for everything forced him down into that steaming water and held him there. Think of his agony as—"

"Enough, Rafe! Please! I can't! I think I'd go mad if I even tried."

His smile was slow. "The water around your little island just got wider and deeper."

Lisl was suddenly depressed.

"Why are you doing this to me?"

"I'm only trying to open your eyes to the truth. There's nothing wrong with being an island. Especially if you're a Prime. We Primes can be self-sufficient on our islands, but the rest of them can't be. Thus the 'No man is an island' lie. We are the wellspring of human progress. They need us to get by. What's wrong is to allow yourself to be deceived into believing you need *them*."

"But I *like* the idea of brotherhood. There's no deception in that."

"Of course there is. You've been culturally conditioned to believe in it. The leeches, the consumers, they want everyone— especially us Primes—to swallow the brotherhood of man myth. It makes it so much easier for them to suck off our juices. Why should they bother stealing from us if we're gullible enough to let them convince us to give of ourselves willingly in the name of brotherhood?"

Lisl stared at Rafe. "Are you listening to yourself? Do you realize how you sound?"

He sighed and lowered his eyes to the sidewalk as they approached Nordstrom's.

"I can imagine: paranoid. But Lisl, I'm not crazy. And I'm not saying we're the victims of an overt plot. It's not that simple. I think it's more of a subconscious thing that has developed down the centuries. It's persistent and pervasive for a very simple reason: It works. It keeps us producing so they can milk us."

"There you go again."

He held up his hands. "Okay. Maybe I'm crazy. But then again, maybe I'm not. One thing I'm sure of is that you and I aren't like them. I want my island to fuse with your island. I want an unbreakable bond between us. Look at these people, Lisl. Your so-called brothers. Is there one of them you can count on? *Really* count on? No. But you can count on me. No matter what, no matter where, no matter when, you can count on me."

Lisl looked at Rafe and saw the intensity in his eyes. She

believed him. And that lifted her spirits. Suddenly she felt like shopping again.

They wandered the crowded aisles, finally stopping at the jewelry counter. The three saleswomen were busy with other customers. Lisl squinted at a wide twenty-inch, eighteen-karat gold necklace out of reach behind the counter. The herringbone pattern appealed to her.

"You like that?" Rafe said.

"It's beautiful."

He reached one of his long arms across and plucked it off its peg. He undid the clasp.

"Here. Try it on."

He reclasped it around her neck, then guided her to the mirror. The gold gleamed as it hung between her breasts, all but obscuring the slim chain and the cowrie.

"I love it."

"Shiny metal makes you happy, does it? Well then, let's get you some more."

He reached again and picked out a pair of gold earrings with onyx centers. Lisl pulled off the little studs she had worn today and allowed him to fasten the new ones onto her earlobes.

"Perfect," he said. "And now the final touch."

A moment later he was slipping an eighteen-karat gold filigree bracelet over her right wrist.

"There!" he said. "The picture is complete." He gripped her elbow and gently propelled her away from the jewelry department. "Let's go."

"Where are we—?"

"Out."

"But we haven't paid."

"We don't have to. We're Primes."

"Oh, God, Rafe!"

Lisl tried to turn back toward the counter but Rafe had a firm grip on her arm.

"Trust me on this, Lisl," he said in her ear. "Follow my lead. I'm the only one you can really trust."

She held her breath and let him guide her toward the exit, sure that at any minute the store detectives would leap upon them and escort them to a back office where they'd be grilled and then arrested. But no one stopped them.

Until the exit. A uniformed doorman stepped in front of them at the glass door that led to the street; his gloved hand gripped the handle.

"Find everything you need?" he said with a smile.

Lisl felt her knees begin to wobble. *Shoplifting!* And with what this jewelry was worth, she'd be charged with grand larceny instead of petty theft. She saw her reputation, her whole academic career heading for the sewer.

"Just looking today," Rafe said.

"Fine!" said the doorman and pulled open the door. "Come back anytime."

"We'll be sure to do that," Rafe said as he guided Lisl ahead of him.

Relief flooded through her as they joined the pedestrians outside and walked up Conway Street. When they were half a block from the store, Lisl snatched her arm away from him.

"Are you in*sane?*" she said, keeping her voice low with an effort. She was furious. She wanted to run away, break it off, never see him again.

Rafe's expression was one of shock, but the hint of a smile played about his lips.

"What's wrong? I thought you liked gold jewelry."

"I do! But I don't steal things!"

"That wasn't stealing. That was merely getting your due."

"I have money! I can afford to buy my jewelry!"

"So can I. I could buy out that whole department in there and cover you with gold. But that's not the point. That's not why I did it."

"Then what *is* the point?"

"That there's *Us,* and there's *Them.* We don't have to answer to them. They deserve anything we do to them, they owe us anything we take from them. They've been dumping on you all your life. It's high time you got something back."

"But I don't want anything from anybody unless I earn it."

His smile was sad. "Don't you see? You *have* earned it. Just by being a Prime. We carry them on our backs. It's our minds, our dreams, our ambitions that fuel the machinery of progress and give them direction. Without us they'd still be boiling tubers over dung fires outside their miserable little huts."

Lisl reached back and unclasped the necklace from around her neck. She removed the earrings and pulled off the bracelet.

"All that may be true, but I'm taking these back. I can't wear them."

And I can't stay with you.

Rafe held out his hand. "Allow me."

Lisl hesitated, then handed him the gold jewelry. Rafe turned and gave it all to the first woman who passed by.

"Merry Christmas, ma'am," he said as he thrust it into one of her hands.

The gesture shocked Lisl. This wasn't petty thievery. Rafe was trying to make a point. When he took her hand, she didn't pull away.

They walked on and Lisl glanced back. The woman was staring after them as if they were crazy. She glanced at the jewelry in her hand, then dropped it all in a nearby litter basket.

Lisl stopped and tugged on Rafe's arm.

"That's eighteen-karat gold!"

Rafe pulled her along. "She thinks it's junk jewelry. Either way, it's shiny metal. That's all."

Lisl turned her back on the woman and the litter basket.

"This is all so crazy!"

"But exciting too."

"Not exciting—terrifying."

"Come now. Admit that there's a kind of exhilaration buzzing through you right now."

Lisl felt the adrenalized tingling of her limbs, the racing thump of her heart. As much as she hated to admit it, it *had* been exciting.

"But I feel guilty."

"That will pass. You're a Prime. Guilt and remorse—they have no place in your life. If you do something that causes guilt, you must do it again. And again. Ten, twenty, thirty times if need be, until the guilt and remorse are gone."

"And then what?"

"And then you go further. You crank it up a notch. You'll see."

Lisl felt a chill.

"I will?"

"Sure. You'll see that it's easier the next time."

"I don't want a next time, Rafe."

He stopped and stared at her. They were at a corner. People were streaming by but Lisl barely noticed them. The disappointment in Rafe's eyes nearly overwhelmed all other perceptions.

"This isn't for me, Lisl. This is for you. I'm trying to cut you loose, to free you to fly and reach the heights of your potential. You can't fly if you won't kick off the shackles they've used to hobble you all your life. Do you want to kick free or not?"

"Of course I do, but—"

"No buts. Are you going to stay chained down here or are you going to fly with me? The choice is yours."

Lisl saw how serious he was, and realized in that moment that she could lose this man. Yes, he was young, and yes, she had lived almost half again as many years as he had, but dammit she could not remember ever feeling this good about herself, about life in general. She felt like a complete woman, an intellectual and sexual being for whom there were no limits. She felt a certain greatness beckoning; all she had to do was follow the call.

And it was all due to Rafe. Without him she'd still be just another math nerd.

Nerd. God, she hated the word. But she'd always been a nerd. She knew it and was brave enough to admit it: She was a nerd to the bone and she was tired of it. She didn't want to be who she was, and here was Rafe offering her a chance to be somebody new. And if she didn't take that chance, what would he do? Would he turn his back and walk away? Give up on her as a lost cause?

She couldn't stand that.

But it wouldn't happen. She was through being a nerd. The new Lisl Whitman was going to take control of her life. She was going to squeeze the last drop of juice from it.

But she didn't want to steal. No matter what Rafe said about other people owing it to her, the idea of stealing stuck in her craw. And no matter how many times she did it, she knew she'd still feel guilty.

She could pretend to go along, though. Pretend that she'd overcome any guilt or remorse about it and then they could quit that and move on to quieter, saner pastimes. Rafe was so radical, so intense, but she was sure that was all due to his youth. A little time and she knew she could mellow him.

She smiled at him.

"All right. I'm ready when you are. When's the next caper?"

He laughed and hugged her. "It's now. It's right up the street. Let's go!"

"Great!" she said, reaching into her bag to hide the sinking feeling inside. She pulled out a stack of envelopes.

"What are those?"

"The Christmas party invitations. I finished addressing them this morning."

She dropped them in the mailbox and sent up a silent prayer that she wouldn't be in jail for her party.

EIGHT

Everett Sanders stepped off the bus from the campus at his usual stop and walked the three and a half blocks home. Along the way he picked up his five white, short-sleeved shirts—boxed, no starch—from the cleaners. He owned ten such work shirts, kept five at home and five in the cleaners at all times. He made his usual stop before the front window of Raftery's Tavern and peered inside at the people gathered there in the darkness to drink away the afternoon and the rest of the evening. He watched for exactly one minute, then continued on to the Kensington Arms, a five-story brick apartment house that had been built in the twenties and somehow had managed to survive the Sun Belt's explosion of new construction.

He had the day's mail arranged in proper order by the time he reached his three-room apartment on the third floor: the magazines and mail-order catalogs on the bottom, then the second- and third-class mail, then the first-class envelopes. Always the first-class mail on top. That was the way it was done. He just wished the mailman would put it into his box that way.

Ev placed the mail in a neat pile where he always placed it: on the table next to his La-Z-Boy lounger, then made his way to the kitchenette. The apartment was small but he saw no sense in moving to a bigger place. What would he do with the extra room? It would only mean more to clean. He never had company, so what would be the point? This efficiency was fine for him.

He spotted a smudge of dust on the glossy surface of the tiny dining table as he passed and pulled out his handkerchief to buff it away. He glanced around the living areas. Everything was in order, everything clean and exactly where it should be. The television was over by the sofa and lounger in the living room; the computer terminal was dark and dumb on the desk in the dining area. The plaster walls were bare. He kept telling himself he should get something to hang on them, but every time he went to look at paintings he couldn't find anything that appealed to him. The only picture he had was an old photograph of his ex-wife that he kept on the night table.

In the kitchenette Ev measured out exactly half a cup of unsalted, dry-roasted peanuts into a paper cup. He returned with this to the lounger. This week's novel was *Hawaii,* a fat one. He'd have to get to today's quota of pages immediately after dinner. He nibbled on the peanuts one at a time as he began opening the mail. First class first, of course.

The invitation to Lisl's party surprised him, and pleased him to no end. What a sweet woman she was to include him in her plans. He was touched. He had a warm feeling for Lisl, and although her intention to prepare a paper for the Palo Alto conference was a direct challenge to his own bid for tenure, it did not alter his feelings for her. She had every right to go for it. And after what he'd overcome in the past, Everett was hardly afraid of a challenge, especially from a respected colleague like Lisl.

But he'd have to turn down her invitation. A party of that sort was out of the question.

He noted that the address was not Lisl's but a place in that exclusive new development, Parkview. Probably belonged to that Rafe Losmara she had been seeing.

Poor Lisl. She no doubt thought she was being so discreet and low-key, but her affair with that rich graduate student was the talk of the department.

Ev wondered what this Rafe Losmara saw in her. He too was reputed to possess a brilliant mind, perhaps the equal of Lisl's, but he was almost ten years her junior. Why was he pursuing an older woman? Lisl couldn't help him academically—she was in a different department than he. So what was his game?

None of my business, he told himself.

And perhaps he wasn't being fair to Lisl. She was an attractive woman—at least Ev had always found her so—and even more attractive now that she was slimming down. There was no reason why she shouldn't have many men chasing after her.

Which made the pool among the other members of the math department all the more offensive. When they'd approached him to see if he wanted to place a wager on how long Lisl's romance would last, he'd coldly dismissed them. He should have given them hell, should have gone to Lisl with it, but he lacked the nerve, and hadn't the heart to bring her hurtful news.

He hoped Lisl and this Losmara fellow stayed together for a long time, just to show up the fools in the department.

But what of that groundskeeper? Ev still saw Lisl taking lunch with him. He wondered how he felt about her relationship with Losmara.

Will Ryerson put off opening the envelope. He knew what it was. He dropped it on the kitchen counter and wandered the main room of the house he'd been renting for the past three years. The tiny ranch was old and damp; built on a concrete slab but that hadn't stopped the termites from establishing themselves in the walls. He swore there were some nights when he could lie awake in the silent darkness and hear them chewing. The house was situated on a large wooded lot in the center of a dense stand of oaks. He never had to go outside to know when fall arrived—the acorns raining on his roof heralded the return of cool weather.

Nothing here belonged to Will but the food, the linens, and the Macintosh on the dining-room table. The house came furnished. And decorated, so to speak. The previous renter had run a roadside stand specializing in velvet paintings. According to the landlord, that tenant had fallen behind in his rent and had simply disappeared one night, leaving behind some of his stock. The landlord had taken a few of the choicer works for himself and had hung the rest in the little ranch, literally covering the walls with them. Everywhere Will turned he faced yards of black velvet smeared with garish colors—yellow lions, orange-striped tigers, sad-eyed clowns, purple-white rearing stallions, and multiple, idealized studies of good old Elvis—the later Elvis, the glitter-sprinkled, high-collared, white-jumpsuited King of Rock 'n' Roll.

Will had found the collection unsettling when he'd first moved in, but he'd become used to them over the years. Lately he'd found himself actually growing fond of one or two. That worried him.

Will picked up the envelope again and stared at it without opening it.

The party.

Lisl talked about little else these days. And she never let up on pestering him to come. She saw it as her big chance to get him

together with Rafe Losmara. Rafe, Rafe, Rafe. Will was tired of
hearing about him. In a way, he wanted very much to meet the
man who had stolen Lisl's heart so completely. He was curious as
to what kind of man—*younger* man, no less—could engender that
level of infatuation in such an intelligent woman. And in another way he dreaded the meeting, fearing he'd discover that Rafe
Losmara had feet of clay.

No use in putting it off. He tore open the envelope.

There it was. After all his refusals she'd gone ahead and invited
him anyway. A holiday party, from eight till whenever, the Saturday before Christmas. At Rafe's Parkview condo.

It sounded nice. Too bad he couldn't go. Not only would he feel
out of place—a laborer mingling with the professors—but there'd
be telephones there.

And then he saw the inscription at the bottom of the inside page.

Will—
Please come. I don't have many friends, but I want them all
at the party. And it won't be a party at all if you're not there.
Please?

Love,
Lisl

Guilt. How could he say no to that? He hated the thought of
letting her down, but he couldn't go. It was impossible.

Or was it?

Maybe there was a way. He'd have to think on it . . .

NINE

Will was on his third cruise through the Parkview complex now. He'd passed Rafe Losmara's condo on each circuit, but each time had been unable to stop and go in. He felt like an awkward teenager, driving past the home of the prettiest girl in school, endlessly circling the block because he was too shy to knock on her door.

No doubt about where the party was. Will could have found it without the address. The gallimaufry of cars cluttering the curbs in front of Losmara's unit told the story.

Finally he forced himself to pull his Chevy into the curb, but he kept the engine running.

"Okay," he muttered. "Decision time."

Was it worth it? That was the question. He was already an hour late. The smart thing would be to turn around and head for home and forget about Christmas parties.

He could see them standing in the windows, drinks in hand, laughing, talking, posing. He didn't belong in there. They were faculty and he was maintenance. And he hadn't been in a social situation for so long he was sure he'd commit some gaffe within the first ten minutes.

But these were all minor excuses. The telephone—that was the obstacle that really counted. What was he going to do about the damn telephone? Telephones. There had to be more than one in Losmara's three-story unit.

And within minutes of entering a room with one it would ring, that long, eerie ring, and then they'd hear that voice, and if Will was close enough he'd hear it too, and even after all these years he couldn't bear to hear that voice again.

But he had a plan. And it was time to act. Time to take a chance.

Will turned off the engine and got out of the car. At the front door to the townhouse he paused, fighting the urge to flee. He could beat this. He could.

Now or never.

Without knocking, he stepped inside and grabbed the arm of the nearest person—a tweed arm with a suede patch over the elbow. A bearded face turned toward him.

"Hi," Will said with all the confidence he could muster. "I've got to check in with my service. Where's the phone?"

"I believe I saw one over on the table next to the sofa in the front room there."

"Thanks."

Immediately Will began to worm his way through the guests, focusing straight ahead, avoiding eye contact with anybody, aiming for the sofa. A white sofa. A white rug. White walls. Everything white. The guests looked out of place, obtrusive. They wore every color *but* white.

There it was. To the left of the sofa. The phone. White, of course.

Will's plan was simple: He'd locate the phones one at a time, make a beeline for them, and disable them.

The first one was right in front of him. He reached for it but a tubby figure suddenly blocked his way.

"Why, Will Ryerson!" said a familiar voice. "Is that you? Praise the Lord, I almost didn't recognize you in that jacket and tie!"

It was Adele Connors, Lisl's secretary friend from the math department.

"Hello, Adele. Look, I've got to—"

"Oh, Lisl was so hoping you'd show up." She glanced around. "Isn't it *strange* here? Doesn't it make you feel *funny*? I mean, look at those paintings," she said, lowering her voice and pointing at the abstracts. "There's something unholy about them. But not to worry. The Lord is with me. And Lisl will be so glad you're here."

"Uh-huh."

He tried to slip around her but there was no room to get by. *My God, the phone!*

"She wanted you here so bad but didn't think you'd show up. So last night I prayed to the Lord that you'd be here today, and see? Here you are!"

He could feel the sweat breaking out all over his body. Any

second now, that phone was going to ring. Any second . . .

"I've got to make a call, Adele."

"You know," she said, "not enough people at Darnell appreciate the power of prayer. Why, just the other day—"

Will pushed past her and lunged for the phone. He yanked up the receiver.

Safe! At least for the moment. It couldn't ring while it was off the hook.

That had been his original plan: Find a phone, lift the receiver, and leave it off the hook. But then it would begin to howl, or someone would see it off the hook and replace it on its cradle. His new plan was better.

Positioning his body between the phone and the rest of the room, Will reached around to the rear of the base and unclipped the jack. This phone was now cut off from the rest of the world. No wire, no calls. Simple but effective.

He hung up the receiver and turned back to Adele. She was looking at him strangely.

"What was so important that you had to almost knock me over to get to the phone?"

"Sorry. Had to check on something. But there's no answer." He looked around the room. "Where's our hostess? I'd like to say hello."

"In the kitchen, I think."

The kitchen. Most likely there'd be a phone there as well.

"Thanks, Adele," he said. "I'll see you later."

Will wove through the living room, went right around a corner, then left toward the back, and there was the kitchen. There was Lisl as well. She was placing canapés on a cookie sheet, spacing them evenly and sliding them into the oven.

Will had to stop and look at her. She wore white, the same white as the rest of the condo, a dress of some soft fabric that clung in all the right places, its whiteness broken only by the red and green splash of holly above her left breast. He had always found her attractive, but she looked beautiful today. Radiant.

Whoever had said white wasn't a good color for blondes obviously had never seen Lisl.

She glanced up and saw him. Her eyes widened.

"Will!" She wiped her hands on a dish towel and hugged him. "You're here! I can't believe it. You said you weren't coming!"

"Your little note changed my mind."

"I'm so glad!" She hugged him again. "This is great!"

As pleasant as the contact was, Will couldn't enjoy it right now.

He glanced left and right over the top of her head, searching the kitchen for the telephone. He spotted it next to the refrigerator— a wall phone.

How was he going to disconnect *that*?

Gently he pushed Lisl back to arm's length.

"Let me look at you," he said while his mind raced. A wall phone—it hadn't occurred to him. "You look great!"

Her eyes were bright, her cheeks flushed. She looked excited. And happy. So good to see her happy like this. But he had to do something about that phone. And *now*.

"You don't look so bad yourself," she said. She reached up and straightened his tie. "But I can tell you're not used to one of these."

"Can I use your phone?" he said.

Her brow furrowed. "I thought you didn't like phones."

"I never said that. I said I just don't have one." He reached over and lifted the receiver. "That's why I'd like to use yours."

"Actually it's Rafe's."

"Just a local call."

"I didn't mean that. Go right ahead. He won't mind."

She turned back to the oven. While Lisl inspected the progress of her canapés, Will pressed the heel of his free hand under the base of the wall phone and pushed up. It resisted so he leaned his body into it. If he could get it free he could—

Suddenly the base came loose and popped off the wall with a clatter. He glanced around and found Lisl staring at him.

"What on earth—?"

He smiled sheepishly. He didn't have to fake embarrassment— he wished he could have been a little more subtle about this.

"It's okay. I'm just not used to these things. Don't worry. I'll get it back on its plate."

He saw that the base was connected to the wall by a three-inch coil of jack wire. He quickly unplugged the wall end, then reset the base back onto the wall plate. He listened to the receiver. Dead.

"The line's busy," he told Lisl as he hung up the receiver. "Can I try again later?"

"Sure."

"How many phones does he have?"

"Three. There's one out in the living room and one upstairs in the . . ." Her voice trailed off. "Did you meet Rafe yet?"

"No. I just got here."

"As soon as these are done I'll introduce you." Her smile was bright with anticipation. "I can't wait for you to meet him."

"Great. Uh, where's the men's room?"

"Right around the corner."

"Be right back."

Will ducked around the corner, spotted the stairs, and ran up to the second story. He glanced in an open door, a bedroom, all in white, the double bed littered with coats, and spotted the phone on a nightstand. Seconds later he was on his way back down to the first floor, light of step, light of heart. All three phones were disabled. Now he could relax a little and try to enjoy himself.

"There you are!" Lisl said, catching him in the hallway as he approached the kitchen. She had her arm crooked around the elbow of a slim young man. "Here's the person I've wanted you to meet for months now."

Lisl introduced Rafe Losmara. Black hair and mustache, fine features, piercing eyes. His open-collared white shirt and white slacks—the same white as Lisl's dress—emphasized his dark complexion. Will realized then that these two were a real couple. And they were letting everybody know.

As he shook Rafe's hand, Will experienced a powerful sensation of déjà vu. The feeling had tickled him before when he had seen Rafe at long distance, but here, close up, it was almost overwhelming.

"Have we ever met before?" Will said.

Rafe smiled. It was dazzling, charming.

"No. I don't think so. Do I look familiar?"

"Very. I just can't place you."

"Maybe we've seen each other around campus."

"No. It's not that. I get the feeling it was years ago."

"I grew up in the Southwest. Ever been there?"

"No."

Rafe's smile broadened. "Perhaps it was in another life."

Will nodded slowly, searching his memory.

"Perhaps."

Another life . . .

Before coming to N.C., Will had spent over a year on New Providence and the surrounding islands; most of that time was lost to him. That had been another life of sorts.

"Have you ever been to the Bahamas?" he asked Rafe.

"Not yet, but I'd like to."

Will shrugged and said, "I guess we'll just have to leave it as a mystery for now. But I'm glad to meet you. Lisl's told me a lot about you."

"All of it good, I hope," Rafe said.

"All of it very good."

Rafe slipped his arm around Lisl's waist and hugged her against his side.

"She's told me a lot about you too. Why don't you stick around after this is over and we'll sit down and get to know each other. Right now I've got to make sure everyone is fed and watered." He gave Lisl a peck on the cheek. "See you later."

Will watched Rafe disappear into the crowded living room. He seemed engaging enough. But what was so familiar about him? It was unlikely he'd met Rafe before—probably just someone very much like him. The answer swam tantalizingly close beneath the surface of his subconscious. Will would have been more than willing to wait for it to reveal itself except that he sensed his subconscious might be warning him about Rafe.

He turned to Lisl.

"Well?" she said. "What do you think?"

Her eyes were so bright, her smile so fiercely proud, Will was powerless to feel anything but happiness for her.

"I don't exactly know him yet, but he seems very nice."

"Oh, he is. But he's very much his own man too. He has his own slant on everything."

"Is his slant much off beam from your slant?"

He thought he saw Lisl's eyes cloud over for a minute, but then they cleared. She laughed.

"Sometimes he surprises me. There's never a dull moment with Rafe. Never!"

Wondering how he should take that, Will followed Lisl back into the kitchen.

Will was working through the living room with his second tray of canapés. Lisl had tried to talk him out of helping but he'd insisted, telling her that he knew no one here and that this was a great way to meet her guests.

And it was.

Besides, he preferred to keep busy. He'd never been one for cocktail parties.

He had to admit though that he was enjoying himself this afternoon. He was nursing a Scotch on the rocks as he wove through the crowd with his tray of pigs in blankets. Everyone was friendly. A few had had a little too much to drink and were getting loud, but no one was out of line.

Then the phone rang.

Will froze and almost dropped the tray. Someone must have plugged it back in. He prayed for the ring to pause and then go on in the stop-and-go pattern of a normal phone call. But it didn't. The ring went on and on, steadily, relentlessly.

And people noticed. One by one they fell silent under the pressure of that endless ring. The conversation noise level dropped quickly by half, then dwindled down to a single slurred voice. And soon even he fell silent. Leaving only the ringing, that damned, incessant, infernal ringing.

Will felt as if he'd been turned to stone. Movement to his left caught his eye and he saw Lisl step into the living room from the hallway.

That ringing! Lisl thought as she entered the room.

Good Lord, what was wrong with the phone? Why did it go on like that? Whatever it was it had brought the party to a screeching halt. The living room looked like a tableau—everyone silent, frozen in position, staring at the phone.

Something unsettling, *unnatural* about that ring. She had to stop it.

Lisl crossed the room and lifted the receiver. An audible sigh whispered though the room as the ringing stopped. Silence, blessed silence. She put the receiver to her ear . . .

. . . and heard the voice.

A child's voice, a little boy's, sobbing, frightened. No . . . more than frightened—nearly incoherent with fear, crying for his father to come get him, that he didn't like it there, that he was afraid, that he wanted to come home.

"Hello!" she said into the receiver. "Hello! This isn't your father. Who are you?"

The child cried on.

"Tell me who your father is and I'll get hold of him."

The child continued to plead.

"Where are you? Tell me where you are and I'll get you help. I'll come get you myself. Just tell me where you are!"

But the child didn't seem to hear her. Lisl tried talking to him again but to no effect. Without pausing for breath he continued crying for his father, his voice slowly rising in volume to a wail. Suddenly he began to scream out his fear.

"*Father, please come and get me! Pleeeeease! Father, Father, Father*—"

Lisl snatched the receiver away from her ear. So loud. She couldn't bear the sound of such naked fear in a child. She looked around. All the strained faces in the room were looking her way, staring at the phone, listening to that small voice. They could hear it too.

"—*don't let him kill me! I don't want to die!*"

"What do I do?" she said. "What do I—?"

Suddenly the voice cut off and the abrupt, deathly silence of the room struck her like a blow.

"Hello?" Lisl said into the receiver. "Hello? Are you still there? Are you all right?"

No answer.

She jiggled the plunger on the base but the line remained dead. Not even a dial tone.

She wanted to cry. A frightened child needed help somewhere and she could do nothing. And without a dial tone, she couldn't even call the police.

As she jiggled the plunger again she spotted the mounting cord coiled on the carpet behind the table. A chill ran over her skin as she lifted the base of the phone. The jack notch at its rear was empty. The phone had been disconnected.

My God! How . . . ?

Lisl turned slowly and stared at her guests. Their pale faces and strained expressions reflected exactly what she felt.

Where was Will?

She didn't see him. She remembered him standing in the center of the room holding a tray when she answered the phone. She remembered the wild look in his eyes as he listened to that insane ring. Like a cornered animal. Where was he now? She glanced down. A tray of cooling pigs in blankets lay on the coffee table.

She heard tires screech outside on the street. Through the picture window she saw Will's old Chevy roar away down the road.

TEN

Manhattan

Detective Sergeant Renny Augustino found a note on his desk that the chief wanted to see him right away. He didn't have anything better to do at the moment so he headed for Mooney's office.

"What is it, Lieu?" Renny said as he dropped into one of the chairs opposite Mooney's puke green desk. A tiny plaster Christmas tree—a product of Mrs. Mooney's ceramics class—sat atop one of the filing cabinets, its lights twinkling chaotically.

Midtown North's chief of detectives, Lieutenant James Mooney, a jowly, fiftyish bulldog, looked up from a paper he was holding in both hands. The fluorescent ceiling lights reflected off his balding scalp.

"Got a message from the PC, Augustino," he said in his whiny voice. "He wants you on his new task force to get that serial killer."

"You sure you got the right Augustino?"

Mooney smiled. He didn't do that often.

"Yeah. I'm sure. Because I checked to make sure myself."

Renny was shocked. The police commissioner wanted *him*?

"Well, ain't that a kick in the head."

"It's your chance, Renny. Handle yourself right with this one and you can get yourself back on track."

Renny looked at Mooney and saw that the chief genuinely wished him well. Suddenly his opinion of Mooney turned around. He hadn't liked the man much; he was competent but had struck

Renny as too concerned with paperwork. He didn't really inspire his detectives. His men had to be self-starters if they were going to be anything better than paper-shufflers. Fortunately there was a fair number of self-starters at Midtown North. But maybe he'd been too hard on Mooney. And maybe that was because he resented anyone with a detective lieutenant's badge, something Renny should have had long ago.

"Yeah," Renny said, rising and extending his hand. "Maybe I can. Thanks, Lieu."

Mooney shook his hand and passed him his papers.

"They want you down at Police Plaza at one sharp. Try not to be late."

Back in the squad room, the other detectives congratulated him as he passed through. Sam Lang, dressed in green corduroy wrinkles, was waiting at Renny's desk, a coffee cup in his left hand, his right thrust out in front of him.

"Some Christmas present, ay, partner?"

"What is this?" Renny said, shaking Sam's hand. "Am I the only guy in the joint who didn't know about it?"

"Maybe if you weren't late all the time you'd be au courant."

Renny glared at him. He hated when people threw in foreign expressions—unless they were in Italian. Then it was okay.

"I got one question, Sam. Why me?"

"Because you're tenacious."

Renny peered suspiciously at his partner over the tops of his reading glasses.

" 'Tenacious' . . . 'au courant' . . . you been dipping into *How to Increase Your Word Power* again?"

"Let me put it another way," Sam said with mild annoyance. "You're a fucking bulldog when you get started on something."

"And how would the PC know that?"

"How else? The Danny Gordon case."

"Yeah. Sure. And where was he when I got busted back to second grade because of the Danny Gordon case?"

"Who cares? What matters is the commish has your name on his list of heavy hitters."

"Would've been nice if he'd asked me if I wanted the job first."

"You mean you don't?"

"I don't know, Sam."

"You're kidding, aren't you? This could get your career back in gear, Renny. I mean, you know they're gonna have to bump you up to lieutenant when the task force catches this guy. How bad can that be?"

"Could be awful. The whole thing could turn out to be another nightmare."

Just like the Danny Gordon case.

Another serial killer on the loose. Zodiac had spawned a bunch of imitators since the summer of '90. The mayor and the police commissioner had been making a big deal out of forming this new hotshot task force to hunt down this latest loon who had frightened most of the city's good-looking women—as well as those who mistakenly thought themselves good-looking—from the streets.

But what if they failed? What if Renny got himself wrapped up in this case and they never found the killer?

He couldn't go through something like that again. Not being able to resolve the Gordon case had torn him apart. Even now, five years later, not a day went by that he didn't think about that kid—or his killer.

"You're not going to turn them down, are you?" Sam said after a big slurp of coffee.

Renny managed a smile.

" 'Course not. Just 'cause I'm crazy doesn't mean I'm stupid."

"Good. You had me going there for a while."

Potts walked up then, a glossy sheet of paper in his hand.

"Fax for you, Sarge."

Sam laughed. "Probably the mayor."

"No," said Potts. "From Southern Bell. Something about—"

Renny was suddenly tense.

"Give me that."

He grabbed the sheet and scanned through it.

Another one of those calls. And in the same town as the last time—Pendleton, North Carolina. That bulletin he'd put out five years ago—to watch for reports of a certain kind of prank call: a strange ring, a child screaming for help. Someone at Southern Bell must have put it in the computer.

Bless you, whoever you are.

"This is it! Son of a bitch, this is him! It's Ryan! He's in North Carolina—Pendleton, North Carolina."

"Who's in Pendleton?" Potts said. "And where's that?"

"I don't know," Renny said as he slipped into his suit coat. "But I'm going to learn a lot about the place real quick."

"You're not heading for the library now, are you?" Sam said.

"Yeah. I'm going to find a book or two on Pendleton to read on the plane. Not going to waste a minute this time."

Sam's face went slack. He dismissed Potts with a wave of his hand. His voice became a tense whisper.

"Plane? What do you mean, plane?"

"Going down there. Have to practice mah drawl. *Noath KehLAHnah*—that sound like I'm from the South?"

"Yeah. South Bronx. Look, buddy boy, are you out of your fucking mind? You ain't goin' nowhere."

Renny had difficulty meeting Sam's troubled eyes.

"I've got to go, Sam. You know that."

"I don't know no such thing! What the hell have we just been talking about? You could get a lieutenant's badge out of that task force."

"That just became a sucker bet," Renny said. He straightened the papers on his desk into two neat piles in no particular order and pushed his chair into the knee hole. "Because I feel the flu coming on and it's going to be a bad case. As a matter of fact, I'm feeling feverish already."

Sam's face broke into a sickly grin.

"You're putting me on, aren't you. That's it, isn't it? Another one of your put-ons."

"Look at this face," Renny said, knowing he must look pretty damn grim. "Is this the face of someone who's kidding?"

"Jesus, Renny! The PC just asked for you personally. You can't walk out now!"

"The Danny Gordon case takes precedence, Sam. You know that." He could feel the heat rising in him. "I've been after this fucker for five years and I'm no closer now than when I started. Christ, you *know* what this thing has cost me! Now I get my first solid lead in God knows how long and you think I'm going to file it for later? No way, Sam! No fucking *way!*"

And that was enough of that. Renny was out of there and into the cold, late-morning grayness before Sam could try to lay any more common sense on him. He hurried down the subway steps and hopped the near-empty F train that was just pulling in. Thoughts of Danny Gordon hovered around him and hounded him all the way to Queens.

When he reached his stop and climbed back up to street level, he saw that the clouds had lowered. Snowflakes swirled among the tiny droplets that sprinkled his face. Sleet. He had no raincoat or umbrella, but he didn't mind. Besides, the grim weather matched his mood perfectly. He lit a cigarette and quick-walked the two blocks to his second-floor apartment.

Renny called American and charged a ticket to Raleigh. He packed quickly, throwing a few clean shirts, a couple of pairs of polyester slacks, and some toiletries into a battered old Samsonite suitcase, then dumped his drawer of socks and underwear on top of everything. He removed his shoulder holster and Smith & Wesson .38 and laid that in among the Jockey shorts. Then he grabbed his raincoat and headed back down the stairs. He could catch the R train and take it to LaGuardia.

But first he had to make a little detour.

Outside it was all snow now. He pulled up his collar and walked south a few blocks, then east until he came to an old boarded-up building. As the snowflakes sifted through his thinning hair and melted on his scalp, he stood and stared up at the facade. The sign to the left of the door was still visible:

ST. FRANCIS
HOME FOR BOYS

This wasn't the first time he'd stood before the place where Danny Gordon had lived. He came here regularly to renew a vow he had made here five years ago.

It was snowing then too.

Danny Gordon was dead. Even though his body had never been found, there was no doubt of that in Renny's mind, no doubt that the priest had killed him. Ryan couldn't hide and travel with a child injured like that. No. He'd finished what he had begun, and then he'd faded away. A perfect disappearing act.

Until now. After all these years, a lead had finally surfaced. Renny was ready to follow it to the ends of the earth.

For Danny.

I don't know where you are, kid, but I know you're dead. But just because you've got no folks, no family, don't think there's no one alive who cares about what happened to you. There is. Me. And I'm going to get the guy who did it. That's Renaldo Augustino's promise.

He turned and walked away through the falling snow toward the subway station, whispering another promise to someone else.

And when I find you, Father Bill Ryan, I'll bring you in . . . but not before I give you a taste of what you did to that poor kid.

ELEVEN

North Carolina

Rafe was right about the stealing. It did get easier. It became so against her will.

With each little theft, Lisl had clung to the guilt, squeezed each incident for whatever remorse she could wring from it, but despite her best efforts the guilt dwindled, the remorse became brittle and desiccated to the point where it crumbled into a fine powder that ran through her fingers like sand.

She had changed. She saw so many things in a new perspective now. Her parents, for instance . . .

She had gone home for Christmas. There had been no way out. She hadn't wanted to leave Rafe but his own family had been tugging at him as well, so they separated for the holiday.

What a nightmare.

And what an eye-opener. She had never realized before how empty her parents were. How shallow, how narcissistic. After she arrived they practically ignored her. All they seemed truly interested in was themselves. They'd wanted her home for the holidays, not out of any genuine desire for her company, but because having your only child home for Christmas was the way it should be. No real concern or interest in anything beyond their front door besides how they appeared to others.

The memory of Christmas night dinner was still fresh in her mind, how she had sat there and listened to them talk. All the pettiness, bitterness, jealousy disguised as wit. The subtle put-downs as they questioned her about how far she wanted to pursue this career thing, about remarrying and giving them grandchildren so they could keep up with their old friends the Andersons who now had three. She'd never seen it before, but these few months with Rafe had opened her eyes.

Depressing. And infuriating.

Lisl asked herself what these two people had ever really done for her as parents. They had fed her, clothed her, put a roof over her head—and she supposed there was something to be said for those benefits since not all parents did even that much for their children—but beyond the necessities of life, what had they given her? What had they passed on to her?

She'd realized with a shock that her life had no center. She'd been raised and sent out into the world without a compass. And unless she did something on her own to remedy that, she would remain emotionally, spiritually, and intellectually adrift.

The day after Christmas she had fled back to Pendleton. She'd been overjoyed to find Rafe waiting for her.

"All right," Rafe now said as they stood on the sidewalk down the street from Ball's Jewelry. They'd just completed their twenty-second shoplifting spree. "Who is the lucky passerby to receive our largess?"

Lisl scanned the faces of the post-Christmas shoppers and gift-returners as they flowed past. Then she glanced down at the gold butterfly pin in her hand, lifted from a counter in Ball's only moments before. She was enchanted by the delicate filigree of its wings.

"No one," she said.

Rafe turned to her, his eyebrows raised. "Oh?"

"I like this. I think I'll keep it."

The words shocked her. They seemed to have taken on a life of their own and escaped independent of her will. But they were the truth. She did want to keep this pin.

A slow smile spread across Rafe's face.

"No guilt? No remorse?"

Lisl searched within herself. No. She could find no guilt. The thefts had become routine, actually. More of a chore—an errand, almost—than anything else.

"No," she said, shaking her head and looking down at the gold butterfly. "And that frightens me."

"Don't be frightened."

Rafe took the pin from her, opened her coat, and pinned it on her sweater.

"Why not?" she said.

"Because this is a watershed, a cause for celebration."

"I feel like I've developed a callus on my soul."

"You've done nothing of the sort. That's the kind of thinking that holds you back. Negative imagery. It's not a matter of calluses. It's breaking free from your childhood shackles."

"I don't feel free."

"Because only one of those chains has fallen away. There are still more. Many more."

"I don't know if I want to hear this."

"Trust me."

Rafe took her arm and they began walking along Conway Street.

"Up till now," he said, "we've been engaging in faceless acts of liberation."

"Faceless? What's been faceless? There've been plenty of faces involved here."

"Not really. We've been stealing from stores. Faceless corporations that do not feel even the slightest prickle of discomfort from what we've done."

"You're not going to turn Marxist on me now, are you?"

Rafe's expression was disdainful. "Please don't insult my intelligence. No. What I mean is that from now on we're going to get personal."

Lisl didn't like the sound of that.

"What do you mean?"

"Not what—*who*. I'd rather show you than tell you. And I wish to do a little research first. Tomorrow will be soon enough." He opened the passenger door to his Maserati and bowed her toward the seat. "Your carriage awaits."

A small, cold lump formed in Lisl's stomach as she got in. Her relief that the thefts would stop was undercut by a growing unease about what would replace them.

TWELVE

The following day Lisl opened her apartment door and was startled to find a seedy-looking stranger standing outside. She'd been expecting Rafe. He was due within the hour and when she heard the bell she figured he was showing up early.

"Can I help you?" she said.

He was thin, haggard-looking, but clean-shaven and smelling of a spicy after-shave. A bulky overcoat rounded off the sharp edges of his wiry frame.

"You can if you're Miss Lisa Whitman."

"Lisl. That's me. Who are you?"

He fished a black leather folder from within his coat and flashed a badge at her.

"Detective Augustino, Miss Whitman. State Police."

She caught a fleeting glimpse of a blue and gold shield before the flap covered it again, then the folder was on its way back inside the coat.

A sudden surge of panic lanced through Lisl.

Police! They know about the stealing!

She glanced down at her sweater where the gold butterfly with the filigree wings was pinned. She had an urge to cover it with her hand—but that would be like pointing it out to him, wouldn't it?

This was it: shame, disgrace, a criminal record, the end of her career.

"What . . ." Her mouth was dry. "What do you want with me?"

"Are you the lady who made the complaint about a crank phone call on December sixteenth?"

Crank phone call? December 16th? What on earth was he—?

"Oh, the party! The call at the party! Oh, that's right! Ohmigod, I thought you were—" She cut herself off.

"Thought I was what, Miss Whitman?"

"Nothing! Nothing!" Lisl fought an insane urge to burst out laughing. "Nothing at all!"

"May I come in, Miss Whitman?"

"Yes! Come on in!" she said, opening the door wider and stepping back. She was so weak with relief she had to sit down. "And call me Lisl."

He glanced at the notepad in his hand.

"So it really is Lisl, with an 'l' on the end? I thought it was a misprint."

"No. My mother was Scandinavian."

Lisl realized with a shock that she had referred to her mother in the past tense, as if she were dead. After that trip home for Christmas last week, maybe she was dead, in a sense. She brushed the thought away.

"Have a seat, Detective . . . ?"

"Augustino. Sergeant Augustino."

As he sat on her tiny couch and took out a pen, Lisl tried to pin down his accent. There was something strange about the way he talked.

"Now, about that phone call—" he began.

"Why are the police involved?" Lisl said. "I reported it to the phone company."

"Yes, but there's been more than one incident like yours. Southern Bell felt it was serious enough to refer it to the State Police."

Lisl remembered the terror in that child's voice.

"I'm glad they did. It was awful."

"I'm sure it was. Could you describe to me exactly what happened, including the surrounding events? In detail?"

"I already gave that information to the phone company."

"I know, but their report is vague. I need your firsthand account to be sure this is the same. Start at the beginning, please."

Lisl shrank from the thought of reliving that call, but if it would help track down the twisted mind that would pull such a sick stunt, she was all for it.

She told Augustino about the party at Rafe's place, the crowded living room, about the strange endless ring that had set everyone's teeth on edge. She watched him leaning farther and farther forward as she spoke. He was so intent that he wasn't taking any notes.

"And since no one else seemed to want to do it," she said, "I picked up the phone. And that's when I heard that voice." She paused, shivering. "How can I describe the terror in that child's voice?"

Lisl glanced at Sergeant Augustino and knew immediately that she didn't have to describe the voice to him. She saw it in his eyes—the look. Almost like the look she caught in Will Ryerson's eyes every so often.

She said, "You've heard it too, haven't you?"

The woman's words jolted Renny.

How the hell did she know? How could she tell?

Shit, yes, he'd heard that voice. He'd had the unnerving experience five years ago—Christ, it was almost five years ago to the freaking day!—of lifting the receiver on one of those drawn-out rings. He'd heard it. And he'd never forget it. How could he? The voice replayed night after night in his sleep.

He studied Lisl Whitman with renewed respect. This was one sharp gal. Good-looking too.

Looks and smarts—a deadly combination. Renny knew he'd have to watch himself. Not only did he lack any official capacity here in North Carolina, he was impersonating a state cop. And that was *molto* illegal.

"No, not really," he lied—not well, he knew. "But I've heard the description so many times I almost feel like I have."

She nodded absently. He could tell she didn't believe him.

"Who's behind this?" she said.

"A very sick man. We're trying to track him down."

She looked him squarely in the eyes and said, "Was that a . . . a real child on the phone?"

"No," Renny said, hoping his eyes didn't betray him. "That was a recording." *It has to be.*

"But what about my phone cord?"

"What about it?"

"Didn't they tell you? It was disconnected."

He didn't remember the phone company rep mentioning anything about that.

"I don't understand."

"The phone . . . it wasn't plugged into the wall when I got the call. How is that possible?"

An awful lot of things about this case aren't possible, lady.

"It's not," he told her. "It must have come loose at the end of the call."

"But it didn't. I distinctly remember looking down and seeing the phone cord coiled on the floor a couple of feet away from the phone."

A chill skittered across Renny's shoulders. She had to be mistaken. But after what he'd seen five years ago, wasn't anything possible?

He pulled himself together. This was no way to think. He'd always followed the old Sherlock Holmes dictum to eliminate the impossible. Well, what she was telling him was pretty goddam impossible. It would only muddy the waters if he gave it any space.

Renny shook his head and changed the subject.

"But this is not the address at which the incident occurred, am I correct?"

Renny congratulated himself on how official that sounded.

"No," she said. "It was at Rafe Losmara's. That should be in the report too."

"It is. But every time I call Mr. Losmara or stop by his place, there's no one home."

"That's strange . . ." she said.

"How long have you known Mr. Losmara?"

"Only a few months."

"Only a few months." Renny sensed he was getting warm. He could feel the excitement building. "So you don't know him that well."

He saw her back stiffen.

"I know him very well."

"Could you describe him to me?" Renny said.

He'd been looking for an answer to that question for nearly two weeks now.

She described Losmara in glowing terms. Obviously these two had a thing going. Lucky Losmara. But Renny found his hot trail cooling rapidly. The man she described was too short, too dark, too small, and about twenty-five years too young.

Not Ryan. No way.

So much for that theory. But that didn't mean that Ryan hadn't been there. Maybe he didn't own the place, but he'd been at that party. No question. Renny would stake his life on it.

"Could I have a guest list?"

"You can't think that anyone at the party—?"

"Of course not. But it's all we have to go on for now. It might be useful."

She rose and went to a small desk in the corner of the living room and began rummaging through the papers that cluttered its surface. Abruptly she held up a sheet of paper.

"Got it! I always knew there was a reason never to throw anything away."

She handed it to him.

"I'll tell you what, though," he said, glancing down at the long list of names. "You could do me a favor and pare this down by eliminating anyone you've known for more than five years or who you're certain has been in the area at least that long."

She picked up a pencil and began drawing lines through some of the names.

"Does that mean you have a suspect?"

Renny chewed the inside of his lip. He'd have to be real careful here.

"We don't have a name, but we do have an old photo."

She handed back the list, then took her seat again.

"Well . . . ?"

Renny pulled the photo out of his breast pocket and placed it on the coffee table between them. He wished he could have arranged for one of those computer-generated drawings that aged a suspect's face.

"A priest?"

Anxiously, Renny watched her face, searching for some hint of recognition as she picked it up and studied it.

"A Jesuit. As I said, this is an old picture. No doubt he looks a lot different now."

She said, "And you say he's been here less than five years?"

"We believe so. That's when he disappeared. Give it a good look. He might have a beard or a mustache these days." He thought he saw her stiffen. "Remind you of anyone?"

She shook her head quickly. "No. No one."

A thrill shot through Renny as he realized she might be lying. Those last two words, the extra, unnecessary emphasis, gave her away. What was that look in her eyes now? Uncertainty? He caught her quick glance at the list in his hand. The photo must remind her of someone at her party.

"Sure?"

"Positive."

If he'd been on his home turf, Renny would have jumped all over her, maybe even gone so far as to bring her down to the station. But he was in a legally precarious position here. If the department got even a whiff of what he was up to, he'd be in big trouble. So he stood and stuffed the guest list in his pocket. He reached across and took the photo from her.

"Thank you, Miss Whitman. You've been a big help. Maybe we'll finally track down this pervo."

She was staring at him.

"Your accent . . . you sound like a New Yorker now."

Damn! Time to beat it.

"Yes, well, I spent part of my youth in Queens. Hard to kick some things, don't you think?"

She said nothing.

"Okay, well, I've got to get back to Raleigh. Thanks again."

He hurried out the door and fairly danced down the steps after it closed behind him. Somewhere on that list in his pocket was the new identity of Father Bill Ryan. He was closing in. He could taste it.

And when he found him, he'd drag him back for trial. But not before he'd extracted down payment on five years worth of rage from his worthless hide.

Wouldn't be long now. Not long at all.

Rafe showed up only moments after the detective had departed. Lisl told him about the encounter but didn't mention how the photo of the priest had reminded her vaguely of Will. But it was so hard to tell. The priest in the photo had been so young and fresh-faced, with a straight nose and unscarred forehead, so different from Will. But still, there was something there. Plus the fact that Will had been working around Darnell less than three years now, and a beard was a good disguise if you were on the run . . .

She shook off the apprehensions. Groundless. Silly. Will was the gentlest of men. She couldn't imagine him hurting anyone, especially a child. And besides, Will had been nowhere near the phone when it rang. She distinctly remembered seeing him standing in the middle of the room.

But why had Will disappeared immediately after?

No matter. She was sure he'd have a good explanation the next time they talked. And she didn't have to worry about the cop bothering him—Will had been so adamant about not coming, she hadn't bothered to put his name on the guest list.

Rafe brushed off her puzzlement as to why the State Police were getting involved, saying it had nothing to do with them, that they had more important things to concern them.

But she noticed that he was unusually quiet and pensive as they drove through town on their way to his mystery destination.

They wound up sitting at the curb near the rear parking lots of County Medical Center for a good twenty minutes or more. With Rafe so quiet she found herself thinking about Will again. Why had he disappeared from her party like that? Right when that awful phone call had come through. She could have used a little comfort from him then.

She wished she could find him and talk to him but she hadn't seen him since the party. Christmas break had a lot to do with that. The students were gone and campus routine was on hold until the second week in January. The few times she'd been back to her office she'd checked the old elm tree but he'd been nowhere in sight.

And she couldn't call him because he had no phone . . .

Phone . . . she wondered if there was any connection between his aversion to phones and the call at the party. But how could there be?

The only way to find out would be to ask him, and that would have to wait until she saw him again. Right now she was chilly and bored.

"What are we waiting for?" she asked Rafe for the fourth time.

"A face. The face we will be targeting. Just watch that nine-twelve over there."

"What's a nine-twelve?"

"A car. A Porsche. That little black one, third from the right in the lot over there."

Lisl spotted the car he meant. A sleek, sporty-looking two-seater. It looked built for speed.

"That's the doctor's parking lot."

"Yes. I know."

Lisl was just beginning to get an inkling of why they might be here when she saw him. A tall, dark-haired man in brushed wool slacks and a camel hair overcoat.

"Oh, God! It's Brian!"

"Yes. Dr. Brian Callahan. Your ex-husband. Very good-looking. I compliment you on your taste. Reminds me a little of Mel Gibson. I suspect he tries to emphasize the resemblance."

Lisl felt something akin to panic gripping her throat.

"Get me out of here."

"Why? Does he frighten you?"

"No. I just don't want to have anything to do with him."

"Why not?"

Lisl didn't answer. How could she? She wasn't sure herself. She hadn't seen Brian for years, and hadn't thought of him much at all since she'd met Rafe. But seeing him now brought back that awful, searing moment outside the attorney's office. The look on his face, the contempt in his voice, the words . . . *I never loved you* . . .

And with the memory came the pain.

She couldn't face him again, couldn't bear to have those hard, cold eyes pierce her again. She had come so far since that day. She couldn't risk letting him drag her down again. And he could do it. She knew he could look at her with that face and make her feel like nothing. Lisl never wanted to feel like nothing again.

Yes. She was afraid of Brian. He had never struck her, never harmed her physically. She almost wished he had. That would have been easier to deal with than the punishment he had meted out to her at the end of their marriage.

"Why not?" Rafe repeated.

"He's simply not worth the time," Lisl said.

"Oh, but he is. You helped put him where he is. You worked to pay the rent, you cooked his meals, you made it possible for him to get through medical school while he was sticking it to anything in a skirt."

"Drop it, Rafe. It's yesterday's news."

"And then when he was ready for his residency and could start making some money on his own, he dumped you."

"Enough."

"Look at him, Lisl. Tall, handsome, prosperous—only a couple of years into private practice and already he's driving an expensive sports car, wearing Armani clothes. And he owes much of it to you."

"I don't want anything from him!"

"Yes, you do." Rafe's eyes were fierce. "You want to be free of him."

"I *am* free of him."

"Legally, yes. But are you?"

Lisl heard Brian's car start, saw him back out of his space, then race to the lot exit. When the gate rose to let him out, he roared away with squealing, smoking tires.

"Let's follow Dr. Callahan, shall we?"

Lisl said nothing. She felt cold and sick as she sat with her arms folded across her chest while Rafe followed Brian through town.

"Dr. Callahan has a heavy foot," Rafe said.

Lisl remembered Brian's love of fast driving. A trip across town with him was an invitation to whiplash.

"You're not exactly a turtle yourself."

"Just trying to keep up with the good doctor."

They followed him through the black section at the southern end of town—"Downtown Browntown" as the students called it—and then into a development of luxury custom homes. The sign at the entrance read Rolling Oaks.

"What on earth is a Rolling Oak?" Rafe said.

Brian's car zipped into a short asphalt driveway and screeched to a halt before a two-car garage attached to a new two-story colonial. The garage door opened automatically and he eased his car inside.

"Nice house," Rafe said. "A 'starter home,' if you plan to be wealthy. Could have been yours."

"I don't want anything of his. I told you that."

"He's got a custom home, you've got a garden apartment."

Lisl realized she was angry—very angry. But somehow admitting that would allow Brian another victory. So she said nothing.

Rafe looked at her a long time, then said, "Doesn't seem fair, does it?"

"Life isn't fair, Rafe. If you expect fairness from life you'll go crazy long before you die."

"Excellent!" he said. "Couldn't have said it better myself. Fairness is a human construct. Life doesn't supply it—*we* do. That's why I brought you here. Now that we know where Dr. Brian Callahan lives, we are going to create a little fairness in his neck of the woods."

Rafe's smile frightened Lisl as he chirped the tires and roared past Brian's closing garage door.

They had a light dinner, and Rafe asked her to stay over. They had just removed the last of their clothing when Rafe pulled a black leather belt out of the drawer and handed it to her.

"What's this for?" Lisl asked.

She uncoiled it in her hands. It was long, close to four feet in length, and two inches wide.

"I want you to use it on me."

Lisl felt a sudden tightening inside.

"What do you mean, 'use it'?"

"I want you to hit me with it."

Her stomach turned. "This is sick."

"What's sick?"

"Look, I love you, Rafe, but I can't get with this masochism thing of yours."

His eyes suddenly blazed.

"*My* masochism thing? Lisl, *you* are the masochist! You've let people put you down, grind you down, chain you down until you've come to accept it as your state of being, your lot in life. Day-to-day *life* is a masochistic event for you, Lisl. You should be on top of the world yet you're content to live under its heel!"

"I don't want to hurt anyone, Rafe."

He stepped up and gently slipped his arms around her.

"I know you don't, Lisl. That's because you're a good person. But there's so much anger in you it's frightening. You seethe with it."

She knew he was right. She'd never been aware of her anger before. But she could not deny its existence now. She had discovered it since meeting Rafe—a boiling rage deep down inside her. And with each passing week she could feel it bubbling closer to the surface.

"I can't help that."

"Oh, but you can. And you will. You've got to let that anger go before you can be the new Lisl."

"I don't know if I want to be the new Lisl."

"Do you like the old Lisl?"

"No." *God, no!*

"Then don't be afraid to change."

His words were so soft, so soothing, the touch of his bare skin against hers was so warm. She floated on the sound of his voice.

"That's why I've led you through these little faceless crimes. They're symbolic. They let you bleed off the anger in tiny, harmless doses, and that brings you closer to the new Lisl. The same is true with the belt."

"No, I—"

"Listen to me, listen to me," he said softly, almost cooing in her ear. "It's a symbolic act. I don't want you to really hurt me. Believe me, I'm into pleasure, not pain. Just think of it as comparable to our little thefts—no one was really hurt. This will be much the same. You won't strike me with any force. You'll just lay the strap across my back and pretend I'm Brian."

"Rafe, please . . ." She was beginning to feel sick.

"Where's the harm? You won't be hurting me and you won't be hurting Brian. You'll only be helping yourself. This is symbolic, remember? *Symbolic.*"

"Okay," she said finally. "Symbolic."

She didn't want to do this, but if Rafe thought it was so important, she'd give it a try. And if it did release some of this anger in her—although she didn't see how it could—that would be to the good. And if nothing else, once she got through it they could make love. That was what she really wanted to do.

Rafe lay across the bed, facedown, the smooth skin of his bare back awaiting the belt.

"All right," he said. "Twenty strokes. Just think of me as Brian and slap it across my back."

Feeling silly, Lisl raised the belt and let its length fall onto Rafe's back.

He laughed. "Come on, Lisl. That was wimpy. This is Brian here. The guy you loved, the guy you trusted enough to marry."

Lisl swung again and put just a little more into it.

"Is that the best you can do? Lisl, this is the guy who was probably cheating on you during your *engagement*. And you know from the divorce hearings that he was putting the moves on his female fellow med students the week you got back from your honeymoon."

She swung harder this time.

"There you go. Just imagine I'm the guy who let you work for him all day to help earn his tuition, and then while you were out taking a night course would sneak a little chippy into your apartment and fuck her right in your own bed."

Lisl remembered the savage look on Brian's face when he'd told her that. The belt made a loud *slap* against Rafe's back when she swung this time. She swung again, even harder.

Slap!

"Good! Here's the guy who took you in marriage not as his wife but as his beast of burden, his meal ticket."

Slap!

"And when he didn't need you anymore, he tossed you away like an old newspaper."

"Damn you!" Lisl heard herself say. Rage suffused her, clouded her vision as she swung the belt with everything she had. And again, over and over, until she saw red . . .

. . . on Rafe's back.

Blood. There was a deep gash across his back.

"Oh, my God!"

Suddenly the rage retreated, leaving her cold and sick and weak. *Did I do that? What's happening? This isn't me!*

She dropped to her knees beside the bed.

"Oh, Rafe, I'm so sorry!"

He turned toward her. "Are you kidding? It's just a scratch. Come here."

He pulled her onto the bed beside him. She could see that he was excited. He began kissing her, warming her, chasing the cold and dread and doubt, building the heat within her until it burst into flame.

Afterward he held her close and stroked her hair.

"There. Don't you feel better?"

Lisl knew what he was referring to but didn't feel like talking about it.

"I always feel good after we make love."

"I meant with the belt. Didn't that leave you feeling a bit cleaner, refreshed?"

"No! How could I possibly feel good about hurting you like that?"

"Don't be silly. You didn't hurt me."

"You were bleeding!"

"A scratch."

"That was no scratch. Turn over and I'll show you."

Rafe rolled onto his stomach and presented his back to her.

His *unmarred* back.

Lisl ran a hand over the smooth skin. There had been welts there only a short while ago. Blood too. She was sure of it.

"How . . . ?"

"I'm a fast healer. You know that."

"But nobody's that fast."

"Which means that you didn't hurt me anywhere near as badly as you thought."

He turned toward her and pulled her down to his side. Lisl snuggled against him.

"You see," he said, "it was all symbolic. You got some of the anger out without hurting me. The anger was real but my wounds were not. You simply magnified them in your mind. The net result: I'm unhurt and you're a little bit closer to being the new Lisl."

"I'm not so sure about this 'new Lisl' business."

"Don't hinder yourself, Lisl. You're on the way to setting yourself free. And when you become the new Lisl, you truly will be a new person. No one who knew you before will recognize you. A new Lisl—that's my promise to you."

"Fine, but this bit with the belt—"

"That's just a part of it—the symbolic part. That must continue. But we won't limit ourselves to the merely symbolic with Dr. Callahan."

"What's that supposed to mean?"

"You'll see. My plans aren't fully formed yet, but you'll be a part of them, never fear. Stage one is all worked out, however. We execute that in a few hours."

"A few hours? It's after midnight!"

"I know. don't worry. It'll be fun. Trust me."

Lisl hugged Rafe close, a shipwreck victim clinging to a lifeboat on a sea of roiling emotions. She trusted him, but she worried about him as well. Rafe didn't seem to recognize the same limits as most other people.

Lisl shivered as she stood by Rafe's side at the telephone booth. She glanced at her watch. Five forty-five A.M. What was she doing at this hour standing in the chilly darkness outside an all-night gas station?

For one thing, she was listening to Rafe call her ex-husband. She could have waited in the car and stayed warm but that hadn't seemed right. She wanted to know exactly what Rafe was up to, wanted to hear every word he said. She was uneasy about this whole trip.

"Rafe," she said, "are you sure—?"

He cut her off with a wave of his hand and put a finger to his lips. He spoke into the receiver in an accented voice pitched a few tones higher than his own. He sounded Indian or Pakistani.

"Dr. Callahan?" he said with a grin and a wink at her. "This is Dr. Krishna from the emergency room at County. So sorry to awaken you at this hour. Yes, I am being very new here. I just started this very evening. Thank you very much. Yes, I have a seventy-six-year-old woman here, a Mrs. Cranston, who says her daughter is a patient of yours. Yes, well, let me see . . . no, I am not having the daughter's name at hand. However, Mrs. Cranston has suffered a displaced fracture of her left hip. She is being in very much pain at this time. No, I am very sorry to say she is not stable. In fact, her blood pressure is falling. Yes, I have done that. Also she is being very obese and I am worried about the possibility of a pulmonary embolism." A long pause, then: "Yes, I will be doing that. And I will be telling her daughter that you are coming in immediately. She will be most pleased. Thank you. I am most looking forward to meeting you, Dr. Callahan."

Lisl stared at him in amazement.

"You sounded just like a doctor. Where did you learn all that?"

He laughed as he led her back to the warmth of the car.

"The same place doctors learn it: a medical textbook. I went to the library and looked up the major complications of a broken hip."

"But why?"

"To get him out of the house, of course."

He helped her into the passenger seat and closed the car door. But instead of getting in the driver side, he headed back to the gas station.

What's he up to? she wondered. He'd been so secretive about his plans for tonight.

A moment later he emerged carrying a cardboard box. He placed it in the space behind the seats, then got behind the wheel.

"What did you buy?" Lisl asked.

"Motor oil."

"Does that have anything to do with Brian?"

"It sure does."

"Can I ask what?"

His smile was enigmatic.

"All in good time, my dear. All in good time."

"You sound like the Wicked Witch of the West."

Rafe let out a high-pitched cackle as the Maserati roared to life.

As they entered the Rolling Oaks development Lisl saw Brian speeding out.

"There he goes. The good Dr. Callahan on a mission of mercy," Rafe said.

"Don't knock that."

"He's covering orthopedic call for the emergency room tonight. He *has* to go or he'll be suspended from the medical center."

"How do you know?"

"I checked. All it took was a telephone call. And besides, he figures on picking up a couple of grand for pinning some old lady's broken hip, so let's not award him a halo yet."

Rafe shut off his headlights before he reached Brian's house. They cruised to a stop just past the entrance to his driveway.

Lisl felt cold. Her stomach fluttered.

"You're not planning something illegal, are you?"

"You mean like breaking and entering? No. But I suppose it could be considered malicious mischief."

"Oh, great!"

"Come on. This is for you, not me."

"A few hours sleep would do more for me."

Rafe got out of the car and lifted the box of motor oil from behind the seats.

"Come on now. And be quiet. We don't want to wake the neighbors."

As he eased his door shut, Lisl got out and joined him on the driveway. The sky was winter-clear, full of glittering stars in the west but growing pale in the east. She could see Rafe twisting the cap off a half-gallon white plastic container of motor oil. He broke the foil seal and handed it to her.

"Start pouring."

"Where?"

"On the driveway, of course. Start at the bottom and work your way up. A good thick coat."

"But—?"

"Trust me. This will be good."

Lisl looked around. She felt exposed and vulnerable out here in the growing predawn light, but she knew Rafe would never leave before he'd accomplished what he'd come here for, so she began pouring.

The oil glugged from the container and splashed on the asphalt but soon she got the hang of pouring it in an even stream, back and forth, slowly backing up as she poured, container after container, letting the viscous golden liquid ooze down the slight decline of the driveway to merge like warm honey into a slick, uniform coat.

"Right up to the garage door there," Rafe said, handing her the last half gallon. "We're not going to give this sucker one little bit of traction."

Lisl complied, then handed him the empty.

"Okay. What now?"

"Now we sit and wait." He glanced at his watch. "Shouldn't be long now."

They returned to the car and Rafe drove it half a block to a corner where he parked at the curb. Almost dawn now. Lisl had a sharp, clear, unobstructed view of Brain's garage and driveway.

They waited. Rafe kept the car idling with the heater on. It was warm. Too warm. Lisl began to feel drowsy. She was ready to doze off when a black sports car roared past them.

Rafe let out a low whistle.

"Ooh, he's ticked. I wonder why? A wild goose chase to the hospital, maybe? Looking foolish in front of the emergency room staff, perhaps? But that's no excuse. A doctor should know better than to hot-rod like that through a residential neighborhood."

Brian's car made a sharp, tire-squealing turn into his driveway——and kept on going.

It swerved as its brakes locked but found no purchase on the oil-slick asphalt, plowing through the garage door and coming to rest at a crazy angle amid its splintered remnants.

Lisl gasped in shock and stared, fighting an urge to get out of the car and run to the site of the accident.

"Ohmigod, is he hurt?" Lisl cried.

"No such luck," Rafe said. "Watch."

The door to Brian's car opened and Lisl watched his white-coated figure stagger out. He was rubbing his head and he looked dazed, but he didn't seem seriously hurt.

She felt a smile slowly work its way onto her lips.

Serves you right, you bastard.

As he moved away from his car to survey the damage, he stepped onto the oiled asphalt. Suddenly his arms began windmilling as his feet did a spastic soft-shoe routine. He went down flat on his back with his legs straight up in the air.

Lisl burst out laughing. She couldn't help it. She'd never seen Brian look so ridiculous. She loved it.

With her hand clapped over her mouth, she watched him roll over and work his way to his hands and knees. The back of his white coat was now black and he had motor oil in his blow-dried hair. He was halfway to his feet when his legs slipped out from under him again and he went down on his face.

Lisl was laughing so hard now she could barely breathe. She beat a fist against Rafe's shoulder.

"Get me out of here!" she gasped. "Before I die laughing!"

Rafe was smiling as he shifted the car into gear.

"Not so scary now, is he?" he said.

Lisl shook her head. She couldn't answer because she was still laughing. Brian Callahan would never be able to intimidate her again.

A question leapt to her mind.

"Why me, Rafe? Why are you doing all this for me?"

"Because I love you," he said, smiling brightly. "And this is only the beginning."

THE BOY
at fifteen years

July 21, 1984

Carol caught him at the front door.

"Aren't you even going to say good-bye?" she said.

During the past two years Jimmy had sprouted to the point where he was now taller than Carol. Slim, handsome, he looked down at her the way a cat might glance at a plate of food it had no taste for.

"Why? We'll never see each other again."

Jimmy had somehow worked a change in his birth records back in Arkansas to show that he was now eighteen. He'd hired a shyster from Austin who'd obtained a court order that had forced her to turn most of the fortune over to him. He'd treated her as so much dirt these past few yeas. So many times she had loathed her son, hated him, feared him. Yet something within her cried out with loss at the thought of his leaving.

"I've raised you, cared for you for fifteen years, Jimmy. Doesn't that mean anything?"

"It's the blink of an eye," he said. "Less. And why should you worry? It's not as if you haven't profited in that time. I've left you millions of dollars to play with."

"You don't understand, do you?"

He looked at her quizzically. "Understand what?"

They stared at each other and Carol realized that he really didn't understand.

"Never mind," she said. "Where are you going?"

"To settle an old score."

"With that red-haired man you keep looking for?"

For the first time, his face showed emotion.

"I told you never to mention him!" Then his face softened into a chilling smile. "No. I'm about to renew an old acquaintance."

He left. Not a touch, not a smile, not a wave, not even a shrug. He simply turned and walked out to his waiting sports car.

As her Jimmy drove off, Carol began to cry. And hated herself for it.

THIRTEEN

New York

Another New Year's Eve.

Outside St. Ann's Cemetery in Bayside, Mr. Veilleur watched the red glow of the cab's rear lights fade into the darkness, then he turned and walked toward the cemetery wall. The cab was to return for him in an hour. He'd given the driver half of a hundred-dollar bill as tip and told him the other half would be his when he returned. He'd be back.

He found a large granite stone jutting from the earth near the wall. He eased himself down on it. The December cold of the frozen earth began to seep into his buttocks.

"I've come to sit with you awhile," he said, speaking to the wall.

No reply came from the unmarked, uneasy grave that lay just over the wall.

Veilleur couldn't get into the cemetery at this hour, especially on New Year's Eve, so he settled for a seat just outside. Magda would not miss him tonight. She did not even know it was a holiday. He pulled out a thermos filled with hot coffee and brandy, and poured some into the cap. He sipped and felt the chill melt away.

"This is the fifth anniversary of your interment here. But I do not come to celebrate, simply to mark the occasion. To sit watch over you. Somebody should."

He sipped some more of the brandied coffee and thought about the future. The *near* future, for he knew his future was severely limited.

The Enemy was steadily growing more powerful. Veilleur sensed the psychic storm clouds gathering, thunderheads of evil piling up on all horizons, closing in. And the nexus point of many of the forces seemed to be here, just over the cemetery wall, in that unmarked grave. Something was going to happen here. Soon.

"What part do you play in all of this?" he asked the grave's restless occupant.

There was no reply. But Veilleur knew he'd find out soon. Too soon.

He sipped his coffee and continued his solitary vigil.

North Carolina

Another New Year's Eve.

Will sat alone in his drafty living room watching Dick Clark host yet another New Year's Rockin' Eve show. God, how he hated this night.

Five years ago . . . five years ago this very night he had committed The Atrocity, the act that had drawn an indelible line between himself and the rest of humanity.

This year would be worse than usual because of the phone call.

So long since he'd heard it. For years he'd managed to avoid it. And then Lisl's party. He shouldn't have gone, but he'd thought he could get away with it. He'd tempted fate.

And he'd heard it. All the way across the room, he'd heard that poor boy's voice.

Will got up and turned off the TV. If he looked at Dick Clark's grinning face much longer he was afraid he'd toss a chair through the screen. All those people milling around in Times Square, ready to jump around like idiots to celebrate the start of a new year.

A new year. Right. For him it was the start of another year in hiding. Day one of year six.

But this new year would be different. This year he'd find the strength to go back, to try to resume his former life. And the best way to do that was to start the year off in prayer.

He pulled his old breviary from his rear pocket—the book he'd been hiding from Lisl since September—and got an early start on tomorrow's daily office.

But tonight the prayers seemed even more meaningless than they had since he'd gone back to them. Usually he could count on the rhythm of the familiar phrases to provide temporary relief from the memories of the horrors of the past. But not tonight. The faces, voices, sights, sounds—they splattered him like raindrops, falling fitfully at first, then increasing to a steady trickle, finally swelling to a rush that flooded the room. He fought the current but it was too strong tonight. Despite his best efforts it swept him into the past.

PART II

THEN

FOURTEEN

Queens, New York

Things started going wrong toward the end of winter that year. It began in March, with spring only a couple of weeks away.

People hadn't called him Will then. His friends and folks called him Bill. The rest of the world called him Father.

Father Ryan. The Reverend William Ryan, S. J.

"I've got you now," Nicky said from the other side of the chess-board.

Bill stretched inside his navy blue sweatsuit and reminded himself for the thousandth time to stop thinking of him as Nicky. He wasn't a little boy anymore. He was a grown man now—a Ph.D., no less. And he had a last name, too. Justin and Florence Quinn had adopted him in 1970 and he carried their name proudly. People called him Dr. Quinn, or Nicholas, or Dr. Nick. No one called him Nicky.

Nicky . . . Bill was proud of him, as proud as he'd have been if Nick were his own son. His SATs had earned him a free ride through Columbia where he earned a B.S. in physics in three years. Then he'd breezed through the graduate program, blowing the faculty away with his doctoral thesis on particle theory. Nick was brilliant and he knew it. He'd always known it. But along the way to gaining maturity he'd lost his old smugness about it. His skin had cleared up—mostly—and his long unruly hair now covered the misshapen areas of his skull. And he was wearing contacts.

That had proved the hardest to adjust to: Nicky without glasses.

"Checkmate?" Bill said. "So soon? Really?"

"Really, Bill. Really."

Another sign of Nick's adult status: He no longer felt he had to call him Father Bill.

Bill studied the board. Nick had spotted Bill both his bishops and both his rooks, and still Bill was losing. In fact he could see no way to get his king free of the web Nick had woven around the piece. He'd lost.

Bill knocked over his king.

"I don't know why you continue to play me. I can't be any sort of challenge for you."

"It's not the challenge," Nick said. "It's the company. It's the conversation. Believe me, it's *not* the chess."

Nick was still a bit of a social misfit, Bill knew. Especially with women. And until he found himself a woman—or one found him—their traditional Saturday night chess games here in Bill's office at St. F.'s would probably go on indefinitely.

"But I seem to become worse at the game instead of better," Bill said.

Nick shook his head. "Not worse. Just predictable. You fall into the same kind of trap every time."

Bill didn't like the idea of being predictable. He knew his main flaw in chess was lack of patience. He tended toward impulsive, seat-of-the-pants gambits. But that was his nature.

"I'm going to start reading up on chess, Nick. Better yet, I'm going to invest in a chess program for the computer. That old Apple II you gave me will be your undoing. It'll teach me to wipe up the board with you."

Nick did not appear terribly shaken by the threat.

"Speaking of computers, have you been tapping into those data bases and bulletin boards like I showed you?"

Bill nodded. "I think I'm becoming addicted to them."

"You wouldn't be the first. By the way, I recently downloaded this new article about cloning. It reminded me of that brouhaha back in the sixties over that friend of yours—"

"Jim," Bill said with a sudden ache in his chest. "Jim Stevens."

"Right. James Stevens. Supposedly the clone of Roderick Hanley. The Stevens case, as they called it, was mentioned in the article. Current wisdom, as stated in the article, says that it was technically impossible to clone a human being back in the forties. But I don't know. From what I've picked up over the years, Roderick Hanley was a real wild card. If anybody could pull off something like that, it was him. What do you think?"

"I don't think about it," Bill said.

And that was almost the truth. Bill rarely allowed himself to think about Jim, because that brought on thoughts of Jim's wife, Carol. Bill knew where Jim was—under a plaque at Tall Oaks—but where was Carol? The last time he'd seen her was at LaGuardia in 1968. She'd called him once after flying off with Jonah, to tell him she was all right, but that had been it. She might as well have fallen off the face of the earth.

During the nearly two decades since she'd disappeared he'd learned how to avoid thinking about her. And he'd become pretty damn good at it.

But now Nick had gone and stirred up those old memories again . . . especially of the time when she had taken her clothes off and tried to—

"It's too bad—" Nick began, but was cut off by the arrival of a pajama-clad whirlwind.

Little seven-year-old Danny Gordon ran in from the hall at full tilt, then tried to skid to a halt in front of the table where Bill and Nick had set up their board. Only he didn't time his skid quite right. He slammed against the table and nearly knocked it over.

"Danny!" Bill cried as the chessboard and all the pieces went flying.

"Sorry, Father," the boy said with a dazzling smile.

He was small for his age, with a sinewy little body, pale blond hair, and a perfect, rosy-cheeked complexion. A regular Campbell's soup kid. He still had his milk teeth, so when he smiled the effect of those tiny, perfectly aligned white squares was completely disarming. At least to most people. Bill was used to it, almost totally inured to it. Almost.

"What are you doing up?" he said. "You're supposed to be in the dorm. It's"—he glanced at his watch—"almost midnight! Now get back to bed this instant."

"But there's *monsters* back there, Father!"

"There are no monsters in St. Francis."

"But there are! In the closets!"

This was old territory. They'd been over it a hundred times at least. He motioned Danny toward his lap. The child hopped up and snuggled against him. His body seemed to be all bone and no flesh, and weighed next to nothing. He was quiet for the moment. Bill knew that wouldn't last too long.

"Hi, Nick," Danny said, smiling and waving across the carnage of the chessboard.

"How y'doing, Danny boy?"

"Fine. Were there monsters here when you were a kid, Nick?"

Bill answered for him. No telling what Nick might say.

"Come on now, Danny. You know there's no such thing as monsters. We've been through all the closets again and again. There's nothing in them but clothes and dust bunnies."

"But the monsters come *after* you close the doors!"

"No they don't. And especially not tonight. Father Cullen is staying here tonight." Bill knew most of the kids at St. F.'s were in awe of the old priest's stern visage and no-nonsense manner. "Do you know of any monster—and there aren't any such things as monsters, but if there were, do you know of any monster that would *dare* show its face around here with Father Cullen patrolling the halls?"

Danny's already huge blue eyes grew larger. "No way! He'd scare them right back to where they came from!"

"Right. So you get back to the dorm and into your bed. Now!"

" 'Kay." Danny hopped off his lap. "But you have to take me back."

"You got *here* all by yourself."

"Yeah, but it's dark and . . ." Danny cocked his head and looked up at him with those big blue eyes. "You know . . ."

Bill had to smile. What a manipulator. He knew that only a small part of Danny's fears were real. The rest seemed to be a product of his hyperactivity. He needed much less sleep than the other kids, so the fantasy of monsters in the closets not only brought him the extra attention he craved, but got him extra time out of the sack as well.

"Okay. Stay put for a minute or two while I talk to Nick here and I'll walk you back."

" 'Kay."

Bill watched as Danny picked up two of the fallen chess pieces and pretended they were dogfighting jets, with all the appropriate sound effects.

"I can't imagine why no one has adopted him yet," Nick said. "If I were married I'd think of taking him in myself."

"You wouldn't get him," Bill said. When he saw Nick's shocked face he realized he'd been more abrupt than he'd intended. "I mean, Danny's adoptive parents will have to have special qualities."

"Oh, really?"

He could tell Nick was a little miffed, maybe even hurt. He hurried to explain.

"Yes. I'm holding out for an older couple who've already raised a couple of kids. A young childless couple is definitely out."

"I don't get it."

"How many times have you seen Danny before?"

Bill was keeping a close eye on Danny as he zoomed around the office with his makeshift airplanes. He knew from experience that the boy could dismantle a room in under ten minutes if he wasn't watched.

"At least a dozen, I'd say."

"And how long were you with him each time?"

Mimicking the sound of an explosion, Danny rammed the two chess pieces together in a midair crash, then let them fall. Before they hit the floor he was on his way toward Bill's desk.

"I don't know. A few minutes I guess."

"Most of which time he was either on his way in and out, or sitting on my knee, right?"

Nick nodded slowly. "I guess so."

Bill leaned back in his chair and pointed to Danny.

"Watch."

In a matter of a minute, certainly no more than two, Danny had tipped over and explored the contents of the wastebasket, climbed to a standing position on the chair and inspected everything on the desktop, pounded on the typewriter, tried to work the adding machine, drawn on the blotter, opened every drawer and pulled out whatever was in his way, picked up and inspected anything that piqued his interest, then dropped it on the floor as soon as something else caught his eye, then crawled into the knee hole and began playing with the plugs on the electric cords under the desk.

"Stay away from the electricity, Danny," Bill warned. "You know it's dangerous."

Without a word Danny rolled out from under the desk and looked around for something else. His eyes lit on Nick's overstuffed briefcase and he zeroed in on it.

Nick reached it first and snatched it off the floor and onto his lap.

"Sorry, Danny," he said with a smile and a quick glance at Bill. "This may look like a wastepaper basket, but it's highly organized. Really."

Danny veered off in another direction.

"See what I mean?" Bill said.

"You mean he's like this all day?"

"And most of the night. Nonstop. From the crack of dawn till he collapses from sheer exhaustion."

"No nap?"

"Never."

"Oy vey. Was I ever like that?"

"You had your own unique set of problems, but your hyperactivity was exclusively mental."

"I get pooped just watching him."

"Right. So you see why I need a pair of experienced parents for Danny. They have to have the patience of Job and they have to go into this with their eyes completely open."

"No takers?"

Bill shrugged and put a finger to his lips. He didn't like to discuss the children's adoption prospects in front of them—no matter how preoccupied they seemed, their ears were usually wide open.

He clapped his hands once and got to his feet.

"Come on, Danny me-boy. Let's get you under the covers one last time tonight."

Nick rose with him, yawning. "I think I'll be getting on my way too. I've still got to drive out to the Island."

They shook hands.

"Next Saturday?" Bill said.

Nick waved. "Same time, same station."

"Bye, Nick!" Danny said.

"Bye, kid," he said to Danny, then winked at Bill. "And good luck!"

"Thanks," Bill said. "See you next week."

Bill held out his hand to Danny who took it and allowed himself to be led down the long hall to the dorm section. But only for a moment. Soon he was skipping ahead and then scampering back to run circles around Bill.

Bill shook his head in wonder. All that energy. He never ceased to be amazed at Danny's endless store of it. Where did it come from? And what could Bill do to govern it? Because until it was brought under control, he doubted Danny would find an adoptive home.

Yes, he was a lovable kid. Prospective parents came in, took one look at him—the blond hair, those eyes, that smile—and said that's the boy we've been looking for, that's the child we've always wanted. His hyperactivity would be explained to them but the parents were sure they could handle it—Look at him . . . it's worth anything to raise that boy. No problem.

But after Danny's first weekend visit they all tended to sing a different tune. Suddenly it was "We have to give this some more thought," or "Maybe we're not ready for this just yet."

Bill didn't hold it against them. Euphemistically speaking, Danny was a trial. That one little boy required as much attention as ten average children. He'd been examined by a panel of pediatric neurologists, put through batteries of tests, all resulting in no hard findings. He had a nonspecific hyperactivity syndrome. Medications were tried but without significant improvement.

So day after day the almost-incessant activity went on. And one after another, Danny simply wore people out.

Which somehow made Bill grow more deeply attached to him. Maybe it was the fact that of all the kids now residing in St. Francis, Danny had been here the longest. Two years. He'd grown from a shy, introverted hyperactive five-year-old survivor of a drug-addict mother who'd accidentally immolated herself while free-basing, into a bright, personable, hyperactive seven-year-old. And it wasn't so hard taking care of him here at St. F.'s. After many hundreds of residents over its century-plus of existence, the building was as childproof as any place could be. Proof even against Danny Gordon.

But the days of the St. Francis Home for Boys were numbered. The Society of Jesus was cutting back—like all the religious orders, the Jesuits were gradually dwindling in membership—and St. F.'s was slated as one of the casualties. The city and other Catholic agencies would fill the void when it finally closed its doors in another two or three years. There were fewer boys in residence now than at any time in the old orphanage's history.

As he tucked Danny into bed and helped him say his prayers, Bill wondered if he might be getting too attached to the child. Hell, why not admit it: He was already too attached. That was a luxury someone in his position couldn't afford. He had to put the child's interests first—always. He couldn't allow any sort of emotional attachment to influence his decisions. He knew it would hurt when Danny left. And although it might take some time to arrange, his adoption was inevitable—yet he could not forestall that pain at Danny's expense.

But he was certainly determined to enjoy Danny while he was here. He had grown attached to some of the other boys in years past—Nicky had been the first—but most of them had started out at St. F.'s a few years older. Bill had been watching Danny grow and develop. It was almost like having a son.

"Good night, Danny," he said from the bedroom door. "And don't give Father Cullen any trouble, okay?"

" 'Kay. Where you goin', Father?"

"Going to visit some old folks."

"Those same old folks you see all the time?"

"The same ones."

Bill didn't want to tell him he was making one of his regular trips out to visit his own parents. That would inevitably lead to questions about Danny's parents.

"When you comin' back?"

"Tomorrow night, same as ever."

" 'Kay."

With that he rolled over and went to sleep.

Bill returned alone to his own room where a half-packed overnight bag waited. If he stepped on it he could probably make it to his folks' place before one A.M.

As usual, Mom had waited up for him. Bill had told her over and over not to do that but she never listened. Tonight she was swathed in a long flannel robe and had her usual motherly kiss and hug for him.

"David!" she called. "Bill's here!"

"Let him sleep, Ma."

"Don't be silly. We have plenty of time for sleep. Your father would never let me hear the end of it if I didn't wake him when you arrived."

Dad shuffled into the kitchen, tying his robe around him. They shook hands, Bill noting that his father's grip was not what it used to be. He seemed slightly more stooped every time he saw him.

The regular ritual followed.

Mom made him and Dad sit down at the kitchen table while she plugged in the Mr. Coffee—all set up, loaded with decaf and water, ready to go. She served them each a piece of pie—it was cherry this time—and when the coffee was ready, they all sat and talked about "what's new."

Which was never much. Bill's routine at St. F.'s was set so that one day was usually pretty much like every other. Occasionally he could report a successful placement or two, but as a rule it was business as usual. As for Mom and Dad, they were both hovering around seventy. They'd never been the types for golf or much socializing, so their existence was sedentary. They went out to dinner twice a week, Tuesdays at the Lighthouse Cafe and Fridays at Memison's. The only break in their routine was the death of an acquaintance. They always seemed to have a new death or major illness to report. Discussion of the details formed the bulk of their conversation.

Not much of a life as far as Bill was concerned, but they loved and were comfortable with each other, laughed together, and seemed happy enough. And that, after all, was what really counted.

But the house was getting to be too much for them. Mom did all right keeping the indoors clean and neat, but slowly, steadily, the outside had got away from Dad. Bill had tried to convince them to sell, get an apartment closer to downtown where they'd have a fraction of their present maintenance and could walk to the harborfront. Uh-uh. They weren't having any of that. They'd always lived here and so they would continue to live here and let's not discuss it anymore.

He loved them dearly but they could be royal pains when it came to this house. Though in a way he couldn't blame them. The idea of selling the old place and letting someone else live in it didn't sit too well with him either. This house seemed like an island of stability in a world of flux and flow.

So, since last summer, a couple of times a month, Bill would devote his Sunday off to the upkeep of the three-bedroom ranch that was the Ryan family homestead. Nearly two decades at St. F.'s had turned him into a skilled handyman. And he was almost caught up. By summer he figured he could reduce his maintenance schedule to once a month.

"I think I'll hit the sack," he said, pushing himself away from the table.

"But you haven't finished your pie."

"Full, Ma," he said, patting his thickening waist. He was carrying more weight than he liked. Mom didn't seem to realize that a man approaching his mid-forties did not need cherry pie at one in the morning.

After good nights, he headed for the bedroom at the far end of the house—his since childhood. He was beat. Without bothering to change out of his sweats, he slipped into the creaky old bed like a tired foot into a well-worn slipper.

Bill awoke coughing, with stinging eyes and nose. Either he was having an allergy attack or—

Smoke! Something was burning!

Then he heard the approaching sirens.

Fire!

He jumped out of bed and turned on the lamp but it didn't work. He pulled the flashlight he'd kept in the nightstand since he was a kid and that did work, but feebly. He stumbled through the white smoke that layered the air of his room and swirled in his wake. His bedroom door was closed. He spotted the smoke eddying in around the edges.

The house was on fire. *Mom! Dad!*

Bill grabbed the doorknob. It was hot—blistering hot—but he ignored the pain and pulled it open. The blast of heat from the hallway threw him back as a torrent of smoke and flame roared into the bedroom. He lurched for the window, yanked it open, and dove through the screen.

Cold fresh air. He gulped it. He rolled onto his back and stared at the house. Flame was jetting from his bedroom window with a deafening roar, as if someone had opened the door to a blast furnace.

And then an awful thought tore through his gut and propelled him to his feet. What about the rest of the house? What about the other end where his parents had their bedroom?

Jesus God oh please let them be all right!

He ran to his right toward the front of the house but froze when he rounded the corner.

The rest of the house was a mass of flame. It gushed from the windows and licked up the walls and climbed toward heaven through holes in the roof.

Dear God no!

Bill dashed forward to where the firemen were setting up their hoses.

"My parents! The Ryans! Did you get them out?"

The fireman turned to him. His expression was grim in the flickering golden light.

"We just got here. You really think there might be someone in there?"

"If you haven't seen a man and a woman in their seventies out here, then yes, they're definitely in there!"

The fireman glanced at the blaze, then back at Bill. His eyes said everything.

With a hoarse cry, Bill ran toward the front door. The fireman grabbed his arm but he shook him off. He had to get them out of there! As he neared the house, the heat buffeted him in waves. He'd seen blazing houses on the TV news over the years but film and videotape had never conveyed the true ferocity of a fire once it had the upper hand. He felt as if his skin was going to blister, as if his eyes were going to boil in their sockets. He crossed his arms in front of his face and pushed forward, hoping his hair didn't burst into flame.

On the front porch he grabbed the brass door handle but winced and let go. *Hot.* Hotter even than his bedroom doorknob had been. Too hot to grip. And then he cursed as he realized it didn't matter how hot it was—the door was locked.

He ran around the shrubs toward his parents' bedroom. The flames were roaring unchallenged from the windows. And yet from within, above the roar, he thought he heard . . .

. . . a scream.

He turned to the firemen and let out his own scream.

"In here!" He pointed to the pair of windows that opened into their bedroom. "They're in here!"

Bill ducked as the fire fighters got the hose going and directed the fat stream directly through the window and into the bedroom.

He heard the scream again. *Screams.* It was two voices now—wailing in agony. His father and mother were in there burning alive!

The fire fighter he had met before ran up to him and began pulling him back.

"Get away from here! You'll get yourself killed!"

Bill fought him off. "You got to help me get them out of there!"

The fire fighter grabbed Bill's shoulders and turned him toward the blaze.

"Take a look at that fire! Take a real good look! Nobody can be alive in there!"

"My God, don't you hear them?"

The fireman stood still a moment, listening. Bill watched his craggy face as he took off his fire hat and cocked an ear toward the house.

He had to hear them! How could he miss those terrified, agonized cries? Each wail tore through Bill like barbed wire across an open wound.

The fireman shook his head. "No. I'm sorry, pal. There's no one alive in there. Now come on—"

As Bill pulled free of his grasp again, the roof over the bedroom collapsed in an explosion of sparks and flaming embers. The blast of heat knocked Bill off his feet.

And that was when he knew they were gone. He felt his chest constrict around the pain. Mom . . . Dad . . . dead. They had to be. The bedroom was a crematorium now. Had been for some time. Nothing could have survived an instant in there.

He didn't—couldn't—resist as the fireman dragged him back to safety. He could only shout out his grief and anguished helplessness at the flames, at the night.

FIFTEEN

Why?

Bill stood alone beside the double grave under an obscenely bright late winter sky. The unfiltered sunlight stung the healing burns on his cheeks, feebly warmed his chest and shoulders, but left his soul untouched. The March wind was a cold knife slicing across the bare knolls of Tall Oaks Cemetery, ripping through the thin fabric of his black pants and jacket.

The mourners were gone; the caretakers had yet to arrive. By tradition he should have hosted a gathering at home for the mourners, but his home was gone. Home was now a tumble of blackened, ice-encrusted timbers.

Why?

Bill had made all the mourners go, practically pushed them away from the graveside. He had wept his tears, he had pounded his fists of rage against unyielding walls until they were bruised and swollen, now he wanted to be alone with his folks one last time before the earth was resealed over them.

How alone he felt at this moment. He realized that subconsciously he had taken it for granted that his parents would always be around. Consciously, of course, he had known that their remaining years were numbered in single digits, but he had envisioned them leaving him one at a time, taken off by natural causes. Never in his worst nightmare had he envisioned the possibility of such a . . . catastrophe. Their sudden departure had left a gaping hole in his life. Even the old ranch house was gone. Where was home now? He felt adrift, as if his anchor had been torn loose three days ago and could no longer find purchase.

A long three days—two for the wake, then the Requiem Mass and funeral service itself this morning—full of pain and the sympathy of friends and acquaintances, days in which he'd tried to leaven his grief by telling himself that his parents had led long, happy, productive lives and hadn't had much time left anyway, and how lucky he'd been to have had them around as long as he did. But none of it worked. Whatever tempering effect that sort of reasoning might have had on his almost-overwhelming sense of loss was repeatedly blasted away by the insistent memory of the two blackened, twisted corpses he had seen removed from the ruins of his parents' bedroom.

Why?

How many times had he offered pat, soothing bromides to a deceased's mourning family when they turned to him with that same question? He had always avoided perpetuating the nonsense that it was God's will, that God was "testing" the living, trying their faith. Circumstance, the capriciousness of reality, those were what tested one's faith. God didn't have to stick his finger into the soup and squash somebody. Disease, injury, genetic accidents, and the forces of nature were all quite capable of ruining and ending lives without the slightest help from God.

And yet here he was, Father Ryan, asking the same question— one chagrined Father Ryan, realizing that he never really had answered the question for others, and he now could do no better for himself.

Chief Morgan of the Monroe Fire Company had provided some sort of an explanation, though. He had pulled Bill aside in the rear of Cahill's Funeral Home during the wake.

"I think we found the cause, Father," he had said.

"Was it arson?" Bill said, feeling the rage rise up in him. He'd been sure the fire had been set. He had no idea who or why, but he couldn't believe the fire could spread so far so fast on its own.

"No. We had the arson team go over the place. No sign of an accelerant. We think it started in the wiring."

Bill had been dumbfounded.

"You mean a short circuit could make a house burn like that?"

"Your folks built that house before the war—the *Second World* War. It was a tinderbox. A good thing one of the neighbors called it in or you wouldn't be standing here."

"Electrical . . . ?"

"Well, the wiring was as old as the house. Not made for modern appliances. Something gets overheated once too often and then . . ." He finished the sentence with an elaborate shrug.

But he had said more than enough to leave Bill feeling weak and sick. Even now as he turned away from the grave and began walking aimlessly, the nausea still churned in his gut. He hadn't mentioned to Chief Morgan that not all the wiring was old. He had spent a couple of weekends over the winter rewiring a few of the rooms himself.

My God, had the fire started in one of the junction boxes he'd replaced? But he'd done the work in January, two months ago. If he'd botched something it would have been apparent before now. The sparks had probably originated in some of the old wiring he hadn't got around to replacing yet. Still, Bill was unnerved by the mere possibility that he had contributed to his parents' horrible deaths.

He stopped and looked around. Where was he? He'd wandered away from the gravesite without actually watching where he was going. He remembered walking through a stand of oaks and was now halfway up the rise on another of Tall Oaks' grave-studded knolls. No upright tombstones at Tall Oaks; everyone got uniform flat granite markers, the implication being that no matter what you were in life, you're all the same in death. Something about that approach appealed to Bill.

A patch of lush, dark green grass off to his left caught his eye. The grass in Tall Oaks was just beginning to come back from its winter brown, but the green of this one small spot was almost tropical.

Curious, Bill approached it, then stopped in shock. He recognized the grave before he was close enough to read the marker. It belonged to Jim Stevens.

A flood of memories swirled around him, especially of the afternoon he had stood on this same spot with Jim's wife Carol and looked down at a similar patch, only that had been dead grass surrounded by living. The grass over the grave today was so green, so perfectly rectangular, almost as if . . .

Bill squatted and ran his hands over the emerald blades. Despite the setting, despite the horrors and misery of the last three days, he had to smile.

Plastic.

He dug a finger under the edge and lifted. The plastic sod came up, revealing a patch of cold, brown, denuded earth beneath. His smile faded as he realized that even after almost twenty years the gardeners at Tall Oaks had been unable to make anything grow over Jim's grave. He glanced up at the flat granite and brass marker.

"What's the story, Jim?" he said aloud. "What's going on here?"

No reply, of course, but he felt his heart give a sudden twist in his chest as he noticed the dates on Jim's marker: January 6, 1942–March 10, 1968.

March 10. Today was March 13—his parents had burned to death three days ago . . . in the early hours of March 10.

Suddenly the wind through Tall Oaks seemed to blow colder, the sunlight seemed to fade. Bill dropped the corner of the plastic turf and rose to his feet.

As he walked down the slope his mind whirled. What was going on here? Jim Stevens, his best friend, had died violently, horribly on March 10, and now two decades later his parents had died just as horribly . . . on March 10.

Coincidence? Of course. But he could not escape the feeling that there was some sort of message there, some sort of warning.

But of what?

He shook off the thought. Superstitious garbage.

He returned to his parents' grave, said a final prayer over their coffins, then headed toward his car.

The boys of St. F.'s were all waiting for him when he returned, swarming like bees around the hive of his office door. He'd been back only once for a few moments since the fire, like a thief in the night, long enough to grab a few changes of clothes before rushing back to Long Island where Father Lesko was letting him bunk in Our Lady of Perpetual Sorrow's rectory for the duration of the wake and funeral, but he was certain the kids all knew what had happened. Especially since so many of them seemed to be having trouble meeting his gaze this morning when he said hello to each of them by name.

What kind of talk had run through these halls last Sunday? He could almost hear it: *Hey! Didja hear? Father Bill's folks got burnt up in a fire last night! . . . No way! . . . Yeah! Burnt to a crisp! . . . Is he comin' back? . . . Who knows?*

Bill knew. He would always come back. And he would keep coming back until they closed this place down. No personal loss, no matter how great, would keep him from fulfilling that vow.

Only a few of the boys were smiling. Weren't they glad to see him?

As he stuck the key into the lock on his office door, Marty Sesta stepped forward. He was one of the oldest boys in St. F.'s, and the biggest. He tended to throw his weight around but he was basically a good kid.

"Here, Father," he said, his brown eyes averted as he thrust a legal-size envelope at Bill. "Dis is from us."

"Who's 'us'?" Bill said, taking the envelope.

"Alla us."

Bill opened the envelope. Inside was a piece of drawing paper, quarter folded. Someone had drawn a sun behind a cloud. Below was a flat green line with some tuliplike flowers sprouting from it. Block-printed words hung in the air: WE'RE SORRY ABOUT YOUR MOM AND DAD, FATHER BILL.

"Thank you, boys," Bill managed to say past a steadily constricting throat. He was touched. "This means a lot. I'll . . . see you all later, okay?"

They all nodded and waved and took off, leaving Bill alone to ponder the incomprehensible wonders of children and what they could wring from a single piece of paper and some crayons. He'd expected a little sympathy from some of them, but never this kind of united display. He was deeply moved.

"Are you sad?" said a familiar small voice.

Bill looked up and saw blond hair and blue eyes. Danny Gordon was standing in his office doorway.

"Hi, Danny. Yes, I'm sad. Very sad."

"Can I sit with you?"

"Sure."

Bill dropped into the chair and let Danny hop up onto his lap. And suddenly the dark winter chill that had enshrouded his soul since Sunday morning melted away. The drifting sensation faded. The gaping emptiness within began to fill.

"Are your mommy and daddy in heaven?" Danny asked.

"Yes. I'm sure they are."

"And they won't be coming back?"

"No, Danny. They're gone for good."

"That means you're just like us."

And then it was all clear to him. The touching drawing, the sympathy from the kids. They'd been long-time citizens of the country to which he'd just emigrated. They were welcoming him to a land where no one wanted to be.

"That's right," he said softly. "We're all orphans now, aren't we."

As Danny jumped off his lap, unable to confine himself to one location a second longer, Bill felt a sudden oneness with the boy, with all the boys who had passed through the doors of St. F.'s during his tenure. More than mere empathy, it was like a merging of souls. The drifting sensation dissipated as his anchor found bottom again and caught.

But he wasn't entirely without family. He knew that although he was indeed an orphan like the other residents of St. F.'s, he still had the Society of Jesus. Being a Jesuit was like belonging to a family of sorts. The Society was a close-knit brotherhood. Whenever he needed them he knew his brother Jesuits would be there for him. In fact, as a priest, there was no reason why he shouldn't consider the whole Church as one huge, extended spiritual family. And in that great body of relatives, the residents of the St. Francis Home for Boys could be looked upon as his immediate family.

True, he had lost his parents, but he never would be truly alone as long as he had the Church, the Jesuits, and the boys of St. F.'s. He would always have a home, he'd always belong.

And that was a good feeling.

Bill put the horrors of last Sunday morning behind him by throwing himself back into the daily routine of running one of New York City's last surviving Catholic orphanages. He felt he'd already faced and survived the worst that life could offer. What else was left to go wrong? Whatever could go sour had already done so—in spades. Things would be looking up from now on.

And for a while, through much of that spring, his life did indeed seem to chart a steadily upward course.

Then the Loms crossed the threshold of St. F.'s.

SIXTEEN

It was a warm Saturday afternoon in early June. Bill was interviewing a young couple in his office. They seemed too young to be seeking to adopt a child. Mr. Lom was twenty-seven, his wife Sara was twenty-three.

"Please call me Herb," said Mr. Lom with a trace of the Southwest in his voice. He had a round face, thick brown hair receding from his forehead, a thick, stubby mustache, and wire-rimmed glasses. He reminded Bill of Teddy Roosevelt. He half expected him to shout "Bully!" at any moment.

"Herbert Lom . . ." Bill said, musing aloud. "Why does that name sound familiar?"

"There's a British actor with the very same name," Herb said.

"That's it." Bill remembered the actor now—Peter Sellers's Inspector Clouseau had driven him mad.

"You've probably seen a number of his pictures. No relation, unfortunately."

"I see. And you want to adopt one of our boys?"

Sara nodded excitedly. "Oh, yes! We want to start a family right away and we want to begin with a boy."

She was tall, dark, and slim with short, deep brown hair, almost boyish in its cut, and luminous eyes. Her application said she was twenty-three but she looked younger. And her drawl was delightful.

Bill had gone over their applications before the interview. The couple had been married only a year; both were native Texans, both graduates of the University of Texas at Austin, although they'd graduated five years apart. Herbert worked for one of the big oil companies; he had been transferred to the New York office recently. His salary was impressive. Both were practicing Catholics. Everything looked good.

Only their ages were against them.

Normally Bill would have rejected their application with a gentle explanatory letter advising them to give more time to their decision to adopt a child. But the details of Sara's social and medical history, combined with the fact that the couple had not limited their request to an infant, prompted Bill to give them a second look.

"You say here that you're interested in a boy between the ages of one and five," Bill said.

That had surprised him. As a rule, what a young childless couples wanted most was an infant.

They both nodded. Sara said, "Definitely."

"Why not an infant?"

"We're realists, Father Ryan," Herb said. "We know the wait for a white newborn can be seven years. We simply don't want to wait that long."

"Plenty of couples do."

Sara said, "We know. But I'm willing to bet that those couples can occupy themselves with tests and procedures and hopes that they'll conceive their own child during the waiting period." She glanced away. "We don't have that hope."

Bill glanced at the application again. According to a summary of Sara's medical history, supplied by a Dr. Renquist in Houston, she had been struck by a car at age eleven and suffered a pelvic fracture with internal bleeding. During exploratory surgery they found a ruptured uterine artery and had to perform a hysterectomy to save her life. The matter-of-fact tone of the summary ignored the emotional impact of that kind of surgery on a child. Bill saw a girl growing through her teenage years as the only one in her crowd who didn't get her period. A small thing in perspective, but he knew how kids don't like to feel they're on the outside looking in—at *any*thing; even if it involves a monthly mess and discomfort, they want to belong. But more than that was the inescapable fact that Sara would never have a child of her own. He was moved by the finality of her condition.

"Are you sure you can handle a toddler or a preschooler?"

She smiled. "I've had years of on-the-job training."

Sara's family history was a definite plus. She was the oldest of six children—and all her siblings were boys. Bill knew that in that sort of family structure, a female first child becomes the second-string mother. Which meant that although childless, Sara was already well experienced in the art of caring for children.

Bill was impressed with Sara. Over the years he had developed a sixth sense for adoption applicants. He could tell when a couple wanted a child merely to complete the family portrait, because having a child was expected of them, because everyone else had one, or because it looked good on a résumé—married with children.

And then there were the others, the special ones, the women in which the nurturing drive was so strong that it went beyond an instinct and became an imperative. These women could not feel complete, would not be a whole person until they had one, two, three children under their wings.

Sara struck Bill as the latter sort of woman. He wasn't reading much off Herb—at worst he was a yuppie wanna-be—but Sara radiated the need to nurture. It warmed the room.

"Very well," he said. "I'm satisfied so far that you two have possibilities here. I think St. Francis can help you."

They beamed at each other.

"Great!" Herb said.

"We'll run a routine check on your references, of course, but in the meantime, I'll let you look at some photos of the boys we have residing at St. Francis now. Later on—"

Suddenly Danny Gordon was charging through the office. He had a rocketship in his hand and he was making rocket noises as he roared it into orbit around Bill's desk.

"Hiya, Father!" he shouted as he passed behind Bill's desk at escape velocity. "You can be the man in the moon."

Bill ran a hand over his mouth to hide a smile.

"You'll be going on a real trip to the real moon if you don't get back to the dorm this instant, young man."

"Back to Earth!" Danny shouted.

As he careened around the desk he came face-to-face with the Loms.

"Whoa! Aliens!"

Sara turned her dark eyes his way and smiled at him. "What's your name?"

The boy skidded to a halt and stared at her for a second, then went into orbit around her chair.

"Danny," he said. "What's yours?"

"Sara." She held out her hand. "Pleased to meet you, Danny."

Danny stopped again, this time for a couple of seconds, but he wasn't still. His feet were tapping and shuffling on the floor as he glanced from Sara's hand to Bill. Bill nodded, encouraging him to do the polite thing. Finally Danny shrugged and shook her hand.

"How old are you, Danny?" she said, keeping a grip on his hand.

"Seven."

"Has anyone ever told you what a handsome boy you are?"

"Sure. Lots of times."

Sara laughed and Bill found the sound delightful, almost musical. And then he noticed something.

Danny was standing still.

Normally by now the boy would have pulled his hand free and been on his way around the room again, racing along the walls and caroming off the furniture. But he was simply standing there talking to her. Even his feet were still.

She asked him questions about rocketships, about school, about playing, and he answered her. Danny Gordon was standing in one spot and carrying on a conversation. Bill was amazed.

He watched them together for a few more minutes, then broke in.

"Excuse me, Danny," he said, "but aren't you supposed to be tending to your chores in the dormitory?"

Danny turned the full power of his big blue eyes on Bill.

"I want to stay here with Sara."

"I'm glad that you do, and I'm sure Sara wants you to stay as well, but we're in the middle of some grown-up work here and I'm sure there's some Danny work left to be done back in the dorm. So say good-bye and I'll see you later."

Danny turned back to Sara, who smiled and gave him a little hug.

"Nice talking to you, Danny."

Danny stared at her a moment, then walked—*walked*—out of the office.

As Bill stared after the boy in wonder, Sara turned to him.

"That's the boy I want."

Bill shook off his amazement and focused on the young woman.

"He's seven. I thought you were interested in an under-five child."

"I thought I was too. But now after seeing Danny I've changed my mind."

Bill glanced at Herb.

"How do you feel about an older child?"

"What Sara wants, I want," he said with a shrug.

"And I want to adopt Danny Gordon."

"That's out of the question," Bill said abruptly.

The statement surprised him. He hadn't intended to say anything like it. The words just seemed to pop out of his mouth.

Herb Lom's expression was shocked; Sara appeared hurt.

"Why . . . why is that out of the question?" she said

"Because he's hyperactive," Bill said.

"He looked like a normally active boy to me. And he was charming."

"What you saw here was an aberration. Believe me, I have it on good authority from a number of specialists. Raising Danny will be a tremendously demanding full-time job."

"That's true of raising any child," she said, looking at him levelly. "And it's a job I'm qualified to do."

Bill would not argue with the first statement, and did not want to challenge the second. He tried an end run.

"Let me get out the pictures of the other boys we have here. If you look through them I'm sure you'll—"

Sara was on her feet, a determined set to her mouth.

"I'm not interested in any other boys. I'm only interested in Danny now." Her features softened. "I don't think it's very fair to let me meet such a lovely child and then tell me I'm not good enough for him."

"I said nothing of the sort."

"Then won't you please reconsider?"

Bill opted to buy himself some time.

"Very well. I'll think about it. But quite frankly, I do not think Danny should be anyone's first child."

"He won't be," she said with a sudden sunny smile. "I practically raised my three youngest brothers. And I want to raise Danny Gordon. And with your help I'm going to do just that."

So saying, she took her husband's arm and they strode from Bill's office.

"You should have seen him this afternoon, Nick," Bill said after Danny had rushed in and disrupted their weekly chess game again. "He was a totally different kid."

Nick Quinn's eyes followed the blur of motion around the room.

"I'll have to take your word for it."

"I kid you not. He shook hands with her and he suddenly became docile. If I believed in magic, that's what I'd say it was."

"I've heard of people who have that effect on animals."

Immediately Bill felt himself bristle within. "Danny's not an animal."

"Of course he's not. I was just drawing a parallel." He scrutinized Bill. "A little touchy, aren't we?"

"Not at all." Then he thought about it. He'd been on edge since the Loms had left. Why? "Well, maybe a little."

"Because someone might adopt him?"

Bill glanced at Nick. He'd grown to be a perceptive son of a B. True, Bill had been wondering whether the prospect of facing St. F.'s without Danny Gordon running around might influence his judgment, but . . .

"I don't think that's it, Nick. It's possible, of course. After two years with Danny I feel as if we have a blood relationship, and it will cost me a piece of my heart to see him go, but this feels different."

"You mean like it doesn't feel right?"

Very perceptive, that Nick.

"Yes. Maybe I do mean just that."

"Well, you did say you thought he had to go to an older couple. These two don't sound as if they fit that particular criterion."

"An older, *experienced* couple. They don't exactly fit that either."

"Then that's probably why it doesn't feel right."

"But Sara says she practically raised her brothers, and I believe her. That would give her credit in the experience column. And if Danny consistently responds to her the way he did this afternoon . . ."

"Then he wouldn't be exactly hyperactive anymore, although quite frankly I can't see anyone slowing that boy down for long."

"You had to be there."

Bill called Danny over and sat him on his lap.

"What did you think of that lady you met here today?"

Danny smiled. "She was niiiice."

"How did you feel when you were holding her hand?"

The smile broadened as Danny's eyes got a dreamy, faraway look.

"Niiiice."

"Can you tell me anything more?"

"Nope!"

And then he was off and running again.

"I gather she was a *niiiice* lady," Nick said with a grin.

Bill shrugged. "Danny's new word. But I think I'm going to put those two together once more."

"To see if it happens again? Good move. Reproducibility is an indispensable factor in the scientific method."

"This is not an experiment, Nick."

Sometimes, though, Bill wished there were a scientific method for this adoption business. There were protocols and procedures, checks and evaluations and waiting periods, all sorts of safety measures and protections for both the child and the adoptive parents. Yet there had been plenty of times over the years when Bill had found himself operating on instinct, flying by the seat of his pants.

Some instinct within him warned against this match, but he suspected the feeling might be fueled by an emotional attachment to this particular child. Finding a good home for Danny, that was what really mattered. And if this woman had some special rapport with Danny, then he had no right to turn her away.

"I just want to see them together again. Maybe it was some kind of freak accident. But if it wasn't, if he responds to her that way again . . ."

"Then maybe you've found him a home. But if that comes about, I see another problem."

"I can let go. I've had to do it before." He'd let Nick go when the Quinns adopted him sixteen years ago. "I'll do it again."

"I had no doubts about that," Nick said, staring at Danny. "But you're going to have to find a way to get him to leave you."

Bill nodded. He'd already foreseen that problem. He figured he'd solve it when the time came.

Bill invited both the Loms back but Sara came alone—Herb was tied up at his office. She arrived the following Tuesday between school dismissal and the dinner hour.

"Have you reconsidered?" she asked brightly when she had seated herself in his office.

She was wearing a white and yellow flower-print sundress that deepened her already dark complexion. Bill wondered if there might be a little Mexican blood mixing with the Texan flowing in her veins.

"I'm in the process of doing so," Bill said, "but I'd like to get into specifics with you about your experience in raising your younger brothers."

They talked for about half an hour. Bill was impressed with Sara's easy familiarity with the ins and outs of child-rearing. But what came through more strongly than ever was her desire for a child, her *need* for one.

And then the inevitable occurred: Danny arrived.

He skidded to a halt when he saw her. A big smile, tiny white teeth—

"Hiya, Sara."

She seemed to glow at the mention of her name.

"You remembered!"

" 'Course I did. I'm smart."

"I'll bet you are! What did you learn in school today?"

Once again Bill watched in amazement as Danny stood calmly before her with his hands clasped behind his back. No hand holding this time; no contact at all. Yet he stood still and answered all her questions, even going so far as to elaborate on his friends and some of the games he liked to play.

And Sara . . .

Bill saw the light in her eyes, the warmth in her expression as she focused on Danny and made him the center of her world for those moments. He sensed the deep yearning within her and allowed himself the possibility that he had made a match—a miraculous one.

Danny turned to him.

"I like her. She's niiiice."

"Yes, Danny. Sara is very nice."

"Can I live with her?"

The question took Bill by surprise. The title of an old song flashed through his brain: "Am I That Easy to Forget?" But he ignored the hurt and concentrated on Danny. He had to be very careful here.

"I don't know, Danny. We'll have to look into that."

"Can I *pleeease?*"

"I don't know yet, Danny. I'm not saying no and I'm not saying yes. There's lots of things to be done before we come to that."

"Can I visit, maybe?"

"We'll look into that too. But Sara and her husband and I have many things to discuss first. So why don't you get washed up for dinner and let us get to work."

"Okay." Hope shone like a beacon behind his eyes as he turned back to her. "See ya, Sara."

She gave him a hug, then held him out to arm's length.

"See ya, Danny."

He trotted off down the hall.

"I think you've got a friend," Bill told Sara.

"I think so too," she said, smiling warmly. Then she gave Bill a level look. "But will that friend be allowed to become my son, Father Ryan?"

"If I've learned one thing in this job, Sara, it's never to make a promise I'm not absolutely sure I can keep—not to the adult applicants, and certainly never to the boys. But we're off to a good start. Let's see where we can go from here."

Her eyes widened, her voice was suddenly small and husky. "You mean you've reconsidered?"

When he nodded she lowered her face into her hands and began to sob. The sight of her tears moved Bill and confirmed his growing conviction that he was doing the best thing for Danny. Only a tiny squeamish part of him remained unconvinced.

SEVENTEEN

The reference checks went smoothly. Both Herb and Sara had excellent academic records at U. of Texas, he in accounting, she in early education. Their credit record was excellent. The home inspection was perfect—a two-story center-hall colonial in a quiet residential neighborhood in Astoria where the Loms were active in the local parish. Bill went so far as to call Sara's old pastor in Houston. Father Geary knew Sara Bainbridge— her maiden name—and remembered her as a sweet, wonderful young woman; Herb came from a wealthy family and wasn't quite the churchgoer Sara was, but the parish priest considered him a good man.

The whole process went swimmingly. The weekend visits came off without incident, and Danny's stays were stretched to a week at a time. He loved it. And he loved Sara. He seemed totally taken by her, completely infatuated. He'd still visit Bill's office on a daily basis, still sit on his lap, still disrupt the Saturday night chess games. But all he talked about was Sara, Sara, Sara. Bill thought she was a fine woman, exceptional even, but God he was getting sick of hearing about her.

By late fall Danny was no longer the same Danny who'd torn around St. F.'s all summer. It wasn't apparent at first, but slowly, in fits and spurts, Bill could see a definite change taking place. Over the course of the investigative and processing procedures Bill had noticed a gradual deceleration in Danny. Not a slamming

on of the brakes; more like a racing truck whose driver was slowly, systematically downshifting as he progressed from the freeway
toward a school traffic zone. The motor was still revving high,
but the speed was falling off. The nuns who taught him in second
grade said he was much less of a discipline problem these days,
and that his lengthened attention span was resulting in improved
schoolwork.

It was almost miraculous. Almost too good to be true.

And that bothered Bill a little. In his two decades with St. F.'s
he'd rarely seen an adoption go so smoothly. And so when he lay
in bed at night, alone with the dark, the lack of glitches would
wake that nagging little voice and spur it to whisper its nebulous
doubts in his ear.

That was why he was almost relieved when the first little glitch
reared its head during the week before Christmas.

Herb had been pushing to finalize the adoption by Christmas,
his reasoning being that he wanted to usher in the new year with
the three of them together as a family. Bill didn't doubt that, but he
had an inkling that with Herb's background in accounting he was
well aware that Danny was good for a full year's deduction as a
dependent if the adoption became official anytime before midnight
December 31.

Which was okay with Bill. Raising a child in New York City
was hellishly expensive and parents deserved any financial break
they could get. That wasn't the glitch.

The glitch was Danny. The boy was having second thoughts.

"But I don't want to go," he told Bill one evening during the
week before Christmas.

Bill patted his lap. "Why don't you hop up here and tell me
why not?"

"Because I'm scared," Danny said as he settled into his usual spot.

"Are you scared of Sara?"

"No. She's niiice."

"How about Herb? Are you scared of him?"

"No. I'm just scared about leaving here."

Bill smiled to himself and gave Danny a reassuring hug. He was
almost relieved to hear of the boy's misgivings. They were common, perfectly normal, and expected in Danny's case. After all, St.
F.'s had been his home longer than any other place in his lifetime.
The residents and staff were the only family he'd known for two
and a half years now. It would be cause for concern if he weren't
suffering a few pangs of separation anxiety.

"Everybody's a little scared when they leave, Danny. Just like they're scared when they come here. Remember when Tommy left last week to go live with Mr. and Mrs. Davis? He was scared."

Danny twisted around to look at him.

"Tommy Lurie? No way! He's not scared of nothing!"

"Well, he was. But he's doing fine. Wasn't he back just yesterday telling everybody how great it was?"

Danny nodded slowly, saying, "Tommy Lurie was afraid?"

"And don't forget, you're not moving far away. You can call me whenever you want."

"Can I come back and visit like Tommy did?"

"Sure can. You're welcome here anytime you want to come and the Loms can bring you. But pretty soon you'll be so happy and busy with Herb and Sara you'll forget all about us here at St. F.'s."

"I'll never do that."

"Good. Because we love you too. The Loms love you. Everybody loves you. Because you're a good kid, Danny."

That was Bill's message to all the boys at St. F.'s, most of whom were basket cases in the self-esteem department when they arrived. Bill began pounding it home from the moment they stepped through the front door: *You are loved here. You have value. You are important. You're a good kid.* After a while a fair number of them came to believe they were worth something.

The message was more than mere rote in Danny's case. Bill was going to miss him terribly. He felt as if he were giving away his own son.

So he sat there with his heart breaking as he held Danny on his lap and told him of all the wonderful times he was going to have with the Loms, of how Bill was going to send a message to Santa Claus to let him know Danny's new address and make sure he brought Danny lots of extra good stuff for Christmas.

And Danny sat, smiling as he listened.

Danny was quiet the rest of the week. But on Christmas Eve, as the final documents were being signed, he began to cry.

"I don't want to go with her!" he sobbed, tears spilling from his eyes onto his cheeks.

Sara was seated by Bill's desk; the battered valise holding all of Danny's worldly possessions rested by her feet. Bill glanced up and saw her stricken expression. He turned and squatted next to Danny.

"It's okay to be a little scared," he said. "Remember that talk we had? Remember what I told you about Tommy?"

"I don't care!" he said, his voice rising in the suddenly silent office. "She's bad! She's mean!"

"Come now, Danny. There's no call for that kind of—"

The boy threw his arms around Bill's neck and clung to him, trembling.

"She's going to hurt me!" he screamed. "Don't make me go! *Please* don't make me go! She's going to hurt me!"

Bill was shocked at the outburst. But there was no denying Danny's genuine terror. He was literally quaking with fear.

Out of the corner of his eye he saw Sara rise to her feet and step toward them. Her eyes were full of hurt.

"I—I don't understand," she said.

"Just some last-minute jitters," Bill told her, trying to assuage the pain he saw in her eyes. "Coupled with an overactive imagination."

"This seems to be more than just a case of simple jitters," Sara said.

Gently, Bill pushed Danny to arm's length and held him there.

"Danny, listen to me. You don't have to go anywhere you don't want to. But you must tell me about these terrible things you're saying. Where did they come from? Who told you these things?"

"No one," he said, blubbering and sniffling.

"Then how can you say them?"

"Because!"

"Because isn't good enough, Danny. Where did you get these ideas?"

"Nowhere. I just . . . *know!*"

Sara stepped forward. Slowly, hesitantly, she reached out and placed her hand on Danny's head, gently smoothing his perpetually unruly blond cowlick.

"Oh, Danny. I would never hurt you. How can you possibly think such a thing?"

Bill felt Danny stiffen at Sara's touch, then relax; saw his eyes roll upward for a heartbeat, then focus again. He stopped sobbing.

"You're going to be my little boy," Sara was saying in a soothing, almost-mesmerizing voice as she stroked his head. "And I'm going to be your mother. And together with Herb the three of us will make a wonderful family."

Danny smiled.

In that instant Bill was nearly overcome by an almost-uncontrollable urge to call the whole thing off, to wrap Danny protectively in his arms, chase the Loms from his office, and never allow them to cross the threshold of St. Francis again.

He buried the impulse. It was the father-son thing rearing its selfish, possessive head. He had to let go of this boy.

"You're not really afraid of me, are you, Danny?" Sara cooed.

He turned and looked up at her.

"No. I'm just scared of leaving here."

"Don't be afraid, Danny, my dear. It's supposed to snow tonight, which means tomorrow will be a white Christmas. Come with us and I promise you this Christmas will be utterly unforgettable."

Something in her words sent a chill across Bill's shoulders but he forced himself to let go of Danny and guide him toward Sara. As Danny's arms went around her hips and Sara's arms enfolded the boy, Bill felt his throat constrict. He turned away to hide the tears in his eyes.

I have to let go!

"I'd better take a rain check, Nick," Bill said into the phone. "It's snowing like crazy."

Nick's voice was tinny over the wire, and genuinely annoyed.

"Since when did a little white stuff ever bother you? Either you get yourself over here now or, snow or no snow, I'm coming over there and dragging you back."

"Really, Nick. I'm good where I am."

"The Quinns will be hurt if you don't show up. And besides, I don't think it's such a good idea for you to be alone on Christmas Eve—especially *this* Christmas Eve."

He understood and appreciated Nick's concern. He'd always spent part of Christmas with Mom and Dad. But this year . . .

"I'm not alone. I'm going to spend it with the boys. Which reminds me that I've got to check on them right now. I'll see you Saturday night. A Merry Christmas to you, and to the Quinns."

"All right," he said resignedly. "You win. Merry Christmas, Father Bill."

Bill hung up and walked down the hall to check on the kids. The dormitory was quiet. Excitement had filled these halls all week, rising ever higher with the decorating of the tree, reaching a fever pitch here a couple of hours ago as he'd overseen the hanging of the stockings by the old never-used fireplace in the dining hall downstairs. But all the boys were in bed now and those who weren't already asleep were trying their best to doze off. Because everybody knew that Santa didn't come until the whole house was sleeping.

Christmas. Bill's favorite time of year. And it was being around the boys that made it for him. They were so excited this time of year, especially the little ones. The bright eyes, the eager faces, the innocence of their euphoric anticipation. He wished he could bottle it like wine and decant off a little at a time during the year to get him through the times when things got low and slow.

God knew there were periods since the fire last March when he could have used a couple of bottles of the stuff. Tomorrow was a milestone of sorts, a dread marker along his personal road: the first December 25th in his life when he wouldn't be able to call his folks and wish them a Merry Christmas.

An aching emptiness expanded in his chest. He missed them. More than he'd ever thought he could or would. But he'd weather tomorrow. The boys would carry him through it.

Satisfied that everyone was asleep or very nearly so, Bill padded downstairs and began unloading the gifts from a locked pantry closet. Most of them had been donated by the local parishioners and wrapped by the sisters who taught the orphans at Our Lady of Lourdes elementary school next door. Good people one and all, pitching in to see that none of the boys went without a couple of presents on Christmas Day.

When the gifts were arranged under the tree Bill stepped back and surveyed the scene: A scraggly limbed balsam laden with a motley assortment of hand-me-down ornaments and garish blinking lights stood guard over piles of brightly wrapped boxes, each tagged with a boy's name. He smiled. Bargain-basement decor, to be sure, but the real giving spirit of Christmas was there. It looked as if Santa had risked a hernia on his trip to St. F.'s this year. Bill was beginning to feel a bit of the old Christmas excitement himself, looking forward to tomorrow morning when he'd be standing in this same spot and overseeing the frenzy of paper-tearing as the overexcited boys unwrapped their gifts with trembling hands. He could hardly wait.

He unplugged the tree lights and climbed the stairs. Halfway up he heard his office phone ringing. He ran for it. If this was Nick again—

But it wasn't. It was Danny. And he was hysterical.

"Father Bill! Father Bill!" he screeched in a high-pitched voice bursting with terror. "You gotta come get me! You gotta get me outta here!"

"Calm down, Danny," he said, keeping himself calm with an effort. Even though he knew it was just another adjustment terror, the real fear in the boy's voice was sending his adrenals into high gear. "Just calm down and talk to me."

"I can't talk! He's gonna kill me!"

"Who? Herb?"

"You gotta come get me, Father! You just gotta!"

"Where's Sara? Put her on and let me speak to her."

"No! They don't know I'm on the phone!"

"Just get Sara—"

"No! Sara's gone! There ain't no Sara! He's gonna kill me!"

"Danny, stop it!"

"Father, please come and get me! *Pleeeeease!*" He broke down into sobs but his words were still intelligible. "Father, Father, Father, I don't want to die. Please come and get me. Don't let him kill me. I don't want to die!"

The fear and abject misery in Danny's voice tore at Bill's heart. He was going to have to abort the adoption, cancel the whole thing. The boy simply was not ready to leave St. F.'s.

"Put Sara on, Danny . . . Danny?"

The line was dead.

Bill yanked open his file drawer and looked up the Loms' number. His hand was shaking as he punched it into the phone. A busy signal buzzed in his ear. He hung up and went to dial again, then stopped. If the line was busy, maybe Sara or Herb was trying to call him. If they both kept dialing, neither of them would get through. He sat back and made himself wait. And wait.

The phone didn't ring.

He forced himself to wait a full five minutes. It seemed like forever. Finally he'd had it. He snatched up the receiver and dialed their number again.

Still busy. *Shit!*

Bill slammed the phone down and wandered around his office, walked the halls. Over the course of the next half hour, he called the Loms' number a couple of dozen times, and each time the line was busy. Over and over he told himself there was nothing to worry about. Danny was in no danger. It was just the boy's imagination, his damned overactive imagination. Sara and Herb would never harm him, never allow anything bad to happen to him. Danny had just worked himself up into a panic and Sara had probably calmed him just as she had this afternoon.

But why couldn't he get through on the damn phone? An idea struck him and he called the operator. He told her it was an emergency and asked her to break in on the line; she came back and told him there was no one on the line. Nothing but dead air.

Had Danny left it off the hook? That had to be the answer.

But Bill could take no comfort in the explanation. He pulled on his coat, grabbed the car keys, and headed for the street. He knew he'd never sleep until he'd actually spoken to Danny and made sure he was all right. Imagined fears were just as frightening as real ones. So no matter how certain he was that Danny was in no danger, he had to be sure that Danny knew it. Then maybe he could rest tonight.

It was a beautiful night, snow falling on a gentle slant, the flakes flaring as they passed through the cones of illumination under the street lamps. The sounds of the borough, already subdued because it was Christmas Eve, were further muffled by the inch or so of white insulation that had already fallen. A white Christmas.

Bill wished he had time to appreciate the scenery but the inner urgency to get to the Loms' house overrode the esthetics of the night.

He guided the old station wagon down the Loms' street, past snowcapped houses trimmed with strings of varicolored lights, then pulled into the curb before number 735. The house was dark. No Christmas trim, no lighted windows. As he hurried up the walk to the front door, he noticed how perfect the layer of snow was, unmarred by a single footprint.

He pressed the doorbell button but didn't hear any chime within so he used the brass knocker. Its sound echoed through the silent night. He rapped it again. Twice. Three times.

No answer.

He stepped back off the front porch and looked up at the second story. The house remained silent and unlit.

Bill was worried now. Really worried. They had to be home. Their car was in the driveway. His were the only footprints on the snow.

What the hell was going on?

He tried the front doorknob and it turned. The door swung inward. He called out a few hellos but no one answered, so he stepped inside, still calling out.

Standing in the dark foyer, lit only by the glow from the street lamp outside, Bill realized it was as cold inside as it was out. And the house felt . . . empty.

A terrible, inescapable sense of dread crept over him.

My God, where are they? What's happened here?

And then he realized he was not alone. He almost cried out when he glanced to his right and spotted the faintly limned figure sitting in a chair by the living-room window.

"Hello?" Bill said, his hand searching for the light switch. "Herb?"

He found it and flipped it. It was Herb, sitting square in a straight-backed chair, staring into the air.

"Herb? Are you all right? Where's Danny? Where's Sara?"

At the mention of her name, Herb's head turned to look at Bill but his eyes never seemed to settle on him, never seemed to focus. After a few seconds, he returned to staring into the air.

Bill approached him cautiously. A part of him deep inside knew that something awful had happened here—or possibly was happening still—and screamed for him to turn and run. But he couldn't run. He couldn't—wouldn't—leave this place without Danny.

"Herb, tell me where Danny is. Tell me now, Herb. And tell me you haven't done anything to him. Tell me, Herb."

But Herb Lom only stared upward and outward at a corner of the ceiling.

Upstairs . . . he was staring upstairs. Did that mean anything?

Turning on lights as he moved, flipping every switch he passed, Bill found the staircase and headed for the second floor. Dread clawed at his throat as he called out the only names he could think of.

"Danny? Sara? Danny? Anyone here?"

The only reply was the creaking of the stair treads under his feet and the faint howl from the uncradled telephone receiver on the table in the upper hall.

He stopped and called out again, and this time he heard a reply— a hoarse whisper from the doorway at the top of the stairs. Unintelligible, but definitely a voice. He ran toward the dark rectangle, lunged through it, fumbled along the wall with his hand, found the switch . . .

. . . light . . . a big bedroom . . . the master bedroom . . . red . . . all red . . . the rug, the walls, the ceiling, the bedspread . . . didn't remember it being so red . . . Danny there . . . by the wall . . . naked . . . his head lolling . . . so white, so white . . . *on* the wall . . . arms spread . . . nails . . . in his palms . . . in his feet . . . face so white . . . and his insides . . . hanging out . . .

Bill felt the room lurch as his legs went flaccid under him. His knees slammed on the floor but he barely noticed the pain as he fell forward onto his hands and gripped the sticky red rug, retching.

No! This can't be!

"Father Bill?"

Bill's head snapped up. That voice . . . barely audible . . .

Danny's eyes were open, staring at him; his lips were moving, his voice was raw skin dragging through broken glass.

"Father, it hurts."

Bill forced his legs to work, to propel him across the red room.
So much blood. How could one little boy hold so much blood?
How could he lose it all and still be alive?

Bill averted his eyes. How could he be so cut up? Who would—?

Herb. It must have been Herb. Sitting downstairs in some sort
of post-epileptic funk while up here . . . up here . . .

And where was Sara?

The nails. He couldn't think about Sara now. He had to get the
nails out of Danny's hands and feet. He looked around for some
way to remove them but all he saw was a bloody hammer. Bill fixed
his eyes on the boy's bloodless face, his tortured, pleading eyes.

"I'll get you free, Danny. You just wait here and—" *God, what
am I saying?* "I—I'll be right back."

"Father, it hurts so bad!"

Danny began screaming, hoarse, raw-throated wails that chased
after Bill, tugging at the very underpinnings of his sanity as he
raced downstairs. He pounded into the living room and hauled
Herb from his chair. He wanted to tear him in half and he
wanted to do it slowly, but that would take time, and he didn't
think Danny had much of that left.

"Tools, fucker! Where are your tools?"

Herb's unfocused eyes stared past Bill's shoulder. Bill shoved
him back into the chair that flipped backward with Herb in it. He
landed in a twisted sprawl on the floor and stayed there.

Bill ransacked the kitchen, found the door to the cellar, and ran
down the steps, fearing all the while that somewhere along the
way he'd trip over Sara's remains. He was sure she was dead. He
found a toolbox sitting on a dusty workbench. He grabbed it and
raced back up to the second floor.

Danny was still screaming. Bill took the biggest set of pliers
he could find and began working on the nails, removing the ones
from his feet first, then moving up to the hands. As his ghastly
white little body slumped to the floor, Danny's eyes closed and he
stopped his hoarse, breathy, barely audible screams. Bill thought
he was dead but he couldn't stop now. He pulled the spread from
the double bed and wrapped the boy in it. Then he headed for the
street, carrying Danny in his arms, racking his brain for the
whereabouts of the nearest hospital.

Halfway to the car Danny opened his eyes and looked up at
him and asked a question that shredded Bill's heart.

"Why didn't you come, Father Bill?" he said in a voice that
was almost gone. "You said you'd come if I called. Why didn't
you come?"

* * *

The next few hours were a blur, a montage of white streets seen through a fogged windshield, of battling skidding tires and locking wheels, of bouncing off curbs and near misses with other cars, all to the accompaniment of Danny's nearly voiceless screaming . . . arriving at the hospital, one of the emergency room nurses fainting when Bill unfolded the bedspread to reveal Danny's mutilated body, the ER doctor's blanching face as he said there was no way his little hospital could give this boy the care he needed . . . the wild ride in the rear of the ambulance, racing into Brooklyn with lights flashing and sirens howling, skidding to a stop before Downstate Medical Center, the police waiting for them there, all their grim-faced questions as soon as they wheeled Danny away to surgery.

And then came the thin, chain-smoking detective with yellow stains between his right index and middle fingers, mid-fortyish, thinning brown hair, intense blue eyes, intense expression, intense posture, everything about him aggressively intense.

Renny had got a look at the kid in the ER.

Twenty-plus years on the force and he'd never seen anything even remotely like what had been done to that kid. Turned his stomach upside down and inside out.

And now his chief was on the phone telling him he could pack it in until the day after tomorrow.

"I'm gonna stick with this one, Lieu."

"Hey, Renny, it's Christmas Eve," Lieutenant McCauley said. "Unlax a little. Goldberg's taking eleven-to-seven and what the hell is Christmas to Goldberg? Leave it to him."

No way.

"Tell Goldberg to cover everything else on eleven-to-seven. This one's mine."

"Something special about this one, Renny? Something I should know?"

Renny tightened inside. Couldn't let McCauley know there was anything personal here. Just play the cool, calm professional.

"Uh-uh. Just a child abuse case. A bad one. I think I got all the loose ends within reach. Just want to tie them up good before I call it a night."

"That could take a while. How's Joanne gonna handle that?"

"She'll understand." Joanne always understood.

"All right, Renny. You change your mind and want to pack it in early, let Goldberg know."

"Right, Lieu. Thanks. And Merry Christmas."

"Same to you, Renny."

Detective Sergeant Augustino hung up and headed for the doctors' lounge he had commandeered. That was where they were holding the guy who'd brought the kid in. He said his name was Ryan, claimed he was a priest but he had no ID and the sweatsuit he was wearing didn't have a Roman collar.

Renny thought about the kid. Hard to think about much else. They didn't know anything about him except what the so-called priest had told him: His name was Danny Gordon, he was seven years old, and until this afternoon he'd been a resident of St. Francis Home for Boys.

St. Francis . . . that was what had grabbed Renny. The kid was an orphan from St. F.'s and someone had cut him up bad.

That was all Renny had to hear to make this case *real* personal.

He'd left a uniform named Kolarcik on guard outside the lounge. Kolarcik was on the walkie-talkie as Renny approached in the hallway.

"They picked up the guy in the house," Kolarcik said, thrusting the handset toward Renny. "Everything there's pretty much like Father Ryan described it."

We don't know for sure he's a priest yet, Renny wanted to say but skipped it.

"You mean the guy was just sitting there waiting to be picked up?"

"They say he looks like he's in some sort of trance or something. They're gonna take him down to the precinct house and—"

"Bring him here," Renny said. "Tell those guys to bring him *here* and nowhere else as soon as he's booked. I want to get a full medical on this guy while he's fresh . . . just to make sure he's not suffering from any unapparent injuries."

Kolarcik smiled. "Right."

Renny was glad to see that this particular uniform was on his wavelength. No way that fucker in Queens was going to take a walk on a psycho plea, not if Renny had anything to say about it.

He opened the door to the lounge and took a look at the guy who said he was a priest. Big, clean-cut, square jaw, thick brown hair graying at the temples, good build. Good-looking guy, but at the moment he looked crushed by fatigue and pretty well frayed on all his edges. He sat hunched forward on the sagging sofa, a cup of Downstate's bitter, overheated coffee clasped in his hands.

His fingers trembled as he rubbed his palms against the cup, as if trying to draw warmth from the steaming liquid on the other side of the Styrofoam. Fat chance.

"You connected with St. Francis?" Renny said.

The guy jumped, like his thoughts had been a thousand miles away. He glanced at Renny, then away.

"For the tenth time, yes."

Renny took a chair opposite him and lit up a cigarette.

"What order you from?"

"The Society of Jesus."

"I thought the Jesuits ran St. Francis."

"Same thing."

Renny smiled. "I knew that."

The guy didn't smile back. "Any word on Danny?"

"Still in surgery. Ever hear of Father Ed? Used to be at St. Francis."

"Ed Dougherty? I met him once. Back in seventy-five at St. F.'s Centennial. He's gone now."

The guy had said the magic words: *St. F.'s.* Only someone who'd lived there called it St. F.'s.

Okay. So he probably really was Father William Ryan, S.J., but that didn't absolutely mean that he had nothing to do with what had happened to that kid. Even priests got bent. Wouldn't be the first time.

"Look, Detective Angostino," Father Ryan said. "Can we make small talk later?"

"It's *Au*gustino, and there's no small talk and no later in something like this."

"I've told you, it was Herb. The husband. Herbert Lom. He's the one. You should be out—"

"We've got him," Renny said. "We're bringing him down here for a checkup."

"Here?" Ryan said. The fatigue seemed to drop away from him in an instant. His eyes came to blazing life. *"Here?* Give me a few minutes alone with him in this little room. Just five minutes. Two." The Styrofoam cup suddenly collapsed in his hand, spilling hot coffee all over him. He barely seemed to notice. "Just one lousy minute!"

Okay. So the priest most likely had nothing to do with hurting the kid.

"I want you to tell me the whole story," Renny said.

"I've done that twice already." The fatigue was back in Ryan's voice. "Three times."

"Yeah, but to other people, not to me. Not directly. I want to hear it myself, from you to me. Right from the moment these people stepped into St. F.'s until you arrived here in the ambulance. The whole thing. Don't leave anything out."

So Father Ryan began to talk and Renny listened, just listened, interrupting only for clarifications.

None of it made much sense.

"You mean to tell me," he said when the priest had finished, "that they had this kid in their home for weekends, whole *weeks* at a time, and never laid a finger on him?"

"Treated him like a king, according to Danny."

"And then as soon as the adoption is official the guy slices the kid up. What's the story there? What's it mean?"

"It means I screwed up, that's what it means."

Renny saw the tortured look in Father Ryan's eyes and felt for him. This guy was hurting.

"You did all the routine checks?"

The priest jumped up from the sofa and began pacing the length of the small room, rubbing his hands together as he moved back and forth.

"That and more. Sara and Herb Lom came up as white as that snow falling outside. But it wasn't enough, was it?"

"Speaking of Sara—any idea where she is?"

"Probably dead, her body hidden somewhere back at that house. Damn! How could I let this happen?"

Renny noticed that he wasn't passing the buck, wasn't blaming anyone but himself. Here was one of the good guys. Weren't too many of those around.

"No system is perfect," Renny said in what he knew was a pretty lame attempt to console the poor guy.

The priest looked at him, sat back down on the sofa, and buried his face in his hands. But he didn't cry. They sat that way in silence for a while until a doctor in surgical scrubs barged in. He was graying, in his fifties, probably robust-looking when he hit the golf course, but he was pasty-faced and sweaty now. Looked like he'd been on a week-long bender.

"I'm looking for the man who brought Daniel Gordon in. Which one of you—?"

Father Ryan suddenly was on his feet again, in the doctor's face. "That's me! Is he all right? Did he pull through?"

The doctor sat down and ran a hand over his face. Renny noticed that it was shaking.

"I've never seen anything like that boy," he said.

"Neither has anyone!" the priest shouted. "But is he going to live?"

"I—I don't know," the doctor said. "I don't mean his injuries. I've seen people mangled in car wrecks worse than that. What I mean is, he should be dead. He should have been dead when he was wheeled in here."

"Yes, but he wasn't," Father Ryan said, "so what's the point of—?"

"The point is that he lost too much blood to have survived. You found him. Was there much blood there?"

"All over. I remember thinking that I never knew the human body could hold so much blood."

"That was a good thought. Was he bleeding when you found him?"

"Uh, no. I didn't think about it then, but now that I look back . . . no. He wasn't bleeding. I guess he'd just run out of blood."

"Bingo!" said the doctor. "Exactly what happened. He ran out of blood. Do you hear what I'm saying: *There was no blood in that boy's body when he got here!* He was *dead!*"

Renny felt the skin at the back of his neck tighten. This doc was sounding crazy. Maybe he'd been on that bender after all.

"But he was conscious!" Father Ryan said. "Screaming!"

The doctor nodded. "I know. And he remained conscious through the entire operation."

"Jesus!" Renny said, feeling like someone had just driven a fist into his gut.

Father Ryan dropped back onto the sofa.

"We couldn't find any veins," the doctor said, talking to the air. "They were all flat and empty. You see that in hypovolemic shock, but the child wasn't in shock. He was awake, screaming in pain. So I did a cut-down, found a vein, and canulated it. Tried to draw a blood sample for typing but it was dry. So we started running dextrose and saline in as fast as it would go and took him upstairs to start suturing him up. That was when the real craziness started."

The doc paused and Renny saw a look on his face that he'd occasionally seen on older cops, thirty-year men who thought they'd seen everything, thought they were beyond being shocked, and then learned the hard way that this city never revealed the full breadth of its underside; it always held something in reserve for the wiseguy who thought he'd seen it all. This doc probably had thought he'd seen it all. Now he knew he hadn't.

"He wouldn't go under," the doc said. "Hal Levinson's been my anesthesiologist for twenty years. He's one of the best. Maybe *the* best. He tried everything he had—from pentathol to Halothane to Ketamine and back and nothing would put that kid under. Even a high-level spinal block wouldn't dent him. Nothing worked." His voice began to rise. "Do you hear me? *Nothing worked!*"

"So—so you didn't . . . operate?"

The doc's expression became even bleaker.

"Oh, I 'operated.' I 'operated,' all right. I went into that kid and put everything in his belly back the way it was supposed to be, then I closed him up. And I closed up the holes in his hands and feet too. And he jerked and writhed with every suture and so we had to tie him down. Yeah, he's all back together. He's up in Recovery now but I don't know why. He doesn't need to recover from the anesthesia because none of it took. He's got no blood and I can't give him any because we can't get a sample to type. He should be dead but he's up there screaming with pain but making no sound because his vocal cords are all shot to hell from all the screaming he's already done."

Renny watched in shock as tears began to form in the doctor's eyes.

"I sewed him up but I know he's not going to heal. He's in pain and I can't stop it. The only thing that's going to help that child is dying and he's not doing it. Who is he? Where did he come from? What happened to him? Are there any medical records on him anywhere?"

Father Ryan snapped his fingers. "Here! He had a full neurological workup right here just last year—through the child study team."

The doc dragged himself wearily to his feet. His expression was even bleaker than before.

"You mean I'm going to find this kid in medical records? That means he really exists and this isn't just a nightmare." He sighed heavily. "Maybe they typed his blood."

As he turned to leave, Father Ryan grabbed his arm.

"Can I see him?"

The doc shook his head. "Not now. Maybe later. After I see if I can get some blood into him."

As he stepped out the door, Kolarcik stepped in.

"They just brought in the guy from the house."

"Lom!" The priest leapt forward. "Let me—"

Renny put a hand on his chest and pushed him back. Gently. "You stay put for now, Father. I'll want you to ID him, otherwise you stay here for the time being."

"If he looks like Teddy Roosevelt, you've got him. But tell me something. Am I under arrest?"

"No. But you're up to your neck in this, so for everybody's sake, stay put."

"Don't worry about that. As long as Danny's here, *I'm* here."

Renny had no trouble believing that.

The handcuffs spoiled the picture, but this guy Herbert Lom really did look like Teddy Roosevelt. Only the glasses were missing. And he was either completely whacked out or was putting on the best damn show Renny had ever seen.

Renny seated himself opposite Lom. The guy's eyes were focused somewhere off in space, like on Mars maybe.

"Your name is Lom? Herbert Lom?" Renny said.

"Don't waste your breath, Sarge," said the uniform who had brought him in, a cocky brat named Havens. "No one could get a word out of him over at the station. His wallet says he's Lom, though."

"Were you at the house?"

"Nah. Wasn't my shift."

"Anybody tell you about the scene."

Havens shrugged. "Said the upstairs bedroom was practically painted with blood."

Just like Father Ryan had said. Renny gave Lom's clothes a careful visual going over.

"These the clothes he was wearing when they found him?"

"Yeah. You don't think we changed him, do you?"

Havens's mouth was going to buy him big trouble someday, but not from Renny. Not tonight. He was too concerned with why there was no blood on Lom's clothes or hands.

"Forensics go over him?"

"Yeah. Scraped his fingernails, vacuumed his clothes, the works."

"He's been Miranda'd?"

"About three times, in front of witnesses."

"And he hasn't asked for an attorney?"

"He hasn't even asked to take a pee. He don't speak and don't do a goddam thing you tell him to, but watch this."

The cop pulled Lom to his feet and he stood there without moving. He pushed him back into the chair and he stayed seated. He got Lom up on his feet again and pulled him forward. After a couple of stumbling steps he began to walk in a straight line. The cop let him go and he kept on walking, right into a wall. Then he stopped walking and stood with his face against the wall.

"Guy's a fucking robot."

Renny didn't argue. He had Kolarcik bring Father Ryan down from the doctors' lounge.

"This him?" he asked the priest when he arrived.

Father Ryan's gentle features twisted into a snarl.

"You filthy—!"

He lunged for Lom's throat and it took everything Kolarcik and the other uniform had to hold him back. Lom didn't even flinch.

The cop was right: Lom was like a fucking robot.

"I'll put that down as a positive ID," Renny said. "In the meantime, Father, would you mind returning to the lounge?"

As the priest was led away, Renny turned to the uniform.

"Take our friend down to the emergency room and have them give him the once-over. I don't want anyone saying we didn't see to his medical needs while he was in custody."

He glanced at his watch. Two A.M. Christmas already. And he hadn't called Joanne yet. There'd be hell to pay for that.

He hurried to a phone.

The ER doc caught up to Renny in the hall about half an hour later.

"Hey, Lieutenant—"

"It's sergeant."

"Okay—Sergeant. Where the hell did you find that guy?"

This doc was young, in his thirties, had long dark hair, an earring on the right, and a neat beard. Looked like a rabbi. The name-tag on his white coat said A. STEIN, M.D.

"Lom? We've got him for attempted murder. Maybe murder, too, if we ever find his wife, so . . . Why are you shaking your head?"

"There's no way your Mr. Lom is going to stand trial for anything."

Renny's stomach gave a lurch at the note of finality in Stein's voice.

"He died?"

"Might as well have. He's as good as brain dead."

"Bullshit! He's faking it, acting like he's got that disease, cata—cata-something."

"Catatonia. But he's not catatonic. And he's not faking. You can't fake what he's got."

"So what's he got?"

Stein scratched his beard. "I'm not sure yet. But I'll tell you one thing: His neurological exam puts him on a level somewhere between an earthworm and a turnip."

"Thanks, Doc," Renny said acidly. "You've been a big help. Now find me a specialist, one who knows that a guy who walks around ain't brain dead. Maybe then I can get a *real* exam done."

Stein's reddening face told Renny he'd scored with that one. Stein grabbed him by the arm.

"Okay, wiseass. You come with me. I want to show you a few things."

Renny accompanied him to a curtained-off cubicle in a rear corner of the ER where Herbert Lom lay on a gurney. Alone.

"Where's Havens?"

"The cop? I sent him for coffee."

"You left a suspect here alone?" Renny said angrily.

"Mr. Lom's not going anywhere," Stein said. He pulled a penlight from his coat pocket and stepped around to the far side of the gurney. "Come on over here and take a look at this."

Renny stepped closer and looked down at Lom's impassive face.

"Look at his pupils. Look how wide they are." Stein flashed the beam of his penlight into each eye, back and forth, one and then the other. "See any change in them?"

The pupils didn't move a hair.

"Fixed and dilated," Stein said. "Now watch this."

He touched his finger to Lom's left eyeball. Renny flinched but Lom didn't. He didn't even blink.

"You don't need a medical degree to know that's not normal," Stein said. "Now check this out. Watch his eyes."

He grabbed Lom's head with both hands, one at the chin and one at the crown, and rotated it back and forth a few times, then moved it up and down like a nodding marionette. Lom's eyes never moved in his head; his gaze remained fixed straight ahead, staring whichever way he was turned.

"We call that 'doll's eyes.' It means his brain's in deep shit. He's got no higher brain function—nothing above the brain stem, if that much. He's a turnip."

"And he couldn't be faking it?" Renny said, although he already knew the answer.

"No way."

"How about drugs? What'd the blood tests show?"

Stein looked away. "We didn't do any."

"You mean to tell me you've got a guy you're calling brain dead and you haven't checked to see if he's full of H or blow or ice?"

"We couldn't *get* any blood out of him," Stein said, still looking away.

An icy-fingered hand began a slow walk down Renny's spine.

"Oh, shit. Not another one."

"You know about the kid too?" Stein said, looking at him now. "I guess everybody in the hospital's heard. What the hell's going on, Sergeant? Somebody brings in a bloodless mutilated kid who can't be anesthetized, and you cops bring in this . . . this zombie with no pulse, no blood pressure, no heartbeat, yet he sits, stands, and walks. I couldn't find any blood anywhere in him—I even stuck his femoral artery, or at least where I thought his femoral artery should be. We cathed his bladder for urine but wound up with a dry tap. This is getting scary."

"Maybe he's brain damaged," Renny said, shaking off the chill. He'd heard enough *Twilight Zone* bullshit for one night. "Can't you X-ray his head or something?"

Stein brightened.

"We can do better than that. We can get an MR—and we can get it stat."

Renny stayed with the inanimate, staring Lom while Stein rushed off to set up the MR or whatever it was.

"You're not fooling me, pal," he whispered as he leaned over him. "I'm going to break up your little game and see that you pay for what you did to that kid."

Renny almost jumped back when Lom's mouth twisted into a toothy grin.

Renny was still shaky as he sat outside the Magnetic Resonance Imaging room. Lom's grin had lasted only an instant before collapsing back into the slack expression he'd worn all night, but that had been long enough to convince Renny that he had a supreme con artist on his hands here.

Which was just great. As if this case weren't already twisted enough, he had to have some Houdini-type trance artist as a prime suspect.

Stein came down the hall and dropped into the seat next to him. He was carrying a pair of X rays. He didn't look so good but he managed a smile.

"Standing guard?" Stein said.

"Actually, I'm sitting."

Renny had stationed himself here when Lom was wheeled in and he'd sit here until he was wheeled out again. There was only one way in or out of Magnetic Imaging and this was it. He was here to see to it personally that Lom didn't pull anything cute—like a disappearing act. Renny would have been inside, right next to the MR machine, except that they'd wanted him to remove anything that contained any iron and leave it outside. Something about warping the magnetic field or something. That meant stripping off his pistol and his badge; they'd even told him he'd have to leave his wallet outside because the field around the MR machine would scramble the magnetic strips on his credit cards.

Sounded like *Star Trek* stuff to Renny, but he wasn't going anywhere around Lom unless he was fully armed. So he'd camped outside.

"I'm telling you, Sergeant, Mr. Lom is *not* going to take a walk. Anywhere."

"And I'm telling you he grinned at me. He's playing you for a sucker, Doc."

"Uh-uh. That was a random muscle twitch."

Renny was about to suggest another muscle Stein could twitch when the MRI technician stuck his head out the door.

"Yo! Dr. Stein. We got ourselves a little problem in here."

Renny was on his feet, reaching for his .38. *I knew it!*

"Where is he? What's he doing?"

The tech was a skinny black guy sporting short dreadlocks. He looked at Renny as if he was nuts.

"Who? The patient? He ain't doing nothin', man. Be cool. It's the computer. It's puttin' out some weird shit."

As Stein followed the tech into the control room he glanced back over his shoulder at Renny.

"Coming?"

Renny was about to tell him that he'd already seen enough weird shit for one night, then decided that a little more wouldn't make much difference.

"Yeah, sure. Why not?"

He followed them to the control console with its rows of monitors. He watched Stein lean forward and stare at one of the screens, saw his face go slack and fade to the color of the eggshell wallpaper behind him.

"You're kidding, right?" Stein said. "This is bullshit, Jordan. If you think this is funny—"

"What's wrong?" Renny said.

"Hey, man," the tech told Stein. "If I could make it show that kinda shit just for fun, you think I'd be workin' this shift?"

"What the hell's *wrong*?" Renny said.

Stein sagged into the chair before the console.

"That's Mr. Lom's head," he said, pointing to the screen before him. "A side view. A sagital cut through the center of his head and neck, top to bottom, right between his nostrils."

Renny could see that. The nose was toward the right side of the screen, the back of the head toward the left.

"Looks like one of those sinus medicine commercials," Renny said.

Stein laughed. The sound had a slightly hysterical edge to it.

"Yeah. His sinuses look fine. But something's missing."

"What?"

Stein tapped the screen with the eraser end of a pencil, indicating the big empty space behind the nose and sinuses.

"There's supposed to be a brain here."

That cold hand did an encore down Renny's spine; this time it was dancing.

"And there's *not*?"

"Not according to this. No sign of a spinal cord either."

"Then your machine's fucked up! He'd—he'd be dead!"

"Tell me about it," Stein said, and turned to the technician. "Slide him farther in and get the chest cavity."

The tech nodded and threw some switches. Before too long, an empty circle lit on the screen.

Jordan the technician said, "Shit, man! Where's his lungs? Where's his fucking *heart*?"

"That's what I said when I saw these," Stein said, handing Jordan the X rays he'd been carrying. "I was trying to tell myself they'd pushed the tube too high but I didn't really believe it."

"Shit!" Jordan said as he held the X rays up to the recessed fluorescents overhead.

"What's wrong?" Renny said, knowing he sounded like a broken record but unable to say anything else. He was completely in the dark here.

Jordan held the films up for him. Renny had no idea what he was supposed to see.

"What?"

"Empty, man," he said. "The guy's whole chest is fucking empty!"

"Aw, come on!" Renny said. He was starting to feel a little sick.

"He's not kidding," Stein said. "Just for the hell of it, Jordan, let's get a look at the abdomen."

Jordan did some more fiddling at the console and soon another image filled the screen. Stein stared at it, then rotated his chair to face Renny. He wore a crazy smile and his eyes looked as if they were receding toward the back of his head.

"He's hollow!" he said. "No brain, no heart, no lungs, no liver, no intestines! He's completely hollow! A walking shell!" He started to laugh.

Renny found Stein's laughter almost as frightening as what he was saying.

"Hey, easy, Doc."

"Easy my ass! We're talking about some sort of zombic here! It can't be! It's *crazy!* It can't fucking be!"

The monitoring room was silent as the three of them sat and stared at each other.

"What we gonna do with this guy?" Jordan said.

"He's a murder-one suspect," Renny said.

Jordan smiled. "Try him and fry him."

"Not in this state. Besides, with all the bullshit that's going down here tonight, he might walk."

The thought of that twisted Renny's insides. Nobody should get off on a head case plea after what he did to that kid.

"He's not walking anywhere tonight," Stein said. He turned to Jordan. "Wheel him out of there. I'm taking him back to the ER and no one—" He glared at Renny. "*No one* is moving him anywhere else until I've got plenty of witnesses to what's going down here."

As long as Lom remained in custody, Renny didn't care where he was kept. And when all this was over, maybe a few questions would get answered.

Like, where was Mrs. Lom?

The waiting was killing Bill. The waiting and the incredible story Danny's surgeon had told. No blood? No anesthesia? Awake during the surgery? Feeling everything? How could that be?

He shuddered. What was happening here? This kind of brutal crime wasn't supposed to make sense, but what had been done to Danny—what was *still* being done to him, apparently—went beyond madness into—what? The supernatural?

Poor Danny. God, he wanted to see him, be with him, find some way to comfort him. Only one thing restrained him from making a scene and demanding, as his legal guardian—*Some guardian*—to be taken to him. The last words Danny had spoken to him in that almost-gone voice still echoed in his mind. Each syllable drove a nail into a different corner of his skull.

Why didn't you come, Father Bill? You said you'd come if I called. Why didn't you come?

"I did come, Danny!" he said aloud around the sob crammed into his throat. "I did! I just came too late!"

And then the phone rang. One ring that wouldn't stop. He'd never heard a phone ring like that. Was that the way hospital phones worked? On and on it went. Bill looked around, wishing someone would answer it. But he was alone in the doctors' lounge, as he had been all night.

And then it occurred to him that maybe it was for him. Maybe Danny was out of Recovery and they wanted him upstairs. But wouldn't they tell the cop outside first?

No matter. He had to stop that ringing. He crossed the room and lifted the receiver.

"Doctors' lounge."

There was a child on the line, a small boy, his voice pitched somewhere between a scream and a sob. Bill recognized it immediately.

Danny's voice.

"Father, please come and get me! Pleeeeease! *Father, Father, Father, I don't want to die. Please come and get me. Don't let him kill me. I don't want to die!"*

"Danny?" Bill said into the phone, his voice rising to a shout. "Danny, where are you?"

The voice started again.

"Father, please come and get me! Pleeeeease! *Father, Father, Father, I don't want to die. Please come and get me . . ."*

Bill tore the receiver away from his ear. The horror of the call was submerged in an almost overwhelming sense of déjà vu. And then he remembered that this wasn't the first time for this call. Danny had cried and screamed those same words last night when he'd called from the Loms' house. His last words just before the phone went dead. His last words . . .

. . . just before Herb had—

Bill couldn't finish the thought. He slammed the phone down and headed for the door to the hall. Some sick bastard had recorded the call and was playing it back. Someone in the hospital. That could be only one person.

The cop named Kolarcik was sitting outside. He jumped to his feet as Bill stepped out in the hall.

"Whoa, Father! You can't leave the lounge, not until the sarge says so."

"Then find him! I want to go see Danny! Now!"

As the cop fumbled for his walkie-talkie he glanced up the hall.

"Hey, here he comes now."

Bill saw Sergeant Augustino and two other men, one white, one black, wheeling a fourth down the hall on a gurney. Their expressions were grim and their eyes held a strange look. As he started toward them Bill wondered what could have happened to make all three men look so strained.

"Sergeant, I want to—"

And then he saw who was on the gurney. It was the filthy, perverted son of a bitch who'd mutilated Danny.

Herb Lom.

Rage like a cold black flame blasted through him, igniting him, consuming him. There was no control, not the slightest consideration given toward control. Bill just wanted to get his hands on Lom. He lunged forward.

"You *bastard*!"

He heard shouts, cries of surprise and warning, but they might as well have been coming from the moon. Kolarcik, Augustino, the two men with him, they had disappeared as far as Bill was concerned. There was only Bill, the hallway, and Lom. And Bill knew just what he was going to do: yank Lom from the gurney, pull him to his feet, and slam him against the nearest wall; and when he'd bounced off that wall he'd fling him across the corridor against the opposite wall, and then he'd do it again and again until there was nothing left of either the walls or Herb Lom, whichever went first. Somehow, it was a beautiful thought.

With his fingers hooked into claws he brushed off the hands that tried to stop him and dove at Lom, reaching for the front of his mint-green hospital gown. His hands slammed down against Lom's chest—

—and kept on going.

With a sickening crunch Lom's chest cavity gave way like weak plaster and Bill's hands sank to their wrists in the man's chest cavity.

And good God, it was cold in there. Far colder than ice . . . and *empty*.

Bill yanked out his hands and backpedaled until he hit the wall where he stood and stared at Herb Lom's chest, at the concavity in his hospital gown that dipped deep into it. He glanced around at Sergeant Augustino and the two men with him. They too were staring at Lom's chest.

"My God!" Bill said. His hands were numb, still aching with the cold.

Kolarcik skidded to a halt beside him and gaped at the gurney, gasping.

"Father! What did you do?"

And then Lom's body started to shake. Little tremors at first, as if he had a chill. But instead of subsiding they became steadily more pronounced, growing until his whole body was spasming, shaking, convulsing so violently that the gurney began to rattle.

Then Lom seemed to collapse.

Bill noticed it first in his chest wall. The depression in the hospital gown began to widen as more of the green material fell into his chest cavity like Florida real estate dropping into a giant sink hole. Then the rest of his body began to flatten under the gown—his pelvis, legs, arms. They all seemed to be melting away.

Good Lord, they *were* melting away. A thick brown fluid was beginning to run out from under the gown and drip off the edges of the gurney. It steamed in the air of the hospital corridor. The stench was awful.

As he turned away, gagging, Bill saw Lom's head collapse into a mahogany puddle on the pillow and begin to stream toward the floor.

EIGHTEEN

Three days in hell.

That poor kid had spent the three days since Christmas Eve in unremitting agony, writhing and turning in his bed. His voice was gone but his open mouth, tight-squeezed eyes, and white, twisted features told the whole story of what he was feeling.

A story Renny could not bear to hear. And though he came by the hospital often he could not bring himself to enter that room more than once a day or stay more than a moment or two.

But the priest, Bill Ryan—Father Bill as Renny had come to think of him—he stuck by the kid's side, sitting by the bed like some guardian angel, holding his hand, talking and reading and praying into ears that weren't listening.

"They say his mind's gone," Father Bill told Renny and Nick on the morning of the fourth day.

This fellow Nick, late twenties and homely as all hell, was some sort of scientific professor at Columbia. He'd been in and out, hanging with the priest since Christmas night. Renny learned that the prof was a former St. F.'s orphan too. Good to see an orphan kid go from nothing to being a hotshot scientist. And seeing as they had St. F.'s in common, the prof was all right in Renny's book.

The three of them were sipping coffee in the parent lounge of the pediatric wing where Danny had one of the few private rooms. Late morning sunlight poured in through the wide picture windows and glared off the remnants of the Christmas snow on the rooftops around them, warming the room until the heat was almost stifling.

"I'm not surprised," Nick said. "And your mind'll be gone soon as well if you don't get some rest."

"I'll be okay."

"He's right, Father," Renny said. "You're heading for a break-down at about ninety miles an hour. You can't keep going like this."

The priest shrugged. "I can always catch up. But Danny . . . who knows how much time he's got left?"

Renny wondered how much time Father Bill had left before he collapsed. He looked like hell. His eyes were sunken halfway into his head, his hair was unkempt from running his hands through it every couple of minutes, and he needed a shave. He looked like an escapee from the drunk tank.

And Renny was feeling like one. He hadn't had much sleep himself. Seemed like he'd been on a treadmill since Christmas Eve, which wasn't sitting well at all with Joanne. Bad enough he'd missed Christmas morning—good thing they didn't have any kids or he'd *really* be in the dog house—but he'd also missed Christmas dinner at his in-laws'. It wasn't that he didn't like his in-laws—they were okay folks—it was just that he was in deep shit with the department. A suspect in an attempted murder case had been transferred to him at Downstate, and a few hours later all he had in custody was a pile of stinking goo.

Renny's stomach gave a little heave at the memory. Over the past three days he had endlessly replayed the scene in the corridor in his mind, but no number of viewings could add any sense or reason to what had happened. One moment he had a suspect in custody, the next he had some lumpy brown liquid. Thank God there'd been witnesses or else no one would have believed him. Hell, he'd been there and had seen the whole thing and still didn't quite believe it himself.

And no matter who he talked to he couldn't get an explanation. None of the docs in this entire medical center could make any sense out of the MR images or the chest X ray, or what had finally happened to Lom's body. In fact there seemed to be a kind of doublethink going on. Since they couldn't explain it, they were sweeping it under their mental rugs. He'd overheard one of the medical bigwigs saying something like: Well, since what they say happened is obviously impossible, their memories of the incident must be faulty. How can we be expected to come up with a rational explanation when the primary data is faulty and anecdotal?

It was a different story up at the 112. The precinct had transferred a suspect to Renny and now the suspect was gone. A pile of goo was not going to be able to go before the grand jury for indictment. So they needed a new suspect. The hunt was now on for the missing wife. And Renaldo Augustino knew he'd better find her if he wanted to hold his head up again in the squad room.

So: Joanne was barely speaking to him at home, his name was mud down at the precinct, and Danny Gordon was still in agony here in the hospital.

Renny wondered why he stuck with this job. He had his twenty years. He should have got out then.

"Are they saying Danny's gone crazy?" Renny said to Father Bill.

"Not so much crazy as shutting down parts of his mind. The human mind can experience only so much trauma and then it begins to draw the blinds. The doctors say he's not really experiencing pain on a high level of consciousness."

"That's a blessing," Renny said. "I guess."

The priest gave him a sidelong glance.

"*If* they know what they're talking about."

Renny nodded tiredly. "I hear you, Padre."

None of the doctors seemed to know what they were doing in Danny's case. They trooped in and out of that room, new bunches every day, about as much help explaining what was happening to the kid as they'd been explaining what had happened to Lom. Lots of talk, lots of big words, but when you cleared away all the smoke, they didn't know diddly.

Nick the professor sighed with exasperation.

"You both realize, don't you, that what's supposedly happening with Danny is impossible. I mean it can't be happening. They say they're putting blood and other fluids into Danny and it's simply disappearing. That's patently impossible. Fluid is matter and matter exists. What goes in as fluid may come out as gas but it just doesn't disappear. It has to *be* somewhere!"

Father Bill smiled weakly. "Maybe it is. But it's not in Danny."

"Wasn't he worked up here before?"

"Completely. Everything one hundred percent normal."

Shaking his head, Nick glanced at his watch and stood up.

"I've got to run," he said, shaking hands with the priest. "But I can be back tonight if you want me to spell you with Danny."

"Thanks, but I'll be all right."

Nick shrugged. "I'll come back anyway."

He waved and left. Renny decided he liked Nick. But he still had to wonder a little. Like, what was the relationship between Nick and Father Bill? An unmarried guy still visiting the priest that took care of him as a kid? What kind of a relationship could they have had when Nick lived at St. F.'s that would hold up after all these years. Renny remembered Father Dougherty from his own days at St. F.'s. He couldn't imagine wanting to pay that cold fish a visit every week, even if he were still alive.

He canned the thought. Just his policeman's mind at work. You got so used to seeing the slimy side of people that when it didn't hit you in the face you went looking for it. But he could see that Father Bill might be a pretty regular guy when he wasn't under this kind of stress, someone you might want to be friends with, even if he was a priest.

"How about Sara?" the priest said when Nick was gone. "Anything on her?"

Renny had been dreading that question. Father Bill had asked it every day, and until this morning the answer had been an easy no.

"Yeah," he said. "We got something. I sent for a newspaper clipping and a copy of her senior page in the U. of T. at Austin yearbook. They arrived today."

"Her yearbook? How can that tell you anything?"

"I do it routinely, just to make sure that the person I'm looking for is really the person I'm looking for."

The priest's expression was puzzled. "I don't . . ."

Renny pulled the folded sheets from his breast pocket and handed them over.

"Here. They're Xeroxes of Xeroxes, but I think you'll see what I mean."

He watched Father Bill's eyes scan the top sheet, come to a halt, narrow, then widen in shock. Renny had had almost the same reaction. The yearbook picture of the Sara Bainbridge who later married Herbert Lom showed a big, moon-faced blonde. The second sheet was a newspaper clipping of a wedding announcement with a photo of the same big blonde in a wedding gown.

Neither of them bore the remotest resemblance to the woman in the photo the priest had given Renny from the St. Francis adoption application.

Father Bill flipped to the second sheet, then looked up at him with a stricken, befuddled expression.

"But this isn't . . ."

"Yeah. I know."

The priest dropped the sheets and staggered to his feet.

"Oh, my God!"

He turned and leaned against the windowsill and stared out at the Brooklyn rooftops in silence. Renny knew he'd just been socked in the gut so he let him have his time. Finally he turned around.

"I really screwed up, didn't I?"

There was an impulse in Renny to say, *Yeah, you did.* But he knew it was just his own anger looking for a convenient target. As a cop he'd had his share of times as target for that kind of anger from citizens and he wasn't going to fall into the trap himself. Besides, what was the point of kicking a decent man when he was down?

"You got taken. You followed the routine and she slipped through. And didn't you tell me you even went so far as to call the woman's old pastor?"

A mute nod from the priest.

"Okay. So how were you to know that the two of you were talking about different people?"

But Father Bill didn't seem to be listening. He started talking to the air.

"My God, it's all my fault. If I'd done my job right, Danny wouldn't be all cut up like that. He'd still be in one piece back in St. F.'s."

"Aw, don't start with that bullshit. It's *her* fault. Whoever took the real Sara's place is to blame. She's the one who took the knife to Danny."

"But why? Why all the subterfuge, the elaborate plotting, and most likely the murder of the real Sara?"

"We don't know that."

True. They didn't know that. But Renny felt it in his gut: The real Sara was dead.

"*Why,* dammit? Just to mutilate a small boy? It doesn't make sense."

"I stopped expecting sense a long time ago."

"And what about Herb?"

"At this point I can go either way on Herb," Renny said with a shrug, trying not to remember what the man had looked like the last time he'd seen him. "But my gut instinct is that Herb was a victim too."

The priest's eyes were bleak as he looked at Renny.

"So then it's Sara—the bogus Sara—we're after."

"Right. And we'll find her."

"I'm not so sure about that," Father Bill said softly.

"What's that supposed to mean?"

Before the priest could answer, a doctor walked into the lounge, one of the nameless, faceless white coats that had been trooping in and out of Danny's room for days.

"Excuse me. Father Ryan? I want to discuss some procedures we'd like to do on the Gordon boy."

Renny saw the priest's body tense, like an animal ready to spring.

"Tests? More tests? What about his pain? All you do is tests but that child is still in agony in there! Don't come to me with more requests for tests until you've healed his wounds and stopped his pain!"

"We've tried everything we know," the doctor said, "but nothing works. We need to test—"

Father Bill took two quick steps toward the doctor and grabbed the lapels of his white coat.

"Screw your tests!" His voice was edging toward a scream. *"Stop his pain!"*

Renny leapt from his seat and pulled the priest off the doctor. He shooed the doctor out of the lounge and got Father Bill into a chair.

"Cool it, Father. Just cool it, okay?"

A nasty thought slithered through Renny's mind. In a crime with no witnesses, the first suspects should be the people closest to the victim. He remembered how everyone he'd interviewed at St. F.'s had commented on how attached Father Bill had been to little Danny. What if he'd been *too* attached? What if the thought of giving the kid up for adoption had been too much for him? What if—?

Jesus! Knock it off, Augustino! This is one of the good guys here. Save it for the street slime.

"Why don't you go home," he told the priest. "You're cracking up from spending too much time in that hospital room."

The priest looked away. "I can't leave him. And besides, it's the only place I know without a phone."

Oh, yeah. Another sign that Father Bill might be cracking under the weight of all this craziness. He kept talking about these phone calls he was getting from Danny where the kid was screaming for help, begging him to come get him. A sure sign that—

The priest jumped as the lounge phone began to ring.

"That's him!" Father Bill said hoarsely, staring at the phone as if it were going to bite him.

"Yeah? How can you tell?"

"That's the way it rings when it's Danny."

The phone did sound weird. One long, uninterrupted ring that kept going. But weird ring or not, Renny knew it wasn't Danny Gordon on the phone. He snatched it up.

"Hello!"

A child's voice, terrified, screaming.

"Father, please come and get me! Pleeeeease! *Father, Father, Father, I don't want to die. Please come and get me. Don't let him kill me. I don't want to die!"*

Renny felt his heart begin to thud in response to the anguish in that little voice. It made him want to run out the door and find him, help him, wherever he was.

But he knew where he was. Danny was down the hall, in bed, hooked up to half a dozen tubes and monitors.

"Is that you, lady?" he shouted into the phone. "This is Detective Sergeant Augustino, NYPD, and you just made the biggest mistake of your life!"

The line was dead. He depressed the plunger and dialed the operator. After identifying himself he asked if she had just put the call through to extension 2579. She said no and checked with the other operators. No one could remember putting a call through to that extension all morning. He slammed the phone down.

"She's somewhere in the hospital!" he said.

"What?" The priest was back on his feet, his eyes wide.

"If the call didn't come through the switchboard, it had to originate in-house. She's probably sitting in some corner playing her tape into the phone."

"You mean it sounded like a tape to you?"

"Come to think of it . . . no."

Father Bill was suddenly running down the hall.

"Danny! She's here to finish him off!"

Renny followed him. He hated the thought of entering Danny's room, of hearing Danny's sound, his voiceless scream, like air escaping a punctured tire. Endlessly. It never stopped. The whole time you were in there it went on and on and on. He didn't know how Father Bill stood it. But he followed the priest into the room. He'd go anywhere, to hell itself to catch the bitch who'd done this to that kid . . .

But Danny was just as they'd left him, twisting and writhing in openmouthed agony. Renny could bear only a moment or two in that room, then he had to flee it, leaving Father Bill alone at the bedside.

Bill seated himself at the side of the bed, pulled a Rosary from his pocket, and began fingering the beads. But he didn't say the usual Our Fathers and Hail Marys. He couldn't find the words. His mind was saturated with Danny's ungodly torment.

Ungodly. A fitting adjective. Where was God when Bill needed Him? When *Danny* needed Him? Where had He been Christmas Eve? On vacation?

Or is He out there at all?

Such a question would have been unthinkable a few days ago. But Bill had run out of excuses.

And he knew them all. All the gentle explanations of why bad things happen to good people, and why even the most devout, most sincere, most selfless prayers often go unanswered. He knew how events often seemed to conspire to work against the best people, against the best things they tried to achieve. But that didn't mean there was a Divine Hand at work, moving people around, shaping events, checking off names of those who could go on living and those whose time was up.

As Bill saw it, death, disease, rape, murder, accidents, famine, plague—they all had earthly causes, and therefore had earthly solutions. As God's creatures we were expected to find those solutions. That was why He equipped us with hands, hearts, and minds.

Neither God nor the mythical Satan were the cause of our woes; if the culprits weren't ourselves or other people, they were time, circumstance, or nature.

Or so Bill had thought.

How did he explain what had happened—what was *still* happening—to Danny?

From everything Bill knew, from everything he had seen during the past few days, the answer was None Of The Above.

None of the above.

Sure, blame whoever had posed as Sara for taking a knife to Danny. She started it all. But what about the rest of it? The endless pain, the wounds that refused to heal, the unresponsiveness to anesthesia, the transfusions—almost fifty liters had been poured into Danny since his arrival—that seemed to be sucked down some black hole never to be seen again—what of them? Danny wasn't eating; his kidneys weren't functioning, so he was putting out no urine; his heart was beating but there was no blood for it to pump. It was impossible for him to be alive—every doctor who'd seen him had uttered those same words at one time or another.

Impossible . . . but here he was.

And what of Herb Lom? A hollow man—not just spiritually, but without internal organs or a nervous system—who had dissolved when Bill punched a hole in his chest.

Good God! . . . the hole in his chest . . . the cold . . . the stench . . . the slime . . .

As much as his faith resisted it, as much as his mind saw it as a surrender of the intellect, he could not escape the feeling, the overwhelming belief that something supernatural was at work here.

Something supernatural . . . and evil.

And Danny was the target.

Why Danny? What had this child ever done to deserve this living hell? He was an innocent, and he was being put through unimaginable torture by a force beyond nature. Something dark and powerful had taken hold of him and was thumbing its nose at the laws of God and man and nature, keeping Danny beyond the reach of humanity's most advanced medical science.

And deep in his gut Bill knew that the torture would go on as long as Danny lived.

Where there's life, there's hope.

Bill had lived by that neat little aphorism for the four and a half decades of his life. He'd believed it.

But no more. Poor little Danny's case broke that rule. As long as he remained alive, there was no hope of relief for Danny. His life would go on—

No. Not life. *Existence* was a better term. For what Danny had now was not life. His *existence* would go on as it had since Christmas Eve—unhealed wounds, unremitting pain, with no hope of relief.

At least not from anything in this world.

Bill pocketed the Rosary and said a silent prayer of his own.

Help him, Lord. Something beyond the natural is causing his torment and so only something else beyond the natural can save him. That's You, Lord. We can bounce back from any blow Your world hands us, but we are helpless against the otherworldly. That's why Danny needs You to step in on his behalf. Not for my sake—put his wounds on me, if that will do it. Just don't let him suffer anymore. If there's something that can be done that's not being done, let me know. Tell me and I'll do it. No matter what it is, I'll do it. Please.

Danny's rasping screams ceased and he opened his eyes.

Bill froze and watched as Danny's eyes stared about the room, searching, finally stopping when they found Bill. He grabbed the boy's hand and squeezed.

"Danny?" Bill said. "Danny, are you there? Can you hear me?"

Danny's lips moved.

"What?" Bill said, leaning closer. "What is it?"

The lips moved again. A whisper escaped.

Bill moved closer still. The breath from the parched tunnel of Danny's throat was sour as Bill put his ear almost against the dry lips.

"What, Danny? Say it again."

"Bury me . . . in holy ground . . . It won't stop . . . till you bury me . . ."

NINETEEN

How long could a week be?

Bill Ryan pondered the question as he swung into one of Downstate's parking lots. As the guard passed him through, a couple of rag-wrapped derelicts hurried toward his car, shouting and waving. They didn't appear to be the typical window-washing winos; they almost seemed to have been waiting for him. Bill drove on. No time today to figure out what they wanted.

He left the station wagon in one of the handicapped spots and entered the hospital through one of the employee entrances.

"Evening, Father," said the smiling uniformed black woman inside the door. "Happy New Year."

Bill could not bring himself to say those words. No way was the year that started tomorrow going to be a happy one.

"Same to you, Gloria."

Only a week here and already he was something of a fixture. The security people knew him, he was on a first-name basis with most of the nurses on all three shifts on Danny's floor, and the walks he took to stretch his legs between vigils at Danny's bedside had familiarized him with most of the building in which Pediatrics was located. All in one week. One endless week. Thank God Father Cullen had been available to fill in for him at St. F.'s.

But if the seven days between Christmas and New Year's had been an eternity for Bill Ryan, he knew it must have been longer by an unholy factor for poor Danny.

Bury me . . . in holy ground . . . It won't stop . . . till you bury me . . .

Danny's eyes had closed after those words and he hadn't spoken since. But those words, those words had tormented Bill for days, echoing through his mind every waking minute. He had asked for guidance, but the advice he'd received was unthinkable.

Or so it had seemed at first.

Things had changed since then. Bill was convinced now that modern medicine offered no hope. The doctors were helpless against whatever force had Danny in its grip. And during the span of Danny's hospital stay that helplessness had wrought a slow but unmistakable change in those doctors. Bill had seen their attitude mutate from deep concern for a savagely brutalized child to bafflement, and from bafflement to cold clinical fascination with a scientific oddity. Somewhere along the line Danny had stopped being a patient and become an experimental subject.

Bill thought he could understand them. The doctors were in the business of curing illness, treating disease, healing wounds, providing answers. But they could not heal Danny, could not help him in the slightest, could provide no answers to Bill's questions. Danny's condition confounded their skills and training, spat on their professional pride. And so the doctors pulled back and switched gears. If they could not help Danny, they would learn from him.

Bill could see it in their flat eyes when he spoke to them: Danny the boy had become Danny the thing. They wanted to experiment on Danny. Sure, they called their plans "testing" and "exploratory surgery," but their real aim was to get inside him and find out what was going on in there.

So far, Bill had been able to stand in their way. But all that would change the day after tomorrow. The head nurse on days had told him that by midmorning on January 2 the hospital would have a court order making Danny a ward of the state and giving it legal guardianship over Danny. The hospital then would have carte blanche; the doctors could experiment on him to their hearts' delight. He'd be the subject of clinical conferences; they'd bring in all the residents and show them The Boy Who Should Be Dead. And when Danny finally died—When would that be? Five years? Ten? Fifty?—what would they do? Bill envisioned Danny pickled in a jar where generations of fledgling doctors could view his still-unhealed wounds. Or maybe his remains would be put on display like the Elephant Man's.

Uh-uh. Not if Bill had anything to say about it.

Word of the court order had spurred him to a decision. The unthinkable became the inevitable.

The nurses at the charge desk on Peds waved hello as Bill passed. He returned the greeting and stopped.

"Where is everybody?"

"Light shift tonight," said Phyllis, the head nurse on three-to-eleven. "Wait'll you see eleven-to-seven—that'll be a real skeleton. Everyone wants to party."

Bill was glad to hear that. He'd expected it, but it was good to have it confirmed.

"I can understand that. It's been tough around here."

Her face lost some of its holiday cheer. "How about you? We're all getting together at Murphy's after we get off. If you want to come over—"

"Thanks, no. I'll stay here."

He would have stopped for a longer chat but didn't dare. The phone calls were coming more frequently now. More than a few minutes within ten feet of a phone seemed to set off that unearthly ring . . . and the terrified voice . . . Danny's voice.

He continued down the hall and found Nick sitting outside Danny's door reading one of his scientific journals. He looked up at Bill's approach.

"Anything?" Bill said.

He knew the answer but he asked anyway.

"Nothing," Nick said.

"Thanks for spelling me, Nick."

He squinted up at Bill. "You were supposed to go home and sleep. Did you?"

"Tried." He hoped he could get away with the lie if he limited it to a monosyllable.

"You look more exhausted than before you left."

"I'm not sleeping well." *That* was no lie.

"Maybe you should get a sleeping pill or something, Bill. You're going to come unglued if you keep this up much longer."

I'm unraveling even as we speak.

"I'll be all right."

"I'm not so sure about that."

"I am. Now you get going. I'll take it from here."

Nick stood up and looked closely at Bill.

"Something's going on that you're not telling me."

Bill forced a laugh. "You're getting paranoid. Go to the physics department party tonight and have a good time." He stuck out his hand. "Happy New Year, Nick."

Nick shook his hand but didn't let go.

"This has been one hell of a year for you, Bill," he said softly. "First your parents, then this thing with Danny. But you've gotta figure things can't get worse. Next year has to be better. Keep that in mind tonight."

Bill's tightening throat choked off anything he might have said. He threw his arms around Nick and held on to him, fighting down the sobs that pressed up through his chest. He wanted to let it all out, wanted to cry out his misery and fear and crushing loneliness on the younger man's shoulder. But he couldn't do that. That luxury was not for him. He was the priest. People were supposed to cry on *his* shoulder.

Get a grip!

He backed off and looked at Nick for what might be the last time. They'd been through a lot together. He'd practically raised Nick. He saw that the younger man's eyes were moist. Did he know?

"Happy New Year, kid. I'm proud of you."

"And I'm proud of you, Father Bill. Next year will be better. Believe it."

Bill only nodded. He didn't dare try to voice belief in that lie.

He watched Nick disappear down the hall, then he turned toward Danny's door. He hesitated as he always did, as anyone would before stepping across the threshold of hell, and sent up a final prayer.

Don't make me do this, Lord. Don't ask this of me. Take this matter into Your own hands. Heal him or take him. Spare us both. Please.

But when he pushed through the door he heard the hoarse, sibilant, whispered moans, found Danny still writhing on the bed.

Closing the door behind him, Bill allowed one sob to escape. Then he leaned against the wall and squeezed his eyes shut. He felt more alone than he had ever thought possible—alone in the room, alone in the city, alone in the cosmos. And he saw no choice but to go through with what he'd been planning all day.

He went over to the bedside and looked down at Danny's thin, tortured, ghastly white face. For an instant the boy's pain-mad eyes cleared, and Bill saw in them a fleeting, desperate plea for help. He grabbed the thin little hand.

"Okay, Danny. I promised to help you, and I will." No one else seemed to be able or willing to—not the doctors, not God himself. So it was up to Bill. "It's just you and me, kid. I'll help you."

* * *

Bill waited patiently through the change of shift, until the incoming nurses had been briefed on each patient by the outgoing crew. The reports were completed more quickly than usual, and with wishes of a happy New Year to one and all the three-to-eleven shift was on its way out of the building in record time. It was party time for them.

Bill made some small talk with Beverly, the head nurse on eleven-to-seven, as she checked Danny's useless IVs during her initial rounds. Then he waited a while longer.

At 11:45 he scouted the hall. No one in sight. Even the nurses station was deserted. Finally he found them. The entire shift was clustered in the room of one of the older children, a twelve-year-old boy recovering from an appendectomy, all watching as Dick Clark's New Year's Rockin' Eve show geared up for the traditional countdown to the drop of the illuminated apple above Times Square.

Bill slipped back to the charge desk and hit the OFF switch on Danny's heart monitor, then hurried back to his room. Working feverishly, he peeled the two monitor leads from the boy's chest wall, then removed the IV lines from both arms and let the solutions drip onto the floor. He untied the restraints from Danny's wrists and slid his painfully thin chest out of the posey. Then he wrapped him in the bed blanket and in an extra blanket from the closet.

He checked the hall again. Still empty. Now was the time. Now or never. He turned back to the bed, reached to lift Danny, then paused.

This was it, wasn't it? The point of no return. If he carried through his plan tonight there would be no turning back, no saying I'm sorry, I made a mistake, give me another chance. He would be accused of a hideous crime, branded a monster, and hunted for the rest of his life. Everything he had worked for since joining the Society would be stripped from him, every friend he had ever made would turn against him, every good thing he had done in his life would be forever tainted. Was what he was about to do worth all that?

Bury me . . . in holy ground. The words seared his brain. *It won't stop . . . till you bury me . . .*

There was no other way.

He lifted Danny's writhing, blanket-shrouded form.

Good Lord, he weighs almost nothing!

He carried him along the empty hall to the rear stairway, then down the steps, flight after flight, praying he'd meet no one. He'd chosen this moment because it was probably the only quarter hour out of the entire year when, unless they were in the middle of a crisis situation, almost everyone's mind was more or less distracted from his or her job.

When he reached ground level Bill placed Danny on the landing and checked his watch: almost midnight. He peeked out into the hall. Empty. At its end, the exit door. And just as he'd hoped—unwatched. The guard's seat was empty. And why not? Georgie, the usual door guard on this shift, had always seemed fairly conscientious, but even he'd have to figure that since his job was to screen the people entering the hospital instead of those leaving it, and since no one could get in unless he opened the door for them, what was wrong with leaving his station for a few minutes to watch the apple drop?

Bill lifted Danny and started for the exit. Up ahead he heard voices through the open door of one of the little offices. He paused. He had to pass that door to get out. No way around it. But could he risk it? If he got caught now, with Danny wrapped up in his arms like this, he'd never get another chance.

Then he heard it: the countdown. A mix of voices, male and female, began shouting.

"Ten! Nine! Eight! . . ."

Bill began to walk, gliding his feet, gathering speed until he was moving as fast as he could without actually running.

"Seven! Six! Five! . . ."

He whisked past the office door, then began to run.

"Four! Three! Two! . . ."

As he reached the door he slowed for half a second, just long enough to allow him to hit the lever bar at the same instant the voices shouted, "One!"

The noise of the opening door was lost in the ensuing cheers as he rushed headlong into the parking lot. He had parked St. F.'s station wagon illegally, hoping his clergy sticker would buy him some leniency. The last thing he needed now was to find that the wagon had been towed away.

He sighed with relief when he saw it where he'd left it. She was a rusting old junker but at that moment she looked like a stretch limo. Gently, he laid Danny on the back seat and arranged the blankets loosely over him.

"We're on our way, kid," he whispered through the folds of fabric.

Then he heard a slurred voice behind him.

"That him? 'S he the one?"

Bill whirled and saw the two ragmen from earlier this evening, one big, the other shorter and slight. How had they got into the lot?

"No, that's not him," said the smaller of the two. "Hush up about that."

The big one stepped closer to Bill and peered into his face. His beard stank of wine and old food.

"You the one?" Another moment of too-close scrutiny, then, "No. He's not the one."

He turned and lurched away.

The little one scampered after him for a few steps.

"Walter! Walter, wait!" Then he hurried back to Bill. "Don't do it!" he said in a harsh whisper. "No matter what you've been told, don't do it!"

"I'm sorry," Bill said, shaken by the man's intensity. "I'm in a hurry."

The little man grabbed his arm.

"I know you! You're that Jesuit. Remember me? Martin Spano? We met long ago . . . at the Hanley mansion."

Bill jolted as if he'd touched a live wire.

"God, yes! What—?"

"Not much time. I've got to catch up to Walter. I'm helping him search for someone. Walter was a medic once. He sometimes can cure people but he can't cure that kid. He can't cure anybody when he's drunk and he's drunk almost all the time these days. But remember what I said. Don't do it. An Evil power is at work here. It's using you! I was used once—I know how it is. Stop now, before it's too late!"

And then he was off, running after his fellow derelict.

Thoroughly shaken, Bill got in the front seat and sat for a moment. Martin Spano—hadn't he been one of those crazy people who'd called themselves the Chosen when they'd invaded the Hanley mansion back in 1968? Spano had been crazy then and was obviously crazier now. But what had he meant—?

Never mind. He couldn't allow himself to be distracted now. He shook off the confusion and drove out of the lot, forcing a smile and waving as he passed the guard in the booth. He drove north, toward the Bayside section of Queens, toward a place he'd spent much of the early evening preparing for Danny.

Renny slammed the phone down and threw off the covers.

"*Damn!*"

"What's the matter?" Joanne asked from the other side of the bed. They'd spent New Year's Eve at home, catching up on their lovemaking.

"The kid's gone!"

"The one in the hospital?"

"Yeah," he said as he pulled on slacks and a sweater. "Danny Gordon. The nurse went in to wish Father Bill a happy New Year and found the room empty."

"The priest? You don't think—"

"They were both in the room before twelve, they were both gone after. What else can I think?" He gave her a quick kiss in the dark. "Gotta go. Sorry, babe."

"It's okay. I understand."

Did she? Renny sure hoped so.

The priest! he thought as he raced toward Downstate. Could he have been the one who cut up on that kid?

Nah! Not possible. No way.

And yet . . .

Renny thought again about how everyone he'd interviewed at St. F.'s had mentioned good old Father Bill's attachment to little Danny, like father and son. How Danny would always sit on his lap. What if that attachment hadn't been entirely on the straight and narrow? You heard about fag priests, about priests molesting kids. It hit the papers every so often. What if the thought of giving the kid up for adoption had scared him? What if he'd been afraid Danny would talk to his new parents about things he'd had to let Father Bill do to him?

Renny increased his speed. He squeezed the steering wheel as he felt his insides tense up.

What if Danny had told the Loms something on Christmas Eve? And what if in their shock and disbelief, in a misguided attempt to give this wonderful and gracious man an opportunity to defend himself, they'd called Father Bill first instead of the police? And what if he cracked when they told him? What if he said he'd come right over and talk this thing out? What if he went completely berserk in the Lom house?

"Jesus!" he said aloud in his car.

It didn't explain everything. Nobody—*nobody*—was ever going to give Renny a satisfactory explanation of what had happened to Herb Lom, so he stuffed that incident into a mental limbo. But the bogus Sara—what was her angle? Was she a red herring? Or was she somehow in league with the priest in some plot to get Danny away from St. Francis to a place where the wonderful Father Bill could have freer and more discreet access to the kid?

And suddenly all the pieces started falling into place.

The priest had spent every waking hour by the kid's side, even slept in a chair in the boy's room. Renny had been taken by this show of such deep devotion. But what if it hadn't been anything like devotion? What if the priest had just wanted to be there when Danny started coming out of it? What if he'd wanted to be the first to know if Danny was going to talk again?

And there was more! The priest had been fighting the endless round of tests and procedures all the docs wanted to perform on the kid. Renny had assumed it was for the kid's sake . . . until now. What if he was really afraid they'd find a way to bring him out of it, or at least get him to the point where he could name his attacker? And now, with the legal machinery moving toward making Danny a ward of the court, the priest was facing certain shutout from having any say in Danny's care. That might have been the last straw. He must have gone into a panic tonight and took off with the kid.

Maybe to finish him off.

Shit!

Renny swerved into the entrance of one of the Downstate parking lots and jumped out of his car. A couple of winos were there. They fairly leapt on him.

"He took the boy!" the shorter one said.

"Who?"

"The Jesuit! He took the boy!"

"You saw him?"

Before the little guy could answer, the bigger wino pushed forward.

"Are you the one?" he said, staring into Renny's eyes.

Renny turned away. He'd heard enough. He flashed his badge at the guy in the guard booth and grabbed the phone. It took a while—he had to go through the hospital switchboard—but he got a line to the desk at his precinct.

"I want an APB on a Father William Ryan. He's a Jesuit priest but he probably won't be dressed like one. He's wanted for kidnapping and for attempted murder. He'll have a sick seven-year-old kid with him. Get his picture out of the file now and get it to all the papers and all the local news shows. Do the usual bridges and tunnels thing. Have anybody and everybody looking out for a guy in his forties traveling with a sick kid. Do it now. Not ten minutes from now—*now!*"

Renny stepped out of the booth and slammed his fist against the hood of his car.

How could he have been such a jerk? The cardinal rule in this sort of crime was to put the first heat on the people closest to the victim. The esteemed Father Ryan had been the closest but Renny had allowed himself to be lulled by the Roman collar, by the fact that he'd come out of St. Francis himself. He'd let that bastard priest sucker him in and squeeze him for all he was worth.

I'm so fucking stupid!

Well, no more. Ryan wasn't getting out of this city tonight. It was New Year's Eve and the shift was spread a little thin, plus the usual bunch of cops was tied up doing crowd control at Times Square, but Ryan wasn't getting away. Not if Renny had a damn thing to say about it. The priest had made him look like a jerk, but Renny realized that wasn't what really mattered, what really burned him. It was how he'd started thinking of the priest as a friend, someone he wanted to hang around with. And Renny didn't offer his friendship easily.

He was *hurt*, dammit.

Something cold and wet landed on his cheek. He looked around. It was beginning to snow. He smiled. The weatherman had predicted a snowstorm tonight. That was good. It would slow traffic, make it easier to spot a guy and a sick kid trying to leave the city.

We're gonna meet again real soon, Father fucking Ryan. And when we do you'll wish you'd never been born.

St. Ann's Cemetery was small and old and crowded, some of the headstones dating back to the early years of the last century. Bill had chosen St. Ann's because it was out of the way and it was consecrated ground.

. . . bury me . . . in holy ground . . .

Now as he drove the deserted street running along the cemetery's north wall he wondered if it mattered.

Consecrated ground, he thought. *What does that mean?*

A week ago he'd have had no trouble answering the question. Now the whole concept struck him as senseless.

But then, nothing made sense anymore. His whole world had been turned upside down and ripped inside out during the past week. He could smell the rot in the very foundations of his faith, could feel them crumbling beneath him.

Where are you, Lord? There's evil afoot here, pure distilled evil that can't be explained away by happenstance or coincidence or natural causes. This isn't fair. Lord. Give me a hand, will you?

Only one other time in his life had he come across anything even remotely resembling what had happened to Danny. That derelict . . . Spano . . . had reminded him. Almost twenty years ago, in a Victorian mansion on Long Island Sound, he'd seen Emma Stevens die not ten feet in front of him with an ax in her brain. He'd watched her lie in front of him, as lifeless as the rug that soaked up her blood. And then he'd seen her rise and walk and kill two people before slumping into death once again.

He'd explained that away by telling himself that if doctors had had a chance to examine Emma while she was lying on the rug with the ax protruding from her skull, they would have found that she only *appeared* dead, and that whatever spark of life was left in her had flared long enough to allow her to finish what she'd started just before she was killed.

But an entire medical center staff had had a week with Danny. They all said he should be dead, but somehow he wouldn't die.

Just like Emma Stevens. Except that Emma had hung on for only a few minutes. Danny had been going for a week and showed no signs of weakening. He might possibly go on forever.

. . . it won't stop . . . till you bury me . . .

Bill wondered if there could be a link between what had happened to Emma and what was happening to Danny. Spano the wino seemed to have hinted at that in the parking lot.

He shook himself. No. How could there be? He was grasping at straws here.

He pulled to a stop in the deep shadows under a dead street lamp. Dead because he'd killed it. He'd bought a CO_2 pellet gun yesterday, come out here last night, and shot the bulb out. Took him a whole cartridge before he finally scored a bull's-eye.

And earlier tonight, shortly after dark, he'd returned to this spot with a pick and a shovel.

Bill leaned forward and rested his head against the steering wheel. Tired. So tired. When was the last time he'd had two consecutive hours of sleep? Maybe if he just closed his eyes for a little while here he could—

No! He jerked his head up. He couldn't hide from this. It had to be done and he was the only one to do it, the only one to realize that this was the only thing anyone *could* do for Danny. There were no other options. This was it.

He'd heard it from Danny's own lips.

With that thought to bolster him, Bill put the wagon in gear and drove up the curb and across the sidewalk until the passenger side of the wagon was hugging the eight-foot wall under an oak that leaned over from the far side. He got out, opened the rear door, and lifted Danny out of the back seat. With the boy's swaddled form in his arms, he stepped up on the bumper, then the hood, then up to the roof. From there it was a short hop to the top of the wall. He swiveled around on his buttocks until his legs were dangling over the inside edge, then dropped to the ground on the other side.

Okay. He was inside. It was dark. The glow from the streetlights didn't reach in here, but he knew where he was going. Just a few paces to the left, against the wall. That was where he had spent a couple of hours tonight after darkfall . . .

. . . hours . . . with a pick and shovel . . .

Oh, God, he didn't want to do this, would have given anything to pass this cup. But there was no one in the wings to take it from him.

Bill paused an instant at the edge of the oblong hole in the ground, then jumped in. When he straightened, the frozen grass on ground level was even with his lower ribs. He would have liked the hole to have been deeper, six feet at least, but he'd exhausted himself here earlier getting it this deep, and there was no time left now. This would have to do.

He knelt and stretched Danny's form out on the floor of the hole. He couldn't see the boy's face in the darkness, so he released his writhing body, and pulled back the folds of blanket. He administered the final sacrament, called Extreme Unction when he was in the seminary, now called the Anointing of the Sick. During the past week he had administered it on a daily basis to Danny, and each time it had lost an increment of its meaning. It was little more than a collection of empty words and gestures now.

Empty . . . like everything else in his life. All the rules he had lived by, all the beliefs on which he had based his life were falling away. The God he'd placed his trust in had not lifted a finger against the force that gripped Danny.

But he went through the motions. And when he was done, he placed a hand on each side of Danny's head, cupping his wasted cheeks.

"Danny?" he whispered. "Danny, will this work for you? I know you told me once that it would, but please tell me again. I'm going against everything I've ever believed in to do this for you. I need to hear it again."

Danny said nothing. He remained lost in agony, giving no sign that he had even heard him.

Bill pressed his forehead against Danny's.

"I hope you can hear me, hope you can understand me. I'm doing this for you, Danny, because it's the only way to end it all for you. All the pain, all the torture will be over in a few minutes. I don't know how much of you is left in there, Danny, but I know some of you still remains. I see it in your eyes sometimes. I don't want you to . . . to die without knowing that I'm doing this to release you from whatever monstrous evil is torturing you. I'm doing it to stop the pain, and to protect you from those doctors making you into some sort of sideshow freak. You know if there was any other way, I'd find it. You know that, don't you?" He leaned over and kissed Danny's forehead. "I love you, kid. You know that too, don't you?"

For an instant, for the interval that falls between a pair of heartbeats, Danny's pain-writhe paused, his breathy screams stilled, and Bill felt the boy's head nod up and down. Once.

"Danny!" he shouted. "Danny, can you hear me? Do you know what I'm saying?"

But Danny's athetoid movements and hissing cries began again. Bill could no longer hold back the sobs. They burst from him and he clutched Danny close for a moment, then he pushed the sobs back down and laid the boy flat again. He covered Danny's face with the blanket—he couldn't throw dirt on his face—then pulled himself out of the hole.

He looked around. No one about. He had to work quickly now. Get to it and get it over with before he lost his nerve. He lifted the shovel from where he had left it beside the hole. He shoved it deep into the pile of loose dirt he had pulled from the ground only hours ago. But as he lifted a shovelful free, he paused, knees weak, arms trembling.

I can't do this!

He looked up at the starless, cloud-shrouded night sky.

Please, God. If You're there, if You care, if You have any intention of taking a hand in reversing the evil that's being done to this boy, do it now. Under different circumstances I'd consider this an utterly childish request. But You know what I've seen, You know what this child has suffered, is still *suffering. We've witnessed the presence of naked Evil here, Lord. I don't think I'm out of line in asking You to step in and take over now. Give me a sign, Lord. How about it?*

It began to snow.

"Snow?" Bill said aloud. *"Snow?"*

What was that supposed to tell him? A snowstorm in July would be a sign. In January it meant nothing.

Except that the ground he had disturbed tonight would go undetected for a long time. Maybe forever.

He threw the shovelful of earth into the hole where it landed atop Danny's writhing blanket.

There, Lord. I've started it. I've played Abraham. I've raised the knife over the closest thing to a son I'll ever have. It's time for You to stop me and say I've passed the test.

He threw in another shovelful, then another.

Come on, Lord. Stop me! Tell me I've done enough. I'm begging You!

He began shoveling the loose dirt into the hole as fast as he could, tumbling in clumps of frozen earth, kicking little avalanches with his feet, working like mad, whimpering, screaming deep in his throat like some crazed animal, blanking his mind to what he was doing, knowing it was the best and only thing for this little boy he loved, throwing off the clutching, restraining bonds of a lifetime of conditioning, two millennia of beliefs, keeping his eyes averted from the hole even though there was nothing to see within its black, hungry maw.

And then the hole was full.

"Are you satisfied?" Bill shouted at the flake-filled sky. "Can I dig him up now?"

There was still dirt left over, so he had to force himself to step onto the fill, to stomp it with his feet, to pack it down over Danny, and then throw some more on top. And still there was more loose dirt left over, so he mounded some of it up and scattered the rest.

And then it was done. He stood there sweating and steaming in the cold as the tiny flakes swirled around him with heartless beauty. He fought a mad urge to start digging again and threw the shovel over the wall so he couldn't change his mind.

Done. It was done.

With a moan that tore loose from the deepest place within him he dropped to his knees atop the grave and leaned forward until his ear was against the silent earth. Fifteen minutes now. Fifteen at least since he'd smothered that wasted little body. No reprieve for Bill now. He had done the unthinkable. But Danny's pain was over. That was all that really mattered.

Was this the only way? God help me, I hope so!

"Good-bye, pal," he said when he could speak. "Rest easy, okay? I'm going away for a while, but I'll be back to visit you when I can."

Feeling utterly lost and empty, he rose to his feet, took one last look, then climbed the leaning oak and jumped down outside the wall. He picked up the shovel, threw it in the back of the station wagon, and began to drive. And as he drove, he began to curse. He screamed out his disgust for a God who'd allow such a thing to happen, he cursed the medical profession for being helpless against it, he swore vengeance on Sara, or rather the woman who had usurped the real Sara's identity. But rising through it all was a tide of loathing, for himself, for everything he had been, for everything he had done in his life, especially what he had done tonight. Self-loathing—it poured from him, it swirled and eddied around him until the inside of the car was awash with it, until he thought he would drown in it.

Somehow he managed to keep driving. Earlier in the evening he'd gone to the bank and emptied out his savings account. He had a few hundred in cash and that was it. There would have been more if he'd settled his folks' estate, but he hadn't pushed on that so it was still pending.

A few hundred wouldn't take him far, but he didn't care. He really didn't have the heart to run. Would have preferred to turn himself in at the nearest precinct house and have done with it. But they'd want to know where Danny was. And they'd keep on him until he told them. And when he finally broke down and told them they'd be out digging up Danny's body so a different crew of doctors could take it apart.

Bill couldn't allow that. The purpose of tonight's horrors had been to lay Danny to rest, to give him peace.

Bill didn't want to face a murder trial either. Too many other people, innocent people, would suffer—the priesthood in general, the Society in particular. That wouldn't be fair. He'd done this on his own. Better to disappear. If they couldn't catch him, they wouldn't know Danny was dead. If he wasn't in court and in the papers every day, the furor would die down. People would forget about him and what he'd done.

But Bill would never forget.

He thought of heading for the East River, of locking the wagon's doors, opening the windows a couple of inches, and driving off one of the embankments. Who knew when they'd find him?

But someone might find him too soon. They might save him. And then he'd have to go through the court scenario.

No. Better for everyone if he kept on the move.

So he drove for hours. The snow accumulated steadily as he wound through the residential streets of Queens, avoiding the area where the Loms had lived, and avoiding the St. Francis area as well. The police would be looking for him now and they'd certainly be watching those two places.

It was near dawn and he was somewhere on the western rim of Nassau County when he saw that his fuel was getting low. He found an open 7-Eleven and filled up at the self-serve. In the store he made himself a cup of coffee and grabbed a buttered bagel. As he was paying the Middle Eastern clerk for everything, he glanced at the little portable TV behind the counter and almost dropped his coffee. His face was on the screen. The clerk saw his expression and glanced at the set.

"Terrible, is it not, when you cannot trust your children to a priest?" he singsonged in his high-pitched voice. "It is getting so you cannot trust anyone."

Bill tensed, ready to run, sure the clerk would see the resemblance. But perhaps because the screen was so small, and Bill had been clean-shaven, well rested, and years younger when that photo had been taken, the man made no connection. He shrugged and turned to the cash register to ring up the gas and food.

Then the phone began to ring. A long ring that wouldn't stop. The clerk dropped the change into Bill's trembling hand and stared at the phone.

"What on earth?" the clerk said.

Bill, too, stared at the phone. *That ring!* He spun and scanned the empty store, then peered through the windows into the snowy dawn. No one was about. He looked back at the phone as the clerk lifted the receiver.

How?

Faintly he heard that familiar, terrified little voice.

"What?" he heard the clerk say. "What are you saying? I am not your father, little boy. Listen to me . . ."

No one knew he was here, no one had followed him—it couldn't be!

Unless . . . unless the caller wasn't hampered by human limitations.

But who? Who or what was tormenting him, mocking him with Danny's cries for help?

One more stratum of proof that his life had fallen under thrall to something as evil as it was inhuman.

His heart pounding like an airhammer, Bill hurried for the door. Out—into the snow, to the safe and sane interior of the station wagon, and back onto the streets.

He realized that if he was going to remain free he'd have to get out of the city, out of the state, out of the Northeast. But to do that he'd have to go through Manhattan.

No—he could go over the Verrazano Bridge, cut across Staten Island, and slip into New Jersey.

He headed south toward the Belt Parkway.

They put the call through to Renny. It was a foreign guy, his voice accented but easily understandable.

"Mr. Detective, sir, I believe I have seen this priest you are searching for."

Renny grabbed a pencil.

"When and where?"

"In the store where I work in Floral Park, not more than one hour ago."

"An hour! Jesus, why'd you wait so long?"

"I did not know it was him until I come home and see his picture on my TV screen. He did not look the same but I believe it was him."

Not exactly a positive ID, but it was all they'd had.

"Was he alone?"

"Yes, he was. There was no child with him, at least none that I saw."

"Did you see what kind of car he was driving?"

"I do not remember."

"Didn't you look?"

"Perhaps, but I was too upset by a telephone call that—"

Renny was suddenly on his feet.

"Telephone call? What kind of call?"

The man described a call exactly like the one Renny had picked up in the hospital, same ring, same frightened child's voice, everything.

What was Ryan up to? And what was the story with the phone calls? Was Ryan making them, using them as a distraction? Or was someone else behind them?

This whole thing was getting loonier by the hour.

Long Island . . . hadn't Ryan grown up on Long Island? Monroe Village or something like that? Maybe that was where he was headed. Headed home.

He reached for the phone.

The morning had lightened but the sun stayed locked behind the low-hanging clouds that sealed off the sky and continued to pump the blizzard at the city. The whole world, the very air, had turned gray-white. Bill had the roads pretty much to himself. After all, it was New Year's Day and snowing like crazy. Only crazies and those who had no choice were out. Still, the going was slow and difficult. The Belt Parkway wasn't plowed and the wagon handled like a barge in a typhoon, slewing this way and that on the curves. He wished he had front-wheel drive.

But things improved when he got on the lower level of the Verrazano. There was blessedly little snow on the protected stretch of bridge. Down the slope lay Staten Island; beyond that, New Jersey and freedom.

Freedom, he thought grimly. *But no escape.*

"So where the hell is he?" Renny said to anyone who would listen.

He was seated at his desk in the squad room trying to coordinate the search for Father Ryan. He waited for one of the other detectives seated around him to offer a brilliant answer but they only sipped their coffee and looked at the floor.

All Renny could do was wait. And waiting was pure hell.

They had the Monroe police force, what there was of it, keeping an eye out for their local boy. Other than that, the bastard could be anywhere on Long Island. Hell, he could have skidded off the L.I.E. and be lying in a ditch freezing to death . . . and that poor kid freezing along with him. He could—

"They think they spotted him on Staten Island!"

It was Connally, rushing through the squad room waving a sheet of paper.

Staten Island? Renny thought. Ryan had been spotted in Floral Park before, due east of the medical center. How could they spot him in Staten Island? That was west.

"When?"

"Less than half an hour ago, Staten side of the Verrazano. Driving an old Ford Country Squire."

"They holding him?"

"Well, no," Connally said. "Whoever it was slipped through. He was alone. No kid anywhere in sight. Might not have been him. The trooper was pulling him over but got drawn away by an accident."

"He got *away?*"

Renny leapt from his chair, spilling his coffee across the top of his drab green desk. He couldn't believe it. Even though it wasn't Connally's fault, he wanted to strangle him.

"Yeah, but they think they got the island sealed off in time."

"They *think?*"

"Hey, look, Renny. I'm only telling you what they told me, okay? I mean, they're not even sure it was him, but they took precautions, and as soon as they got the phone working, they—"

Renny felt a thrill go through him like an electric shock.

"The phone? What was wrong with the phone?"

"The one in the toll booth. They said there was a hysterical kid on it and they couldn't get him off it."

"That was him in the wagon!" Renny shouted. "Goddammit, that was him! We've got the son of a bitch! We've *got* him!"

Made it!

Bill snatched the ticket jutting from the slot in the machine and started up the southbound ramp of the New Jersey Turnpike. He must have reached the Goethals just in time. He'd been watching in his rearview mirror as much as he dared while the wagon fishtailed up the slippery span. Through the haze of falling snow, as he reached the crest of the bridge, he spotted a group of flashing blue lights converge behind him at its Staten Island base.

If they were confining their search to Staten Island, he was home free. But he couldn't count on that. So the best thing to do was to put another state between himself and New York. He noticed on his toll ticket that Exit 6 was the Penn Turnpike Extension. That was where he'd go. Take that about a hundred miles into Pennsylvania and leave the car in a shopping mall. Then he'd buy a bus ticket and double back to Philadelphia. From there he'd Amtrak south, all the way to Florida. And after that, who knew? Maybe hitch a ride on a fishing boat to the Bahamas. That would put him less than a hundred miles from Florida but he'd be in a British territory, essentially a foreign country.

He felt so tired. He tried to look to the future but could see nothing there. And he couldn't look back. God no—not back. He had to forget—forget Danny, forget America, forget the God he had trusted, forget Bill Ryan.

Yeah. Forget Bill Ryan. Bill Ryan was dead, along with everything he had ever believed in.

He had to get away to a place where no one would recognize him, a place where he could lose himself, lose his memories, lose his mind.

A place with no phones.

A heaviness grew in his chest. He was alone now. Truly alone. No one in the world he could turn to. Anything he had ever loved or cared about was either gone or closed to him. His folks were gone; his family home was a vacant lot with a charred spot at its

center; he was barred from St. Francis; and the Church and the
Society would turn him in and disown him if he went to them
for help.

And Danny was gone . . . poor dear Danny was gone too.

Wasn't he?

Of course he was. Safe and at peace, smothered beneath four
feet of frozen, snow-covered earth. How could he be otherwise?

Shuddering, he shook off the horrifying possibility and accel-
erated, leaving it behind. But its ghost followed him south through
the white limbo of the blizzard.

PART III

NOW

JANUARY

TWENTY

Pendleton, North Carolina

Saturday morning and it was top-down weather.

Bill reveled in the warmth of the sun on his shoulders and the back of his neck as he pulled from a parking slot on Conway Street. Warm for late January, even a North Carolina January. He'd just picked up a bargain-priced CD of *The Notorious Byrd Brothers* and he was itching to play it. How long had it been since he'd heard "Tribal Gathering" and "Dolphin Smile," tunes they never played on the radio, especially down here.

He pressed the scan button on his radio—one of the old Impala's few nonvintage accessories—and stopped it when he heard someone singing a plaintive, countrified version of "Yellow Bird." A wave of nausea sloshed against the walls of his stomach as he was jerked back to the Bahamas, back to the two lost years he had spent among that cluster of tiny islands straddling the Tropic of Cancer.

He'd arrived in West Palm by train late on New Year's Day. First thing the next morning he rented a sixteen-foot outboard, loaded it up with extra gas, and followed one of the tour boats out toward the Bahamas. He ran out of fuel a quarter mile short of Grand Bahama and had to swim the rest of the way in. When he came ashore at West End, he sat on the beach for a while, barely able to move. He was now on British soil, which meant he had to add his native country to the things he had left behind.

Besides his life, he had only one other thing left to lose. He wrote *William Ryan, S. J.* on the wet sand, turned his back, and began walking.

His clothes were dry by the time he reached Freeport.

He experienced most of the next year or so through a haze of cheap rum. There were drugs too. Why not? What did he care? He didn't trust God anymore, at least not the God he'd been raised to believe in. And he didn't think of himself as a priest anymore, either. How could he? He could barely think of himself as human. Not after what he'd done. He'd smothered a child he'd loved more than anything in this world. Buried him alive. No matter that he'd done it out of love, to put the boy out of reach of the forces that were torturing him—he'd *done* it! He'd dug the hole and placed the child within and then he'd filled it.

An atrocity—*The* Atrocity, as he came to call it. And the memory of the weight of the dirt-laden shovel in his hands, the image of that small, struggling, blanket-shrouded form disappearing beneath the cascades of falling earth, was more than he could bear. He had to blot it out, all of it.

He lived in back-street rooms in Freeport on Grand Bahama, in Hope Town on Great Abaco, in Governor's Harbor on Eleuthera. His money didn't last long and he soon wound up on New Providence, bedding down on the sand each night—as hollow as the empty shells scattered around him—and during the day wandering Cable Beach selling bags of peanuts or shilling for the ride operators off Paradise Island, getting two bucks a head for every passenger he rounded up for the banana boats and five each for the parasails, spending it all on anything he could smoke, swallow, or snort to blot out the memory of The Atrocity.

He spent more than a year continually stoned or drunk or both. He recognized no limits. Whatever it took, he'd take. A couple of times he overdid it and nearly did himself in. More than once he seriously considered getting together enough stuff for a fatal overdose, but he kept putting it off.

Finally, his body rebelled. His flesh wanted to live even if his mind did not, and it refused to stomach any more liquor. He sobered up by default. And he found a clear head bearable. The Atrocity had receded into the past. The wounds it had left hadn't healed, but they had evolved from open sores to a cluster of steadily throbbing aches that flared only occasionally into agony.

And that agony plunged him again and again into the blackest despair. He was in a drugged stupor at the time, so he didn't remember the first anniversary of The Atrocity, but he'd never forget the second: He'd spent most of that New Year's Eve with the bore of a borrowed snub-nosed .357 Magnum pressed against his right eyelid. But he couldn't pull the trigger. By the time the sun rose on the new year, he'd decided to live a while longer, to see if he could set what was left of his life into some semblance of order.

He found he hadn't lost his knack with the internal combustion engine, so he managed to land a part-time job at Maura's Marina on Potter's Cay under the Paradise Island Bridge. His way with motors soon won him the respect and admiration of boatmen on both sides of the law, so when he began entertaining the notion of returning to the States, he asked the right people for advice and was shocked at how easy it was to buy a new identity.

Born again . . . as Will Ryerson.

They'd advised him to choose a name close to his own to make it easier to cover slips when speaking or writing the new one. Will Ryerson now seemed more like his real name than Bill Ryan ever had.

But Father Bill wasn't dead. Despite everything that had happened, the priest part of him still wanted very badly to believe in God. The Jesuit within him still pushed at the envelope of Will Ryerson's persona. So he'd made concessions to it. He'd begun to say his daily office again. He kept hoping he'd find a way to go back. But how? There was no statute of limitations on murder.

But during these past three years in North Carolina he had found a new equilibrium. He was not happy—he doubted he would ever be really happy again—but he had come to terms with his existence.

And now, on this sunny Saturday morning, he spotted one of the few bright spots in his life strolling along the sidewalk. A slim knockout of a blonde trailing a wake of turned heads. Lisl. And she was alone. She was hardly ever alone anymore. He stopped at the corner, blocking her path as she stepped off the curb.

"Hey, girlie! Wanna go for a spin?"

He saw her head come up, saw her upper lip start to curl as she readied a curt reply, then saw her smile. What a smile. Like the sun burning through low-lying clouds.

"Will! You've got the top down!"

"Perfect day for it. I'm serious about the spin. How about it?"

He was hoping she'd say yes. It seemed like an age since they'd had some decent time together to talk.

She hesitated for a second, then shrugged. "Why not? I'd have to be crazy to refuse."

He leaned over and pushed open the door for her.

"Been a long time, Leese."

"Too long," she said, sliding in and slamming it closed.

"Where do you want to go?"

"Anywhere. How about the highway? I want to go fast."

Bill headed out of town, wondering at the perversity of life. Here he was, a shabby, bearded, ponytailed, defrocked priest looking fifty in the eye, riding in a convertible under a perfect sky with a beautiful thirty-two-year-old windblown blonde. He felt like the high school burnout who'd just picked up the queen of the prom.

Maybe happiness wasn't an impossible dream.

"What are you grinning at?" Lisl asked.

"Nothing," he said. "Everything."

As he was overtaking someone on a bicycle, Lisl said, "Watch out for the geek."

Bill looked at her sharply. They'd passed this kid on his bike at least a hundred times in the past and she'd never made a crack like that. Although Bill didn't know his name, the kid was a familiar sight around town. He'd never spoken to him, but he could tell by his features, by the single-minded intensity with which he pedaled his bike, by his clothing and the incongruous fedora he wore every day, that he was mentally retarded. Bill could imagine the kid's mother making his lunch, stowing it in that dinky little knapsack on his back, and sending him off every morning. Probably worked at the Sheltered Workshop on the other end of town.

"Get up on the wrong side of bed this morning?"

"Not at all," Lisl muttered as they passed the kid. "They shouldn't allow mutants like that on the road."

"You're pulling my leg, aren't you? I don't know that kid, but I'm proud of him. Dressing himself, riding to work, and doing some manual labor probably taxes his abilities to their limit, yet he's out here on his bike every day, rain or shine, making it to work and back. You can't take that away from him. It's all he's got."

"Right. Until he has a spasm and gets hit by a car and his folks sue the driver for everything he's worth."

Bill reached over and felt her forehead. "You all right? Coming down with a fever?"

Lisl laughed. "I'm fine. Forget it."

Bill tried to do just that as they hit Route 40 and drove north, sailing along, talking about what they'd been doing, what they'd been reading, but in everything she said he detected subtle nuances of change. This Lisl was different from the woman he'd known for the past three years. She seemed to have calcified in the weeks since her Christmas party, as if she were building up a hard shell around herself. And all she seemed to want to talk about was Rafe Losmara.

"Any further word from the State Police on that weird telephone call?" he said, as much from a sincere desire to know as from a wish to move the conversation away from Rafe.

"No. Not a word. And I don't care. As long as I never have to hear that call again."

The way she shuddered reminded him of the old Lisl, and that was a relief.

Bill had been shaken up when Lisl had told him that the call was being investigated. And he still couldn't figure out how the North Carolina State Police had connected him with the call, or had wound up with that old photo of him. Had to be Renny Augustino's doing, especially since it sounded like the same photo the New York police had released five years ago. That one had been old even back then. Bill was now twenty pounds lighter and ten years older than the priest in that photo.

He was different in other ways too. That Christmas week in hell five years ago, plus the first year, the lost year of living on the edge in the Bahamas, had wrought their own set of changes. He'd hung out with scum during that year and had thought they were too good for him; he'd been cut and he'd had his nose mangled more than once in the drunken fights he'd started. Time had added deep furrows to his cheeks and alongside the scar on his forehead, and a bumper crop of gray to his hair. He was pulling that hair off his face now, usually tying it back, exposing the receding hairline at each temple. All that, plus the full beard, made him look more like a darker, heavier set version of Willie Nelson than the young, baby-faced Father Bill in the old photo. So he shouldn't have been surprised that Lisl hadn't recognized him. Yet he was. He wasn't used to good luck.

Traffic began to slow as the road became more crowded.

"Where's everybody going?" Lisl said.

"It's a warm sunny Saturday. Where else would everybody be going?"

Lisl sank back in the seat. "Of course. Big Country."

The giant amusement park *cum* African safari complex had opened a few years ago and had quickly become the biggest attraction on the eastern end of the state. The locals loved all the new jobs and the boost to the economy, but nobody liked the traffic jams.

"Want to go? We haven't been to the safari in a long time."

"No, thanks," she said with an emphatic shake of her head. "I'm not in the mood for crowds."

"No," he said, smiling, "I can see that you aren't."

Maybe she had PMS.

They finally came upon one of the contributing factors to the traffic jam—a stalled station wagon, an ancient Ford Country Squire, just like the one St. Francis used to own. The hood was up and a man in jeans and a flannel shirt was leaning over the engine. As they passed, Bill saw the stricken looks on the faces of the four kids in the back, the naked anger and resentment on the face of the overweight woman in the front passenger seat, and then he got a look at the man staring in bewilderment at the dead engine before him. Something in the fellow's eyes caught Bill in the throat. He read it all in a heartbeat—a laborer, not much dough but he'd promised to take the wife and kids to Big Country for the day. A rare treat. And now they weren't going anywhere. The tow truck and ensuing repairs would probably eat up much of his spare cash, and even if it didn't, the day would be spent by the time they got rolling again. If the man's eyes had shown plain old anger or frustration, Bill could have kept going. But what he saw in that flash was defeat. One more footprint on the back of an already struggling ego.

Bill swerved onto the shoulder in front of the wagon.

"What are you doing?" Lisl said.

"I'm going to get this guy going again."

"Bill, I don't want to sit here and—"

"Only be a minute."

He hurried over to the wagon. He knew the Country Squire engine like he knew his Breviary. If it wasn't anything major, he could fix it.

He leaned on the fender and looked across the engine at a man who was probably ten or fifteen years younger but didn't look it.

"She die on you?"

The fellow looked up at him suspiciously. Bill expected that. People tended to be leery of offers of help from bearded guys with ponytails.

"Yeah. Died while we were stopped during the jam. She cranks but she won't catch. I'm afraid I don't know much about cars."

"I do." Bill started spinning the wing nut on the air filter cover. When he'd exposed the carburetor he said, "Get in and hit the gas pedal. Once."

The fellow did as he was told and Bill noticed right away that the butterfly valve didn't move. *Stuck.* He smiled. This was going to be easy.

He freed the valve and held it open.

"All right," he called. "Give her a try."

The engine turned and turned but didn't catch.

"This is what it was doing before!" the driver shouted.

"Just keep going!"

And then it caught. The engine shuddered and shook and then roared to life with a huge belch of black smoke from the rear. These engines tended to do that. To the tune of children's cheers from the wagon's rear compartment, Bill ran to his own car, popped the trunk, and got some spray lubricant from his work box. He lubed the hinges on the valve, replaced the cover, and slammed the hood.

"Get that carburetor cleaned and that choke checked out as soon as you can," he told the man, "or this'll happen again."

The fellow held out a twenty to him but Bill pushed it back.

"Get those kids an extra hot dog."

"God bless you, mister," the woman said.

"Not likely," Bill said softly as they pulled away.

He returned the waves of the smiling kids hanging out the rear window, then walked up to his own car.

"There!" he said to Lisl as he started the Impala. "That didn't take too long."

"The Good Samaritan," she said with a sad shake of her head.

"Why not? It cost me nothing but a few minutes of doing the kind of thing I like to putter around with in my spare time anyway, and it literally saved the day for six people."

Lisl reached over and touched his hand.

"You're a good man, Will. But you shouldn't let everyone who comes along take advantage of your good nature. They'll eat you alive if you do."

Bill turned off at the next exit, looped on the overpass, and got back on the freeway heading south toward town. He was baffled by her attitude.

"No one took advantage of me, Lisl. I saw a fellow human being who needed a hand; I had no place I was hurrying to, so I lent him one. That's all. No big thing. I come away feeling a little better about myself, he goes away feeling better about other people. And somewhere inside I have this hope that I've started some kind of chain letter: Maybe the next time he sees someone who needs a hand, *he'll* stop. That's what it's all about,

Lisl. We're all in this mess together."

"Why do you need to feel better about yourself?"

The question caught him off guard. *Lady, if you only knew.*

"I . . . I think everybody does, a little. I mean, how many people don't feel they could be better or do better? I like to feel I can make a difference. I don't mean changing the world—although, come to think of it, if you make a change for the better in one person's life, you *have* changed the world, haven't you? An infinitesimal change, but the world, or at least a part of it, is better for your passing." He was pleased with the thought.

"If you want to be a sacrificial lamb, I'm sure you'll find plenty of people standing in line for a piece of you."

"But I'm not talking about sacrifice. I'm talking about simple good fellowship, acting like just another crewman on Spaceship Earth."

"But you're not a crewman. You're an officer. Think about it, Will. Can any of *them* do anything—really *do* anything—for you?"

He thought about that, and was frightened by the answer. Who out there in the world could help him? Was there anyone who could put his life right again?

"No," he said softly.

"Exactly. Primes stand alone. We're islands. We have to learn to exist apart from the rest."

Bill stared straight ahead at the road. *Lisl, you don't want to be an island. I know what it's like. I've been an island for five years, and it's hell.*

And then something she'd said struck a discordant note in his brain.

"Primes? Did you say Primes? What's that?"

She then launched into this involved dissertation on Primes and "others," punctuated everywhere with the phrase "Rafe says."

"What a load of elitist bullshit!" Bill said when she was through. "Does Rafe really believe that garbage?"

"Of course," she said. "And it's not garbage. That's your cultural conditioning speaking. Rafe says—"

"Never mind what Rafe says. What does *Lisl* say?"

"Lisl says the same thing. You and I and so many others have been conditioned to deny who we really are so that we can be more easily used. If you look around you, really look at the world, you'll see that it's true."

Bill stared at her.

"What's the matter with you, Leese?"

She turned on him, her face contorted with anger.

"Don't say that to me! My parents always said it and I don't want to hear it ever again!"

"Okay, okay," Bill said soothingly, startled by the outburst. "Be cool. I'm not your parent."

He spent the rest of the ride back to town trying to explain the shortcomings of Rafe's perverted egoism, how egoism in itself wasn't wrong, but when it refused to recognize the validity of all the other *I*'s around it, the result sacrificed not only logic but compassion as well.

But Lisl wasn't having any of it. She'd bought into Rafe's philosophy completely.

Slowly, a deep unease wormed through Bill.

What was happening here? It was almost as if Rafe had been reshaping Lisl from within—right under Bill's nose.

He saw how it had happened. Someone as vulnerable as Lisl was a sitting duck. A poor self-image, emotionally battered, and suddenly there was this enormously attractive young man telling her she's not the ugly duckling she's always considered herself, but a swan. A little love and affection to ease the deep emotional pains from her divorce, a little tenderness, a little patience, and Lisl opened up to him. But having her physically wasn't enough, apparently. He'd gone on to seduce her mind as well. Once her defenses were completely down, he began to fill the vacuum of her valueless upbringing, whispering a twisted philosophy that offered an easy road to the self-esteem she'd been denied for most of her life. But it was false self-esteem, gained at others' expense. And during the course of his remodeling job, Rafe had made himself Lisl's sun; she revolved around him now, her face turned always toward him, only him.

As they pulled into town, Lisl asked Bill to drop her off at the downtown lot where she'd left her car.

"Thanks for the ride, Will. It was great. But I want to get you and Rafe together real soon. He'll open your eyes. Wait and see—it'll be the best thing that ever happened to you."

She waved, then turned and headed for her car. Bill felt a terrible sadness as he watched her go.

I'm losing her.

Not losing her body, not her love—they weren't the important things for Bill where Lisl was concerned—but her mind, her soul.

Rafe. What was he doing to her? His involvement here seemed almost . . . sinister. But that had to be Bill's latent paranoia rearing its head. There was no plot here. Rafe was simply drawing Lisl into his own warped view of the world. Warped people tended to do that.

But in doing so he was turning Bill's only friend in the world into a stranger. Bill wasn't going to allow that. Lisl was too innocent, too decent a person at heart for him to sit back and watch all that was good within her get sucked down the black hole of a philosophy like Rafe's.

He had to help her fight back, even if she didn't want to fight back.

Bill knew he was late coming to the battle. He hadn't even known it was being waged until today. But he could not sit on the sidelines any longer.

The first order of business was to learn a little more about Rafe Losmara.

TWENTY-ONE

Everett Sanders sat alone in his office and chewed his twentieth white grape. He hadn't been able to find any decent peaches yesterday, so he'd settled for the grapes. He folded the Ziploc bag he'd brought them in and slipped it back into his brown paper lunch bag. He stashed the bag in his briefcase.

There. Lunch was done. Time for cigarette number six. He lit up and reached for his novel of the week: *The Scarlatti Inheritance* by Robert Ludlum. He was enjoying it immensely; so much so that he had read well past yesterday's quota of pages last night. He pulled the little notebook from his breast pocket. Yes, there it was. Last night's entry. He had actually completed today's quota before he'd finally turned in.

Which left Ev in something of a quandary. Any more reading during his lunch break today would put him further ahead, opening the possibility of having nothing to read on Saturday. Of course he could always start next week's book—usually first opened on Sunday afternoon—on Saturday, but that would move everything out of sequence for the coming week and he might be faced with an even worse problem next weekend.

A domino dilemma. Perhaps a book of short stories might solve the problem . . . he could sample a few as needed and then—

No. It was novels he liked and novels he would read.

Why not skip reading altogether today? It was Wednesday, after all, and he did have the meeting tonight. If he stayed a little later he could come home and go directly to bed at his usual hour of 11:30, immediately after the late news. All he had to do now was find a way to kill the lunch-hour time and he'd be almost home free.

But he had no backup plan for this lunch hour. That meant free time. Ev didn't like free time. It wasn't good for him. He knew from past experience that if he allowed his thoughts to roam free too long, they would roam the wrong way.

He was tempted to turn on his terminal and work on his paper for Palo Alto, but he had allotted time elsewhere in the day for that. He couldn't do that now.

Ev began to feel the first twinges of anxiety.

He went to the window and looked out to where Lisl used to take her lunch. He hadn't seen her with the groundskeeper lately. Maybe it was too cool these days for lunch al fresco.

As he smoked his cigarette and stared out at the deserted knoll, he began to experience another reason for avoiding unoccupied time: loneliness. A cluttered day left no time to ponder the emptiness of his existence.

And it is *empty, isn't it?*

He sighed as he exhaled the last of his cigarette. But that was how it had to be, at least for the time being. Perhaps in a few years, if he found the right someone, someone who could understand and accept him, he might be ready to make another commitment. He'd be past forty-five then. Kind of late in life to be thinking of marriage again. But other people did it all the time, so why couldn't he?

Perhaps because his first marriage had been so painful. Poor, long-suffering Diane—what he had put her through. She'd hung on longer than anyone had a right to expect while their marriage had died a lingering death, all because of him. Someday he might have the courage to try again and get it right the second time, but such a thing was impossible now. He still loved Diane.

He lit cigarette number seven and strolled into the hall. He had a sudden craving for human company but did not expect to find it in the department at lunch hour. Most of the faculty retreated to the lounge where they could eat in peace without interruption from students with questions and problems. Still, it was worth a look.

He pulled up short as he passed Lisl's office. The door was open and someone was in there. He backed up a step. Lisl, working away at her terminal. Industry. He liked that, especially in a woman. He hesitated, then knocked on her door frame.

"Working hard?" he said.

Lisl turned with a startled expression, then she smiled. She had a wonderful smile.

"Ev! How are you? What's up?"

"Nothing. Just wandering the halls, looking for someone to talk to. But if I'm disturbing you—"

"Don't be silly. Come in, come in. Let me exit this"—she pressed a couple of keys and her terminal beeped—"and we'll talk."

She rose from her terminal and approached her desk, motioning him to one of the chairs. She'd lost more weight and was very trim now. Absolutely smashing in her snug sweater and knee-length skirt. Not at all what one would expect in a mathematics professor. That gave Ev a twinge of concern. Lisl's level of attractiveness bordered on the unprofessional. A student might find it very difficult to concentrate on her words when she was parading before the class. He wondered if he should mention it to her . . . purely as a friend. Then again, maybe he should mind his own business.

"So," he said as he sat down, "working on your paper?"

"Yes. It's coming along pretty well. How about yours?"

"Oh, I'm bogged down on some of the calculations, but I think it's all going to work out in the end."

He wondered what her topic was but knew it wouldn't be proper to ask. He was sure she'd have a good paper, but he was also sure his would be better. He was very excited about it.

Silence hung between them.

"So," she said finally, "what have you been up to lately besides your paper? Anything exciting?"

He had to laugh. *Exciting? Me?* Excitement implied spontaneity, and for Ev spontaneity meant trouble. He had painstakingly arranged his life to eliminate the unexpected, structured his days so that each one followed a predictable pattern, so that every Tuesday was just like every other Tuesday. Excitement? There was no room in his life for excitement. He had carefully seen to that.

"Well, I'm reading a rather exciting novel at the moment—an oldie but a goodie, you might say. It's—"

"Excuse me," said a voice behind him. "Am I interrupting something?"

Ev turned and saw that Losmara fellow Lisl had been keeping company with. He wondered what she saw in him. He was not at all the sort Ev would have matched with Lisa. Too delicate. Lisa seemed the type who'd be more at home with a beefier male, one with more physical presence. But none of this was any real concern of his. Over the years he'd learned to mind his own business.

"Hi, Rafe," Lisl said. "You remember Dr. Sanders?"

"Of course," Losmara said, stepping forward and extending his hand. "I've been auditing a few of your lectures."

"Have you now?" Ev said, rising and shaking hands. "I don't remember seeing you there."

The young man smiled. "I usually take a seat in a back row. I'm there just to listen, to keep a honed edge on my math. You can't let your math get rusty in my end of psych."

Ev felt his attitude toward Losmara warming. Maybe there was more to him than he'd thought, some real depth behind that dandified, rich-kid appearance.

"I hope they're useful."

"They're telling me what I want to know."

Ev saw a look pass between Lisl and Losmara and realized he was a fifth wheel here.

"Well, I've got some odds and ends to clear up in my office. Nice talking to you, Lisl. And good luck to you, Mr. Losmara."

They shook hands again and Ev left the two lovers alone. He still didn't approve of faculty-student affairs, even when there was no academic relationship, but he had to admit that Rafe Losmara's attitude toward learning indicated that he had the makings of a fine scholar.

"You're auditing Ev's lectures?" Lisl said after she'd closed her office door.

Rafe smiled. "Know thine enemy."

"Ev's not an enemy."

"You wouldn't think someone as prissy and ineffective as he could pose a threat, but don't be surprised when he gets tenure and you're left out in the cold."

"He won't if my paper's as good as I think it is—as you say it is."

"The relative quality of your papers is irrelevant. In the end the only thing that will matter is sex."

"Sex?"

"Yes. He's a male. You're a female. He'll get the post because of his 'Y' chromosome, because of what hangs between his legs."

"Bull, Rafe."

He'd alluded to this before but Lisl refused to buy it. Still wouldn't.

Rafe shrugged. "Suit yourself. Stick your head in the sand and hope for the best. That's the way Primes always get cheated out of what they deserve—they let the leeches snatch it from under their noses."

"Ev's not a leech. He's one of us."

"Ev?" He barked a laugh. "Everett Sanders? A Prime? You've got to be kidding!"

"He's got a brilliant mind, Rafe. One of the cleverest mathematicians I've ever met. He stands alone, he doesn't need the approval of the crowd—an island if there ever was one. All the things you say distinguish a Prime."

"He's a nonentity, a misfit, little more than an actor," Rafe said. His voice dripped with scorn. "He plays at being a whiz but he's nothing more than an accomplished poseur."

When Rafe got like this—sniping at her opinions, goading her—she could almost hate him.

"You're not qualified to judge his work!" Lisl snapped.

The remark had the desired effect. Rafe turned to her with raised eyebrows, a smile playing about his lips.

"But I'm not judging his work, Lisl. I'm judging the man. I say he's one of *them,* and with a little help from you, I can prove it."

Lisl took a deep breath. She was almost afraid to hear this.

"What sort of help?"

"His keys. Get me his keys for half an hour and I'll have what I need."

"How can I—?"

"Make up a story. You lost your key to the front door of the building or something. Charm him, but get those keys."

"And what are you going to do with them?"

"Never mind." His half smile broadened into a grin. "You'll know soon enough. Do you accept the challenge?"

Without replying, Lisl walked past him, through the door, and down the hall. She knocked on Ev's open door.

"Ev?" she said as he looked up from his desk. "I left my storeroom key home. Can I borrow yours?"

"Of course, Lisl."

He went to his suit coat that was neatly hung on a hanger behind the door, reached into a side pocket, and produced a jangle of keys. He picked out one and held it up for her as he handed her the entire ring.

"This one's for the storeroom," he said.

"I'll get these right back to you," she said.

"No hurry, Lisl," he said with a smile. "I trust you."

Damn, she thought as she thanked him. *Why'd you have to say that?*

Lisl's pace was slower as she headed back to her office. She had a queasy feeling in the pit of her stomach, a sudden urge to run back and wrap the key ring in Ev's bony fingers and tell him never, never, *never* to let her get near them again. But she couldn't give into that sort of groundless feeling. What would Rafe think?

There were times—and this was one of them—when she wondered if she let what Rafe thought matter too much to her. But she couldn't help it. It did matter. *Rafe* mattered. And she was so afraid he would find her out, afraid she'd do something to give herself away. Because she was convinced she wasn't really a Prime. Sure, Rafe called her one and didn't seem to have any doubts about it, but Lisl was riddled with them. She felt like a fake. She'd read where a lot of accomplished people—neurosurgeons, judges, statesmen—felt the same way . . . felt deep inside that their lives were shams, that their success had been a combination of luck and cleverness and that they were nothing at all like the brilliant individuals people perceived them to be, that they lived in fear of the misstep that would reveal their true nothing selves.

Lisl had experienced vaguely similar feelings all through college and her post-graduate training. The work had been a breeze, her professors had told her time and again what a brilliant mind she had as they'd raved about her papers, yet deep inside she'd never believed them. Rafe, she was sure, would lay the blame for all her insecurities on the way her parents had treated her, but finger pointing wouldn't help Lisl get past the idea that all her academic accomplishments were nothing more than a bubble that one day would burst and allow the world to see the naked, frightened, inadequate little girl inside.

Lisl was sure Brian had peeked inside the bubble. That had to be why he'd left her. She wasn't going to let Rafe find out. She'd go on acting like one of his Primes as long as she could get away with it. It was mostly an attitude, of dividing up the world into people who mattered and people who didn't, the few worth knowing and the great many not worth thinking about. She'd been practicing. It didn't come naturally but she was getting the hang of it. And maybe if she acted like a Prime long enough, she'd actually become one.

So she'd let Rafe have the keys, but she wasn't going to let him pull any of his tricks on Ev. Ev was too nice a man.

She returned to her office and dropped the key ring in his outstretched palm.

"Here they are," she said. "But I hope you're not planning any nastiness."

Rafe shrugged. "Dirty tricks? They're fun, but we've pulled enough of them on Brian during the last month to carry us the rest of the year, don't you think?"

Lisl had to smile. Yes, they had indeed. They'd purchased subscriptions to *The Advocate* and other homosexual publications for his office waiting room; Rafe had applied for membership in NAMBLA—the North American Man-Boy Love Association— in Brian's name; and on a couple of occasions they'd sat in his waiting room and slipped samples of hardcore gay pornography between the pages of *People* and *Time* and *Good Housekeeping*. Dr. Brian Callahan's sexual orientation was now seriously in question among his peers at the medical center.

The pièce de résistance had been the sign they had taped to the passenger side of Brian's black Porsche one night shortly before he'd driven it home from the hospital. In fluorescent orange letters on black paper it had read: BACK OFF! THIS CAR KILLS NIGGERS WHO TOUCH IT!

It had been dark in the parking lot and Brian had approached on the driver side. He had no inkling of the sign's existence until he pulled to a stop at a light in the downtown black section and a group of infuriated youths attacked the car. Lisl and Rafe had been following a few car lengths behind. They watched the kids pound on his windows, break off his radio and car phone antennae, and kick dents in his doors and fenders. Lisl was shocked when she caught herself avidly hoping they'd get a door open and vent some of their rage on Brian himself. The idea that she could hunger for something like that sickened her. Everyone had a dark side, but hers seemed so close to the surface now. That worried her.

But Brian roared away before they could touch him. Before he got away, the kids tore off the sign and shredded it, so no doubt he still was baffled as to what had precipitated the attack on his car.

But she'd noticed him taking a longer, more circuitous route home these days.

"They seem kind of childish now," Lisl said, worrying anew about the darkness she had discovered within herself.

"That's because they've served their purpose. They taught you that he does not have all the power, that you actually have power over him. You can make his life miserable when you choose and you can leave him alone when you choose. When *you* choose— that's the lesson. And now that you've learned it we can move on to other things, leaving Dr. Callahan lying awake at nights wondering who, wondering why, wondering what next?"

"I don't want to leave Ev like that."

"Don't worry. We're just going to do a little snooping on Professor Sanders. That's all. See what makes him tick."

"Nothing more. You promise?"

"I won't need anything more to prove to you that he's a phony."

"You're wrong this time, Rafe. I think Ev is one of those people where what you see is what you get."

"There is no such person," Rafe snapped. "And I'll prove it to you tonight when we search his apartment."

Lisl's stomach lurched. Wasn't that breaking and entering? And wasn't that going just a bit too far? But she couldn't back down. Not now. She couldn't surrender to Rafe's theory about Ev. Because she knew he was wrong.

"We can't do that. Not—not while he's there."

"He won't be," Rafe said. "It's Wednesday night. He goes out every Wednesday night."

"He does?" She had difficulty imagining Ev going out at all. "Where?"

"I don't know. Maybe we'll follow him sometime. But tonight we'll take advantage of his unfailing routine and check out his digs, see what makes him tick."

"Is this fair, Rafe?"

He laughed. "Fair? What's fair got to do with it? This is a leech posing as a Prime! We've got to set things right."

"Why do we have to—"

"In fact," Rafe went on, beginning to move about the office, slashing the air with his hand, "I've got a feeling Dr. Everett Sanders is a fag."

"Knock it off, Rafe."

"No. I'm serious. I mean, consider his name—Ev. What normal man lets himself be called *Ev*? It's effeminate. And he's such a priss, so neat and particular. Like a maiden aunt. And have you ever seen him with a woman?"

"No. But I've never seen him with a man, either. Maybe he's just asexual."

"Maybe. But he's hiding something. You can count on that. Have you seen his CV?"

"No. Why would I—?"

"There's ten years missing. He graduated cum laude from Emory, worked for a few years, then entered the masters program at Duke, went on for his doctorate, then came here to Darnell."

"What's wrong with that? Lots of people work in the real world before going on for postgraduate degrees."

"Right. But there's a ten-year blank spot in his curriculum vitae."

"Ten years?"

Rafe nodded and placed his hands on her shoulders, his fingers brushing the base of her neck, raising delicious gooseflesh along her arms.

"Like he dropped off the face of the earth. He's not telling anybody what he did with those years, which means he's hiding something. And we're going to find out what it is."

He began to knead the tense muscles in her neck and shoulders, magically relaxing them. She closed her eyes and reveled in the soothing sensations. As always, Rafe's touch caused her doubts to dwindle, her fears to fade. Nothing mattered more than keeping him by her side. As she listened to Rafe's soft voice, she found herself falling in line with his way of thinking. Her interest was piqued now.

What *was* Ev hiding?

Everett Sanders, Ph. D., where the fuck are you?

Renny sat and smoked a cigarette on the stoop outside the apartment house. Waiting. He'd been waiting here most of the day. This guy Sanders had to show up sooner or later. He hoped for sooner.

He was almost out of names. And just about out of hope. He'd checked out all but two of the people on Lisl Whitman's guest list. If he didn't hit pay dirt with this one or the final one, he'd be forced to write this whole trip off as a complete bust. No way. Too much time and money and goodwill back at Midtown North down the tubes for that. He needed to score here.

More than just a score—he needed to strike it rich. He needed Everett Sanders, Ph.D., aka Father William Ryan, S.J., to walk up the steps, head bowed, lost in thought. Renny would recognize him in an instant and say, "Hey, Father Bill. How's Danny doing?" Then he'd land a right hook and knock him back to the sidewalk. And extradition be damned, he'd haul him back to Queens for arraignment.

A dream. A pipe dream.

As he was scuffing his latest cigarette butt into oblivion on the stone stoop, a bony guy in a tan raincoat started up the steps. At first glance he looked older, but close up Renny pegged him as somewhere in his mid-forties. This sallow, bifocaled ghost wasn't Ryan, that was for sure. And hopefully he wasn't Sanders, either. Because if he was, that left only one more name to check.

"Excuse me," Renny said, reaching for his badge. He'd been using his NYPD shield but not giving anyone a good enough look at it to realize that it had been issued a long way from North Carolina.

The man stopped abruptly and stared at him.

"Yes?" His voice was cool, dry—like the desert at night.

"Would you be Professor Sanders?" *Please say no.*

"Why, yes. Who are you?"

Damn! "I'm Detective Sergeant Augustino with the State Police"—a quick flash of his medal in midsentence—"and I'm investigating an incident at Dr. Lisl Whitman's party last month."

"Party? Incident?" The man's expression was genuinely confused for a moment, then it cleared. "Oh, you mean the Christmas party. Why would you be investigating her party?"

"There was a sort of obscene phone call and—"

"Oh, yes. I remember her mentioning that. It seemed to have upset her terribly. But I'm sorry—I can't help you."

Renny put on a smile. "You may be able to help more than you know. You see, lots of times—"

"I wasn't there, Sergeant."

Automatically, Renny looked down at the slip of paper in his hand.

"But your name's on the list."

"I was invited but I didn't go. I don't go to parties."

Renny gave Dr. Sanders's prim, fastidious exterior another quick up-and-down.

No, I guess you don't.

"Well then, maybe you can help this way." He pulled the Father Ryan photo from his inner pocket and held it out to Sanders. "Ever seen this guy before? Anywhere?"

Sanders started to shake his head, then stopped. He took the picture from Renny and stared at it, cocking his head this way and that.

"Strange . . ."

Renny felt his heart pick up its tempo.

"Strange? What's strange? You've seen him?"

"I'm not sure. He looks vaguely familiar but I can't quite place him."

"Try."

He glanced at Renny through the upper half of his glasses.

"I'm doing just that, I assure you."

"Sorry." *Twit.*

Finally Sanders shook his head and handed the picture back.

"No. It won't come. I'm quite sure I've seen him somewhere but just when and just where I can't say."

Renny bit down on his impatience and pushed the picture back at him.

"Take your time. Take another look."

"I've looked quite enough, thank you. Never fear. I never forget a face. It will come to me. Give me your number and I'll call you when it does."

Out of habit, Renny reached for his wallet where he kept a supply of cards—New York City cards. He diverted his hand to his breast pocket for his pen and notebook.

"I'm right here in town for the moment." He wrote down the number of the motel where he was staying. "If I'm not in, leave your number and I'll get back to you."

"Very well." He took the slip of notepaper and started up the steps toward the front door.

"Sure you don't want to take another look?"

"I've committed it to memory. I'll be in touch. Good day, Sergeant."

"Good day, Professor Sanders."

What a tight-ass.

But Renny didn't care if Sanders farted in C above high C, as long as he remembered the guy who reminded him of Father Ryan.

There was a new lightness to his step as he hopped down to the sidewalk and headed for the last name on his list—Professor Calvin Rogers. Too old, apparently, to be Ryan. A wasted trip, probably, but Renny wasn't leaving anything to chance. After all, look what a five-minute conversation with this Professor Sanders had turned up.

Yeah. Renny had a gut feeling Sanders was going to turn this trip around.

"I don't believe we're doing this," Lisl said in a low voice as she followed Rafe into the vestibule of Ev's apartment building.

"Nothing to it," he said, and handed her a shiny new key, fresh cut from Ev's own this afternoon.

Reluctantly she took it. She had the jitters.

"I don't like this, Rafe."

"It's not as if we're going to steal anything. We're just going to look around. So let's get going. The sooner we get in there, the sooner we'll be out."

Unable to argue with the logic of that, and wanting very much to have this over and done with, Lisl unlocked the vestibule door. With Rafe in the lead, half dragging her up the narrow stairs, they climbed to the third floor. Outside apartment 3B, Rafe handed her another key. Her fingers were slippery with perspiration now.

"What if he's in there?"

"Put your ear to the door," Rafe said.

Lisl did. "The phone's ringing."

Rafe nodded, smiling. "Remember that call I made before we left?"

"When you left the phone off the hook?"

"Right. This is the number I called. There was no answer then, and if it's still ringing, it means he hasn't come back while we were in transit."

Wondering at the deviousness of Rafe's mind, Lisl checked the hall to make sure no one was watching, then unlocked Ev's apartment door and hurried inside. When the door was closed behind them, she allowed herself to relax—just a little.

Rafe found the light switch, then the phone; he lifted the receiver long enough to stop the ring, then replaced it.

Silence.

"Now," he said. "Where do we begin?"

Lisl looked around. Her immediate impression was that nobody lived here. The only personal item was the computer terminal, a duplicate of hers, with a dedicated line to Darnell's Cray II. Remove that and the apartment was like a hotel room after the cleaning crew had passed through—freshly spruced up and waiting for someone to rent it. It wasn't decorated like a hotel room, not with this motley collection of furniture, but it had that just-cleaned, everything-in-its-place look and feel. She wondered idly if there was a paper ribbon across the toilet seat.

"Let's get out of here," she said.

"We just got here." He strolled from the front living room to the study at the rear, into the bedroom, and back again. "The man lives like a monk—a neatnik monk with vows of cleanliness and orderliness."

"Nothing un-Prime about that," Lisl said.

"Yes, there is. It shows an obsessive-compulsive personality. A Prime would be able to overcome it."

"Maybe he's a damaged Prime, like me."

Rafe gave her a long look. "Maybe. But I'll reserve judgment until after we've made our search."

"All right, but let's hurry. I don't want him coming back and finding us here."

"He won't. But be careful to put everything back just the way you found it. And let me know when you come across anything that looks like a bank book. We both have a pretty good idea what Darnell is paying him and we know he can live better than this. Where's his money going?" His grin became wolfish. "Maybe somebody's blackmailing him."

Lisl opened the refrigerator. It was pitiful inside. Nonfat yogurt, orange juice, fruit, corn oil margarine, some lettuce, a red pepper, and some low-fat Swiss cheese.

Rafe glanced in over her shoulder.

"He eats like you do."

"Maybe he's a health nut—or he's got a cholesterol problem."

But Rafe had already wandered over to Ev's computer terminal.

"My, my," he said, flipping through a notebook on the desk. "Here are all his access codes for his files in memory. Dear Ev believes in security."

They began going through the drawers. There weren't many in the apartment, so it wasn't long before Rafe came across Ev's financial records. He shook his head and whistled as he paged through them.

"Rent, utilities, and food . . . rent, utilities, and food . . . that's all he uses his money for. The rest is all in CDs and zero-coupon bonds in IRAs and Keoghs. He's loaded."

Lisl couldn't repress a smile of satisfaction.

"There. I told you. He's a Prime. He'll be able to retire in another ten years."

"We're missing something," Rafe said.

"Like what?" She was getting annoyed now. "What could we be missing? There are no drugs or alcohol here, not so much as a bottle of sherry, no gay magazines, no child porn, no notes from a blackmailer. Give it up, Rafe. The man's clean. And he's a Prime."

"We still don't know where he is tonight, or every other Wednesday night for that matter. Once we know that, I'll rest my case . . . or bow to yours."

"How are we supposed to find that out?"

"Simple. Next Wednesday night we'll follow him."

Games . . . Rafe loved games. But at least following Ev wasn't illegal—not like snooping through his apartment.

"All right. We'll do that. But let's get out of here. Back to my place." A fiery desire was growing within her. "I know something we can do that's a lot more fun. And legal too."

They made sure everything was just as they had found it, then they hurried back to Rafe's car. Lisl took the lead on the way out.

Bill edged his old Impala out of the parking lot and into the flow along Conway Street. Traffic was light and he was in no hurry. He'd just seen *Who Framed Roger Rabbit?* for the third time and he was in a great mood. Each time he found something new to marvel at. He'd tried watching it at home once on a rented cassette but it wasn't the same. When he'd read that The Strand was running a big-screen revival, he'd jumped at the chance for another look.

As he pulled to a stop at a light, he noticed a familiar-looking sports car to his right on the side street, waiting to make a left turn. A Maserati. In the bright, diffused peach glow of the mercury vapor lamps that lined Conway, Bill recognized Rafe Losmara at the wheel, speaking animatedly to someone next to him. Once again Bill was struck by the feeling that they'd met before. Something tantalizingly familiar about his face.

He wondered who Rafe was with. He almost hoped it wasn't Lisl. He didn't want to see her hurt but he was convinced that Rafe was no good for her, that his twisted values were behind the appalling deterioration in Lisl's character.

Maybe Rafe was out with somebody else tonight. If so, perhaps Bill could find a way to use that as a wedge between Lisl and him. All the standard objections rolled through his mind—*It's none of your business, she's a big girl, a grown woman, you're not her father, not even her uncle, and even if you were, she has a right to choose her lovers and her values*—and he let them roll right out again. All valid, but his feelings for Lisl overruled them. Lisl was heading for a fall—Bill knew it as sure as he knew his real name—and he wanted to catch her before she did. Because she might not come back from this crash. And if Bill couldn't save the one friend he had left in the world, he might not come back, either.

As the Maserati made the turn and swung around the front of Bill's car, he recognized Lisl in the passenger seat. He cursed in disappointment and shot one last glance at Rafe.

A wordless cry escaped Bill as the street seemed to tilt under his car. Close up, in the strange mercury glow that gelled the air, Rafe's mustache seemed to fade away, and his face . . . it looked . . . just like . . .

Sara!

And then he was past, gone, out of sight, his car a receding blob of red. But the vision remained, floating before Bill's eyes.

Sara!

Why hadn't he seen it before? The resemblance was unmistakable. He could be her brother!

What if he *was* her brother?

But how could that be? And why would he be here? What possible purpose—?

Lisl! Was he going to hurt Lisl like his sister had hurt Danny?

The blare of a horn from behind startled Bill and he looked up. The light was green. His slick palms slipped on the wheel as he pulled over to the curb and shut off the engine.

He sat behind the wheel, trembling, sweating, trying to get a grip as the wild thoughts raced through his head.

Wait. Stop. This was crazy.

Rafe had looked like Sara for an instant. So what? That was scary, but he wasn't Sara, and the odds of someone related to Sara showing up as a graduate student at the same university where Bill was working under an assumed identity were astronomical.

And yet . . .

Bill couldn't shake the feeling that a veil had parted for an instant and allowed him a peek at a deadly secret. He couldn't ignore it. He had to follow it up. Now. But he couldn't do it himself. He couldn't raise his profile. He needed help. But who? How? He searched for a way, a name. And he knew: Nick.

He scooped the pile of change out of his ashtray and started the car. He drove until he saw a phone booth, stopped, jumped out, and lifted the receiver.

The sweat was pouring out of him now.

Just once . . . just this once, let me get a dial tone.

There was dead air, then a click. The operator? His heart was pounding. A minute . . . that was all he needed. Just a minute of conversation, even if it was with Nick's answering machine.

"Hello? Hello?"

And then came the voice, the awful, too-familiar child's voice.

"Father, please come and get me! Pleee—!"

With a groan, Bill slammed the receiver down and ran for his car. Behind him the pay phone began to ring . . . continuously. He could still hear it echoing in his mind over the sound of his roaring engine as he gunned out of earshot.

He headed for home and along the way he searched his memory for everything Lisl had ever told him about Rafe Losmara. He had it all arranged in his mind by the time he reached his computer. He accessed the DataNet network and found the bulletin board. He typed out a message to Nick.

    TO EL COMEDO
    NEED BACKGROUND CHECK ON ONE RAFE LOSMARA . . .

He gave as much background as he could, Rafe's undergraduate school, year of graduation, anything he could remember from Lisl's glowing rambles about him, but he scrupulously avoided any mention of Rafe's present circumstances or whereabouts. He had to be careful here. Too much current data in the message would allow some nosy busybody in the network to contact Rafe and let him know that he was being investigated.

Bill closed with a circumspect note that he hoped would spur Nick to dig as deeply and quickly as he could:

    . . . CHECK FOR POSSIBLE RELATION TO THE MISSING MYS-
    TERY WOMAN WE WERE LOOKING FOR LAST TIME WE WERE
    TOGETHER. CHECK WITH OUR POLICE FRIEND. MAYBE HE CAN
    HELP OUT. PLEASE HURRY. URGENT, URGENT, URGENT!
                                        IGNATIUS

Bill signed off and leaned back in his chair. He didn't have to leave it all to Nick. At lunch break tomorrow he could hit the university library and see if there was some way he could get hold of a copy of the Arizona State yearbook from last year.

Probably all a wild goose chase. No way Rafe and Sara could be related. Just a freak combination of light and shadow, nothing more.

Bill couldn't repress a shudder at the memory of how *much* Rafe had looked like Sara in that instant.

He picked up his Breviary and tried to concentrate on his daily office.

This isn't working.

In the dark of her bedroom, Lisl coiled her arms around Rafe's neck and thrust her pelvis down against his. She'd wanted tonight to be different. Insisted, in fact. No belt, no symbolic beating, no taunts, no shouting, no catharsis—just lovemaking, pure and simple. So that was what they had done: strip, turn the lights off, and meet under the sheets.

But it wasn't working. Rafe had only half his usual tumescence, had even had difficulty penetrating her. Even now, sliding within her, she sensed his softness, his listlessness.

Suddenly she was angry. He wasn't going to cooperate. Was this how it was? If they didn't approach sex his way, he'd participate, but just barely? In a sudden burst of fury, she bit him on the shoulder.

Rafe started and groaned in her ear; she felt him harden within her as he began moving more ardently against her. She bit him again, deeper, tasting blood this time. Lisl couldn't help laughing as she felt him harden further, becoming stiff and straight as a broom handle. And like a witch, she rode him into the night.

TWENTY-TWO

Everett Sanders stood at the curb along the lower rim of the south parking lot and pretended to be a casual bystander watching three members of the grounds crew replace a section of hose in the underground sprinkler system. But his interest wasn't casual and he really wasn't watching the work.

He tried not to be obvious about it, but he wanted to get a close-up look at one of the workers. The one with the beard and the short ponytail. Lisl's friend.

Ever since that state policeman had shown him the photo, Ev had been plagued by a tantalizing sense of familiarity about that face. He'd always been good with faces—terrible with names, but he never forgot a face. He could run into a student he'd taught for a single semester and hadn't seen for years and immediately remember the course, the student's usual seat, and his or her final grade. But he'd be lost as to the name.

So when the policeman had shown him the photo, he'd been positive he'd seen that face before. It had taken him a whole week, but he was now ninety percent sure that the young priest in the photo and Lisl's groundskeeper friend were one and the same. Lisl and the fellow had lunched together outside last Friday and again yesterday. Ev had used his binoculars to watch him while they sat together under the bare elm but it hadn't been enough. The man's end of the conversation had been animated, with much head movement and many hand gestures, and Ev hadn't been able to get a good look.

He had decided yesterday that he would have to get closer to obtain that final ten percent of certainty. For he insisted on being completely sure before he pointed his finger at a man. A little disconcerting to break out of his usual daily routine—especially on a Wednesday afternoon when his time was always tightly budgeted—and wander the grounds looking for a mysterious stranger, but he reminded himself he was doing this to protect Lisl.

But he had found him and now little bursts of excitement twitched in his nerve endings as he edged closer. This was almost like private detective work, like being Sam Spade or Philip Marlowe for a day.

He noticed that although the man in question worked well with the others, he didn't seem completely a part of them. He talked with them, laughed at their jokes, but didn't seem to truly belong. Ev had the feeling that there was something within the man that kept him forever one step removed.

Like me.

"You get any closer, mister, you gon' fall in."

Ev was startled by the voice. As the other groundsmen laughed, he glanced up and smiled at the big shovel-wielding redhead who had spoken.

"I don't mean to disturb your work."

"Oh, you ain't disturbin' nothin'. But you sure ain't helpin', neither."

Ev wasn't sure if there was an undercurrent of hostility in the man's voice, or if he was just pulling his leg.

"I was just curious as to how deep in the ground you had to lay the hosing."

"Shoot! Ah don' know 'bout you, man, but Ah ain't abouta lay mah hose in the ground, Ah kin tell you that! Nossir!"

Amid renewed laughter, Lisl's groundsman looked up at Ev with his clear blue eyes. He was down on his knees, adjusting a coupling.

"Aren't you Professor Sanders?"

Ev was somewhat taken aback at being recognized.

"Why . . . yes."

"I thought so. Well, Professor, down here we don't have to bury the hose too deep at all. A few inches will usually do. But up where you get a deep freeze, you've either got to lay the hose below the frost line or drain the system every fall."

Ev could tell by the trace of a northern accent in the man's voice that he knew about cold winters. He studied the face, looking for that last ten percent of certainty, but couldn't find it. And up close, the nose was all wrong.

The man shot a glance at the redhead.

"I'm surprised at you, Clancy," he said. "How'd you let that remark about freezing hose get by?"

Clancy smiled. "Ah guess Ah was too shook up thinking 'bout havin' to wait till fall to get mah hose drained."

And in that instant, as Lisl's groundsman laughed with the others, Everett found what he'd been looking for. It was in the eyes. When he smiled, his lids, eyes, and eyebrows crinkled in a way that was identical to the photo.

"Thank you," Ev said, hiding his satisfaction.

"You clear on all this now?" Clancy said.

"Yes. I've learned precisely what I came to know."

He hurried back to his office, intent on calling the State Police immediately, but by the time he reached his desk he'd had second thoughts. Everyone had secrets—Lord knew, Everett had his own. Did he have a right to do the State Police's work for them and expose this man's?

The question plagued him the rest of the afternoon. He'd almost come to the decision to tear up the slip of paper with the state cop's name on it when he saw Lisl in the hall. She glanced at him, gave a quick wave, then turned away. She'd been acting that way for nearly a week. Almost as if she were avoiding him. Had he done something to offend her? He couldn't think of anything. But seeing her reminded him of just how disturbed this groundsman must be. He remembered how upset Lisl had been by that phone call in the middle of her Christmas party. It had ruined the whole day for her. The memory of her distress the following week angered him.

Perhaps his fingering this man as her tormentor might change her opinion of Ev. He knew she thought of him as a very stiff and very dull man. Which he was. Ev was the first to admit it. He was no fun. But maybe Lisl would warm up to him a little if he did this for her. He didn't want much. Maybe a smile, a touch on the arm once in a while. There was no warmth in his life, hadn't been any for too long.

A little warmth. That wasn't too much to ask.

Ev stepped back into his office and dialed the number the detective had given him. A motel switchboard answered—the Red Roof on the edge of town. The operator rang the room half a dozen times, then said that Mr. Augustino wasn't in. She offered to take a message. Ev told her he'd call back later. He wanted to make sure the detective got the information firsthand.

He closed up his office and took the number with him. He'd call again from home.

I must have Lisl on the brain today.

Ev stood at his living-room window and looked down on the street. He'd been passing by a moment ago while cleaning up after dinner—eight ounces of baked chicken, a cup of frozen peas, and a small can of corn niblets—and could have sworn he'd seen Lisl passing under the streetlight below. But when he'd looked again, she was gone. Must have been someone else. After all, what would Lisl be doing wandering around down here? She was probably out having dinner with that Losmara fellow. And after dinner they'd probably go back to his place or hers and . . .

He glanced at the clock on the wall, then at his watch. They both read 7:32. He knew it was the right time because he checked them regularly against the Weather Channel's clock. Time to go. The meeting didn't start until 8:00 but Ev always liked to get there early and grab a cup of coffee while the urn was still fresh. Especially since he'd forgone his after-dinner coffees and cigarettes to save them for the meeting. Heavy smoking and coffee drinking were the rule at the meetings, and he didn't want to go over his daily limits.

The Weather Channel had said there was a possibility of rain so he put on his raincoat and stuffed his Totes rain hat in the pocket. He made a last check of the apartment, made sure all the dinner dishes and utensils were put away, then headed for the street.

As was his custom, he stopped at Raftery's front window and watched the drinkers inside for exactly one minute. As he was turning away he caught a flash of blond hair down the street. For a moment he thought it was Lisl standing in a doorway. But when he squinted through the darkness for a better look, he saw nothing.

He continued on his way, wondering why Lisl would be on his mind like this. He knew he'd been thinking about her more than usual, but that was because of the photo the detective had shown him. At least he hoped that was why. Ev was well aware of how prone he was to obsessions. He didn't want her to become one. Not Lisl. Not a colleague.

He continued on his way. It was only a few more blocks to the St. James Episcopal Church. When he got there, he bypassed the imposing granite front steps and went around to a small wooden door on the north side.

"There!" said Lisl, unable to resist gloating. "There's his big bad secret. A clandestine meeting in the church basement."

She rubbed her chilled hands together as they stood in a shadowed doorway across the street from the church. The excitement of following Ev along the darkened street, of ducking out of sight every time he paused or turned around, had left her feeling a little wired.

She glanced at Rafe, who had remained silent since Ev had entered the church.

"Come on, Rafe," she said. "Cheer up. Don't take it so hard because he didn't sneak off to some gay leather bar. You can't win them all."

"What do you think our friend Everett is doing in there?" Rafe said finally.

"Who knows? Maybe he's a deacon or something."

"Has he ever struck you as a religious man?"

Lisl considered that. She couldn't remember Ev ever referring to God, even once. She didn't know of many people who got into higher math and still believed in God.

"No. But we both know from last week that his apartment is a model of frugality, sobriety, and orderliness. I don't think it's much of a leap to accept him as a churchgoer."

"Perhaps not. But I'm still not convinced he's not hiding something."

"Give it up, Rafe. He's one of us. He's a Prime." She liked the idea of recognizing Ev as an official member of the club.

"Maybe. But I won't be convinced until I know what's going on in there."

"It's a *church*, Rafe."

"I'm aware of that. But I'm also aware that churches traditionally allow civic and community groups to use their basements and function rooms. I wonder what group is in the basement tonight?"

"What difference does it make?"

"For all we know it could be a self-help group for child molesters or transvestites or—"

"Really, Rafe. Must you?"

She couldn't see his face in the darkness, but she hoped he wasn't wearing that sardonic half smile of his. They stood there in silence for a while and watched other figures approach the church and enter the side door; men outnumbered women three to one; they were mostly middle-aged but a few looked barely out of their teens; some came in pairs but the vast majority arrived alone. By 8:10 the flow stopped.

"Well, what do you think?" Rafe said when it seemed that everyone who was coming had arrived. "I counted a couple of dozen. An unwieldy number for a good orgy."

"You know, Rafe, you're impossible at times."

"I don't mean to be. I just want to know. Knowledge is power, as they say."

"Then go over there and find out."

"No. I want you to go. Because if I come back with a tale of some wild Satanic rites, you'll think I'm putting you on. You see for yourself and then come back and tell me. Whatever you say, I'll believe, and that will be that."

More sneaking around. Lisl didn't like it, but now her own curiosity was aroused. If Ev wasn't attending a church meeting in the basement of St. James every Wednesday night, what *was* going on down there?

"Okay. I'll take a look. But then that's it. If it's nothing screwy, we drop this whole thing and get off the poor guy's back. Agreed?"

"Agreed."

Lisl hurried across the street to the looming shadow of the church and went directly to the door she had seen Ev use. She didn't pause. If she did she knew she might actually think about the silliness of this whole evening and what she was doing and reconsider it.

She pulled open the door slowly and saw a deserted stairway. She entered and tiptoed down the two flights to the basement. She saw light and heard voices at the end of the hallway and cautiously made her way along until she found the meeting room. The doors stood open, spread wide into the hall like wings. She peered into the room from a safe distance.

Folding chairs were set up in short rows facing the opposite end of the low-ceilinged room. Most of the chairs were occupied and the few people left standing were sliding into the rows to get a seat. Everyone held either a cigarette or a Styrofoam cup of coffee or both. The air was already thick with smoke; clouds of white billowed in the glare of the naked fluorescent bulbs clinging to the ceiling. Ev was seated at the end of the last row. Alone.

Lisl hung back in the dimness of the hall and watched.

A balding man stood at the head of the group. He too had a cup of coffee and a cigarette. He was speaking but the words were garbled. Lisl crossed the hall to hear him. She slipped behind the nearer open door and listened. She had a clear view of Ev through the slit between the wall and the door.

"—the same faces as usual here. Our 'regulars.' But we haven't heard from some of you in a long time. We all know why you come here, but I think some of you old-timers hang back too much, thinking we know all about you. But we don't. So how about it? How about one of you founding members getting up and giving us the benefit of your experience?"

He waited but no one moved. Finally he pointed to the back row.

"Everett. How about you? We haven't heard from you in a long time. How about it?"

Ev stood slowly. He looked uncomfortable. He cleared his throat twice before speaking.

"My name's Everett," he said, "and I'm an alcoholic."

Knotting the fingers of her hands together, almost as if in prayer, Lisl leaned toward the strip of light before her and listened.

Everett was nervous at first. He hadn't done this in a while, but he was overdue for some testimony. It was time.

His nerves eased as he began talking. He knew the patter of his story like he knew basic calculus. He'd told it often enough.

"It started for me when I'm sure it started for most of you—as a teenager. I wasn't a drunk right away. That took time, and lots of practice. But the warning signs were there, right from the start. All my friends drank now and again when we could liberate some booze from our folks or persuade some stranger to buy us a case of beer, but I always seemed the happiest when we could get some and the most disappointed when we couldn't.

"And once I started to drink I couldn't stop. I didn't realize it then, but when I look back now I can see that even as a kid I didn't know how to stop. The only thing that kept me from seeing it then was the fact that our supply was always limited. Our purloined booze always ran out before I could get myself good and sick.

"My fraternity house at Emory fixed that. We bought beer by the keg and I got thoroughly ripped on a regular basis. But only on weekends, at our parties, where I became something of a legend for the amount of alcohol I could put away. During the week, though, I managed to keep up an A average. I was the envy of my peers—the honor student who could party with the best of them. This was in the mid to late sixties, when pot became the campus drug of choice. But not for me. I was too all-American for that hippie locoweed.

"Not that I didn't try it. I did. At one time or another along the way I've tried everything. Plenty of times. But I remained loyal to my friend the bottle. Because nothing else could ever find that special spot within me that needed touching. Only booze could reach that place and soothe it. I was at Woodstock, and like too many of the people there, I don't remember much about that weekend other than endless rain and oceans of mud. I had to see the movie to find out what it was really like. But I wasn't wrecked on pot or mescaline or the bad brown acid that was going around. Oh, no. That would have meant I was some hippie freak with a drug problem. Not me. I had my friend along. I was wasted on the case of bourbon I'd brought from my good old home state of Kentucky."

He shook his head as he thought of the years that followed. So much pain there. He hated dredging it up, but he had to. That was what this was all about. He couldn't allow himself to forget the misery he had caused himself . . . and others.

"You can all guess how the rest of the story goes. I graduated, got a job with a technical firm that had just moved into the Sun Belt, began working in computer technology. In those days it took a roomful of equipment to do what a desktop PC does today. If I were still with the company today, I'd probably be a millionaire. But the booze used the pressures of the job to tighten its hold on me.

"Then I fell in love with a wonderful woman who was made foolish by her own love for me. Foolish enough to believe that she could be more important to me than my old friend the bottle. Little did she know. We married, we started a life together, but it was a ménage à trois—my wife, me, and the bottle. You see, I still thought of the bottle as my friend. But it was a jealous friend. It wanted me all to itself. And slowly but surely it poisoned my marriage until my wife gave me an ultimatum: her or the bottle.

"Those of you who have been there can guess which one I chose."

Ev took a deep breath to fill the emptiness inside him.

"After that it was a steadily accelerating downward spiral for me. I lost one job after another. But my superiors always gave me a decent recommendation when they let me go. They thought they were doing me a favor by helping me hide it from the next company that had the misfortune to hire me. This prolonged my intimate relationship with my friend the bottle because it delayed my inevitable bottoming out.

"And did I ever bottom out. I went through detox three times before I finally realized that my friend of twenty years wasn't really my friend. He had taken over my life and was destroying me. The bottle was in the driver seat and I could see that if I didn't take back the wheel, he was going to run me off a cliff.

"So that's what I did. With the help of AA, I took back control of my life. *Complete* control." He smiled and held up his coffee cup and cigarette. "Well, not complete control. I still smoke and I drink too much coffee. But everything else in my life is under strict control. I've learned to manage my time so that there's no room left in my life for booze. And there never will be again."

He considered mentioning his daily challenge—standing outside Raftery's Tavern every time he passed and staring in the window for exactly one minute, daring the booze to try to lure him in—but decided against it. Someone else here might decide to try the dare . . . and lose. He didn't want to be responsible for that. He figured he'd said enough.

"So that's it. I've been dry for ten years now. I went back to school, got my doctorate, and now I'm doing exactly what I want to do. I'm back in the driver seat—for good. Thank you for listening."

As he sat down to a round of applause, he thought he heard hurried footsteps in the hall outside. He heard the upstairs door slam. Had someone left while he was speaking? He shrugged. It didn't matter. He'd spoken his piece, done his share. That was what counted.

Lisl composed her emotions as she crossed the street. Ev's story had shocked and moved her. Before tonight he had seemed little more than a collection of compulsive mannerisms. Mr. Machine. Now he was a person, a flesh-and-blood man with a past and a terrible problem, one he had been able to overcome. He'd beaten the bottle, but he didn't trumpet it around like some recovering alcoholics on the faculty; it was Ev's private victory, one he'd kept to himself. Lisl was proud of him, and suddenly proud to know him. And if he wanted his past kept secret, it was safe with her.

She stopped on the sidewalk before the shadowed doorway.

"Let's head back to the car, Rafe."

He stepped out into the light and looked at her expectantly.

"Well?"

"Well, nothing. It was a prayer meeting, that's all. Just a bunch of people sitting around reading from the Bible and stuff like that."

Rafe only stared at her. She hooked her arm through his and started them walking back the way they had come. His voice was very soft when he spoke.

"You wouldn't be telling me a story now, Lisl, would you?"

"And what if I was? What difference would it make?"

"Primes shouldn't lie to each other. I've always been completely honest with you. I expect the same."

Fine. Now she was trapped between two guilts: betray Ev's secret or betray Rafe's trust. She wished they'd stayed home in bed tonight.

"Can't we just drop this whole subject? I'll concede to your position that Ev isn't a Prime and we'll let it go at that, okay?"

Rafe stopped and turned her toward him. His intense stare made her uncomfortable.

"You're protecting him," he said. "Don't do that. He's one of them. He's not worthy of your misdirected loyalty. He wouldn't do the same for you."

"You don't know that."

Rafe sighed. "All right. I'll take you off the hook you've impaled yourself on. I know it's an AA meeting."

Lisl was shocked—and furious.

"You *know?* You've known all along?"

"I followed him here a couple of weeks ago."

"Then why this cloak-and-dagger charade stuff tonight?"

"Because if I'd told you last week that he's an alcoholic, would you have believed me?"

"Yes," she said immediately, then thought about it. "No. I guess not."

"Exactly. That's why I had to let you find out for yourself. Now there's no question in your mind that he belongs with them instead of us."

"On the contrary. The very fact that he's overcome his alcoholism is proof that he *is* a Prime. If he weren't, he'd be drunk in a gutter somewhere instead of on the Darnell faculty."

They started walking again.

"I don't know about that. If you think about it you'll see that he really hasn't beaten his problem with alcohol, he's merely found a way to hide from it. He's organized his life in such a way that he never comes within arm's reach of liquor, which is why you've never seen him at faculty parties. That's not conquering the problem, that's running from it. It's the coward's way."

"That's not fair. Alcohol is a toxin for him. I've read that a good percentage of alcoholics have different brain chemistries than the rest of us, and that alcohol does things to them that it doesn't do to you or me. It's not cowardice to avoid something that's poison to your system."

"If he were a Prime, he'd be able to surround himself with liquor and not touch a drop. Or better yet, he'd be able to control himself—have a drink or two and then switch to ginger ale. But he's not a Prime."

"Prime, shmime," Lisl said, wearying of the subject. "Who cares whether Ev is or isn't? What's the point?"

"Very simply, Lisl," he said slowly, and she could hear real anger in his voice, "the point is this: Everett Sanders is your intellectual inferior, yet he is going to move ahead of you in the department simply because he is a man. It's the same pattern as always. They move one of their own ahead and leave you behind where they can still get the benefit of your work and brains and innovation yet give the credit and status to a lesser mind. It infuriates me every time I see it happen and I will not permit it to happen to you!"

"Easy, Rafe. You don't know if that's going to happen. There's no sense in getting yourself all riled up when—"

"Lisl, it's already been decided."

The words struck her like a blow. She stumbled against Rafe as her feet refused to walk any further.

"*What?* How can you say that?"

"I overheard your pal Sanders talking to Dr. Masterson at lunch last month—"

"Last *month?* And you didn't tell me?"

She could see his face in the glow of the streetlight. His expression was tortured.

"I didn't know how to tell you. I knew it would hurt you. I . . . I was afraid it would crush your spirit."

For the first time since she'd met him, Rafe seemed unsure of himself. And all because of his feelings for her. At any other time it would have warmed Lisl, but the good feeling was swept away by the arctic wind of her growing anger.

"What exactly did they say?"

"I caught only part of it, but I heard the chairman saying that he hoped your paper wasn't very good, because if it was he'd have to do some fast talking to explain to you why he was giving Ev tenure instead of you. He asked Sanders if he had any suggestions on how to let you down easy so you wouldn't start applying to other universities."

"What did Ev say?"

"I don't know. I was too angry to listen. It was right after that I started auditing Sanders's classes. I wanted to do something but I didn't know what. At least I didn't then. I know now."

"What?" Lisl said eagerly. She felt betrayed, hemmed in, and utterly helpless. If Rafe knew a way out, she'd take it.

"Follow me."

He took her hand and led her across the street toward an apartment building. She recognized it immediately.

"Ev's place? What are we going to—?"

"Just trust me. You'll see."

Using the duplicates of Ev's keys, he led her inside and up to the apartment.

"Isn't this a little risky? I mean, he could come back at any minute."

"Those meetings average a good two hours or more." He opened the door and led her to the kitchen counter where he turned and faced her. "We've got plenty of time."

"For what?"

Rage reached inside his jacket pocket and held out a slim glass tube.

"For this."

She took it and held it up to the light. A test tube, filled with clear fluid. It looked like water but Lisl knew it wasn't. Suddenly she was uneasy.

"What is it, Rafe?"

"Pull the stopper and sniff."

She did. There was a very faint odor, too faint to identify.

"I don't know . . ."

"Absolute ethanol. Pure alcohol. Nearly odorless, almost taste-less when mixed with fruit juice."

"Oh, no," she said as she felt her stomach begin to tighten. "You can't be serious."

Rafe went to the refrigerator and brought back an open half gallon of orange juice. He placed it on the counter between them.

"I've never been more serious in my whole life. Pour it in, Lisl."

"No. I can't do that to Ev!"

"Why not?"

"Because it's poison for him!"

"It's only an ounce, Lisl. Two tablespoons."

"That doesn't matter. Even a drop could start chemical reactions in his brain and knock him off the wagon. We could be sending him off on a real bender."

Rafe shrugged. "If that's what he wants, then so be it."

"Rafe, it'll have nothing to do with what he *wants*—he won't be able to control it!"

"If he's a Prime, he *will* be able to control it. If he's one of us he'll be able to shake off two tablespoons of ethanol and stay on track. And if he can do that, maybe he *should* get tenure. But if he can't . . ."

"We could be ruining his life."

Rafe shook his head. "That's a bit melodramatic, don't you think? He knows the problem. He's controlled it before. Even if he's not a Prime, he can control it again. But if he does go on a bender, it will open Masterson's eyes—and the university administration's, as well—to the caliber of the man they've handpicked for tenure over you."

"It's not fair, Rafe."

Rafe's eyes grew cold, flinty.

"Fair? *What's* fair? You've been playing by the rules, devoting your spare time to this paper, thinking you really had a shot at the spot while all the while the choice has already been made. Can't you just hear Ev going to Masterson and whining, 'You're not really thinking of giving the position to *her,* are you?' And meanwhile you're going to Masterson for advice and he's thinking what a sucker you are! Don't talk to me about *fair,* Lisl!"

He opened the mouth of the cardboard container and pushed it toward her.

"Pour."

"Maybe I should drink it myself—about half a dozen of them would help me right now."

"No drugs, Lisl," Rafe said, leaning over her shoulder, speaking softly into her ear. "Nothing to muffle the inhibitions that people like Sanders and Masterson and your parents and all the rest have conditioned into you. You must face those inhibitions, Lisl, and you must subdue them, beat them into the mud until they are powerless to hold you back. You must be strong, you must toss away all excuses. Never blame your actions on outside influences. No excuses, no scapegoats—'It was the drugs.' 'It was the booze.' It must be you and you alone—nothing between you and what you do. And you must be proud, Lisl. No shame. Ever."

The diamond-shaped opening yawned before her. She tried to be cool, be rational about this, but the thought of Masterson encouraging her to write her paper even though he had already made his decision stoked the fiery anger that had begun to blaze within her. And Ev—Ev was in on it.

With a groan, she upended the tube over the opening.

"Yes!" Rafe said in a harsh whisper.

He took the container, closed the top, and shook up the contents. Then he replaced it in the refrigerator.

"Let's go," he said, turning to Lisl and taking the empty test tube from her fingers.

Lisl stood there unmoving, feeling numb, queasy.

What have I done?

Rafe took her arm and she allowed herself to be led from the apartment, down the stairs, and to his car. She felt as if she were moving in a dream.

"I want to go back," she said. "Let's pour that juice down the drain and forget about the whole thing."

"No, Lisl. Remember what I told you. No regrets, no looking back. We make our own rules. We answer only to ourselves."

"That's what frightens me the most."

"You'll see," Rafe said as he started the car and pulled into the traffic. "This will bring everything into focus for you. You've just passed your test of fire. You've thrown off one more set of chains. Now comes Everett Sanders's trial. Now he gets a chance to prove what he's made of." He reached over and squeezed Lisl's hand. "I'm so proud of you."

"Are you really?"

"Yes. Enormously."

Then why do I feel so ashamed?

TWENTY-THREE

Ev had been feeling strange all day. Slightly woozy, slightly off kilter. Jittery. On edge. Lethargic and yet hyped up. Oddly elated yet all the while suffused with an aura of impending doom.

Sitting at his office desk, staring at the late afternoon sun that poured through the window, he tried to sort out the odd conglomeration of symptoms that had plagued him since he'd left his apartment this morning. But it was difficult to sort out anything today. His powers of concentration, usually so sharp-focused, had all but deserted him.

So uncomfortable. Sweaty one moment, chilled the next. He felt as if his heart were racing yet he'd checked his pulse numerous times and found it chugging in the low nineties—high for him but certainly not extraordinary. He wondered if it could be the start of a virus—February was flu season, after all—but although he felt feverish, he'd stopped by the infirmary and his temperature had been normal.

Blood sugar. Could he be hypoglycemic? Unlikely. He'd had his usual breakfast of o-j, toast with Fleischmann's margarine, Grape-Nuts with skim milk, and coffee; his lunch had been the usual tuna-fish salad on whole wheat that he had every Thursday. So why would his blood sugar be down? Maybe it was the coffee. Maybe the accumulated caffeine from twenty cups a day for umpteen years was finally catching up to him. He couldn't think of anything else that would get to him like this.

Maybe his body was telling him it was time to cut down. Perhaps that would salve these jangled nerves.

"Ev? Are you all right?"

He swung about in his chair. It was Lisl, standing in the doorway, a worried look on her face.

All right? Why would she ask that? Was something wrong? Did he look sick?

"No. I'm fine," he said, hoping he sounded convincing. "Just fine. Why do you ask?"

"Oh, I don't know. I just wanted to know." She bit her upper lip. "I mean, you looked a little pale."

He looked pale? Lisl looked awful. Her face was drawn and haggard, with dark circles under her eyes. She looked like she hadn't slept a wink all night.

Ev rose and approached her.

"I'm fine, Lisl. But what about you? You look—"

She turned and hurried down the hall. Bewildered, Ev stood in his doorway and watched her go. First she was so solicitous about how he felt, then she turned and left him while he was talking to her. She seemed unnerved. The only time he could remember seeing her this upset was back in December when she had told him about that phone call—

The phone call! Had she received another one? Damm it, he'd forgotten to call that detective. What was wrong with him today? As a rule, he never forgot things like that. Well, he wouldn't waste another minute.

He pulled the telephone number from his wallet and dialed it immediately. This time the detective answered when his room was rung.

"Yeah?" said a New York–inflected voice.

"Is this Detective Augustino? This is Professor Sanders. We spoke last week about—"

"Right, right. On the steps. Did you place the guy in the photo?"

"Yes. I believe he's one of the groundskeepers here at the university."

"No shit! You're sure? You're really sure? What's his name?"

Ev could almost feel the excitement pouring through the wire from the other end.

"I don't know."

"You don't *know?*" The voice became irate. "What do you mean, you don't know? What kind of a scam do you—?

"Listen, Detective. I've seen the man around here for years but

I simply do not know his name, just as I'm sure you don't know the name of the janitors who clean your barracks in Raleigh. He's changed his appearance quite a bit since that photo was taken but I'm convinced he's your man. Now if this is the sort of thanks I get—"

"You're right," the detective said through a sigh. "Sorry. Do you know where I can find him?"

"No. But I'm sure if you check with personnel tomorrow they'll be able to help you."

"Tomorrow? What's wrong with today?"

"The administrative offices are closing even as we speak. They reopen at eight in the morning." Ev found he had no further patience for this obnoxious state cop. "You're welcome," he said, and hung up.

He felt shaky as he rose and reached for his coat. At least that was over with. He'd be glad to get back home where he had everything under control.

He passed Lisl's office on the way out but her door was closed. It looked like she'd left for home ahead of him.

Ev felt a mounting anxiety during the bus ride home, an almost-desperate desire to reach the far side of his apartment door and lock it. He couldn't fight the rising fear that something terrible was going to happen if he didn't.

When he stepped off the bus, he headed for home at double time, but forced himself to stop outside Raftery's for his daily test of will. He glanced at his watch, then began his one-minute stare through the nicotine-fogged window.

All the regulars were there, lined up on their usual stools at the bar, sipping their Scotches and their gins, talking and laughing. But instead of the disdain he usually felt for such wasted time, money, and liver cells, Ev was almost overcome by a wave of nostalgia.

Those were the good old days, when he could walk into his neighborhood tavern in Charlotte and be greeted by a chorus of hellos, where he could sit among friends and talk and swear and laugh and drink from late afternoon until the early hours of the morning. The fellowship, the camaraderie, the sense of belonging, for some reason he missed it today more than any other time in recent memory. The longing for companionship was an expanding void within him. If he could only have that back, just for a few hours—

Ev caught himself with his fingers on the brass door handle, pulling it open. He snatched his hand away as if he'd received an electric shock and all but ran for his apartment.

Once inside, with the door safely locked behind him, he slumped in the recliner and panted from the exertion of running up the three flights of stairs. He hadn't even stopped to pick up his mail.

What's wrong with me?

It had to be his blood sugar. There was no other possible reason why he should feel so shaky. He had to eat something to get it up.

He went to the fridge and saw the o-j on the top shelf. Wasn't that what diabetics used when their sugar was low? He grabbed the container, poured himself a glassful, and gulped it down. Then he returned to the recliner and waited. He'd give it twenty minutes to see if it had any effect.

It took only half that. By the end of ten minutes he was feeling much better. Calmer, more relaxed. The near panic of moments ago was almost completely gone.

Amazing what a little orange juice could do.

He went over and poured himself another glassful.

TWENTY-FOUR

"Have you seen Ev?"

Lisl froze at the sound of Al Torres's voice. She'd looked for Ev earlier this morning but his office door had been closed. That wasn't unusual, though. She knew he had early classes on Fridays.

It had been okay for her to be looking for him. She had a reason. He'd seemed a little strung out yesterday but had been acting perfectly normal; she'd wanted to see if he was any better today.

But no one else should have been looking for him.

Unless . . .

"No," she said, keeping her eyes trained on her desktop. "Why?"

"He missed his first two classes this morning. And he didn't call in. That's not like Ev at all."

Oh no, oh no, oh no!

Lisl suddenly wanted to be sick. She tried to speak but no words would come.

Al went on: "Administration wants to know if anybody's heard from him."

Lisl could only shake her head and not look at him.

"You okay, Lisl?" he said.

She ventured a glance at him and managed to say, "Not feeling too good." She wasn't lying.

"Jeez, no. I guess you're not. I've heard there's a bug of some sort going around. I'll bet that's what Ev's got. Maybe you're coming down with it too. Anyway, if you hear from him, tell him to call administration."

When she heard her office door close, Lisl lowered her face into her hands and began to sob.

What have I done?

She'd spent much of the night in agony, struggling to sleep. She'd lifted the receiver a dozen times to call Ev, to tell him to stay away from his orange juice, to dump it down the sink. She even managed to dial his number once but hung up on the first ring.

How could she say that to him? How could she tell him that when he'd trusted her with his key ring she'd made a copy of his apartment keys, that she'd invaded his home and dosed his orange juice with alcohol. How could she get those words past her lips? Impossible.

She'd even toyed with the idea of calling up and somehow disguising her voice with a handkerchief like they did in the movies, but she didn't believe that would work.

It had taken her two sleeping pills to get to sleep the night before, and it took the same last night before she finally dozed off, and even then she'd had to placate herself with the thought that if Ev had got through yesterday without going on a bender, he would probably come through this whole ordeal with flying colors. Then she'd be able to thumb her nose at Rafe and this particularly wild theory of his.

Rafe . . . why had she listened to him? He made her feel so good so much of the time, but every so often he'd convince her to do something that made her feel rotten. And he was *so* convincing. Everything made so much sense when he was whispering in her ear. It was only later that she wished she had listened to her own heart. She knew he had her best interests at heart, that he was fighting for her, it was just that Rafe didn't heed the boundaries that limited most people's actions. Rafe didn't seem to recognize any limits.

And apparently neither do I.

Lisl slammed her fist on her desk. She still couldn't believe she had doctored Ev's juice. Yet she had. Deliberately. With full knowledge of the threat it posed to that poor man. What had come over her?

But more important now: Where was Ev?

She pulled her address book from her top drawer and looked up his number. She was sure the department secretary and the administration office had already called him but she had to try herself. She dialed and listened to the phone ring on the other end. She didn't count the rings but it had to be near twenty by the time she hung up.

She rose and was surprised by how wobbly her legs felt. What if Ev had gone out last night and bought a case of vodka? In her mind's eye she saw him sprawled on his kitchen floor in a drunken stupor or in a coma from alcohol poisoning.

She had to go over there.

Renny wasn't exactly sure how to handle this. He'd wandered the grounds since eight A.M., searching for someone who looked like the priest, but nobody he'd seen had even come close. And he couldn't exactly go up to one of these guys and ask, could he?

Then it had occurred to him that he could queer this whole bust if Ryan recognized him.

So now Renny was standing before a counter in the university personnel office, hoping he could bluster his way through this.

"Yes, sir?" said the pert young brunette with the red-framed glasses. "Can I help you?"

Renny did the badge flash.

"Sergeant Augustino, State Police. We have reason to believe that one of your groundskeepers might be a fugitive from out of state. I need to see your personnel records."

"A fugitive? Really?"

Renny watched as she chewed her lip and glanced around the office. If she was looking for help, there was none to be had. It was no accident that Renny had chosen coffee-break time to pop into personnel.

"What are we waiting for?" he said.

"Well, I'm not sure. I mean, shouldn't you have a search warrant or something like that?"

"I have a warrant for his arrest. That enough?"

"Oh, dear," she said, looking around again, but the office was just as empty as before. "What's his name?"

Renny gave her a tired look.

"He won't be using his real name. Now come on. We're wasting time." He leaned forward and gave her a hard look. "You wouldn't be protecting someone, would you?"

She flushed. "No. Of course not. It's just . . ." Her shoulders slumped in resignation. "All right. What records do you want?"

"Any groundskeepers hired in the last five years."

Renny stood and drummed his fingers on the counter, looking calm and patient, but inside he was urging her to hurry her ass before one of her supervisors came back. She went to one desk, then to another, then to a computer, then she disappeared into the back. Finally she reappeared with a small stack of buff folders.

"I brought all I could find. Some of them don't work here anymore but I brought them anyway."

Renny grabbed the stack and opened the one on top. He stifled a curse.

"No photos."

She shrugged. "Some do, some don't."

He flipped through quickly, reading the names, searching for photos: Gilbert Olin, Stanley Malinowski, Peter Turner, Will Ryerson, Mark DeSantis, Louis—

Whoa!

He shuffled back to Will Ryerson. Right age, right height and weight, hired almost three years ago. Will Ryerson . . . William Ryan. Renny's pulse ripped into overdrive.

Gotcha!

He memorized the address, then made a show of looking through the rest of the folders. Finally, he slid the stack back to the woman.

"Nope. Doesn't look like he's here. Another false lead. Thank you for your help. Have a nice day."

And then he was out of the office and hurrying down the hall, wondering where he could get hold of a city map and find out how to get to Postal Road.

Got you, you bastard. Got you at last!

Lisl started by knocking on Ev's door, then graduated to banging with her fist. When she got no answer, she fished the key from her purse and unlocked it.

"Ev?" she said, closing the door behind her. "Ev, are you here?"

All was quiet. She looked around the apartment. Ev was nowhere in sight. The place felt empty, but that might not mean anything. With her pulse pounding in her throat, she headed for the bedroom.

God, what if he's dead? What will I do?

She paused on the threshold of the bedroom, then forced herself to peek inside.

Empty. The bed was made, the spread pulled tight and unwrinkled.

Not sure whether to be relieved or even more upset than she already was, she let out the breath she'd unconsciously been holding. Where could he be? Everything in the place was perfectly in order, just like she and Rafe had left it Wednesday night—

Except for the kitchen. The orange juice carton sat on the counter; a pulp-streaked tumbler huddled against it. Lisl grabbed the carton. A low moan escaped her when she felt how light it was. In a sudden fit of anger—at Rafe, but mostly at herself—she hurled the empty carton against the wall, then grabbed the glass and did the same. The carton bounced, the glass shattered.

Why did I do it?

Lisl sagged back against the refrigerator and closed her eyes, waiting for an answer. None came. She set her jaw and straightened up.

All right. She'd gotten Ev into this, so she had to help him get out of it. But first she had to find him. And she was going to find him if she had to comb every bar in town.

Lisl headed for the door but stopped before she reached it. What if Ev wasn't in a bar? What if he was in a hospital?

She ran to the phone and called the Medical Center switchboard, a number she still remembered from her days as the wife of an intern.

No, there had been no one named Sanders admitted during the night.

She sighed with relief, then wondered why she should be relieved. At least if he were in a hospital it would mean he was being cared for. If he was lying unconscious in an alley somewhere . . .

She ran out to comb the nearby bars. But it was slow work, and after covering only three places in the space of an hour and getting nowhere, she realized she couldn't do this alone. She needed help.

But who? Rafe wouldn't lift a finger to help Ev. In fact, he might even talk her out of looking for him. She could think of only one person she could count on. But that would mean explaining what she had done. How could she explain the unexplainable?

She headed for the next bar. Alone.

Sick.

Ev felt terrible. Sick to his stomach and sick at heart as he leaned against his apartment door and twisted the key in the lock. He lurched in and staggered the short distance to the recliner. He dropped into its comforting familiarity and closed his eyes.

Off the wagon. He'd fallen off before, but the last time had been so many years ago he'd begun to think he'd never fall off again. He pressed his fists against his eyes. He wanted to shout, he wanted to cry, but he wouldn't allow it. What purpose would that serve? He wouldn't wallow in self-pity or recriminations, or look for someone else to blame. He'd been down those roads before and they were dead ends. He had to make something positive out of this. Everything was a learning experience. What he had to do was turn this episode around and see if he could learn something from it.

Well, the lesson was obvious, wasn't it? A drunk is a drunk, and no matter how long you've been dry, you shouldn't get too comfortable with your sobriety. Yesterday was a good example of how fast it can desert you.

But why? Why had he gone off the wagon? He'd felt strange all day yesterday—it *had* been yesterday, hadn't it? Of course it had. He'd seen the newspaper in the box on the corner. It was Friday afternoon. He glanced at his watch: 4:16. He'd lost almost a whole day to booze. Not the first time for that either.

But what frightened him was how it had come without warning. An odd sensation all day, then he'd come home as usual. He'd been sitting here drinking orange juice, and when he'd finished it, he'd gone out for more. But he never made it to the market. As he passed Raftery's he'd hesitated only a heartbeat, then he was inside ordering a Scotch.

No warning. One moment outside, the next moment inside, drinking.

But Lord how good it had tasted. Even now his mouth watered with the memory of it. One of the few memories left from yesterday. A montage flickered through his brain, a procession of drinks, of buying a bottle, of upending it and gulping it down like a desert wanderer finding a cache of cool spring water.

His next memory was of waking up sick, dirty, aching, shaking in the early afternoon sunlight under a sheet of cardboard behind an appliance store. He still had his wallet so he'd bought himself something to eat and another long procession of drinks—all coffees.

He pushed himself out of the recliner and headed for the bathroom. On the way, something crunched under his foot.

Glass. Fragments of the tumbler he'd used for the orange juice were scattered all over the kitchen floor. The o-j carton was on the floor too. There was a stain on the wall, as if someone had smashed the glass against the wall.

Someone. Who? *Me?*

Who else? The door had been locked when he'd come in. Nothing was disturbed. He was the only one with a key.

He must have come back and gone out again last night. He shook his head. If only he could remember. It was scary to lose little pieces of your life.

Despite his throbbing head, he swept up the fragments, put them in the juice carton, and tossed everything into the garbage. Then he continued on to the bathroom for a shower.

Half an hour later, clean, shaved, wearing fresh clothes, he felt almost normal. He'd go to the Friday night meeting of his AA group, something he hadn't done in years. He'd find another AA group that met on Saturdays and he'd go to that meeting too. He'd go every night until he was sure he was in control again.

But it was only five o'clock. Hours to go before the meeting. His hand shook as he lit a cigarette. What was he going to do till then? He wanted a drink, he *craved* another damn drink. Good thing there wasn't any in the apartment. He went through the ritual of making himself a cup of coffee and worried about how he was going to stay sober until the meeting. He didn't have an AA contact anymore—Ev's had moved away a few years ago and he'd never bothered to get another. He'd thought he didn't need one.

Work. Work was better than any contact, at least for him. He could lose himself in the calculations for his paper and the time would fly by.

He sat down at his console and went through the routines required to access Darnell's Cray II. Then he used his private access codes to call up his personal files. The terminal beeped. He was stunned by the message.

ERROR. FILE NOT IN MEMORY.

He shook his head. Must have hit a wrong key somewhere in the sequence. That wasn't like him. More fallout from the binge. He input his access codes again, and was rejected again.

No. This was impossible.

Shaking now, he input an alternate access route to his backup files. Another beep. Another error message.

Oh, no! Oh, please, no!

He tried again. And again. The same result every time. The files were gone! *Gone!*

He got up and walked around the room. This couldn't be! He was the only one who knew his access codes. No one could even *find* those files, let alone erase them.

No one but me.

He stopped in midstride. He'd been back here last night—the broken glass proved it. What had he done? Had he accessed his files and wiped them out in some drunken fit of self-destructive rage?

That was the only answer. A year's worth of work—gone! It would take him forever to rework those calculations.

He hadn't fallen off the wagon and lost a night—he'd lost a *year!*

In a daze, he reached for his coat and wandered toward the door. He had to get out, take a walk, get away from that useless, empty terminal.

Maybe to Raftery's.

Bill rinsed the last of the dirt off his hands and forearms and reached for a paper towel. A good day. Despite Clancy's constant chatter about his sexual prowess, they'd managed to fix the last of the faulty fittings in the north lawn's sprinkler system today. It would be ready to go when growing season started.

He was just about dried off when Joe Bob stepped into the washroom.

"Hey, Willy! There's a lady outside wants to see you."

"Who dat?" Clancy called from across the room. "His momma?"

Amid the laughter, Joe Bob said, "No way. This blond babe's young enough to be his daughter. I think she's faculty. And she's built like a brick shithouse."

That description fit only one person Bill knew: Lisl. He wondered what she wanted.

The laughter changed to hoots and catcalls as Bill crossed the washroom toward the door, shaking his head and smiling at their good-natured crudeness. They'd all been half convinced there was something a little strange about him because he never joined in on their "can-you-top-this" recountings of their sexual escapades. They actually seemed happy for him now, and he couldn't help being warmed by the groundswell of good feeling, no matter how wrongheaded.

"Didn't I tell you guys," Joe Bob said as Will pushed through the swinging door, "it's always the quiet ones who get the quality pussy."

He found her outside the garage door. As soon as he saw her tense, pale face he knew something was very wrong.

"Lisl! Are you okay?"

Her eyes filled with tears and her lips quivered as she nodded.

"Oh, Will, I . . . I've done something awful!"

Will glanced around. This wasn't the place for her to be telling him about something awful. He took her elbow and guided her toward the parking lot.

"We'll talk in my car."

He helped her into the passenger seat. By the time he'd slid in behind the wheel on the other side, she was sobbing openly. He didn't start the car.

"What is it, Lisl?"

"Oh, God, Will, I don't want to tell you. I'm so ashamed. But I need help and you're the only one I can turn to."

Words from the past scrolled through his brain.

Bless me, Father, for I have sinned . . .

"It involves Rafe, doesn't it?" he said, hoping to get her going.

Her head snapped up. She stared at him.

"How did you know?"

"Lucky guess." He didn't want to tell her that he'd sensed that the garbage philosophy Rafe had been feeding her would lead to trouble. "Go ahead. Let it out. I won't turn away from you. No matter what."

There was gratitude in her eyes, but no lessening of the pain there.

"I hope you feel the same way when I'm finished."

Bill listened with growing horror as Lisl recounted the events of the past week and a half. He almost groaned aloud when she told him about Rafe producing the vial of ethanol. He saw the rest of the scenario in a flash but he had to let Lisl talk it through.

"And now I don't know where he is," she said as she finished describing her search of the bars in the area around Ev's apartment. Tears were sliding down her cheeks. "He could be anywhere. He could be dead!"

Bill sat behind the wheel and stared straight ahead. He fought to overcome his shock and revulsion and frame a reply. He had to say something—but what? What could he say to ease her pain? And should he even attempt to ease her pain? What she had done was . . . abominable.

"What on earth, Leese? What on earth prompted you to do such a thing?"

"I didn't mean to hurt him! I'd never do anything to hurt Ev!"

"How can you say that after spiking his orange juice?"

Her lips quivered. "I was so sure he was a Prime. I thought he could overcome it. I was *sure* he could. Rafe was putting him down and I thought that would prove to Rafe that Ev was one of us."

Bill tried but couldn't neutralize the acid in his voice.

"Who's *us*? People who sabotage another person's life? I don't think Professor Sanders falls into that group."

Lisl dropped her head into her hands.

"Please, Will. I need your help. I thought you'd understand."

"Understand? Lisl, I don't know if I'll ever understand what you did. But I *will* help. For Sanders's sake, and for yours. Because I still believe in you. And because I hope this will open your eyes to the garbage Rafe has been feeding you. *Primes!*" Merely saying the word left a sour taste in his mouth. "The whole concept is morally and intellectually bankrupt. And so is Rafe."

Lisl stared at him. "No. Don't say that. He's brilliant. He's—"

"He's the reason you're feeling miserable and why Everett Sanders is out on a tear. Hooking up with that guy was the worst thing that ever happened to you."

"He's not all bad. For the first time in my life I felt good about myself."

"How good are you feeling now?"

She looked away without answering.

"Lisl, it's a false self-esteem when you have to look down on someone else before you can feel good about yourself. Real self-esteem comes from within."

Lisl's face hardened for an instant, then crumbled.

"You're right," she sobbed. "You've been right all along, haven't you?"

Bill took her in his arms and held her like a crying child. Poor Lisl. She'd been dragged into hell and hadn't known it. But even worse was the hell she had caused Everett Sanders.

After a moment she straightened up.

"Will you help me find Ev?"

"Yes. But first I want to see if I can find out something about Rafe."

"There's no time."

"This will only take a minute. Does your office computer have a modem?"

"Yes. The department subscribes to a number of data bases. How will that—?"

He started the Impala and threw it into gear.

"Just get me to your computer."

He drove over to the math building and parked in front. Lisl led him to her office. While she was setting up her terminal for him, he unplugged her desk phone and looked for a place to put it. All the other offices on the floor were locked up tight. As he held the phone in his sweaty hands, his anger grew. He didn't have time for this. He opened the window and tossed it out. He watched it bounce and roll on the grass three stories below, then turned and found Lisl staring at him.

"Will? Are you all right?"

"I haven't been all right for a long time," he said. He pointed to the computer. "Are we ready to dial?"

"All set."

He took her seat and punched in DataNet's phone number, then entered his access code. With Lisl hanging over his shoulder, he searched the bulletin board for a message to Ignatius. It took only a few seconds to find one.

TO IGNATIUS:
NOT MUCH AVAILABLE ON THE MAN IN QUESTION YET BUT PROBABLY A PHONY. EXISTS IN ARIZONA STATE UNIVERSITY COMPUTER BUT NOT IN YEARBOOKS. GREAT ACADEMIC REC-ORD BUT CAN'T FIND ANYONE WHO REMEMBERS HIM. NOT THE WORST OF IT. WAS DOODLING WITH HIS NAME AND NOTICED IT'S AN ANAGRAM OF SARA LOM. IS THAT WHY YOU WANTED HIM CHECKED OUT?

EL COMEDO

" 'Checked out'?" Lisl said, straightening up behind him. "You were having Rafe investigated?"

But Bill barely heard her. He couldn't have answered her anyway. His mouth had gone dry. Spicules of ice were crystallizing in each cell of his body, freezing him in position as he stared at the screen.

. . . *Losmara . . . an anagram of Sara Lom . . .*

He transposed the letters in his mind. Yes. He could see it now. How come he hadn't seen it before?

He felt as if a vast abyss were opening before him, taunting him, beckoning to him, offering him all the answers to everything he wanted to know . . . and to more that he never wanted to know.

Good God, this didn't make any sense! Rafe was related to Sara—there was no denying the family resemblance once he'd picked up on it. But why was he using an anagram of his sister's name? No—not Rafe's sister. The real Sara Lom had disappeared. Rafe's sister had appropriated her name. Which made it logical to assume that Rafe was a fake as well. But why? In God's name, *why?*

Lisl's words echoed his thoughts.

"What's going on, Will?"

"I don't know, Lisl. But I'm pretty sure of one thing: Rafe Losmara is not who he says he is."

"You mean he's an impostor? That's impossible! You can't get into a graduate program at Darnell without high GRE's and some pretty impressive letters of recommendation."

"You said he's a whiz with computers, didn't you? These big state universities have twenty to forty thousand students enrolled at a time. They use computers to keep track of them. I don't know how he did it. He might have used a phony transcript to transfer in as a senior, attended a few key classes and wowed a few key faculty members, got into the computer and created an impressive academic record, and he was set: In the space of nine months—one academic year—he's created a completely bogus identity with a three-point-nine grade point and glowing letters of recommendation."

"But this is all supposition," Lisl said. "You've got no proof!"

"True. But I know it in my gut. Because I know someone else who was fooled by a scam very much like this one."

"Who?"

"Me."

"Will, you're talking crazy. Why would he go to all this trouble to create a false identity? And what's this anagram business in that message?"

"I don't know. But I'm going to find out."

"So am I!" She picked up her bag and turned toward the door. "I'm going over to Rafe's right now and—"

"What about Ev?"

She stopped. Her shoulders slumped.

"Oh, God . . . Ev. How could I forget about Ev?" She turned her tortured face to him. "What's the matter with me?"

"You're being torn into little pieces, that's what's the matter." Bill rose and put an arm around her shoulders. "We'll straighten out the rest of it soon. But first we've got to find Everett Sanders. Right?"

She nodded without looking at him. "Right."

"Okay. Here's my idea. You start at the north end of Conway Street, I'll start at the south. We'll check every bar along the way and meet somewhere in the middle. If we haven't found him by then, we'll start moving in other directions." He gave her shoulders one final squeeze. "Don't worry. Together we'll find him."

He walked her out to her car and saw her off on her way to Conway Street. As he hurried to his own car, he congratulated himself on becoming such a smooth liar. For he had no intention of looking for Everett Sanders now. Later, yes. But right now he was heading for Parkview Condos.

As he drove, Bill began to sweat. A rank fear-sweat. It poured out of him. He was heading for a showdown with a man who was linked to the woman who'd called herself Sara Lom, the woman Bill had thought he'd never find, the woman who'd mutilated Danny Gordon and left him for Bill to find.

But she'd done more than mutilate the child. She'd left him alive yet placed him beyond the reach of any medical science known to man.

And that was what terrified Bill now, what made the darkness seem to press against the windows of his car. He was heading toward the unknown. Sara and Rafe—or whoever they really were—were linked to something hideous, something unnatural, maybe supernatural. He could almost believe they were linked to Satan himself—but he didn't believe in Satan. He'd found it difficult to believe in much of anything anymore. But if inhuman evil could be embodied in one being, that being was the woman he'd known as Sara. And by blood or something else, Rafe was related to her.

But he couldn't allow himself to be afraid. He couldn't hesitate for an instant in his confrontation with Rafe. He wished he had a gun—something to cow Rafe into telling him what he wanted to know. But he'd have to do it all on his own. And for that he'd need ice in his nerves and fire in his blood.

So he thought about Christmas Eve five years ago and what Sara did to Danny, and about the agonies Danny had suffered during the ensuing week.

And very soon the fear was gone. By the time he screeched to a halt before Rafe's condo it had been replaced by a blistering rage.

The Maserati was in the driveway; the big living-room windows were lit. No hesitation, no second thoughts. Bill raced up the steps, didn't knock, slammed against the door, and burst in.

"Losmara! Where are you, Losmara?"

"Right here," said a calm, soft voice from the right.

Bill found Rafe sitting on the white sofa in his white living room. He was dressed in the white slacks and soft white shirt he'd worn at the Christmas party. Bill stood over him and pointed a finger in his face.

"Who the hell *are* you?"

Rafe didn't even flinch. His legs were crossed, his arms were folded across his chest. He looked Bill straight in the eyes and spoke calmly.

"You know very well who I am."

"No. You're a phony. You and your sister. Both sickos playing sicko games. But it's going to stop. And you're going to tell me how I can find your sister."

"I have no sister. I'm an only child."

Bill felt the fury surging higher within him. He wanted to take Rafe's throat in his hands and rattle him like a rag doll. And maybe he would. But not yet. Not yet.

"Cut the shit. Whatever the game was, it's up. I've found you out. 'Losmara' . . . 'Sara Lom'—they're word games. You're not pulling something here with Lisl like your sister pulled with Danny and me back in New York. I'm stopping it here and now."

"Whatever are you talking about?" Still no sign of alarm, no emotion at all. He hadn't even asked Bill to leave. "And what do you believe I'm 'pulling' with Lisl?"

"You're destroying her, corrupting everything that's good and decent in her."

A smile. "I'm destroying nothing, corrupting nothing. I've *done* nothing to Lisl. I've merely offered options. Any choices she's made are wholly her own."

"Sure. I've heard your options: something bad or something worse."

Rafe shrugged. "That's a matter of opinion. But you forget there was always the option of choosing neither. I've never forced a thing on Lisl."

"You were dealing from a loaded deck!"

"I have no intention of wasting my time debating with you. But let me point out that one inescapable fact remains: Everything Lisl's done has been of her own free will. I pointed out certain paths to her, but it was she who chose to set out upon them. Never once did I threaten her—with anything. I did not make her choices; she did. The responsibility for anything she's done lies with her."

Bill's rage was nearing critical mass.

"She was vulnerable! You took advantage of her weaknesses, knocked down her defenses, twisted her up in knots. Then you put that vial of alcohol in her hand in Everett Sanders's apartment.

That was like giving her a loaded gun."

"But she's an adult, not a child. And she knew what she was doing when she pulled the trigger. Your outrage is misdirected, my friend. You should be shouting at Lisl."

That did it. Bill grabbed the front of Rafe's shirt and yanked him out of the chair.

"I'm *not* your friend! Now I want some answers and I want them *now*!"

The phone began to ring. That long, protracted ring. The sound so startled Bill that he released Rafe's shirt.

Immediately Rafe stepped over to the phone and lifted the receiver. He listened for a second, then turned and extended it toward Bill.

"It's for you, Father Ryan."

Bill stumbled back. Danny Gordon's pleas echoed faintly from the receiver.

"Father, please come and get me! Pleeeeease! . . ."

But breaking through the horror was the realization that Rafe had called him Father Ryan.

"You know?"

"Of course."

"But how?"

"Does it matter? I think it's more important that you answer little Danny. He wants you to come help him."

"He's dead, you bastard!"

Bill was about to leap at Rafe but the younger man's condescending smile and slow shake of his head stopped him cold.

"Don't be so sure of that."

"Of course he is!" Bill said. "I—I buried him myself!"

The infuriating smile continued through another slow shake of the head.

"You may have buried him . . . but he didn't die."

Bill knew it couldn't be true. *He's lying! He's got to be lying!* But he had to ask.

"If he's still alive, where is he?"

Rafe's smile broadened.

"Right where you left him."

Bill's knees threatened to buckle but he locked them straight. Still, he swayed. He could barely hear his own voice over the roaring in his ears.

"No!"

"Oh, yes. Oh, most certainly yes. For more than five years he's been lying in the bottom of that hole you dug for him in St. Ann's

Cemetery. Waiting for you. Hating you."

Bill stared at Rafe. There was no reason in the world to believe a single word from this . . . this *creature's* mouth, yet somehow he believed this.

Because in the darkest corners of his soul, within the most obscure convolutions of his brain, in the deepest crevices of his heart, there had always lurked the faintest suspicion that he had been duped, fooled by the force that controlled Danny's fate into committing the atrocity of burying Danny alive in the hope of ending his pain. When he would awaken sweating and palpitating in the darkness of his bedroom, it was the memory of that final night that haunted him, but laced through it was the unspeakable possibility that Danny might not have died in that hole. Bill had never faced that fear, but now he had no choice.

He squeezed his eyes shut.

No! It's impossible!

Impossible . . . but the impossible had been true five years ago when Danny remained alive and in torment, a bottomless pit for the transfusions and medications being pumped into him. So the impossible could be true now.

He opened his eyes and looked at Rafe.

"God dammit, who *are* you? *What* are you?"

Rafe smiled and suddenly the lights began to dim.

"I'd dearly love to show you," Rafe said. "But it doesn't serve my purpose at the moment. However, I will grant you a brief glimpse."

The room grew darker and colder, as if some hidden vortex were sucking all the heat and light from the room. And then the black swooped in, a darkness so perfect that Bill's nervous system screamed as direction went awry, as up and down lost all meaning. But this was not a quiet darkness, not a simple absence of light; this was a *devouring* of light. A living blackness, a slithering, shuffling, shambling, *hungry* blackness, ravenous not for his flesh but for his soul, his essence, his very being. As Bill dropped to his knees and hugged the floor, digging his fingers into the pile to keep from tumbling toward the ceiling, a noxious grave-born odor seeped into his nostrils, caressed his tongue—sour, acrid, moist, carrying a hint of putrescence—gagging him.

And then he saw the eyes, hovering before him. Huge, round, the whites like glazed porcelain, the irises crystalline black, but not nearly as black as the bottomless sinkholes into infinity at their center. From those pupils there radiated such palpable malevolence that Bill had to turn away, squeeze his eyes shut to shield himself from the beckoning madness.

And just as suddenly there was light beyond his lids. He opened his eyes. The living room was lit again. He gasped for air. What had just happened? Had he been hypnotized somehow—or was that the real Rafe?

Bill shook off the body-numbing horror and looked around. Rafe was gone. He staggered to his feet and searched from room to room, upstairs and down—Rafe was nowhere in the condo. Shouting Rafe's name, he stumbled toward the door.

So many questions still unanswered. Who was Rafe? Was he even human? He didn't seem to be. What was his connection to Sara? How could he possibly know about Danny? Bill's numbed mind could barely frame the questions, his tongue couldn't speak them. And there was no one here to answer them.

Danny . . . alive. It couldn't be true, but he had to know. Because if by some unholy power Danny was still alive in that grave, Bill couldn't allow him to stay there a moment longer.

He had to go back. Back to New York, to that cemetery. He had to know!

He ran for his car.

The priest almost caught Renny with his pants down—literally.

Getting into Ryan's house had been easy. The little ranch was set back from the road and surrounded by trees. Completely shielded from its neighbors. Renny broke a pane in the back door, reached in, turned the dead-bolt knob, and he was in. When he saw all the velvet paintings on the walls, the tigers, the clowns, the Elvises, he thought he'd made a mistake. He couldn't imagine the Father Ryan he'd known going for this stuff. But Will Ryerson *had* to be Ryan.

Renny used the first hour or so to search the place but found little of interest. Somewhere along the way he noted the absence of a phone. That bolstered his conviction that he was on target— the last time he'd seen him, the priest had been terrified of phones.

He spent most of the remainder of the day sitting around, watching TV, keeping the sound low. He even brewed himself a pot of coffee and made a sandwich from the cold cuts in the fridge. Why not? Ryan wouldn't be needing them.

But along around five he turned off the TV and seated himself in the front room, his pistol drawn, waiting.

And waiting.

He'd already waited five years for this meeting. He could wait a few more minutes. But these last minutes were killing him, dragging on like slugs on sandpaper.

What's going to happen here?

After all these years, what was he going to do when he came face-to-face with the priest? Renny hoped he wouldn't blow it. He had to keep his cool, because he knew what he wanted to do: nail him to the wall and gut him, just like he'd done to that little kid. But he'd be sacrificing himself then, too.

No. He'd decided to play it straight. Arrest him, take him to the state capital, and start extradition proceedings.

Prison was better than anything Renny could do to the guy. And it was slower. The priest would be a short-eyes to the other cons. As soon as he got to Rikers, he'd find out firsthand about the very special treatment reserved for child molesters by all those guys who practically grew up in prison.

Prison would be much slower. Hell would be a quick little picnic in the shade compared to life in prison for a short-eyes priest.

For the first time since he'd become a cop, Renny was glad New York State didn't have a death penalty.

As the clock crept toward six and the room darkened, Renny began to get antsy. It was a fifteen-minute drive at most from the campus to here. Wasn't he coming?

And then Renny's bladder began sending him increasingly urgent messages. Never failed when he had too much coffee. He went to the window and peered out at the road. No cars in sight. He chanced a quick trip to the bathroom. He was in the middle of relieving himself when he heard tires crunch to a halt on the driveway gravel. Cursing under his breath, he zipped up and rushed down the hall. As he entered the living room, he nearly collided with someone.

The other man cried out and leapt back.

"Who the hell are you?"

Renny reached for a lamp switch and turned it on.

And gaped. Maybe he *had* made a mistake. The bearded, silver-haired guy before him looked nothing like Father William Ryan. Had a ponytail, for crissake! Then Renny took a closer look and recognized him.

Their eyes locked.

"Remember me, Father Bill?"

The guy stared at him, obviously confused, and more than a little frightened by the gun in Renny's hand. Then the confusion cleared.

"Oh, Jesus."

"Jesus ain't gonna help you, you bastard. In fact, I think he'd be the last one who'd want to."

Renny had expected fear, terror, desperation, pleas for mercy, offers to buy him off. He'd been anticipating them with relish. He did see shock and fear in the priest's eyes, but it wasn't fear of Renny. He was afraid of something else. But overriding all of it was a look of exasperation.

"Now?" Ryan said. "*Now* you catch up to me?"

"I may be slow, but I get the job done."

"I haven't got time for this now, dammit!"

Renny was shaken for a second or two. *Haven't got time?* What kind of a reaction was that? He raised the pistol.

"You know how the saying goes: Go ahead—make my day."

"Listen, I've got to get back to New York!"

"Oh, don't worry. That's exactly where you're going. But by way of Raleigh, first."

"No. I've got to get to New York now."

"Uh-uh. You've got to be extradited first."

Renny was doing this by the book. He wasn't about to give some legal snake a chance to screw up this collar. He stared hard at the priest, waiting for the hate to surge up in him, to make him ache to pull the trigger. But it wouldn't come.

Where was all the rage he'd saved and nurtured these five years? Why wasn't it making him crazy now? How could he look at this sick bastard and not want to kill him on the spot?

"That will take too long," Ryan said. "I've got to go right now."

"Forget it. You're—"

The priest turned and headed down the hallway toward the bedroom. Renny hurried after him, aiming his pistol at the back of Ryan's head.

"Stop right where you are or I'll shoot!"

"Then shoot!" Ryan said. "I'm going to New York, and I'm going now. You can arrest me there. That way you won't have to worry about extradition or any of that."

Renny watched in a daze as Ryan pulled off his work shirt and slipped into a long-sleeved striped jersey. This wasn't the way it was supposed to go. What was Ryan up to? A trick of some sort? He had to be extra cautious now. Ryan was a big guy, and crazy as a loon.

Suddenly he noticed him reaching into a slit in the fabric of his box spring. He cocked his pistol.

"Don't try it!"

Ryan pulled his hand out and flashed a wad of bills.

"My savings account."

He grabbed a rumpled sports coat from the closet and brushed by Renny, heading for the living room again.

"Stop, God dammit, or I swear to God I'll shoot!" He lowered the barrel. "You know what it's like to get shot in the knee?"

Ryan stopped and faced him. His eyes were tortured.

"Danny's still alive."

"Bullshit!"

"Just what I would have said. But the person who told me may know what he's talking about."

"Don't give me that! You snatched him and killed him!"

His eyes turned bleak. "I thought I did. I buried him in St. Ann's Cemetery in Queens."

He's admitting it! He's confessing to murder!

Now the rage was coming, rising, filling Renny's mouth with a bitter, metallic taste.

"You bastard!"

"I did it to save him! If I hadn't, he'd *still* be in a hospital somewhere with tubes coming out of every orifice, still suffering the torments of the damned while a bunch of white coats clucked over him! You didn't really think I'd do anything to hurt that boy, did you? He was damaged beyond all hope of repair!"

"Damage *you* did to him! You were abusing him and you couldn't let him go, so you mutilated him!"

He watched the priest's shoulders slump.

"Is that the accepted theory?" He shook his head sadly. "I guess I kind of expected that."

"You got what you deserve, and you're going to get more—a *lot* more. And don't think any bullshit stories about the kid being alive will let you cop an insanity plea. No way."

Ryan didn't reply immediately. He seemed lost in thought for a moment, then he straightened and looked hard at Renny.

"There's only one way to find out, isn't there? We'll have to go back and dig him up."

The idea staggered Renny. Was Ryan crazy enough to lead him to the spot where he'd buried the kid? That would clinch the case against him.

The priest picked up his car keys.

"You coming? I'll drive."

He headed out the front door. Renny ran after him.

TWENTY-FIVE

Queens, New York

He thinks I'm crazy, Bill thought, glancing over at Detective Augustino in the passenger seat. He guided the rental car out of its stall in the Avis garage at LaGuardia and onto the eastbound ramp of the Grand Central Parkway. *Maybe I am.*

He'd explained it all to Augustino on the way up. He'd told him about what he had done on New Year's Eve, and why he had done it. He also told him about Rafe's resemblance to Sara, about the anagram of the names. But as he listened to himself speak he realized how utterly deranged his story sounded. Even he began to have his own doubts, and he'd lived through it.

Danny alive? Why did he even consider it? Even for a second? Of all his ravings, that had to be the most lunatic.

Yet Rafe had told him. *Rafe!* How could Rafe know anything about it if he weren't directly involved?

Augustino's explanation for the whole convoluted mess? "You imagined it all—because you're nuts."

Nuts. This wasn't the first time Bill had considered the possibility, and he was sure it wouldn't be the last. But tonight he sensed he was approaching some sort of watershed that would either confirm or confute his sanity.

As he drove through the dark first hours of Saturday morning, he wasn't sure which he was hoping for.

They found an all-night Shoprite Superstore and bought a pick and shovel in its garden department; they added a flashlight to the bill, then drove the final leg to St. Ann's Cemetery. Bill cruised slowly along the north wall. They'd long since replaced the bulb he'd shot out five years ago, but he recognized the old leaning oak. The detective had been quiet most of the way, but when Bill drove over the curb and onto the grass, he began shouting.

"What the hell are you doing?"

"This is it," Bill said, braking and turning the engine off.

"This is nothing! What are you talking about?"

He opened his mouth to speak but the words wouldn't come. He couldn't believe he was back here, actually talking about it with a stranger. A cop, no less. He tried again.

"This is where I buried him."

Had he? Had he actually done that? It seemed ages ago, a bad dream.

"I thought you said *in* the cemetery."

He looked at the detective. "We can't exactly cruise through the front gate at two in the morning, can we?"

"Maybe this isn't such a good idea," Augustino said. "I can get an exhumation order—"

Bill shoved the flashlight into his coat pocket, opened the door, and stepped out. He opened the rear door and grabbed the pick and shovel.

"Go ahead. Meanwhile, I'll be on the other side of that wall, digging."

In his heart, in his mind, he was sure that Rafe had been lying. He had convinced himself of that during the trip north. But long-suppressed doubts had been set free and were worming through his gut, welling up in the back of his throat. Bill needed to be sure. Waiting for an exhumation order was out of the question. He wanted to put this horror behind him once and for all. Tonight. Now.

He stepped up onto the hood of the car, threw the pick and shovel over the wall, then climbed after them.

Renny hesitated as he watched Ryan haul himself up to the top of the wall. This was getting crazier by the minute. He was letting a madman, a defrocked priest who was a child molester and child *killer* to boot, lead him up and down the East Coast. And now he was supposed to follow Ryan into a deserted cemetery?

I must be crazy!

But it was too late to turn back.

"Shit!" he said.

He slammed a fist against the dashboard. Then, muttering a stream of curses, he followed the priest over the wall.

It was dark on the other side, and for an instant he was mortally afraid. Somewhere nearby was a mad killer with a brand-new pick. He dropped into a crouch and pulled his pistol.

Then he saw the beam of the flashlight a dozen feet away. Ryan stood there like a statue, shining the light on a patch of ground before him. Renny approached warily.

"This is the spot," Ryan said. His voice was hoarse, barely a whisper.

"There's no marker. How can you be sure without a marker?"

"I know where I dug it. You don't forget something like that. And look—no grass."

Renny stared down at the bare patch of ground. Thick, winter-browned grass surrounded the area, but not here.

"Has this been dug up?" Renny said, scuffing his feet on the bare earth. "Somebody beat you to it?"

The priest bounced the business end of the shovel off the hard, cold earth.

"Not recently."

"So there's no grass there. So what?"

The priest's voice was barely audible.

"This isn't the first time I've seen something like this."

Renny couldn't see Ryan's face, but he sensed real fear in the man. Suddenly he became aware of how cold it was here in New York in February. He very much wished he were back in N.C. right now.

"Let's get this over with."

He held the flashlight while the priest did the digging. It was tough work breaking through the granite-hard top soil and at times Renny was tempted to help out, but he couldn't risk it. He couldn't turn his back on this man and let him turn this spot into a double grave—if indeed it was a grave at all.

The priest made quicker progress in the deeper layers below the frost line. When he got the hole hip-deep, he tossed the shovel aside and sank out of sight.

Renny moved closer. Ryan was on his knees, scooping up the dirt with his bare hands.

"What are you doing?"

"I don't want to hit him with the shovel."

He's not going to feel it, you jerk!

But Renny was struck by the reverence in Ryan's tone. That little boy seemed to matter an awful lot to him—even dead.

And after five years at the bottom of that hole, he couldn't be anything *but* dead. But his body could still tell stories. Recovering it would put a whole bunch of nails in Father William Ryan's legal coffin.

"Almost there," the priest said, panting. "Just a little bit fur—"

He jerked back.

"What's wrong?" Renny said.

"Something moved."

"Come on, Ryan!"

"No . . . under the dirt there. Something moved. I felt it."

Renny stepped up to the edge and shone the light into the bottom of the hole. He didn't see anything moving.

"Probably just a mole or something," he said, trying to sound calm.

"No," said the priest, his voice so hushed Renny could barely hear him. "It's Danny. He's still alive. Oh, God, he's still alive!"

He began to paw at the earth, frantically.

"Easy, fella. Just take it easy."

Christ Almighty, don't go to pieces on me now.

"I feel him!" The priest was shouting as he tossed huge handfuls of dirt into the air, showering Renny and himself with cold, damp earth. "I feel him moving!"

And damned if the dirt in front of the priest didn't seem to be heaving and rippling, as if something was squirming and struggling beneath it. Renny swallowed what little saliva remained in his mouth. A trick of the light. It couldn't be anything but—

But then something broke through the surface and writhed in the light. At first Renny thought it was some sort of giant white worm, then realized it was an arm, a thin little arm, twisting and flailing in the air. But not a whole arm. It looked tattered and moth-eaten, the skin stiff and dry, the flesh rotted away in areas to expose the underlying bone.

Renny gagged and almost dropped the flashlight, but the priest kept on digging, sobbing as he clawed at the earth. Finally he uncovered the remnants of what looked like a blanket. He grabbed two fistfuls of the fabric and yanked upward. The material ripped with a soggy sound, the overlying layer of earth parted, and what was left of Danny Gordon sat up in his grave.

Or maybe it wasn't Danny Gordon. Who could tell? It was child-sized, but whatever it was, it had no business moving and acting alive. It belonged in a grave. It belonged dead.

Renny felt the strength rush out of him as he watched the thing in the jittering beam of the flashlight. Where its head and upper torso were exposed the flesh was as tattered and rotted as the arm that still wr.thed in the air like a snake. It reached for the priest and Father Bill didn't hesitate. He took the worm-eaten thing in his arms and clutched it against his chest. Then he raised his head and cried out to heaven in a voice so full of anguish and despair that it damn near broke Renny's heart.

"My God, my God! How could you allow this? How could you *allow* this?"

Renny probably would have been able to handle it if he hadn't seen the eyes. He'd managed okay through the smell, through the sight of a dead thing moving like it was alive, but then came that moment when it turned its face toward the light and he saw the perfect blue eyes, moist, bright, shining, untouched by rot. Little Danny Gordon's eyes, fully alive and aware in that decaying skull.

Renny's nerve snapped then. He dropped the flashlight and ran. A part of him hated himself for bolting like a panicked deer, but a larger, more primitive element had taken hold, shrieking in fear, overruling any action but flight. He reached the cemetery wall and leapt but couldn't get a grip on the top. He caromed off and ran to the leaning tree nearby, scrabbled up its rough bark, swung to the top of the wall and leapt down, landing next to the rental car. He slumped against the fender and heaved, but nothing would come up. So he stood there panting and sweating, his eyes closed.

He'd been right! The priest had been right! The kid was still alive—buried for five years and still alive! *Five years in the ground!* This couldn't be happening.

Yet it was, dammit! He'd seen it with his own eyes. No question about it—something hellish going on here.

From the far side of the wall he could still hear Father Bill's voice, ranting at the empty winter sky.

And then he heard something else. Footsteps approaching.

Renny straightened and looked around, stiffening at the sight of a bundled-up figure limping toward him across the frozen ground. A big guy, but not too steady on his feet. He supported himself with a cane in one hand; something boxlike dangled from the other and bounced against his leg as he walked.

"Get out of here," Renny said, his voice tight and raspy. For want of something better to say, he added, "Police business."

The old man didn't even slow his pace; unperturbed, he continued forward. When he stepped into the glare from the streetlight, he stopped and stared at Renny. He wore a heavy topcoat. The brim of his hat kept much of his face in shadow, but from what Renny saw of his white beard and lined cheeks, he could tell he was old.

"You've opened the grave, I gather," the old man said.

Christ, who else knows about this?

"Look," Renny managed to say, "this is none of your business. If you're smart, you'll go back to wherever you came from and stay the hell out of this."

"You're quite right about that, but . . ." He paused and almost seemed to be considering taking Renny's advice. Then he sighed and held up the object he was carrying. "Here. You'll need this."

Renny saw now that it wasn't a box but a can—a two-gallon gasoline can. Its contents sloshed within.

"I don't understand."

The old man jerked his head toward the cemetery.

"For whoever was buried in that unmarked grave. It's the only way to end it."

Instantly Renny knew he was right. He didn't know where this old guy had come from, but he realized this was the solution.

But it meant going back over the wall, seeing that thing that was all that remained of Danny Gordon. He didn't want to do that, didn't know if he could.

It was quiet on the other side of the wall now. Father Bill was alone in there with that thing that had been—and in a way still was—Danny Gordon. Alone. Because Renny had run out on him. And Renaldo Augustino had never run out on anyone in his life. He wasn't about to start now.

He grabbed the gasoline can and hopped up on the car hood. As he straddled the top of the wall, he looked back at the old man.

"Don't go anywhere. I want to talk to you."

"I'll wait in your car, if you don't mind. I came by cab."

Renny didn't say anything. He looked down at the dark side of the wall. There was the last place he wanted to be. But he'd come this far already; had to see it through to the end. He slid over the edge and down. As soon as he hit the ground he spotted the flashlight, pointing toward him from where he had dropped it. Setting his jaw, he took a deep breath and hurried toward it on rubbery legs.

Bill sobbed as he held Danny's reeking, squirming remains in his arms. How could this be? Five years in the earth! Had he been alive—alive but slowly rotting—and in agony all that time? Who or what was responsible for this? Why was something like this *allowed*?

He heard a sound and stretched to raise his eyes above ground level. Detective Augustino was returning, carrying something, stumbling toward him on legs that looked like they were ready to give out any second. For an instant he reminded Bill of Ray Bolger's Scarecrow.

Augustino picked up the flashlight and pointed it into the grave. Bill winced in the brightness.

"Let him go and come out of there, Father," said Augustino's voice from behind the light.

Bill was startled by the "Father"—it was the first time the detective had called him that since their reunion a few hours ago. But he wasn't going to abandon Danny.

"No!" Bill said, clutching the animate remains of the boy more tightly against him. "We can't just cover him up again!"

"We won't just cover him up." The detective's voice sounded flat, almost dead. "We're going to put an end to this once and for all."

Bill looked down at Danny's ravaged face and into the tortured blue eyes. If only he could end his pain . . .

He laid him back and crawled out of the hole. He saw the gasoline can at Augustino's feet.

"Oh, no," Bill said. The response was instinctive. The thought was appalling. "We can't."

"Look what's already been done to him. Can you think of anything worse?"

No. He couldn't. He could barely think at all. Yet somewhere deep inside he knew fire would work. The cleansing flame . . .

"It's got to be done," the detective said. "Want me to do it?"

Bill could hear very plainly in his voice that it was the last thing in the world Augustino wanted to do.

"No. It's my job. I put him into her clutches; I'll get him out."

He grabbed the can and unscrewed the cap. The odor of the fumes set something off within him and he began to cry as he poured the gasoline into the hole.

"Forgive me, Danny. It's the only way."

When the can was empty, he turned to the detective. Augustino already had a matchbook out. Bill took it from him and paused.

"I can't do this to him."

"Then do it *for* him."

Bill nodded—to Augustino, to the night, to himself. Then he emptied his mind, struck one match, used it to light the rest of the pack. As it flared, he dropped the whole thing into the hole.

The gas exploded with a *wooomp!* and the heat staggered him back. There was no cry from the hole and he could see no movement within the flames—he was grateful for that. But he couldn't watch. He had to turn his back, walk away, lean against the tree. Part of him wanted to cry, part of him wanted to be sick, but he was tapped out, dry, empty. He was little more than skin wrapped around a void.

Only anger remained.

What had happened to Danny wasn't some sort of cosmic accident. It had been *done* to him. And the ones who had done it were still out there. Bill resisted the urge to scream out his rage at the night; he held it in, nurturing it, saving it for those who were responsible. He swore he'd find them.

And make them pay.

Renny stood over the hole until the fire died down to a few sputtering flames. Father Bill came up and stood beside him as he played the flashlight beam over the glowing ashes. He glanced at the priest's face. Something scary was moving behind those blue eyes.

"Is it over?" the priest said.

"Yeah," Renny said. "Has to be."

Nothing moved down there. Danny Gordon was quiet at last. Little more than his bones left now. The rotted flesh that had clung to him before had crisped and fallen away. Renny could see his naked skull, but no eyes. He was gone.

"Peace, kid," he said. "Peace at last."

He picked up the shovel.

"You want to say a few words?"

"I'm sorry, Danny," the priest said. "I'm so sorry." And then he was silent.

"No prayers?"

Father Bill shook his head. "I'm through with prayers. Let's cover him up."

They filled in the hole quickly, then started back toward the wall.

"I suppose you'll be taking me in now," Father Bill said.

Renny had been thinking about that. His whole world had been turned upside down in the past hour. He'd put his career on the line to bring this man to justice, and now he no longer had the vaguest idea of what would constitute justice in the face of what he had just seen. Father William Ryan was not the monster Renny had thought him to be for the past five years. But he had nurtured his hatred for the man so long that it was difficult to let go of it now. Yet he had to. Because everything was different now. And what did a career mean—what did the *law* mean—after what had happened to Danny Gordon?

"I don't know," Renny said. "You got a better idea?"

"Yeah. Go back to North Carolina and pick up Rafe Losmara and bring him back to my place and keep him there till he tells us what we want to know."

"And what do we want to know?"

"What the hell was done to that boy!"

"Maybe we won't have to go to North Carolina to find out. There's a guy in the car who might have some answers."

The priest stopped and stared at him.

"Who?"

"I don't know. But he's the guy who brought the gasoline."

Suddenly Father Bill was running for the tree. He monkeyed up the trunk and was over the wall before Renny had taken half a dozen steps.

Bill approached the car warily, almost afraid of who he might find there—maybe even Rafe Losmara himself. When he peered through the blurry glass, he was relieved to see that the man sitting in the back seat appeared to be a lot bigger and older than Rafe. He opened the driver door and saw by the light of the courtesy lamp that he was much older. Eighty at least. Maybe eighty-five.

"You brought the gasoline?"

The old man nodded. "I guessed you'd need it." His voice was dry, leathery.

"But who are you? And how did you know we'd be here? Even *we* didn't know we'd be here until tonight."

"The name is Veilleur. The rest is difficult to explain."

Bill slumped under the weight of what he had done tonight. The fatigue was catching up to him.

"It can't be as difficult as what we just went through in there."

"No. I imagine not. But you did the only thing you could. He is at peace now."

"I hope so," Bill said as the detective jumped in on the passenger side.

"He is. I can tell."

Bill studied the craggy face and found that he believed the old man.

"But *why?*" Bill said. "Why did this happen to that little boy? He never hurt anyone. Why was he put through that hell?"

"Never mind the whys for now," Augustino said, lighting a cigarette. "I want to know *who.*"

"I don't know the why," the old man said. "But I may be able to help with the who."

Bill twisted around in his seat; he noticed that Augustino did the same. They spoke simultaneously.

"Who?"

"Drive me home first. And on the way, tell me what you know about the one in the cemetery, and what brought you back to him now."

TWENTY-SIX

Pendleton, North Carolina

It was almost closing time when she found him.

Lisl's feet were killing her. She'd spent the entire night trudging the length of Conway Street and down some side streets as well. Toward the end she'd become desperate and searched through places she had no business even walking by, let alone wandering through. She endured the catcalls, the lewd remarks, the cheap feels. As far as she was concerned, she deserved every one of them.

And where was Will? He'd said he'd be starting at the south end and they'd meet in the middle, but she hadn't seen him since he dropped her off. She'd gone back to her car and had cruised around, looking for him, but it was almost as if he'd disappeared. She hoped he was all right.

Sometime after midnight, as she was passing near Ev's apartment house, she looked up at the third floor and saw a light in one of his windows.

He's home! Thank God, he's home!

Served her right. Here she was trooping all over town looking for him while he was sitting comfortably at home.

But *was* he sitting comfortably? Or was he dead drunk? An image of Ev lying on his bathroom floor in a pool of vomit flashed through her brain.

One way to find out was to call. She cruised a couple of blocks farther down the street, looking for a phone. She spotted a booth on a corner and pulled into the curb next to it. Her hand trembled as she fumbled a coin into the slot. What she wanted right now was to hear Ev pick up the phone and ask her in a perfectly sober voice what on earth she was doing calling him at this hour. Wouldn't that be wonderful? She wanted to learn that Ev was fine and that this entire night of anxiety and self-loathing had been for nothing.

Well, not for nothing. She'd learned an awful lesson tonight, and she'd looked inside herself and seen some things she was ashamed of, things she'd have to change.

But she had to talk to Ev first, make sure he was okay. That was top priority now.

But the pay phone was dead. It ate her quarter and wouldn't give her a dial tone. As she searched on foot for another, she passed a bar called Raftery's. She had been in there earlier looking for Ev. Maybe they had a phone.

Inside, Raftery's was dark and smoky and boozy-smelling, just like every other place she'd been in tonight. She remembered having high hopes for this place when she'd searched it earlier because it was the closest to Ev's apartment. It had been packed a few hours ago, but the crowd had thinned considerably now.

She spotted a pay phone on the back wall near the restrooms and headed for it. As she moved past the bar, still rimmed with drinkers, she spotted a solitary figure slumped in a corner booth. Thinning hair, a slight frame, glasses . . .

"Ev!"

She practically shouted his name. People stared at her as she pushed her way through the maze of intervening tables. She'd found him. But her initial elation was fading as she realized where she had found him, and her awareness of the shape he was in.

"Ev?" she said, sliding into the other side of the booth. "Are you all right, Ev?"

His bleary eyes focused on her through his glasses. For a moment he seemed confused, then his face broke into a smile.

"Lisl! Lisl, what a surprise!" His voice was loud, the words slurred. Her name came out *Lee-shul.* "It's so good to see you. Here, let me get you a drink!"

"No thanks, Ev. I really —"

"C'mon, Lisl! Loosen up a little! It's Friday night! It's *party* time!"

Lisl gave him a closer look to make sure this ebullient barfly was really Everett Sanders. He was.

Drunk as a skunk—and my fault.

She pushed back the self-recrimination. Plenty of time for that later. Right now she had to try to undo some of what she'd done.

"I've had enough for the night, Ev. And so have you. Let me take you home."

"Don't want to go home," he said.

"Sure you do. You can sleep it off there."

"Not home. Don't like it there."

"Then we'll go someplace else."

"Yeah. Someplace that swings! Not like this graveyard!"

"Right."

Someplace where we can get you some coffee.

She took his arm and helped him out of the booth. He swayed when he stood up, and for a moment she feared he might topple over. But he steadied himself on her. He could barely walk, but together they made it to the cooler, fresher air outside.

"Where're we going?" he said as she guided him into the passenger seat of her car.

She hurried around and got in the other side.

"To get some coffee."

"Don't want coffee."

"Ev, I want you to sober up. I've got to talk to you about some things and I can't do it while you're loaded."

He looked at her groggily. "You want to talk to me? You've never wanted to talk to me before."

The simple statement caught Lisl by surprise. The truth of it touched her as deeply as it cut her. She smiled at him.

"Well, that's changed as of tonight—along with a lot of other things."

"All right then. Let's get coffee."

She drove to the Pantry on Greensboro Street and ran inside while Ev waited in the car. She got two large coffees to go and hurried back outside. When she got back in the car, Ev was snoring. She tried to wake him but he was out.

Now what?

She could take him back to his apartment house but there was no way she could get him upstairs. Same with her place. She wished Will were here.

She opened her coffee and drank some. It felt good and warm going down. Getting chilly out and she wasn't dressed for it. Neither was Ev. The only thing to do was drive around with the heater on and keep him warm until he woke up.

She dreaded that moment. Because she was going to have to make a decision then about how much to tell Ev. But until then, she'd keep the car moving.

She put it in gear and headed for the highway.

TWENTY-SEVEN

Manhattan

Bill waited impatiently for the old man to return from his wife's bedroom. Apparently she was pretty sick. Sick enough to need a full-time nurse. And Veilleur appeared wealthy enough to afford one. Bill knew nothing about the current state of Manhattan real estate, but he knew a top-floor condo overlooking Central Park like this didn't come cheap.

During the drive from Queens, Bill had told Augustino and Veilleur everything—from what he'd done New Year's Eve all the way to Rafe Losmara's revelation that Danny was still alive in his grave.

The detective came over to where Bill was standing at the window, looking down at the empty, illuminated traverses snaking through the dark of Central Park.

"You know, Father, I think I had you all wrong."

"Don't call me Father," Bill said. "I'm not a priest anymore. The name's Bill."

"All right, Bill. Call me Renny." He sighed. "I've spent a lot of years thinking some pretty awful thoughts about you."

"Perfectly understandable."

"Yeah. And now I'm thinking some pretty brutal thoughts about this Losmara guy and what I'd like to do to him and his sister—because I don't think the legal system's going to be much use here."

Bill turned toward the bedroom as he heard some high-pitched

English words mixed with some other language that sounded East European.

Renny said, "Sounds like Mrs. Dracula—having a nightmare."

Veilleur returned to the living room then. He eased himself into a chair and indicated the facing sofa for Bill and the detective.

"Sorry for the delay," he said, "but I wanted to make sure the nurse was in her own room and my wife settled quietly for the rest of the night before we talked."

"Is she a light sleeper?" Bill asked, more out of courtesy than any real interest.

"Yes. She tends to get her nights and days mixed up."

Bill started when he noticed the telephone by his elbow.

"That won't be bothering you anymore," Veilleur said. "But let's get back to this young man in North Carolina. You say he calls himself Losmara?"

"Yes. Which is an anagram of Sara Lom, the woman from five years ago I told you about."

"Both of which are anagrams of another name." He smiled tiredly and shook his head. "Still playing games."

"What's the other name?" Augustino asked from Bill's right on the sofa.

"Rasalom."

"What kind of a name is that?"

"A very old one."

"Is that their family name?" Bill said.

"Who?" The old man looked confused.

"Rafe and his sister."

"There is no sister. Only one—Rasalom. Within certain limits, he can change himself. The one you called Sara and the one you call Rafe are the same person."

"No," Bill said, closing his eyes and letting his head fall back. "That can't be."

But why couldn't it be? After what had happened to that hollow thing called Herbert Lom, to Danny, why was he balking at this minor trick.

He opened his eyes and stared into Veilleur's.

"We're out of our depth here, aren't we?"

"This is out of everyone's depth," Veilleur said.

"What are we up against?"

"Rasalom."

"And who the hell is *that*?" Augustino said.

Veilleur sighed. "After what you two have seen tonight, I suppose you're ready to believe. It's a very long story and I'm very tired, so I'll capsulize it for you. Rasalom used to be a man. He was born ages ago. Rasalom isn't even his real name, but a name he took and has used in various permutations ever since. Ages ago, as a youth, he gave himself over to a power that is inimical to everything we consider good and decent and rational. He became a focus for the hostile forces outside this sphere, and for all that is dark and hateful within humanity. He gains strength from what is worst in us. Like a hydroelectric dam, he stands in the flow of human baseness, venality, corruption, viciousness, and depravity and draws power from it."

"Power?" Bill said. "Just what does that mean?"

"The power to change things. To alter the world, make it into a place more to the liking of the force he serves."

Beside him, Bill heard Augustino snort in disgust.

"Gimme a break, will you? I mean, this sounds like fairy-tale stuff."

"I'm sure you said the same thing when your priest friend here told you that a boy who'd been buried for five years was still alive."

"Yeah," Augustino said, nodding slowly and shrugging. "You got a point there. But it still sounds like a Nintendo game. You know, stop the Evil Wizard before he finds the Ring of Power and rules the world. That sort of thing."

"Except it's no game," Veilleur said. "And did you ever consider why that sort of story is so powerful, why it recurs again and again, fascinating one generation after another?"

"No, but I've got a feeling you're going to tell me."

"Racial memory. This war has been fought before . . . and almost lost. With results so devastating, human history had to restart itself. Rasalom keeps trying, though. But he has failed each time because he has always been countered by someone representing an opposing force."

"Come on!" Augustino said. "The old war between Good and Evil story."

Bill was tempted to tell him to shut up and let the old man talk.

"Except that the Good here isn't terribly good," Veilleur said, seemingly unperturbed by the detective. "It tends to be rather indifferent to our fate. It's more interested in opposing the other force than in doing anything for us. And when it appeared that Rasalom had finally been stopped for good, the opposing force went elsewhere."

"When was that?" Bill said.

"In 1941."

"So how come he's back?"

"He has a knack for survival and he was very lucky. This is not the first body he's worn. It's all very complicated. Suffice it to say that he found a way to be reborn in 1968."

1968. Why did that year send ripples across Bill's brain?

"How do you know so much about this?" Augustino said.

"I have been studying him a long time."

"That's all fine and good," Bill said. He wasn't buying all of this, but the old man had been laying out his story so matter-of-factly that Bill found himself believing him. He should have been writing him off as a kook, but after tonight he wasn't going to be too quick about writing anything off as too crazy to be true. "But what is he up to? Why pick on Danny? Why pick on Lisl? There's no road to world domination there."

"Who can say what goes on in Rasalom's mind. I can tell you this, however: He receives his greatest satisfaction from human self-degradation. When he can bring out the worst in us, when he can induce us to lose faith in ourselves, convince us to choose to be less than we can be, to choose the low road, so to speak, it's . . . I think it's like a cosmic sort of sex for him. Plus, he grows stronger with each incident."

Bill couldn't help but think of Lisl. That certainly sounded like what Rafe—or Rasalom, if Veilleur was to be believed—had been doing to her.

"But why Danny and Lisl? Why would he be interested in them?"

"Oh, I doubt very much that they were his real targets."

"Then who?"

"Think about it. They were both very close to you. Losing the little boy sent you into a tailspin from which you barely recovered. Might that not happen again if something similar occurred to the young woman in question?"

His heart pounding with sudden horror, Bill straightened up on the couch.

"Are you saying—?"

"Yes," Veilleur said, nodding. "I think *you* are Rasalom's target."

Bill stood up. He had to move, had to walk around the room. More craziness! It couldn't be! But it explained so many things. And there was a hellish consistency to it.

"But *why,* God dammit! Why me?"

"I don't know," Veilleur said. "But I may know someone who

does. We can't talk to her right now. But in the morning, I'll call her. For now I suggest we all get a little rest."

Bill continued to prowl the room.

Rest? How could he rest if all Danny had suffered and what Lisl was going through were because of him?

TWENTY-EIGHT

North Carolina

Lisl locked the car with Ev sleeping peacefully inside and walked into the truck stop. A couple of times during the last half hour he'd stirred and she'd thought he was going to come around, but he never actually opened his eyes. She hoped he woke up soon so she could get him back to his apartment and get some sleep herself.

She was beat. Almost dawn now and she was verging on twenty-four hours with no sleep. As an undergrad she'd had no trouble pulling all-nighters at exam time, but that had been over a decade ago. She'd become accustomed to her sleep these days.

If nothing else, the endless drive had given her plenty of time to think. Her thoughts had turned inward and she hadn't liked what she'd found. How had she become so warped? How had she allowed Rafe to twist her up into someone who could pour alcohol into an alcoholic's orange juice? She hated Rafe for doing that to her. And simultaneously she felt her insides heat with desire at the thought of him.

God, she was a mess. She was going to need help to straighten herself out after this.

But first she had to get Ev straight.

She shivered in the dawn breeze and her hand shook as she reached for the door to the coffee shop. This must have been her eighth stop since leaving the Pantry in Pendleton, and she'd bought coffee at every one. Too little sleep and too much caffeine.

Tired and wired. She smiled at the phrase. Not bad. She'd have to remember that.

She wondered how many miles she'd put on her car tonight. She'd swung by Will's house first. The lights were on, the door was unlocked, but he wasn't there. So she'd taken 40 north to the interstate and had cruised 95 ever since. Traffic had been light. She'd set the cruise control on fifty-five and settled into the right lane. But the truck traffic was picking up now. Maybe it was time to head back toward Pendleton.

Inside the coffee shop the counter was crowded with truckers having breakfast. She guessed most of them had spent the night in the cabs of those big eighteen-wheelers lined up in the parking lot, but some looked like they'd just come off the road. She'd gained new respect tonight for long-haul drivers.

She was aware of appraising stares from many and even heard a few whistles. She glanced at herself in one of the mirrored walls and saw a pale, haggard-looking woman with circles under her eyes and wind-tangled hair.

They've got to be kidding!

Maybe driving all night not only made truckers tired, but desperate and nearsighted as well.

She poured herself a coffee from the take-out pot, added two sugars, and grabbed a wrapped donut. Another whistle followed her out the door after she'd paid.

Halfway to her car, she froze in the middle of the parking lot. The passenger door was open. But she'd locked the car. She ran toward it. There was a puddle of vomit under the door. The car was empty. Ev was gone.

She set the coffee and donut on the trunk and stepped up on the bumper for a better look. Frantically, she scanned the parking lot but saw no one who looked like Ev. And then, all the way around behind her, she spotted a lone figure, thin, lost-looking, stumbling toward the highway.

She ran after him, shouting his name, and caught up to Ev near the edge of the roadway.

"Lisl?" he said, squinting at her in the dim light. He looked dazed, but he didn't seem drunk anymore. "What are you doing here?"

"I drove you here."

"You? But how? I don't remember. And where are we?"

She could barely hear him over the roar of a passing truck, but the confusion in his eyes said it all.

"I found you in a bar. You were . . ."

She saw his shoulders slump, his head drop until his chin touched his chest.

"I know. Drunk." With a moan that echoed from the deepest part of him, Ev dropped to his knees and buried his face in his hands. "Oh, Lisl, I'm so ashamed." He began to sob.

The utter misery in the sound made Lisl feel as if someone were tearing her heart out of her chest. She sank down beside him and threw her arms around him.

"Don't, Ev. Please don't. It's not your fault."

He didn't seem to hear her. He lifted his head and stared out at the thickening traffic.

"I thought I had it licked. I had my life completely under control. I had a career, I was making progress, I was working on a paper, everything was going perfectly."

"Nothing's changed, Ev. You still have all that to go back to. You can forget about tonight and pick up things where you left off."

"No," he said, still not looking at her. "You don't understand. I'm an alcoholic. I'll always be an alcoholic. I thought I had it under control, smothered, locked away, but I can see now that I'll never really control it. It's like a ticking bomb that can go off at any time. If I can fall off the wagon like this after all these years, when everything's going so well for me, what's going to happen the first time something goes wrong? Don't you see, Lisl? I'm a slave to this thing! I thought I'd won but I didn't. I'm a loser! And I'll go on being a loser! I think I'd rather be dead!"

"No, Ev!" she said. His doomed, hopeless tone frightened her. "Don't talk like that! You didn't fall off the wagon, you were pushed. You didn't lose in a fair fight. You were ambushed."

Finally, he looked at her.

"What are you talking about?"

"Your orange juice. There was alcohol in it."

"No," he said, shaking his head. "That's impossible. I bought it at the A & P. There couldn't be . . ."

His voice trailed off as he stared at her. Lisl wanted to turn away but couldn't. She had to face this, and face it now.

"How do you know?" he said.

"I know . . ." The words clogged in her throat, but she squeezed her eyes shut and forced them out. "I know because I put it there."

There. She'd said it. The awful truth was out. Now she had to face the music. She opened her eyes and saw Ev staring at her, face slack, mouth agape.

"No, Lisl," he said in a hushed voice. "You wouldn't—
couldn't—do that."

"I did, Ev. And I'm deeply ashamed. That's why I'm here with
you now."

"No, Lisl. You have too much integrity to do something like
that. Besides, you couldn't have known I was an alcoholic."

"I did, Ev." God, she wanted to run down the highway rather
than speak these words. "I followed you to a meeting in the
basement of St. James. I knew exactly what you were."

"But how? Why?"

"When I borrowed your keys last week, I . . . had copies made."

The shock in Ev's eyes was quickly fading to hurt.

"You made copies? After I trusted you with my keys? Lisl, I
thought you were a friend!"

"Friend?" she said, suddenly overcome by a need to justify
herself. "*Friend?* Do you call someone who has lunch with the
department chairman and whines not to let a *woman* be tenured
before him a friend?"

"Me? Lunch with Dr. Masterson? Where did you hear that?
I've never had lunch with Masterson. I never have lunch with
anyone."

And in that awful instant Lisl knew that Ev was telling the truth.
Rafe had lied to her.

"Oh, God, no!" she moaned.

Why? Why would Rafe lie about Ev? Why had he been so
intent on turning her against him? She fought an urge to explain to
Ev about Rafe, to make him see that it wasn't her fault, that Rafe
had made her do it. But he hadn't made her do anything. He'd lied
to her, but that was beside the point. Even if his stories about Ev
had been true, that didn't justify spiking Ev's orange juice. There
was *no* justification for that. What was she going to say? The Dev-
il made me do it? There was no one and nothing to hide behind.

She looked at Ev now and saw the profound hurt in his face.
She'd have much preferred anger. Hatred, maniacal rage—she
could deal with having angered someone. But not hurt. She felt
like crawling away on her belly.

"Lord, what's wrong with me?" he said.

"But don't you see, Ev?" she said, desperately searching for a
bright side to this. "You can't blame yourself for falling off the
wagon. If you'd been left alone, if I hadn't planted that bomb
in your refrigerator, if you'd been allowed a free choice, you
wouldn't have started drinking again. Don't blame yourself. It's
my fault, not yours."

"I almost wish it were my fault," Ev said in a worn, desolate tone.

"No. Don't say that."

He struggled to his feet and she rose with him. He began wandering around her in a jagged circle.

"It's true. I don't have many friends, Lisl. In fact, I don't have any. I was never good at making them when I was sober. That was one of the reasons I drank. But I thought *we* were friends, Lisl. Well, not really friends, but colleagues at least. I thought you had some respect for me, some consideration. I never dreamed you'd do something like this to me."

"Neither did I, Ev. Neither did I."

"What did I ever do to you to make you hate me so?"

"Oh, Ev, I don't hate you!"

"Lord, how stupid I was!" he said. His voice was rising. "What an idiot! I trusted you! I . . . *liked* you. What a fool! What a goddamned fool!"

"No, Ev! I'm the fool. And I am your friend. I'll help you get things right again."

"And what about my work? What about my paper for Palo Alto?"

"What about it?"

"It's gone. Wiped out! Even my backup files. Wiped out! That was no accident! If you had access to my refrigerator, you also had access to my codes. Lisl, how could you? You could have brushed me aside if you wanted to get to the top. You didn't have to crush me like some sort of insect!" He stopped moving and put a hand to his face. A muffled sob escaped. "How could I have been so wrong about you?"

Lisl stood straight, silent, stunned. Ev's paper—gone? Who could have—?

And then she knew. Rafe. He'd spotted Ev's access codes next to the terminal in his apartment. Rafe must have wiped them out. But what could he be thinking? What could be his purpose? Could he believe by any stretch of the imagination that he was helping her?

"Ev, I didn't touch your files."

But Ev wasn't listening. He was wandering away from her, stumbling across the brown grass toward the highway. His words were garbled by the roar of the traffic, but snatches drifted back to her.

" . . . thought I had it all under control . . . wrong . . . fool . . . actually thought I had something . . . had nothing . . . thought I could rely on Lisl at least . . . didn't have to squash me . . . what's the use . . . can't take it anymore . . . can't start all over again . . ."

"Ev! Come back!"

At first she thought he was just trying to get away from her, and she couldn't say she blamed him. Even Lisl didn't feel like getting into a car with herself. He looked as if he was going to get on the shoulder and start thumbing for a ride.

But Ev didn't stop at the shoulder. He kept on walking straight out, into the right lane.

Oh, no! Oh, my God! What's he doing?

Lisl screamed his name, but if he heard her he didn't acknowledge it.

She began running after him. By sheer blind luck the right lane had been empty and he'd crossed it unscathed, but now he was stepping into the middle lane and there was a truck roaring through the half-light from the left. Lisl heard the horn, heard the agonized scream of the brakes blend with her own as the eighteen-wheel juggernaut bore down on Ev's frail figure. Lisl saw him turn toward the hurtling mass of chromed steel. And in the last instant before it thundered into him, he turned his face toward her. For a heartbeat his tortured, miserable eyes locked on hers, and then amid a spray of crimson he dissolved into the front grille of the truck.

Lisl could only stand on the shoulder and scream until her voice gave out and the emergency squad came and someone led her away.

TWENTY-NINE

Manhattan

Mr. Veilleur was up at first light, clanking around the kitchen. Bill hadn't realized how hungry he was until the odors began seeping through the apartment. Eggs over easy, bacon, rye toast, and the best coffee in recent memory. All served by Mr. Veilleur himself.

Veilleur didn't eat with them. Instead, he put together a breakfast tray and accompanied the nurse into his wife's bedroom. Bill waited impatiently for his return, looking at his watch, thinking about Lisl, wondering if she'd found Everett Sanders, and what she'd told the poor guy. Bill knew she was probably counting on him for help, but this was more important.

When Veilleur returned to the kitchen half an hour later, Bill cornered him at the sink.

"This person who can tell us what's going on—when can we see her?"

Veilleur glanced at the clock on the wall.

"I can call her in a few minutes. I don't want to risk it while her husband is home."

"Why not?"

"Because," Veilleur said with a wink, "Mrs. Treece and I have been meeting in secret."

Bill wandered back to where Renny was watching *Good Morning, America* and wondered why he couldn't get a straight answer from anyone.

A few minutes later Mr. Veilleur stuck his head in the room.

"Mrs. Treece will be over in half an hour."

Bill asked if he could use the phone. Veilleur told him to go ahead. He was almost afraid to touch it, but he forced his hand to pick up the receiver and put it to his ear. When he heard a dial tone, he had a sudden urge to cry.

Maybe it's over—really, finally over.

He called North Carolina and got Lisl's number, then dialed her apartment. He let it ring a good while but there was no answer. If she wasn't home, it probably meant she'd found Sanders and had taken him back to his place. He tried information again for Everett Sanders's number but it was unlisted.

He hoped everything was going all right down there without him.

While waiting for Mrs. Treece to show up, he heard Mrs. Veilleur's accented voice shouting from the bedroom.

"Glen! Glen! Where's my breakfast? I smell breakfast cooking! Isn't anyone going to give me any? I'm hungry!"

Bill nodded and listened as Veilleur went in and patiently explained to his Magda that she'd just had breakfast and that lunch was still hours away.

"You're lying to me!" the woman said. "Nobody's fed me for weeks! I'm starving here!"

Suddenly Bill knew Mrs. Veilleur's problem, and the need for a full-time nurse: Alzheimer's disease. And abruptly Mr. Veilleur changed from a mystery man with a jealously guarded store of arcane knowledge to someone very human coping with a terrible burden.

But why had she called him Glen? The name on the mailbox downstairs had listed him as Gaston. He shrugged it off. Probably just a nickname.

The doorman called up shortly thereafter to announce that Mrs. Treece had arrived. A few minutes later there was a knock on the door and Veilleur opened it.

She was older, her hair shorter and more styled, her face thinner, more lined, but it was her.

"*Carol!*" Bill said as soon as his throat unlocked. "Carol Stevens!"

The woman stared at him in shock, without the slightest hint of recognition in her eyes.

"No—no one's called me that for—"

"Carol, it's me! Bill Ryan!"

And then she knew him. He could see it in the widening of her eyes as the old memories reconciled with the changed man before her. Her lips quivered and she looked as if she was going to cry. She opened her arms and rushed toward him.

"Bill! Oh, my God! It really is you!"

And then his arms were around her, crushing her to him as he swung her off the floor. He heard her sobbing against his neck and felt his own eyes fill with tears.

Finally he let her down but still she clung to him.

"Oh, God, Bill, I thought you were dead!"

"In a way, I was," he said. Carol . . . so good to hold her . . . like being brought back to life. "But not anymore."

The last time he'd seen her had been in 1968 when she'd boarded that plane with her father-in-law, Jonah Stevens. That had been right after the other horrors—Jim's violent death, the bizarre murders in the Hanley mansion, the crazy talk about her unborn child being the Antichrist.

Her child! Carol had been pregnant the last time he'd seen her.

A slow chill began to crawl through him. Veilleur had said the woman coming this morning might be able to answer Bill's questions about what had happened to Danny and what was happening to Lisl. Carol's child would have been born in 1968, making him just about . . .

Rafe's age.

He stepped back and looked at her, then at Veilleur, then back to Carol.

"Are you . . . is she . . . Rafe's mother?"

"Who's Rafe?" she said.

Mr. Veilleur said, "I believe we've found your son, Mrs. Treece."

"Jimmy?" she said, her fingers digging into Bill's arms. "You've found Jimmy?"

Jimmy. She'd named the boy after her late husband, Bill's old friend Jim Stevens.

Bill described Rafe to her and she nodded slowly.

"That sounds like him."

She fished in her purse and came up with a wrinkled photo. She handed it to Bill. His knees weakened as he stared down at a slim, dark, handsome teenage boy who looked more like Sara than Rafe.

"That's him," he croaked.

"What's he done?" she said softly.

Bill could barely stand, let alone speak. Still clutching the photo, he stepped back and found a seat. Rafe was Carol's son?

But Veilleur had said Rafe was some sort of evil immortal whose real name was Rasalom.

"Someone had better explain this to me," Bill said.

Veilleur closed the nurse in the bedroom with his wife, then the four of them seated themselves in the living room. Carol was introduced to Renny. Bill noticed that the detective looked as confused as Bill felt.

"Last night I told you both about Rasalom," Veilleur said. "He was killed—or at least appeared to have been killed—in 1941 at a place called the Keep in a small pass through the Transylvanian Alps."

"Who killed him?" Renny said. Bill supposed it was a natural question for a cop to ask.

"I did," Veilleur said. "The power I had served for so long released me then and so I assumed it was over at last. Apparently I was wrong. Over the past few decades I have pieced together the following sequence of events. It seems that at the time of Rasalom's death, Dr. Roderick Hanley was successfully growing a clone of himself here in New York. For some reason, perhaps due to something unique about a clone, Rasalom was able to move into the body of the child who would eventually grow up to be James Stevens."

The name hit Bill like a punch.

"Then it's true?" Bill said, looking at Carol. "All those stories about Jim being a clone were true?"

Carol nodded. "Yes. All true."

"But Rasalom could not control the clone's body," Veilleur said. "He could use the body as a vessel for his life force and nothing else. He was trapped, an impotent passenger in Jim Stevens's body—until Jim fathered a child. When that happened, he moved into the new life the instant it was conceived within Carol."

"All that Antichrist talk," Bill said, remembering Jim's violent death and the pursuit of Carol by the Chosen.

Carol shrugged helplessly, almost apologetically.

"But I never really believed all the things my Aunt Grace and those awful people with her said about my baby. So I fled with Jonah to Arkansas where Jimmy was born. He was a perfectly normal infant during the first few months, but it wasn't long before I began to suspect there was something wrong with him, something . . . *malignant* about him. I blamed my feelings on all the horrors I'd gone through while I was carrying him, all the terrible things that had been said about him, about him being the

Antichrist and all that. But after a while I realized that there was no question about it: Jimmy was not a normal child. Physically, he grew and developed at a normal rate, but mentally he was unlike any child who has ever lived."

She paused and Bill noticed that she shuddered.

"How?" he said.

Staring at the corner of the ceiling as she spoke, she gave a brief summary of fifteen years spent with a child who was never really a child, who had never needed a parent.

"Finally, at age fifteen, he walked out on me. After he was gone, I distributed the balance of the fortune to various charities— I wanted no part of it—and came back to New York. I met a man, we got married, I'm . . . getting by. Mr. Veilleur contacted me a few years ago. We've been meeting and talking about Jimmy. I don't know if I believe him about Jimmy being this Rasalom he talks about, but I don't know if I disbelieve him either. It explains so many of the terrible things that have happened since he was conceived." She looked at Renny, then at Bill. "But what's he done to you?"

Bill told Carol about Sara and what she had done to Danny five years ago; he told her about Rafe and how he was twisting Lisl, and what they had done to Ev.

"But Mr. Veilleur doesn't think they were his real targets," he concluded. "He thinks Rafe or whoever he is has really been out to hurt me. Is that possible?"

Carol nodded. "He hates you."

Bill was struck speechless for a moment.

"Me? What did I ever do to him?"

"You almost killed him."

As Bill listened in awe, she went on to remind him of her botched attempt to seduce him that afternoon in the Hanley mansion, of how the seduction had ended when she'd started to miscarry the child she hadn't known she was carrying.

"He almost died then," she said, "and he blames you, Bill."

"Me? But I had nothing—"

"You had everything to do with it," Veilleur said. "Mrs. Treece has told me of the incident. It's plain to me that Rasalom influenced her from within her womb, causing her uncharacteristic behavior. But it was your refusal to yield to her, to hold to your vows—it didn't matter that the God to whom you made those vows doesn't exist—it was your determination to continue on the course you had chosen for your life, toward what you believed was right that caused the near miscarriage." He shook his head in dismay. "And it was a complete miscarriage of fate that you got her to the hospital in time to save her child. For it was that child who has come back to ruin your life."

Bill's mind rebelled against what he was hearing.

"He did that to Danny because I refused her? And now he's after Lisl for the same reason?"

"I believe he also set fire to your parents' house," Veilleur said. "It was no accident that they died on the same date as your friend Jim Stevens. He was sending you a message. *You* have been the target all along, Father Ryan. You hurt him and he does not forgive."

"But they were innocent!"

"But useful to Rasalom. Think: You'd already taken vows of poverty, chastity, and obedience. He could not ruin you financially or slaughter your wife and children, so he chose another route of attack."

"Why didn't he just kill me?"

"Too quick. No sustenance from that. Even physical pain gives him only a fraction of what he derives from psychic pain, from fear, hatred, self-doubt. His purpose appears to have been to utterly ruin you from within. To do that he stripped you of your support system—your family, your friends, your freedom, your religious order, your god, your very identity. He wants you to doubt yourself, to question the worth of your life, the usefulness of continuing it. He destroyed everything that gave meaning to your life, that made you who you are, expecting you to turn against your values and wallow in doubt and misery and self-pity. And then, hopefully, to commit the ultimate act of despair: suicide. He almost succeeded five years ago, but you refused to give up. So now he's returned to finish the job."

Bill sat there numb, in shock.

"But why is he wasting his time with me? If he's so powerful, if he's out to change the world into some awful place, why expend so much effort on me?"

"First of all, it gives him great pleasure. And in a hellish way it's a testimony to you that he felt he had to level such a devastating assault against you. He must respect your strength of character. He may even fear you. But the real reason he's taken the time to shatter your life is that he's afraid to reveal himself just yet. He's been biding his time, accumulating power, amusing himself while he grows stronger."

"He was afraid of a red-haired man when he was growing up," Carol said. "But we never saw him. Who was that?"

Veilleur sighed. "Me."

They all stared at the old man. Finally Renny said what was on Bill's mind.

"You've got to be kidding!"

"Not as I am today," Veilleur said quickly, "but as I used to be. I am the red-haired man Rasalom fears—or rather I was. He still thinks I am a vigorous, younger man, brimming with all the power of the opposing force, waiting for him to show himself so that I can bring the full power of that force to bear on him."

"So," Bill said. "You were the last to oppose him? Who before you?"

"No one."

"But you said this has been going on for ages."

Veilleur nodded.

"Then you're . . ." Bill couldn't grasp it, didn't want to try right now. "But then who represents this opposing force now?"

Veilleur's expression was bleak.

"No one. When Rasalom appeared to be dead, the battle appeared to be won, so the opposing force left this sphere. And I began to age as everyone else . . . one year at a time. So now there is no one on earth to oppose him."

Suddenly Bill was afraid—for the world, but especially for Lisl.

"I've got to go back," he said, rising to his feet.

"Bill, you can't be serious!" Carol said.

Bill felt his fear swell into waves of murderous rage, roaring through him like a storm surge.

"He killed my parents, mutilated Danny Gordon, and God knows what else. I'm not sitting pat up here while he does whatever he pleases with the people I left behind."

Renny was on his feet too.

"I'll go with you. I've got some unfinished business with this bozo myself."

"I want to come too," Carol said. "Maybe I can talk some sense into him."

"Do you really believe that?"

"No," she said, her lips trembling. "But I feel I've got to try."

"I believe I'll come too," Mr. Veilleur said.

"Are you up to it?"

Bill felt the full intensity of his blue-eyed gaze.

"You can't stop him, but you can frustrate him, hamper him. I have this feeling that you're a man who can do it. It will be a small victory, meaningless in the long run, but I'd like to see it. I'll have to stay in the background, of course. Under no circumstances must he know about me. Understood?" One after another, he stared at each of them. "If he sees me like this he will know he's free to make this world—quite literally—a living hell."

As Mr. Veilleur went to give the nurse instructions as to the care of his wife during his absence, Bill began calling the airlines to check out the flight schedules. He was possessed by a dreadful rising urgency to get back to Pendleton.

THIRTY

North Carolina

Ev was gone.

They'd removed what was left of him from the front of the truck, put him on a stretcher, and roared off to the nearest hospital. Lisl vaguely remembered being guided to the back seat of a State Police cruiser that then followed the wailing ambulance. Before the ride, and after while sitting in the waiting area of the hospital emergency room, she answered countless questions; but now she could remember neither the questions nor her answers. She only remembered that E. R. doctor coming out and saying what everybody already knew: Everett Sanders was DOA.

She'd prepared herself for the news and so she was able to maintain a calm front when it came. They wanted to hold her for observation, saying she looked as if she was in shock, but Lisl adamantly insisted she was okay. Finally they took her back to the truck stop and her car. She drove away and got as far as the next rest area; she pulled in, stopped in a deserted corner of the parking lot, and went to pieces.

And finally, when she could cry no more, when her sob-wracked chest and abdomen could take no more, Lisl sat and stared blindly through the windshield. She kept her eyes open as much as possible because every time she closed them she saw the sad, defeated, accusing look on Ev's face in the instant before the truck slammed into him.

Never in her life, not even in the depths she'd plunged to after her divorce from Brian, had she felt so utterly miserable, so completely worthless.

All my fault.

No . . . not all her fault. Rafe's too. Rafe had played a major role in Ev's death. That didn't exculpate her one bit, Lisl knew, but Rafe more than deserved to share her guilt. He'd erased Ev's computer files, perhaps the final shove that had sent Ev on that fatal walk onto the interstate. Rafe should know that he'd contributed to a man's death.

Lisl reached for the ignition key. Her limbs felt weak, leaden, as if they belonged to someone else. She had to concentrate on every movement. She got the car started and headed back to Pendleton.

The morning sun was unreasonably bright, glaring in her eyes as she drove. Traffic was Saturday-morning light but she stayed to the right, not trusting her exhausted reflexes at the higher speeds. The sun had disappeared behind a low-hanging sheet of cloud by the time she reached Pendleton. The town was coming to life then but the Parkview complex was still quiet. She pulled up to Rafe's condo and didn't hesitate. She went straight to his front door and pounded on its glossy metal surface. Silence inside. She pulled out her key and unlocked the door.

"Rafe?" She stepped inside. "Rafe?" She stopped on the threshold of the living room and stared in shock.

The room was empty. Stripped. The furniture, the paintings, even the rugs—gone.

What's going on?

"Rafe!"

She hurried from room to room, the clack of her shoes on the hardwood floors echoing through the emptiness. Each was the same. All traces of Rafe's presence had been completely stripped away.

Except in the kitchen.

Something was on the counter. Lisl hurried over and saw that it was a slip of paper and . . . a test tube. She picked it up and sniffed its open end—a trace of the mild odor of ethanol. She knew this tube. The last time she had seen it she had just emptied its contents into Ev's orange juice.

She lifted the slip of paper with her other hand and peered at it. Numbers and code words in Rafe's handwriting—computer access codes.

Ev's codes.

Weak, numb, feeling lost and very much alone, Lisl turned in a slow circle and stared at the condo's empty rooms.

Gone. Rafe had packed up and vanished. No good-bye, no note of explanation. Just gone. Not even a snide, nasty note, telling her that she hadn't lived up to his standards—she would have preferred that to nothing. She now knew what his standards were and she wanted no part of them.

But the test tube and the access codes—they transfixed her. To take everything else and leave only them was calculated cruelty. Brilliant cruelty. Hard evidence of what she had done, reminders that she had made possible everything that had happened.

She stared down at them, then closed her eyes.

Ev's face stared back at her from the inner surface of her lids.

With a cry she gripped the cowrie slung from her neck and pulled, breaking the gold chain. She flung the necklace across the room and fled Rafe's apartment.

She drove to Will's place but it was just as she'd left it in the early hours of the morning—empty. At least his furniture was still here, but where was Will? It didn't look as if he'd been back since she'd been here.

An awful thought struck her: Was he in on this too?

No, that was too crazy, too paranoid. Indeed, Rafe had something weird going on in his head, but Will wasn't part of it, she was sure. But where was he?

She gave up and headed for home. On the way, it began to rain.

For an instant, as she entered her apartment, she had the feeling that Rafe might be there waiting for her. But no, it was empty.

Empty . . . just like her, just like her whole life. She'd never felt so alone, so cut off. If only there was someone she could call, talk to. But she'd never had any really close friends here, and since becoming involved with Rafe she'd grown away from the few she might have called. And her parents—oh, God, she couldn't talk to them even about simple things, so how could she discuss *this*? Will was the only one, and he'd disappeared.

She went into the bedroom and fell across the rumpled sheets. Sleep. That might do it. Just a few hours respite from the grief, the guilt, the loneliness. She'd be able to function then.

But function at what? Go back to the math department? After what she'd done? Slide up in the pecking order with no fuss because Ev was no longer in the way? How could she do that?

Lisl sat on the edge of her unmade bed and tried to visualize her future. She saw nothing. It was as if she'd been struck blind. In a sudden panic she reached into her night table for the bottle of Restoril.

Sleep. I've got to get some sleep!

But no way was she going to get any with Ev staring back at her every time she closed her eyes.

She took the bottle to the bathroom and swallowed two capsules—twice the normal dose, but she was sure she'd need it. She looked at herself in the mirror, at her hollow, haunted face, her guilty eyes.

You worthless piece of shit.

Amid a rush of fresh tears, she poured a dozen more capsules into her hand and washed them down, then a dozen or so more, and again, until the bottle was empty. It had been almost full—maybe ninety capsules. She dropped it into the sink and shuffled back to her bed to wait for sleep, and for peace, permanent peace. This would fix it. No more guilt, no more pain.

She lay on her back and listened to the rain outside. She stared at the ceiling, forcing her eyes to fix on a crack above her, keeping them open to ward off visions of Ev's last moment alive.

Finally the growing lethargy tugged on her lids, closing them. As the silent, faceless darkness rose around her, engulfing her like warm water, she embraced it.

Peace.

She thought she heard a noise in the room. She tried to open her eyes but could barely part her lids. Someone was standing over her. It looked like Rafe. He seemed to be smiling, but she could not react. She was floating now, being pulled downstream . . .

. . . downstream . . .

As soon as they landed, Bill went to a phone. He called Lisl's number. No answer. He ran out to the parking lot and drove his Impala back to the terminal where he picked up Carol, Renny, and Mr. Veilleur.

"I want to check out Lisl's place first," he said.

When he reached Brookside Gardens, he left his three passengers in the car.

"I'll only be a minute."

He ran through the downpour to her front door and knocked. When he got no answer, he tried the latch. The door was unlocked. Bill stepped inside, calling her name. He didn't want to frighten her, but he had this feeling . . .

He found her sprawled across her bed. She looked dead. He leapt forward and pressed his hand to her throat. Still warm, and there was a pulse. But she was barely breathing. He shook her but couldn't rouse her. He ran to the bathroom for some water to splash on her and found an empty pill bottle in the sink. The label read: "Restoril 30 mg.—one (1) at bedtime as needed for sleep."

His heart broke for her. She took things so hard. She probably hadn't been able to find Ev and had come back here depressed. Probably thought her friend Will had deserted her too.

If I'd stayed here . . .

But there was no time for this. He had to get help. Bill ran to the phone to call an ambulance. She'd hate being admitted to the hospital where her ex-husband was on staff, but there was no choice.

No dial tone. He jiggled the plunger: dead.

Cursing the breakup of Ma Bell, Bill ran to the front door and signaled to the car for help. As Renny got out and ran through the rain, Bill returned to the bedroom. He skidded to a halt at the doorway. A man was standing by the bed.

Rafe.

"You bastard!" Bill said, starting forward. "What have you done to her?"

Rafe looked at him coldly. No pretense now, no attempt to hide the gleam of icy malevolence in those dark eyes.

He really does hate me!

"As I told you yesterday, Father Ryan—I've done nothing. Lisl has done everything herself. I've merely offered her"—he smiled—"options."

"I know all about your 'options,' " Bill said, "and I'd like to introduce you to a few of mine, but right now I've got to get her to a hospital."

As Bill passed him on his way to the bed, Rafe pushed him back. He was so much smaller than Bill, his physique almost delicate, yet Bill grunted with pain as a crushing impact on his chest sent him staggering back against the wall. He sank to the floor, gasping for breath.

"She'll be all right," Rafe said in a bored tone. "She didn't take enough to kill herself." He shook his head disgustedly. "Couldn't even do that right."

Bill rose to his knees, ready to hurl himself at Rafe, when Renny burst in.

"Hey, what's going on? What happened to her? And who's this guy?"

"That's Rafe Losmara—the one I told you about."

Renny's eyebrows lifted. "Yeah? The guy who supposedly passed as the broad five years ago?"

Bill saw a questioning look pass across Rafe's face. Veilleur's warning echoed through his mind. He wanted to warn Renny about saying too much. But Renny had his hands on his hips and was walking around Rafe, studying him.

"Yeah, I can see where he might have been able to pull it off," Renny said, then looked at Bill. "This is the guy we're supposed to be afraid of?"

Bill glanced at Rafe to see his reaction. He watched in shock as the mustache above the arrogant smile began to thin, the individual hairs falling out and sprinkling the floor like tiny pine needles from a dying tree. His features softened, rearranged themselves ever so slightly until, seconds later, Bill was looking once more into the face of Sara Lom. The face smiled and cooed in Sara's voice.

"You're not really afraid of me, are you, Danny?"

Bill could not move. It was all back—all the horror, all the grief, the self-doubt, the guilt. He was helpless before this creature.

Then a voice spoke behind him. Carol's voice.

"Oh, Jimmy! That can't be you!"

Sara's sweet face turned rotten, hideous with anger as it glared at Bill.

"Her? You brought *her* here? How did you find out?"

Bill's mind was working again, racing. He had to get poor overdosed Lisl to a hospital—now! But he had to be very careful here. He could feel the naked evil in the room like a cold sickness in his marrow, growing, strengthening, as if layers of insulation were peeling away, setting it free. With each passing minute, Mr. Veilleur's story was becoming less and less improbable.

"I figured it out," Bill said quickly, spinning the lie as he sidled toward Lisl's inert form. "The inexplicable things that happened to Danny and Lom—I knew there was something unholy going on. Then I remembered all the Antichrist hysteria about Carol's baby. You resemble Sara and you're the right age. I put everything together."

"Don't flatter yourself. You haven't put a thing together. I'm not your pathetic Antichrist."

"I never thought you were," Bill said as he reached the far side of the bed.

Rafe made no move to block him. He no longer seemed interested in keeping him away from Lisl. Bill knelt beside her and gripped her arm.

Cold! Good God, she was *cold!* He dug his fingers into her throat, probing for a pulse, but her arteries were still, her waxen tissues inert, doughy . . . lifeless.

"Lisl?" He shook her. *"Lisl!"*

Bill pressed his ear to her chest—silence. He pushed back an eyelid—a widely dilated, sightless pupil stared back at him.

"Oh, good God, she's dead!"

No! He sagged over her, his forehead resting against her cold skin. *Oh, please, no! Not again!* He straightened and began pounding on the mattress in a wild rage, incoherent curses hissing between his clenched teeth. When he noticed that Lisl's body had begun to pitch and roll with his pounding, he stopped and let his head slump down onto the bed.

He felt so leaden, so useless. His parents, then Danny, now Lisl—all because of him. When was it going to stop?

He glared up at Rafe.

"But you said she hadn't taken enough to kill her! That she—"

As he looked down at Bill, Rafe shook his head and smiled—an infuriating mixture of pity and derision.

"Did you really expect the truth from me, Father Ryan? Won't you ever learn?"

Bill launched himself from the floor, straight at Rafe, ready to kill. And Rafe bounced him back. He seemed to do little more than flick his wrist but Bill was sent sprawling again.

"Jimmy!" Carol shouted.

"Yeah, Jimmy," said Renny, stepping up and standing nose to nose with Rafe, "or Sara or Rafe or Rasalom or whatever the fuck you call yourself, you're under arrest—"

Rafe's hand shot out and grabbed Renny by the throat. He lifted him off the floor.

"What did you call me?"

Bill saw the shock and fear in Renny's mottling face. He shook his head.

"Only one living being knows that name!" Rafe said. "Where is he? He's here, isn't he? Tell me where he is!"

Renny shook his head again.

Bill heard Rasalom—he began thinking of Rafe as Rasalom then—make a noise like a growl, a sound somewhere along the echoing hall between fury and panic. He seemed to expand, grow larger, taller.

"Tell me!" He took his free hand and rammed it through Renny's ribs, sinking it to the wrist in his chest cavity. "Tell me where he is or I'll tear your heart out and feed it to you!"

Bill saw the agony in Renny's face, saw the life fading from his terrified eyes. He had to know then that he was a dead man, but he offered no answer, made no plea for mercy.

Instead, he spit in Rasalom's face.

Rasalom staggered back a step as if he'd been sprayed with acid instead of spittle, but an instant later he'd shaken it off. With a howl of insensate rage, he hurled Renny from him, sending his body spinning, spraying, dappling the walls and ceiling with crimson as he arced over Lisl in her deathbed and thumped to the floor on the far side.

Carol was screaming as Bill regained his feet and ran to the detective's side. Blood bubbled from the hole in his chest; his eyes were glazing. Bill pressed his hand over the wound to stop the flow of blood, knowing it was useless but trying anyway.

The detective was going fast. Bill wanted to give him something to take with him.

"Renny!" he whispered. "That was the bravest thing I've ever seen. You hurt him. He can be hurt, and *you* hurt him!"

A smile wavered on Renny's blanched lips.

"Fuck him," he said, then he was gone.

Another one—another good one gone.

Bill straightened up and turned. Rasalom looked huge now, but Bill was too angry to be afraid.

"You bastard!"

As he started toward him, Rasalom grabbed Carol by the throat and held her in the same death grip.

"Where *is* he?"

Carol! Would he really kill Carol?

"She's your mother!"

"My mother has been dead for millennia. This"—he lifted Carol clear of the floor as she struggled in his grasp—"was no more than an incubator."

"Who *are* you?" Bill cried.

Rafe turned on him, his voice rising, his face changing again. And his eyes—the pupils widened into unsounded darkness, like windows into hell.

"Who am I? Why, I'm you. Or parts of you. The best parts. I'm the touch of Richard Speck, Ed Gein, John Wayne Gacy, and Ted Bundy in all of you. I am the thousand tiny angers and fleeting rages of your day—at the car that cuts you off on the freeway, at the kid who sneaks ahead of you in line at the movies, at the old fart with the full basket in the eight-items-only express checkout at the supermarket. I'm the locker-room residue of the names, the scorn, the pain heaped on all the pizza-faced, flat-chested, pencil-dicked, lard-assed geeks, nerds, and dumbshit bastards who had to change clothes in front of their peers. I'm the nasty glee in the name-callers and the long-suffering pain, the self-loathing, the smoldering resentment, the suppressed rage, and the never-to-be-fulfilled promises of revenge in their targets. I'm the daily business betrayals and the corporate men's room character assassinations. I'm the slow castrations and endless humiliations that comprise the institution called marriage. I'm the husband who beats his wife, the mother who scalds her child, I'm the playground beatings of your little boys, the back seat rapes of your daughters. I'm your rage toward a child molester and I'm the pederast's lust for your child, for *his* own child. I'm the guards' contempt for their prisoners and the prisoners' hatred for their guards, I'm the shank, I'm the truncheon, I'm the shiv. I'm the bayonet in the throat of the political dissident, the meat hook on which he is hung, the cattle prod that caresses his genitals. You've kept me alive, you've made me strong. I am *you*."

"Not even close," Bill said, approaching warily. He wondered if he could instill a little fear into Rasalom himself. "The one you're looking for is up north, getting ready to crush you!"

Bill crouched to leap as Rasalom poised his free hand over Carol's chest. Suddenly Rasalom stiffened.

"No! He's here! He's—!"

He dropped Carol and brushed by Bill on his way into Lisl's living room. Bill hurried after but stopped at the doorway. A few feet ahead of him, Rasalom had stopped too, half crouched in a wide-legged stance. In the center of the living room stood Mr. Veilleur, leaning on his cane.

Their eyes were locked.

"Can this be you?" Rasalom said in a hushed voice. He began to circle Veilleur as a snake hunter might approach a cobra. "Can this really be you, Glaeken?"

Veilleur said nothing. He stared straight ahead as Rasalom moved behind him. Finally, they stood face-to-face again. Rasalom's smile was ugly as he towered over Veilleur's gnarled, shrunken figure.

"This explains everything!" he said in a half whisper. "Since my rebirth I've sensed that I've had this world to myself. I had no awareness of you. But I didn't trust my perceptions. You've tricked me before, so I was wary. I stayed out of sight, avoided anything that might draw attention to me." The smile faded. "All for nothing! Decades of soaking up power for this final confrontation—wasted! Look at you! You've been aging since you thought you killed me at the Keep. Glaeken, the great warrior, the champion of mankind, the wielder of Light against Darkness, of Reason against Chaos, is nothing now but a pathetic old man. This is *wonderful!*"

As he edged closer to Veilleur, Bill felt a touch on his arm. Carol was beside him, watching her son in horror. Bill put an arm around her shoulders and pulled her close. He had a feeling something awful was about to happen in the next room. He didn't want to see, but he could not look away.

"The power's left you, hasn't it?" Rasalom said, his face only inches from Veilleur's. "It's deserted this entire sphere. Which means I'm completely unopposed here." Rasalom laughed and backed away, spreading his arms and turning. "What an Armageddon this is! There's only one army here. The field is mine!"

He stood silent for a moment. Bill watched him stare at Veilleur—or Glaeken, if that was the old man's real name. The only sound was the gentle patter of rain outside. But there was a growing storm in Rasalom's face as it darkened with rage. Suddenly he screamed and lunged at Glaeken, each hand a blur as it knifed toward the old man's throat. Bill squeezed his eyes shut as Carol buried her face against his shoulder. But when there was no sound of impact, he chanced a look.

Rasalom's fingertips hovered a hairbreadth from Glaeken's unflinching skin.

"You'd welcome this, wouldn't you?" Rasalom said. "Then it would be all over for you. But as much as I would love to reach inside you and rip out your spine one vertebra at a time, it's not going to be that easy. No, Glaeken. I'm deferring that pleasure. I'm going to break you first. You've fought me for ages to protect this so-called civilization of yours, so I'm leaving you alive to watch how quickly it crumbles." He held a balled fist before Glaeken's eyes. "Your life's work, Glaeken"—he flicked his fingers open and snatched his hand away—"gone! And you're helpless to stop me. *Helpless!*"

Bill felt a tremor in the floor, then. He looked into Carol's frightened, troubled eyes and knew she felt it too. The tremor graduated to a shudder. Outside he heard a roaring sound, in the skies, growing louder. Suddenly all the windows exploded inward. Bill dove for the floor, taking Carol with him as a million shards of glass knifed through the air.

From the floor where he huddled with Carol, Bill chanced a peek at the two men in the front room. They were barely visible through the tornado of debris that whirled around them. And then there was another explosion, this one outward. It slammed Bill's head against the floor, stunning him for an instant. He was aware of masonry cracking like rifle shots, of wall beams snapping like bones. And then the walls blew out.

When he lifted his head, Bill saw Glaeken and Rasalom standing as they were before. Rasalom turned and looked at Bill, and in that instant he saw what was to come, a world of eternal darkness, a nightmare existence devoid not only of love and compassion, but of logic and reason as well, a night world of the spirit.

Rasalom smiled and turned away. He made a mocking bow toward Glaeken, then strode toward the blown-out front wall.

"I'll be back for you, Glaeken. When civilization is dead and the remnants of humankind are little more than maggots feeding upon its putrescent corpse, I'll be back to finish this."

And then he was out and into the rain and gone.

Carol began to sob against Bill's shoulder. He moved her away from the canted doorway to the ruined living room, away from the bodies of Renny and poor, twisted, tormented Lisl. As she huddled beside him, Carol looked up into his eyes.

"That's not Jim's son," she said with a quaking voice. "That's not my child."

"I don't think he ever was," Bill said. Holding her close, he turned his attention to the old man who still hadn't moved or spoken.

"Glaeken?" Bill said finally. "Is that what I should call you?"

"It will do," the old man said. It was almost a shock to hear his voice after his steadfast silence before Rasalom.

"What happens now? Can he do what he says?"

"Oh, yes." Glaeken's blue eyes locked with Bill's. "From the start he has sought to claim our world for the power he serves, to make it a fit place for that power. So many of you these days think of this world as a terrible, violent place, but it is better now than it has ever been—believe me, I've seen the changes. But there is still more than enough hatred, bitterness, malice, violence, viciousness, brutality, and everyday cruelty behind our closed doors to make Rasalom strong enough to convert this world into a place suitable to his sponsor's needs. He will provide a fertile environment in which to germinate the seeds of evil in all of us. Love, trust, brotherhood, decency, logic, reason—he will sap them from humanity until we are all reduced to tiny islands of wailing despair."

"But how? Maybe he can cave in these walls, but that doesn't mean he can wave his hand and turn us all into beasts. We're tougher than that."

"Don't count on it. He will start with fear, his favorite weapon. It brings out the best in some, but in most by far it brings out the worst. War, hate, jealousy, racism—what are they but manifestations of fear?"

Carol lifted her head from Bill's shoulder.

"And nothing can stop him?" she said. "You stopped him before. Can't you—?"

"I'm not quite the same as the last time Rasalom and I met," Glaeken said with a sad smile. "The opposing power was tricked into going elsewhere."

"Then there's no hope?" Bill said.

He'd already been down where there was no hope. He didn't want to go back there again.

"I didn't say that," Glaeken said, his blue eyes focusing on Bill again. "We may be able to find someone to draw the power back. I'll need help. I think it would be quite fitting if you joined me. And you, Mrs. Treece? Will you sign up for our little army?"

Carol seemed to be in shock, but she managed a nod.

"Yes. Yes, I will."

"Excellent." Glaeken turned toward the door. "Let's go then."

"What about . . . them?" Bill said, glancing toward the bedroom door.

"We'll have to leave them."

Lisl . . . Renny . . . lying there like slaughtered cattle.

"They deserve better than that."

"I don't disagree, but we can't afford to become involved with the police who are undoubtedly on their way as we speak. They'll detain us, perhaps even jail us, and we haven't a moment to lose."

Reluctantly, Bill was forced to accept the old man's logic. He and Carol followed Glaeken outside into the rain. He shivered with the chill of it.

"When will he begin?"

"I don't know," Glaeken said. "But I believe it will start in the heavens. That's his way. He may start subtly, so we must keep watching the skies so we won't miss his opening shot. We want to know when the war begins, and we have to be ready."

Bill glanced up and saw only the low, gray lid of clouds pressing down on them.

In the heavens . . . what would happen up there? He had a feeling that looking up would become a reflex in the weeks to come.

"But what can we do against a power like his?"

"There are a few things we can try." The old man's eyes narrowed with anger as he tapped the tip of his cane on the pavement. "He called me *helpless*," Glaeken said in a low voice, his blue eyes blazing for an instant. "No one has ever called me that. We'll *see* how helpless I am."

F. Paul Wilson welcomes comments:

Box 33
Allenwood, New Jersey 08720